MELTING POINT

Cici Williams is a psuedonym for Amy Gaffney, who hails from Kildare and is a graduate of UCD's Creative Writing MA. In 2021 she was shortlisted for the Penguin Michael Joseph Christmas Love Story Competition. Her poetry is published in *Poetry Ireland Review* Issue 125, and the *Irish Times* Hennessy New Irish Writing. Amy's short story *Mother May* I was shortlisted for the Irish Book Awards in 2019, in the Short Story of the Year category. She has mentored at University of Limerick's Winter Writing School and has been a panel member at various discussions there, and also hosted the Reading Corner at the Murder One Crime Writing Festival in Dublin in 2019. Amy has also written two books under the pseudonym Rosie Hannigan, *The Moonlight Gardening Club* and *The Sunrise Swimming Society*.

Cici Williams

MELTING POINT

avon.

Published by AVON
A division of HarperCollins*Publishers* Ltd
1 London Bridge Street
London SE1 9GF

www.harpercollins.co.uk

HarperCollins*Publishers*
Macken House, 39/40 Mayor Street Upper
Dublin 1, D01 C9W8, Ireland

A Paperback Original 2026
1

First published in Great Britain by HarperCollins*Publishers* 2026

A catalogue record for this book is available from the British Library.

ISBN: 978-0-00-878503-1

Set in Sabon LT Std by HarperCollins*Publishers* India

Printed and bound in the UK using 100%
Renewable Electricity at CPI Group (UK) Ltd

For the women who've been told to toughen up.
For the ones who fight for every inch.
For the ones who thought they had to choose—
between ambition and affection, gold and love,
desire and dedication . . .

The right kind of love doesn't dampen your fire.
It fuels the burn.

This is for the women who push limits,
and the partners who match their heat—
not to tame the flame, but to race with it,
to push harder—and stoke the fire into an inferno.

Together and unstoppable.
Past the point of no return.

1

Sam

Saturday, 7th February 2026—Livigno, Italy

Snow was falling, the night sky dark against the snow-capped mountain ridges that surrounded the town. It wasn't like the wild, snow-blasted peaks back home in Silverpeak, Colorado—but the Italian Alps had a quiet kind of majesty Sam was starting to appreciate. Chalet-style stores, wooden-clad houses and cozy hotels lined the narrow street that was lit up by string after string of lights. There was no better place to be on the night after the opening of the Winter Olympics. Sam leaned back against the snow-dusted wall of a log cabin and pinched herself—literally—for the second time. Not that she could really feel it through her new Zero Below winter jacket and gloves, but still. *You've done it! You made it to the Winter Olympics before turning twenty-four! No matter what happens, no one can take that from you!*

Sam couldn't stop grinning. They'd made it to the Olympics, she and Finn, her best friend in all the world.

It was almost unbelievable. They'd shared this dream ever since they had met. Sam rubbed her gloved hands together. Her breath fogged out in front of her. She was—finally—an athlete at the Winter Olympics. Last night she'd stood with her teammates, shoulder to shoulder, in the awesome San Siro Stadium in Milan for the opening ceremony. It had been all and more than she'd ever thought it would be, but nothing in the world had prepared her for the rush of sensation that had washed over her entire body as athlete after athlete had marched into the arena. The cheers from the crowd still rang in her ears. When she closed her eyes, she could still see the dazzling lights and smell the adrenaline—sharp and metallic, almost like frost—thick in the air. The buzz had taken her by surprise. She'd chanted and cheered until she was hoarse, her heart hammering as awe, honor, fear and excitement had flooded her veins. The only thing that could have made it better was having Finn by her side. But with his first ski qualifier today, he had skipped out on the ceremony and gone ahead to the cutest mountain town she'd ever seen and where she now found herself.

The three-hour team bus journey from Milan to the tiny town of Livigno—home to the snowboarding and freestyle skiing events—had meant she'd been just in time to see Finn ace his qualie and secure his place in his finals on Tuesday. Tomorrow, it was her turn. The women's big air snowboard qualifier was the first of her qualies, and the thoughts of it made her skin tingle. Excitement twisted in her stomach—butterflies the size of avalanches—reminding her that it was real. She was *here*, in *Livigno*, and she had only ten days to make the most of her chance to take home a gold medal. Pinching herself hard enough to feel it this time, Sam stamped her feet, grinning at the satisfying crunch of snow underfoot.

Ten days, and two chances. That's all she had to make her dreams come true. If she listened to what the commentators were saying, she had every chance of taking the gold in the two categories she was competing in, but it wasn't a good thing to listen to what everyone else was saying. The last thing she wanted to be was complacent.

She'd lost out on being a part of the 2022 Beijing Olympic team. She'd been pipped at the post by Becky Stanford. Sam frowned. Her father, the famous and stoic Jake Harrington, trained both her and Becky, and Sam just knew her father thought Becky was the one to watch. It was subtle, but it was there. It was in the way he nodded proudly when Becky made a clean run. It was the tight claps, the rare smile, the murmured "That's it" that Sam craved for herself. He'd never said she wasn't good enough—he didn't need to. His silence said it all.

Becky was here now too, a teammate and competing in the same two competitions as she was, but Sam had a feeling that this was *her* time to shine. She was going to take home a gold; she just knew it. She was competing in two of her absolute favorites, so she was sure she'd take home at least one—maybe even two—gold medals. Becky had better watch out—Sam had never been in such good shape. Finn had missed out on Beijing too. Although his had been down to an injury, not ability. But here they both were now, together at the Winter Olympics in Italy. Everything was perfect, absolutely perfect, except for the loud chatter and squealing from a cluster of teenagers in the street. Sam surveyed the chaotic scene in front of her and choked back the urge to laugh out loud.

Outside the Bivio Bistrot, dusted with snow, Finn Bradley, tipped to win gold at the Winter Olympics in at least one freestyle ski category, was swamped by adoring fans. He'd always had fans, but this crowd was something else. Sam smiled and leaned against the wall. She could totally see the attraction—of course she could. You'd have to be blind not to notice how gorgeous and hot Finn was. And over the past few years Sam had witnessed just how many people noticed his irresistible appeal. And boy did he know it too; he worked his magnetic charm with flair. Sam rolled her eyes thinking of the few times she'd awkwardly bumped into unfamiliar faces in their shared accommodation at competitions. Not that she was jealous or anything—he was a red-blooded male after all. He was entitled to see whoever he wanted to see. Just as she was. Just as they'd always urged each other to do.

Sam waited, amused, as Finn awkwardly bent his six-foot-two frame down to fit in a photo with a petite blushing blonde. He looked great, he looked fit, and he looked embarrassed. Finn ran a hand through his dark unruly hair that had never looked neat, not as long as Sam had known him. It stuck up at an odd angle that made him look as if he'd been up to no good, and her heart beat a little faster while her hand twitched to smooth it down as she sometimes did. It had been years since she'd felt this way, but she tamped down the feelings that stirred inside her. It was hard not to want him, even now after all these years. He'd really grown up since they'd first met. He had deep midnight blue eyes, full pouty lips and the kind of jawline that she was sure sent many women searching for their favorite nightstand toy.

Sighing, Sam shifted against the wall. It wasn't just his face that won him so many fans, he'd a body to die for too. She knew it for a fact—she'd seen it in the gym, the sauna, the pool and last week when she'd accidently walked in on him getting changed. He'd been completely naked, and she'd been lost for words, stuttering and stumbling backwards from the bedroom as he'd dashed to grab anything to hide his . . . well, the less she thought about that part of him the better. She couldn't think about that. Nope. It wasn't allowed. It wasn't wise. And if she did, she'd ruin everything they'd been working for.

Shaking off the memory, Sam tugged at the zip of her Zero Below jacket. Finn had given it to her last week after he'd received a promotional bundle from their current favorite brand. The soft pink shade of the puffy jacket wasn't something she'd have chosen for herself, but Finn had stepped back and whistled when she'd put it on. His words replayed in her head: *pink suits ya, Sam*. Such a simple thing to say but she'd shivered under his gaze. He'd carried on emptying the package, his strong, lean back to her, as she'd turned to check herself out in the mirror.

He wasn't wrong, she conceded as he battled through the crowd toward her, the pale pink made her green eyes sparkle and her skin glow. She was glad she'd given in to his insistence that she take the jacket, even though she'd bought a new one only a few weeks ago. She'd worn it tonight to please him. It was a small thing that she knew would make him very happy.

"Congrats on placing in the final!" Sam called out as he broke free from the crowd. Finn shrugged and grinned at her, his cheeks pink as she pretended to shake an imaginary trophy from side to side. "You're first chance to take home a gold! How does it feel?"

"Crazy, you know." Finn scrunched up his nose and brushed the air to wave the question away, as if this moment wasn't that important—as if it wasn't what they'd been working for together since they were sixteen. He clattered up the steps and smiled at her as his fans dispersed, pausing midway to double-take a glance at her.

"You wore it!" His grin was huge.

"Of course I did!" Sam shook her head at him. "You knew I would."

"Yeah, I did." Finn laughed. "If only the press were here to see us."

He struck a pose in his jacket, pulling a ridiculous face and crossing his eyes. Sam slapped his arm and laughed. No matter what he did he just couldn't manage to look anything but hot. What on earth was wrong with her today? Why was she checking out her best friend?

"Oh, dear Lord!" Sam laughed. "Stop it before someone *does* see you! There'll be no more promotional goodies for you, no chance of a sponsorship deal, or any scholarships when they see how totally terrible you really are!"

Finn instantly straightened up and leaned against the wall, one arm over his head. He turned to Sam and ran his eyes up and down her body. Sam giggled as he fluttered his eyelashes at her.

"How you doin'?" Finn smoldered at her, making her

insides go all gooey. With a shake of her shoulders, Sam stuck her tongue out at him.

"I'm good, thanks for asking, now come on . . . we're late—the whole team are in there waiting!" Sam said just as a cute brunette with warm brown eyes stuck her head out the restaurant door.

"There you are!" Maya trilled as she took in the pair before her. She paused and stared at them. "That would make the perfect Insta post . . . Where's my phone? Hold that pose!"

Sam and Finn didn't move. When Maya said *hold that pose* you held that pose until she said otherwise. Maya took her job as the team's social media content creator very seriously, and it was clear to everyone that she was extraordinarily talented at her job. Sam held her breath and hoped her pulse wasn't visible because being this close to Finn was sending her into cardiac arrest. God, he smelled so goddamn good! Like snow-dampened cedarwood, warm skin and something spicy, something that was making her heartbeat skip its rhythm. Clean, masculine and so maddeningly tempting. She leaned toward him, inhaling hungrily.

"Great! Got it!" Grinning, Maya busily tapped her phone screen. Sam jumped slightly, but Finn didn't move. He held his pose as Sam tweaked his nose.

"You can move now." She raised her eyes to his, a laugh catching in her throat.

"I know." He smiled down at her. His deep blue eyes locked on hers. "But you look so . . ."

Sam swallowed. "I look so . . . what?"

7

He tweaked her nose back and glanced away but still didn't move. "Like you have some kind of secret you're keeping from me."

"Well, maybe I have." Sam shifted away from him, her mouth dry. "But that's for me to know and you to find out!"

"Finn!" Maya looked up from her phone and laughed. "You can relax! Now hurry up! Food's ordered!"

* * *

Inside was loud, cozy and crowded. The relaxed décor of the chalet-style bistro along with a fantastic menu made sure that the place was a hit with competitors and spectators of the Games. It was right next to one of the three official hotels the Olympic Committee had set aside for the athletes and had instantly become the place to go for food and fun. Sam's tummy rumbled and she was glad that Maya had had the foresight to book their large group some tables. Squeezing through the crowd she spotted her brother, Leo, with his arm thrown around her fellow competitor, Becky. Becky waved at them immediately, a warm smile on her pretty, sun-kissed face. Leo was, as usual, holding court at the warm pine table. He looked up and rolled his eyes as Sam and Finn sat down.

"Finally!" he leaned forward and bellowed down the table in Sam's direction, interrupting Becky as she had started to say hey. "We thought we'd have to send out a search party for you two."

"No need, we're here now." Sam smiled tightly at her brother. Just because he was six years older than her didn't mean he knew everything, although he certainly behaved as if he did. Leo turned back to Becky and the two people opposite him and carried on with his conversation as if he hadn't been rude to Becky only moments before. Sam blew out a long slow breath and slowly released her jaw. Ever since their father had left them in the lurch five years ago, right after the car accident that had paralyzed their mother and ruined Leo's skiing career, Leo had become a right pain in the ass, dominating the family as if he actually did anything of use at all. Lately he'd been spending all his time with Becky. It was great. It meant that Sam and her mother had the house to themselves and didn't have to listen to his snarky comments about girls' movies, laundry or who'd take the bin out if it wasn't for him.

Sam looked away from Leo, trying to keep the anger from bubbling up inside her. Who the hell did he think took out the garbage when he wasn't around? She did—their mother couldn't. Emptying the garbage was difficult for her in her wheelchair. She couldn't lift her arms high enough to get the bag out. God knew what the hell Becky saw in him.

Finn caught her hand and squeezed it.

"Don't let him get to you," he whispered. "You know he's only trying to rile you."

"I don't know why he bothers," Sam whispered back. "God, I hate him sometimes, I really do. He's . . . he's . . ."

"He's your brother," Finn said. "He's supposed to be a prick."

"No," Sam said. "He's supposed to protect me, take care of me and love me. Like Maya's brother does."

"No one is as nice as Shawn. He's one of the best." Finn

shrugged. "But I can be your protector . . ." His voice drifted as a large pizza was set on the table in front of him.

"Hold that thought," he said. Sam looked at Maya who smiled back at her. When it came to food Finn was a lost cause. He had the ravenous appetite of a teenage boy and never seemed to stop eating. He took a large mouthful of a steaming-hot slice. A master of the art, he didn't leave a long string of cheese behind on his chin as Sam always seemed to.

"Oh God," Finn groaned. "This is good, this is the best—I've never had pizza like this before."

"That's because you're in Italy," Sam said. She swiped at her chin with her napkin.

"Fair point," Finn said. His eyes followed a dark-haired Italian woman as she weaved her way past their table. "Is there anything the Italians can't do?"

Sam nudged him with her elbow. "Italians do it better, they say."

Finn's eyes were still on the woman. She waved at him and mouthed the word *ciao*. "Is that a fact?"

"Well, Madonna said it in the Eighties," Sam said. "And she wasn't wrong!" The Italian woman's dinner partner looked up to see what was going on and locked eyes with Sam. Sam felt her cheeks redden under his scrutiny. His full lips twitched. His eyes raked her over once more. A bubble of anticipation filled Sam's stomach. Was he going to wave at her too? Dropping her napkin onto the table, Sam brushed a strand of blonde hair back from her face. She glanced down and then back up, just as she'd seen the Italian woman do. As she raised her eyes the bubble in her stomach popped.

The Italian god was no longer looking at her. He'd actually turned his back to her and was engaged in an animated conversation with Finn's object of desire.

"Looks like we've been weighed," Finn said paraphrasing one of their favorite watch-together films: *A Knight's Tale*.

"Measured . . ." Maya chimed in.

"And definitely found wanting." Sam picked up another slice of pizza. "It's not as if I'm after a relationship—I'd settle for a one night and one night only kinda thing."

"I'd settle for a half-hour kinda thing," Finn said. He sighed.

"Oh my God, Finn—are you that desperate?" Sam laughed.

"Ahem, Miss I'm Not Here For Fun I'm Here To Win— did I not just hear you say you'd take a one-night stand?"

"Yeah, but I was only joking!" Sam blushed.

"Has it been that long?" Finn nudged her with a laugh. "Oh my God, has it really been . . . since . . ."

"Shhhhh." Sam glared at him. "You don't need to announce it to the whole table."

"Oh, okay," Finn said. "I was actually trying to announce it to the whole room. Have you considered maybe going on *Love Is Blind*? Maybe going for someone not based on their looks might be the way to go!"

"Finn!" Sam thumped his shoulder. The idea of appearing on the show that they watched together no matter where they were in the world made her grimace. Sure, it was fun to watch other couples find love—they never missed their watch parties and loved psychoanalyzing and dissecting the on-screen relationships as they unfolded—but a blind date didn't appeal to her. Neither did his comment about choosing someone for their attractiveness first and foremost.

"Sorry!" He rubbed his arm. "Ouch! When did you get so tough?"

Sam leaned her chin on her hand. It was seven months, four days and three hours since she'd last had sex with her ex. And it had been bloody good. The downside was that it had been breakup sex. She'd known as soon as it was over that it had been Ethan's way of getting her out of his system. She just wished it had been hers. The initial breakup had been easy, really, but the breakup after the breakup sex had been awful.

"I kept thinking he'd change his mind," Sam said quietly to Finn.

"You're better off without him." Finn threw his arm around Sam's shoulders. "You do know that, don't you? Look how far you've come since he's been gone."

"True." Sam leaned into her friend's strong shoulder.

"You're on fire, Sam." Finn squeezed her gently. "Don't let him get into your head now—not when a medal is on the line. Remember—this is what we've been working for."

"I won't, I promise." Sam looked down at her now cold pizza.

"Maybe we should extend our pact," Finn said, reminding her of their teenage promise. "We don't fall for *anyone* while we're competing."

"Huh!" Sam snorted. "Some hope of you managing that!"

"I can do it," Finn said huffily. "I'm not the slut you think I am!"

Maya looked up from her phone. "Oh yes you are."

"Maya!" Finn shook his head. "I'm surprised at you!"

"Well, you're no saint," Maya said. "You haven't been in a relationship that's lasted for more than a month. You lose interest when you've got them in the sack."

"Me? Why I am practically a virgin." Finn pouted as the table suddenly went quiet. His arm slipped from Sam's shoulders as the entire table turned to look at him. Peeking down the table, Sam saw a smirk on her brother's face.

"Guess you'd better stick to the slopes then—it's the only place you seem to be getting some action." Leo's brash voice carried down the table. Finn reddened. Leo flashed a smile, and the conversation level rose. After a moment Finn took a gulp of his beer.

"Never mind him," Sam said as Finn took another slug of his drink. "You know how he is."

"I do," Finn said. "I know he's your brother, Sam, but sometimes I just wish I could punch his lights out."

"Well, don't let me stop you," Sam said. "Give him a punch for me while you're at it."

"Roger that," Finn said. "I'll keep that in mind when the chance arises."

A shriek from the end of the table made them both jump.

"Oh my God! Yes! YES! YESSSSSSS!"

Sam flinched, almost knocking over her beer, as the shrieks got louder.

"Who's having an orgasm?" Finn asked, turning around. "Lucky bastard."

Sam groaned as she stared down the table. Typical of her brother. He'd only gone and stolen the evening from

13

the entire team by proposing. There he was, on his knees and grinning like a lunatic as Becky jumped and screamed, a small box clutched tightly in her hand.

"Oh God," Sam grumbled. "Oh, come *on*. Is this really happening?"

Finn's shoulders shook with laughter. "Well, I can't punch him tonight now."

"I can't believe this," Sam mumbled. "What an idiot."

"Which one?" Finn laughed.

"Both!" Sam expostulated. "What on earth are they doing? It's too close to the competition to be distracting Becky like this. She's only got this chance—this next week and a half. He should have waited until after."

"Yes, he should," Finn said as a waiter twisted the cork from a bottle of Prosecco. "Love always gets in the way. He knows that."

"Honestly, you'd swear he was doing it to sabotage her." Sam watched Becky slip a huge diamond ring onto her finger. The soft lighting made the ring sparkle. Poor Becky. She'd have to put up with Leo now—forever. But she looked happy, so happy. Maybe . . . Sam shook her head. No, having a relationship while competing at the highest level wasn't a good idea. She and Finn had always said so. *Urgh*, now she'd have to go down and congratulate the happy couple or else Leo would be angry with her.

2

Finn

Finn raised the glass in the air as cries of "To Leo and Becky!" filled the room. Sam and Maya were hugging Becky, admiring the ring and he just knew Sam was hating every minute of it. Her smile was too bright and her posture too straight. She had that cynical look on her face, the same one she had when they watched *Love Is Blind* together and she didn't agree with a couple getting together. Becky and Leo posed for Maya as she took snap after snap and then okayed the ones she was allowed to post on the team Instagram page. He watched Maya haul Sam into more photos, smiling as she posed for a few shots before her patience ran out. That was Sam for ya, she'd little time for romance or love—even when she'd been with Ethan, and whatever the guy before him was called.

Finn swirled the Prosecco in his glass, then knocked back the last drop. Ethan. He'd been good for Sam, but she'd kept him at arm's length. She'd never committed to him the way he'd committed to her. You couldn't blame her though; she'd had her heart set on getting to the Olympics and Ethan didn't understand that. He wasn't a sports kind of guy. And Sam—well, she hadn't understood Ethan either. The relationship seemed to be all surface and nothing else—not even lust. Nevertheless, the guy had been devastated when Sam had broken up with him. Though Finn had been relieved to have Ethan out of the picture, he felt sorry for the guy. Sam, at her best, was adorable, hot and sassy. She was that at her worst too but with a laser-sharp tongue and an ability to freeze people out that an iceberg would be proud of. Ethan had been hooked on her, but as usual Sam didn't let him in.

Finn blew out a long stream of air. Would she do the same to him if she knew how he really felt about her? Ever since he'd been her impromptu date to her prom, he'd managed to keep his feelings for her under wraps, but it was getting more and more difficult as time went by. It all seemed so useless and stupid, really. He swallowed some Prosecco, vaguely recalling how he'd been so savagely aware of time that night, or the lack of it. How they'd been so honest with each other—how she'd opened up to him about wanting this moment that they were now in, and how he'd shared his dreams with her too. He'd never had anyone listen to him, hear him or see him the way Sam did. And it was beginning to kill him that time was slipping away while he fell more and more in love with her but couldn't do anything about it.

The waiter brought out a second bottle of Prosecco, topping up glasses as Becky and Leo kissed in the warm, golden light. It was a beautiful place to get engaged, in fairness. The restaurant was cozy, the town outside cute and picturesque. There was snow, and snow made everything

16

wonderful. Romantic even. Romance wasn't any good if you weren't with the right person. Maya may have been close to the truth when she'd called him out for his philandering ways, but at least he was respectful. He'd never ghosted anyone; he was kind, considerate and fun. And he'd always understood their boundaries—and expected the same in return. It hadn't always worked out. Some of the women had been after him for the glory of being able to say they'd been with Finn Bradley, to brag on their socials about him, not to mention to further their own careers on his credentials. It wasn't a nice feeling to realize you were being used—he'd never used someone as blatantly as that. His fame and his talent were something he never took for granted—ever. Even as a teenager he'd been keenly aware of how lucky he was. That was why he and Sam had made that pact to never fall for each other, not while they were going for gold.

He sighed and looked at her. She looked so beautiful, even more than the day he'd first seen her. The golden light made her glow. Her green eyes seemed darker and her lips full and kissable. But those weren't the only things that made him want her. It was the little things she did. The way she never forgot his or his mom's birthday, the little surprise care parcels she hid in his bags when he was away competing. She had a knack for somehow managing to slip something into his luggage that he'd find at the moment he needed it most. The last time it had been his lucky river stone, the one that he'd needed that time more than ever. He hadn't been able to find it when he was packing, but, somehow, she had. And she'd tucked it into his wash bag because it was the first thing he'd unpack, so it would be the first thing he'd see.

Knowing that she must have searched everywhere for it had made him feel warm and fuzzy, something she was really good at doing to him.

Finn tapped his fingers on the table, brushing crumbs away impatiently as the familiar feeling that they'd made a mistake began to rise inside him. Maybe they'd made a mistake making that promise—after all, what do you really know about love when you're seventeen? Maybe now they were here, competing for the highest honor, they might forget about the pact. Maybe now they could be together . . . No. Finn shook his head at no one in particular. There was no way it would happen. Sam wouldn't allow it—not now, not after everything they'd been through. When they'd both missed out on the Beijing Olympics, she'd been furious and inconsolable. There was absolutely no chance that Sam would consider changing things now. Not when they were this close. They'd both worked too hard to get where they were to mess things up by falling in love. Because that's what would happen—it would all get messed up.

He loved her, that was for sure, far too much. The last thing she needed was for him to admit that, and that the highlight of his week was their watch party, that making her laugh made him feel like he'd won the world. That he'd walk away from an Olympic medal if she said he had to—without a second thought.

He couldn't tell her that he loved how she challenged him. Or that he lived for their random weekends away when she needed some space from her dad—weekends where he pretended, for a little while, that they were a couple. And that watching her leave him at the airport always cracked his

18

heart a little bit more. He wouldn't do that to her. She was his best friend. And that meant it was his business to make her Olympic dream come true—no matter what.

"Finn!" Sam's voice broke into his morose thoughts. She waved at him to come and join them. She looked miserable despite her smile. Her eyes beseeched him to save her from the celebrations and, ever the best friend, he shuffled by his teammates until he was at her side.

"Who'd have thought the prick had it in him to ask her to marry him? She's far too good for him," Finn murmured in Sam's ear, inhaling the scent of her as she grasped his arm. She always smelled good: a mix of vanilla and jasmine and musk. "What perfume are you wearing?"

"The one you got me last Christmas—d'oh," Sam said through her teeth as she smiled brightly at yet another *don't worry, it'll be your turn soon* from one of their teammates. "If someone says that to me again, I'll kill them, with my bare hands, Finn. I swear to God—I'll rip them limb from limb."

"Gotcha." Finn pulled her back from teetering over. She really was agitated over this. Furious even. "I'll be your alibi, cross my heart and hope to die."

"Oh, thank you," Sam said with gusto. "I'll hold you to that."

Finn braced himself as he saw her arrange her face into a smile as an old ex of his, Harper Reynolds, Sam's current biggest opponent, from the Canadian snowboarding team, walked toward them looking like a Parisian catwalk model. Not a hair out of place, she was as freshly groomed as the snow they all loved best. *Damn.* Harper was sporting a diamond on her ring finger—one she hadn't taken long to get after Finn had broken up with her just over a year ago. Finn groaned inwardly and stepped back slightly. He felt genuinely bad for stringing Harper along when he'd always known she was on the lookout for a long-term romance. She'd been the one to end it between them as soon as she'd realized that he only had room in his heart for Sam. He was grateful that she'd never told Sam anything about the conversation they'd had when they'd broken up.

"Samantha, wow! What great news!" Harper sing-songed as she flicked a glance over Finn. Her eyebrow rose slightly as if to ask him if he'd told Sam how he felt yet. "Can you believe it? Your big brother is getting married! And Becky has clinched the Valestré deal! What a night for celebrations!"

Sam's face paled. Finn took her hand. That deal was supposed to be hers. He squeezed Sam's hand as she stammered her reply, "W-well, they're barely engaged, Harper, but I'll pass on your congratulations," Sam said. Her hand tightened around his.

"And I believe congratulations are in order for you too. I'm happy for you." Finn interrupted the moment, his heart breaking for Sam. That deal was huge, and it would have given her so much independence. They'd spent hours talking about how important it was—even muting their favorite show. This was going to devastate her.

"Thank you, yes, we're . . . so happy. Setting a date soon—it'll be a summer wedding of course." Harper held her hand up for them both to admire her ring.

"Gorgeous," Sam said dutifully. "Congratulations."

20

Harper's eyes softened as she looked at her ring. "Thanks. He picked it out himself. And what about you?"

"Me?" Sam's nose wrinkled. "What about me?"

"Anyone special in your life?" Harper asked quietly. Finn held his breath. Not another one—Sam was going to explode.

"Oh no, no, no." Sam twitched to move forward. Finn threw his arm around Sam's shoulders and pulled her in close as Harper half raised an eyebrow. He silently mouthed a "no" to Harper.

"Oh, well, enjoy the celebrations. See you out there tomorrow," Harper babbled before turning and quickly going back to her table.

Finn could feel Sam bristling with anger. Her face was pink, very pink, and she clenched her fists by her sides.

"Outside," he murmured in her ear. "Come on—let's cool off."

* * *

"Can you believe it—*he gave the sponsorship to Becky*!?" Sam stormed through the door and out into the street where the snow had left little drifts up against the buildings and curbs. The snow had stopped, and the stars had come out. Her breath billowed in front of her as she stomped across the street.

Finn stuck his hands deep into his jeans pockets. It had gotten significantly colder since the sun had set. "I'm sorry. Do you really think he did that?"

"Of course he did!" Sam raised an eyebrow at him. "I

21

know my dad—and that deal was mine, Finn. Right up until this moment I thought . . . I thought that it was." She swiped her hands over her hair, loosening blonde tendrils that settled around her face. "Look, I know why they prefer Becky over me. It's my big mouth. It gets me in trouble all the time. But he's my dad—he should've wanted this for me. Not for her!"

"I agree," Finn said. "This sucks, Sam. I can't believe it. And I'm so sorry. But, Sam, do you really think it's because of your—how did you put it—big mouth?"

"It has to be—what else could it be? He's warned me to stop bringing up the lack of opportunity for women in sport. He's told me *stop being so feminist*! But if I don't talk about it, who will!? Argh! I'm so frustrated and angry."

"I can tell. Want to talk about it?"

"It's crazy, Finn!" Sam paced up and down the street, more wisps of blonde hair escaping from her long braid as she ran her hand over her head again. "Here we are—the day before my first Olympic qualie, and I have to deal with this: an engagement *and* losing a sponsorship because my own father couldn't advocate for me! Crazy! Doesn't anyone else see how huge this is—this is so huge!" Her cheeks were flushed and her green eyes sparkled. Finn couldn't stop looking at her. Although he'd never told her and never intended to, he'd always been turned on by Angry Sam, and right now he couldn't help but wonder if she looked this way after sex, or if she'd be softer and gentle. Hopefully a little of both.

He shook himself. *What the hell? This wasn't the way friends—best friends—thought of each other.* Damn, now that he'd imagined her in bed, it was hard to get the image out of his head, but he had to. It had been like this for ages now; she was all he could think about. And he'd an inkling that she'd had a few thoughts about him ever since she'd walked in on him naked last week. She said it was an accident but what if it wasn't? What if she'd— No, Sam wasn't like that. Not even now when her teammate had gotten engaged—it was as if she didn't even see the romance in it all. She was focused on her sport first and foremost, and always had been ever since they'd met, but even more so after they'd made that stupid pact to keep their friendship and going for gold first and foremost. To keep their mutual attraction to each other out of their minds until they'd achieved their dream of taking home an Olympic gold medal. It was killing him. He sighed. He'd put Sam out of his mind a long time ago, ever since she'd spit on her hand to shake on their deal.

They'd been walking home after her prom—Coach Harrington had called him and made him take her when her date had bailed—and he'd jumped at the order. Anything to spend more time with her. He'd been freezing that night, having offered her his jacket as they'd strolled hand in hand back through the town. He remembered he'd felt like a real man doing what he'd always seen his dad doing for his mom, and how they'd talked all night long.

He could still hear her laughing at Maya getting a piggyback from her date because her feet were sore. Maya had given up on her heels after bravely dancing in them for hours, claiming that for one night only she was going to dance like tomorrow didn't exist, and that no one was to ever mention that she danced barefoot to anyone, ever.

He'd laughed as Sam had lifted her dress to show her flat shoes.

"Clever move," he'd said, unsure of what else to say.

"I need my ankles," she'd retorted. "I value my comfort."

"Don't you ever wear heels?" he'd ventured.

Sam had tilted her head at him and smiled before answering. "Not often. Do you?"

He'd burst out laughing. "Touché!"

"You'd better believe it," she'd said. "Do you have a thing for shoes, heels—is that it?"

He'd gone the deepest shade of cranberry under her gaze. No girl had ever been so forward with him. "Um, no . . . It's more like, well, shoes are pretty, and women have nice feet. Why the hell am I telling you this?"

"I dunno, Finn, why are you telling me this?" Sam had nudged him with her elbow as they'd walked companionably side by side.

"Let's change the subject." He remembered stopping outside the hardware store, not wanting the night to end. "Slow down or we'll be home in no time."

That's when it had really gotten serious.

3

Finn

Sam had seemed to understand what he meant without him needing to explain it to her. She'd leaned against the bus stop bench as the sky grew lighter, staring up at the stars, and had told him that she was making a wish. He did too. Even now he remembered wishing that they'd be together forever, because he was positive that there was no other way to be. But instead of telling her that, he'd wound up spilling his dreams to her. Telling her about how he needed to make money so that he could take care of his mom, how shattered he was since his dad had died, how he was crap at school, but everyone said he'd make bank if he kept skiing. And since skiing seemed to be the only thing he was good at, it was clearly the right road for him to take. She'd held his hand and then held him as he talked, her arms warm around his body, her head on his chest as if it was meant to always be there. He remembered thinking how real and solid his love felt, and at the same time thinking that they were kids and too young to feel this way. After all, seventeen was too young to know about love, wasn't it?

Then he remembered her saying it so softly that it had felt like a dream.

"I like you, but I can't have you." Her voice had been so small. Her blush made her look even more beautiful.

"Sam . . ." He'd hesitated. Then the words had come out before he could've stopped them. "You can have me—but only for tonight."

"What?" She'd shivered as he'd cupped her chin in his hand.

"We have tonight—let's make it count. Tonight is ours."

"Tonight *is* ours." She'd echoed his words. "Tomorrow, we go back to normal."

He'd nodded. "I can do that, I think. Sam, can I kiss you?"

That was when she'd reached for him; her hands, soft and warm, had cupped his face as she brushed his hair back from his forehead. Her touch had sent shivers down his spine, and he'd leaned in slowly to kiss her. The space between them had vanished as Sam leaned forward and pressed her lips against his. Softly at first, and then more purposefully as her hand had gently slipped around his neck.

Now, in the cold snowy streets of Livigno, he wondered if he'd change anything if he could go back to that moment. It was a futile thought—he knew that—but he wished that he could kiss her again, take her hand and have it mean something more than friendship. They did everything together, were everything to each other besides lovers. Didn't that count as something like love? But even if he'd been able to change his actions, he wouldn't have been able to change Sam's.

Because, that night, in true Sam style, she'd pulled back from their kiss, breathless and only thinking of him. Laying her head back on his chest she'd sighed.

"You'd better get training hard," she'd whispered into his chest. "You've a lot to lose if you don't."

"I know. I just wish it could be different."

She'd looked up at him. "Don't do that, Finn. Don't wish for that because then you'll have to give up something. And that something will be all of this." She'd gestured to the mountains around them. "Skiing is your way out—you are a star in the making, Finn Bradley. Don't ever forget that. And I won't let you forget. I'll be with you every step of the way."

"Promise?" he'd sniffed, his heart sore at the turn in their conversation.

"Yeah, promise." He could still see the determination on her face as she kept talking. "You, no, we—the two of us—we need to put our careers first. When we're at the top of our game, that's when we can call the shots."

He'd nodded. "I hear you, but I don't want to."

"You have to," she'd said. "For now, at least. We can't risk my dad walking away from training you, not now. You need him, Finn. He knows everyone, and I mean that. Everyone. You need his guidance and his connections first and foremost."

"Urgh. I know—you're right. It sucks."

She'd laughed at his petulance. "It does, but hey, we won't be kids forever."

"No, we won't." He'd smiled at her. "All we have to do is take over the world."

"One competition at a time." Sam had nudged him. She'd

offered her pinkie finger to him. "Promise me this: we put our careers first, friendship second, and we forget about this between us . . ."

Finn had wrapped his pinkie around hers for a moment. "Okay, I promise. We can revise the plan later."

"When we win," she'd said, clearing her throat. She'd pulled her hand away, then spat on it and stuck it out in front of her. "Shake on it."

"When we win," he'd agreed before taking her hand in his, spit and all. "But for now, I'd better get you home before your dad finds out the time."

Every step toward her house had been leaden, heavy with time and lost love. His stomach had tightened as they turned into her driveway. There was no going back now. They'd made their agreement, and he had to stick by it. It was the right thing to do. She'd be fine, no matter what. Her dad would never walk away from training her, but Coach Harrington would drop Finn in a heartbeat if he thought there was something going on between them.

Looking down at Sam as they'd walked, he'd felt his heart break a little. For some reason he'd had the awful feeling that he was lost to her now. That this was the moment they should have fallen in love with each other, forever. Yet it had passed, and it felt like he'd failed a test. Someone else would find Sam, and love her with all their heart—because why wouldn't they? She was amazing. As she'd slipped her key in the front door, she'd turned back to look at him.

"Thank you," she'd said quietly. "I had a wonderful night."

He'd simply turned and walked away, wondering if he'd

made the right decision. Could he ever just be her friend—or had he lost her forever?

But again, Sam had challenged him. She'd kept their promise, and he'd had to endure the pleasure and absolute torment of being in her company more and more as they trained together under Coach Harrington's watchful eye. She'd taught him something though: there was nothing she wasn't able to do once she'd set her mind on it. And she'd kept her part of the bargain. Not once had she overstepped the boundary of friendship. It was driving him insane!

Their pact was six years old now and it felt like a lifetime. A long and lonely lifetime. Hadn't they'd grown up enough to possibly manage thinking of each other as more than friends? Surely, she'd thought of him in compromising situations too? He raised an eyebrow at Sam as she continued ranting. He'd no idea what she'd just said but damn, she looked absolutely delicious. What he wouldn't give to have a taste of her.

"I wish you'd tell me what happened between you and Harper," Sam said, her rant having moved on and away from Becky and the stolen sponsorship. He knew she would quietly mull it over though and tear herself apart over the choices and decisions she'd made until she'd convinced herself that it was all her own fault. She'd moved on to other topics because she was hurt and needed to think about it. "You two seemed so . . . perfect together. You couldn't keep your hands off her," she continued.

"Ah, well," Finn mumbled. "Yeah, I'll tell you sometime. Not today."

Not ever. He was never going to tell Sam why he couldn't

stay in a relationship with Harper—or with anyone—for more than a few months. That wasn't to say he hadn't tried.

And it was true. He'd been so hot for Harper—but that's all they'd had between them—heat and lust. He'd tried to make it more, especially as Harper had let him know that she was ready for more. But no matter how hard he tried to move beyond the lusty sex they'd had anywhere and everywhere, he just couldn't move from sex to love. His heart hadn't been in it. In the end it had ruined everything. His inability to commit to Harper, his constant desire to be with Sam, even if it was just on the slopes—well, it had the power to ruin everything.

A little voice in his head murmured: *you've always been into Sam, but you just had to go make that "no falling for each other" pact all those years ago, didn't you—and this is why you're in this position now—standing in the snow, freezing your balls off with a raging boner for your best friend.*

"Shut up!" Finn muttered right as Sam turned to face him. Incredulity swept over her face.

"What did you just say?"

"Nothing, just telling my inner demons to shut up." Finn scrunched up his face. "I'd managed to forget I'd dated Harper and, well, the memory wasn't great."

"Oh, Finn. I'm sorry." Sam slipped her arm through his. "Here I am ranting away when all this time she's been here and you . . . are you doing all right?"

His jeans tightened and he tried to clear his mind as she squeezed his arm. Damn, what if she realized he had a massive hard-on right now? How the hell could he explain that? Her hands were cold, and she pressed against him, her breasts soft and warm on his arm. Harper was a distant memory when Sam was around.

"It's freezing," he said as she shivered against him. "I'll, eh, let me, um, I'll get our jackets."

"Jackets?" Sam frowned. "Don't you think we should go back in?"

"Do you?" He turned the question back around. *Please let her say no.*

Sam peered around him into the bistro. Finn turned too. The whole place was alive and loud. The team were gathered around their table still cheering Leo and Becky's engagement while Maya took photo after photo. Harper and her team were there too, scooched up at the table as if they were all best friends. That's what free Prosecco and dessert did to people—it brought them together when they'd normally not be seen dead together in the same room. Sharing Sam with the whole team and with Harper wasn't appealing to him.

"Urgh," Sam said. "It looks . . . uncomfortable."

"It does," Finn breathed out. Although Leo and Becky looked very happy. They were both beaming into each other's faces as if nothing else existed. It was weird to see Leo so relaxed and smiling. Finn watched with a strange feeling as Leo leaned back in his chair and pulled Becky into the crook of his arm, kissing the top of her head as she blushed and snuggled closer into him. *It wasn't jealousy, was it? No, it couldn't be.* He wasn't into Becky at all, never had been. Leo and Becky just seemed so . . . He struggled to find the words to describe what he was looking at. Sam nudged him.

31

"They seem so settled, don't they? In a good way, I mean. Like calm, relaxed . . . like they know they're doing the right thing." She sounded wistful.

"Settled." Finn tried the word. Trust Sam to be able to say exactly what he was thinking. "Yeah, they do look settled." While he himself felt . . . unsettled.

"I really don't want to go back in. Not after the Valestré news," Sam said. "Hey, I know it's late, and I should be in bed, really, but I need to clear my mind for tomorrow, get my head in the game. I think I'll take a walk. Oh, Maya mentioned that there's a food market nearby—do you fancy coming with me? See if they can top the *Samwich*?"

"I do." Finn's stomach flipped as he spoke. *I do* . . . wedding vow words . . . He slipped away from her. "I'll get our jackets. Be back in a second."

He was back in less than a minute with the jackets in his grasp.

"I googled the market," Sam said. She zipped up her jacket. "I think it's this way. Did you think to grab my hat?"

"In your pocket." Finn pulled his own hat down around his ears, an old battered luminous orange beanie.

"You brought that old thing to the Olympics!" She beamed at him, making his heart swell. He'd worn that beanie to all of her competitions since they'd gotten serious about their sports when they were teens. He'd chosen the color because she could spot him in the crowd from the top of the slope, no matter where they were. He was glad he hadn't forgotten to bring it to her most important moment ever. This weather was perfect, and if he wasn't wrong, there was more snow on the way. The air had that metallic smell that always brought snow and it had gotten even colder. Looking up he saw that the stars were now hidden behind a thick blanket of clouds.

Sam's teeth were chattering as she tugged her hat down over her hair. Her fingers were tinged pink from the cold. Finn slipped his gloves from his pocket and handed them to her.

"Put those on, you look like you're about to lose a finger," he instructed as she smiled up at him right as the snow began to fall.

"My hero." Sam smiled up at him. "What about you—aren't you cold?"

"Nah, I'm good." Finn shivered as they made their way along the street. A good brisk walk would warm them both up and hopefully get the blood circulating around his body and not stuck in his cock. He picked up the pace with Sam easily keeping up with him. This was more like it, just him and Sam in the snow, having fun, relaxed and enjoying each other's company. Nothing and no one between them. The snow squeaked under his boots and Sam giggled.

"I love that sound," she said as they rounded a corner. "I don't think I'll ever hate it."

"Never."

"Do you think we'll be able for all of this when we're old and creaky?" She gestured around her as they walked. Couples and families were out enjoying the festive atmosphere.

"Walk, you mean?" Finn laughed.

"Hahah, very funny." Sam giggled. "Compete. Or even just get out here—or anywhere."

"I don't know," Finn said. "I suppose that depends on how good life is to you."

"Humph." Sam squinted up at him. She seemed thoughtful. "How good life is to you. What does that mean?"

"I think what I mean is that we don't know where life will take us, I suppose."

"That's deep, for you."

"For me?!" Finn gasped. "Ouch, Sam—that hurt."

"No, it didn't." She laughed. "You know what does hurt? Coming down that slope, thinking you've just outperformed your competitors, then catching an edge and getting slammed—that hurts."

"Well, yeah," Finn said. Frowning, he carried on. "But life can slam you pretty hard too if you're not ready for it—or even if you are."

"Finn, is there something you want to talk about?" Sam kept the pace. "You're future-tripping!"

"You started it!"

"Huh! I . . . yeah, I did, didn't I?" Sam stopped in her tracks as they came upon the food market. "I guess seeing Leo and Becky make such a big move got to me."

"In what way?" Finn took her arm and led her toward the first food stand where the menu seemed reasonable but was almost all pizza.

"Oh, I don't know," Sam said quietly. "What's next for Becky? She's twenty-seven and Leo is twenty-nine. A big wedding? Babies?" She pulled a face. "As if Leo wasn't baby enough. She won't keep that sponsorship if she gets pregnant."

"Sam, that's low." Finn moved them on away from the pizza stand. "Let's try over here." His stomach rumbled.

"You are never not hungry." Sam smiled up at him as he sniffed the air.

"Do you smell that? Hot dogs!" Finn pointed his nose in the air.

"Talk about being a baby." Sam rolled her eyes.

Finn lowered his nose. "What?"

"All men, they're all babies. All they want is someone who can level them up."

"Level them up?" Finn frowned. "What does that even mean?"

Sam sighed. "God, Finn, you're gonna hate me for this—I don't want to get into it."

"No, get into it," Finn said. He stared down at her. "We can talk about anything, can't we?"

"Oh, Finn, I don't know—I don't want to fight." Sam grimaced. "And I know it's *not all men* but . . . No. I'm not having this conversation. Not with you—I like you too much."

She made to walk away but he caught her arm.

"Not fair, Sam, you can't say something like that and leave it hanging. Just tell me. I'm a big boy now—I can take it."

"That's just it. You're all just big boys." Sam looked up at him, a crease forming between her eyebrows. Whatever was going on in her head was clearly upsetting her. Finn took a breath and relaxed his shoulders.

"I'm sorry. I really want to understand what you mean. I won't take it personally."

Sam's eyebrows relaxed and she gave a little smile. "You promise?"

"Pinkie promise." Finn held up his little finger. Sam wrapped her finger around his.

"It's like this," she started. "Leo is a pain in the ass; we all know that. But for some reason Becky has fallen for him. He seems great, I get that, but I see him at home and he's not all that. The man doesn't even do his own laundry for crying out loud."

Finn nodded. "Go on." *Mental note, make sure Sam knows I can use the laundry machine.*

"Becky is ambitious. We've had conversations about the future." Sam squeezed her pinkie finger tighter around Finn's. "She doesn't want to give this all up. I'm not surprised about the deal, I suppose. I'd have taken it, if it'd been offered to me, without a second thought for her."

"She won't have to give this up," Finn said.

"She will, because Leo is going to wear her down. He's going to get his own way, and she'll give in to him and when he's used her all up, he'll move on, and her life will be left in pieces."

"Sam, that's not going to happen." Finn wriggled his pinkie from hers to grasp her hand tightly. "He's not your father."

"Oh God. That has nothing to do with it!" Sam pulled her hand from his.

"Okay, if you say so." Finn pressed his lips together, knowing she'd made up her mind on the matter. "But it's not all men—"

"I know that!" Sam exploded. "But it's *nearly* all men—and *you* said you weren't going to take this personally."

"Sam," Finn said quietly. "This isn't about Leo and Becky, is it?"

"Urgh, Finn. Of course it is." Sam marched away in the direction of the hot dog stand. Finn hurried after her.

"I said I didn't want to talk about it with you," Sam said harshly as he caught up with her. "I don't want to fight with you—you're the only person I can really talk to."

"We're not fighting," Finn said taking her hand again. *Or talking.* "Come on, let's get something to eat—some dessert maybe?"

"Dessert would be good." Sam's tone softened. "Something chocolatey."

"Would waffles with chocolate and hazelnuts—"

"Yes. Hell yes." Sam nodded furiously, all of the fight leaving her at the mention of the delectable dessert. "But I already know it won't—can't—compete with the *Samwich*!"

"I know." Finn smiled. "Nothing can compete with the *Samwich*."

"Do you think they have anything here remotely close to a *Samwich*?" Sam glanced around. "I could really do with some peanut butter banana goodness right about now."

"I highly doubt it," Finn said. "But if you'd unpacked already, you'd have seen that I managed to sneak peanut butter, graham crackers and a tub of salted caramel into your luggage. All you need now are bananas."

"You did not!" Sam squealed and threw her arms around him. "Maya is gonna lose her mind! She still can't understand what's so delicious about it."

"Clearly she's a crazy woman," Finn said, loving the huge smile that was on Sam's face now. It had been an inspired idea to copy her kindness and sneak the goods into her bags.

"What's not to like about a *Samwich*—it's basically a s'more only with peanut butter and banana."

"I agree, she's just a crazy lady," Sam said as they made their way toward the waffle stall. "You know, aside from your sluttiness, you're almost the perfect man."

"I'll take that as a compliment," Finn said, his heart sinking a little. Did she really think of him that way? Slutty. The word sank like concrete inside him, making his stomach hurt. Slutty implied all manners of things, and none of them good.

"You should," Sam said, seemingly oblivious to his discomfort. "Oh! Strawberries!"

"You get the waffle; I'll get the strawberries and chocolate sauce—and I'll share." Determined not to argue again, Finn forced a laugh. "But I get the last bite."

"Hmmmm." She grinned, her nose wrinkling in the way he loved. "But let's share it—like they do in the movies!"

He watched her order their treats as the snow started to fall again. She treated him like he was her best friend, which technically he was, but then she said things like that—things that made his mind go to all the places he'd been trying so desperately not to go. Things that made him wonder if she sometimes thought about what it would be like to be something more than friends. Things that he wanted more than anything in the world—Sam, just Sam, to say she wanted to be his, only his, forever.

4

Sam

Leaning against the stall, Sam's mouth watered as the waffles cooked on the pan in front of her. The sweet, hot air lifted her spirits, and she threw a smile at Finn who was paying for the strawberries and melted chocolate pot at the next stand. He winked back and her heart caught in her chest. He was looking at her a little differently, as if he was maybe flirting with her—which he couldn't possibly be. Flirting wasn't something they did. He was probably trying to take her mind off losing the Valestré sponsorship, but that wasn't something she'd easily get over. No. But it was good of him to try, so she'd do her best to be more cheerful. It was the least she could do. Tilting her head, she waited for him to rejoin her.

"Here, get this into you." He speared a chocolate-coated strawberry and held it out to feed her. Grinning, she gently took his hand and guided the strawberry into her mouth. His hand trembled under her touch, and she let go.

"Are you okay?" she mumbled around the strawberry. "You're shaking."

"Cold," Finn said. "Just cold. I think it's going to snow all night. Good for your qualie tomorrow."

Sam wiped the chocolate from her lips. He was lying; she knew it. He was avoiding looking directly at her. And he kept pressing his lips together the way he always did when he wasn't happy about something. There was definitely something in the air, not just the snow or her lost sponsorship, nor the prevailing desire to win at the Games. She couldn't quite put her finger on it, but it felt a little like nervousness, only it wasn't radiating from everyone. It seemed to come from just her, and from Finn. He definitely seemed to be a little on edge, and he definitely did not want to talk about whatever was making him so nervous.

"Can you believe it?" Sam said as she took the hot waffle from the stallholder. "We made it, Finn. Pinch me! I can hardly believe it. We're actually at the Olympics together. You're already through to a final, and I have the first of my qualies *tomorrow*—the big air. And I know it's one of my favorites but, oh God, I'm so nervous. What if I mess it up?"

"You won't mess up because you're so nervous. Think about it—it would be weird not to be nervous," Finn said. "Listen, I was so scared in the run-up to Beijing that I went way past nerves. I went too hard and was too intent on winning that last International Ski and Snowboard Federation qualifying competition. I think it's what messed me up. I should've just stayed nervous, then maybe I wouldn't have injured myself. Nerves mean you're ready; I think being scared is worse."

"Oh." Sam felt a weight in her stomach. "I didn't realize you were . . . scared."

"And I didn't want to go without you, of course," Finn said.

"Yeah, yeah, blame me why don't ya!" Sam cradled the waffle in her hands, enjoying the heat and the sweet smell.

"Well, there was an element of that," Finn said. "Just a little."

Sam glanced up at him. "Really?"

"Yeah, but don't tell your dad."

"I won't." Sam looked away. Finn wasn't himself. She wished she could blame it on the Games, but it wasn't just that. It was something else. Ever since she'd gotten here, he'd been a little bit worried. No, that wasn't it. And he wasn't anxious. She'd never seen her friend like this, like an avalanche waiting to happen. She felt that one loud noise could set him off. And Leo's proposal to Becky seemed to have gotten to him. Well, the whole night had gotten to her too.

They walked around the market for a while, then to the edge of town and stared up at the mountains. Standing in the silence, staring up at the mountains she'd be competing on, Sam felt like it was a monumental task that she wasn't quite ready for. Now that her dream was happening, a fear of losing was beginning to swamp her.

"It feels surreal to be here—I mean to be here competing," Finn said as he wiped his fingers on the tiny napkin the stallholder had provided. "I think this is my first time to really feel the . . . pressure."

Sam looked at him. His face was still as he contemplated the mountains. The streetlamps highlighted his cheekbones and made his hair look even darker than it was. He took her hand and squeezed it tightly and pursed his lips together, and although she couldn't feel her toes by that stage, she didn't want to leave. The hotel room she was sharing with Maya held no appeal for her, not when she could be here, in the snow with her best friend.

"The pressure." Sam leaned against him, slipping her arm into his so they were linked together. "Yeah, I feel it too but, Finn, we can't let it get to us."

"I know." He sounded sad. "But what if we don't bring home a medal, Sam? What then?"

"I don't know," Sam replied. "We try for 2030?"

"Really—2030?" Finn's voice deepened as if he was laden with troubles.

"Why not?" Sam's eyes widened. "Isn't an Olympic medal the goal?"

Finn nodded. "I suppose. I just thought that we'd both have one each by now, and that we could . . ."

"Could what?" Sam held her breath. *Was he possibly talking about their pact? Hardly.*

"Move on with our lives," Finn said.

"Move on?" Sam let go of his arm. "Do you mean . . ." she paused, not wanting to bring up the promise they'd made each other in case that wasn't what he meant ". . . not . . . *ski*?"

Finn nodded. Then he shrugged. "I don't know. Maybe. Don't you ever think about a life beyond all of this?"

"A life beyond all of this," Sam said thoughtfully.

What *would* a life beyond all of this mean?

She closed her eyes for a moment and tried to picture what might happen if they won the medals they'd dreamed of since they were teenagers.

42

Would he remember their promise? Would he follow through on his word?

What if he didn't want that life—a life with her—anymore? Would he go away and find a life with someone else—someone who wouldn't tolerate Sam in his life? That was a possibility, one that she didn't want to ever think about.

Opening her eyes she said quietly, "I've never let myself imagine a life beyond all of this."

Finn shrugged and said nothing. The still of the night enveloped them both as they stood at the foot of the mountains that held the answers to all of their dreams, to all that they'd worked so hard for. Crunching footsteps behind them made Sam turn. Maya, swamped in a huge satsuma-colored down coat, was taking a picture of them, her bare hands pink from the cold.

"You guys won't believe how cute you two look right now." She slipped a pair of matching mittens on, her nose scrunching up as she did. "These are a nuisance. I forgot my touchscreen gloves. Left them on the bed back home. Me. Can you imagine! I never forget anything." She joined them. "What are you doing out here? It's really cold."

"She's right," Finn said. "We should probably get back. I've a four thirty alarm call."

"Six thirty for me." Sam frowned as Finn walked ahead of them.

Maya didn't seem to notice anything was going on. She linked her arm with Sam's and together they trudged toward their hotel, waving at Finn as he diverted toward his own hotel just down the street from theirs, which was where Coach Harrington and the skiing team were based.

43

"Jammy," Maya said as she took in the glamour of Finn's hotel: a large three-story modern-style chalet with a huge front porch and a swish-looking bar. "I wish we'd gotten that hotel—ours is gorgeous but it's not a patch on this one. You could be in there, you know, in a real bed, with a kitchen—like Finn has. How did he manage to pull that one—get a suite—while we got a room that's on their website as The Classic Double?"

"You forgot the hot tub." Sam laughed. "He got the suite with the hot tub."

"There's a hot tub?" Maya squeaked. "You're kidding me."

"I'm not." Sam nudged her. "He even has two floors, and the hot tub is on the top deck—and it has a mountain view."

"Dear Lord, will you stop tormenting me!" Maya shook her head. "Listen, I know you're trying to be Miss Independent, and I know that you have beef with your dad and don't want to be in the same space as him—but we could be in that hot tub right now!"

"It's not worth it," Sam said. She considered telling Maya about the lost sponsorship but decided against it. "He'd think that I've forgiven him for leaving us, and I haven't. It's hard enough that he's still my coach . . . I don't think I could share a hotel with him."

Maya blew a curl from her eyes. "I know . . . but seriously forget about the hot tub. Think about the bed! Finn said his bed is enormous—that it's the most comfortable bed he's ever slept in."

"Gah!" Sam snorted. "I'm sure—and he'd be the expert there—he's slept in a lot of beds."

Chuckling, Maya pulled the card key to their room from her mitten as they kicked the snow from their boots outside their hotel. "I've heard tales about how good he is in bed."

Sam covered her ears. "I don't want to know! Argh! Maya! He's like a brother to me! Stop!"

Maya laughed as they went inside, pulling off their snow jackets as they made their way to the mirrored lift at the end of the warm and cozy lobby. Sam was more than happy with their hotel. It wasn't as plush as Finn's, true, but it was a step up from the accommodation she knew some of the athletes had suffered through at other events. She missed Finn being close by, but their room allocations were out of their control, and they were going to be together during the day, so it really didn't matter that much.

Up in their room, Sam watched as Maya filled the tiny kettle for their hot water bottles. It was such a novelty, having an electric kettle in their room, and being able to have a complimentary hot chocolate really did help her relax. She slipped into her pjs and sat on the bed as Maya, ever the diva, swanned into the bathroom to do her ritual double cleanse and skin routine. Picking at the fluff on the comforter Sam bit her bottom lip. What she'd said to Maya about Finn outside the hotel rankled: *he's like a brother to me* . . . It wasn't even true. He was *more* than a brother to her, but in what sense? He was her best friend, her confidant, the first person she wanted to share good, and bad, news with.

Even if he hadn't been there when Harper had let the news of the Valestré sponsorship slip, he'd have been the first person she'd have gone running to. He made her laugh like no one else did and he knew all of her favorite things. He could tell from the tone of her texts that things were getting to her and that she was about to ask him to run away on a weekend break with her. And he always made *Samwiches* for their watch parties, even when they weren't together. Freakily, he always knew when she wanted a Starbucks hot chocolate, and when she wanted a peach iced tea. He said he could tell by the way she walked! Stomping meant hot chocolate because she needed sweetening and warming up, a light walk meant she was in a good mood that could only be made better by the addition of anything peachy. And occasionally hot cider because the season demanded it, and she needed to try new things every once in a while.

New things every once in a while. Did that have anything to do with what he'd said earlier? She mulled over it; he'd said he wondered what they'd do after this. She hadn't thought that far ahead. Well, she'd lied. She had thought about it, but she never expected anything to come of it and had pushed those dreams aside. Feeling silly that she hadn't ever realized time was passing and they weren't going to be able to compete forever, Sam filled her hot water bottle and sat back against her headboard. She needed something to cuddle.

She'd left her phone on the locker to charge when they'd gotten in, and it lit up as she settled back. It was Leo. His fifth WhatsApp message. Sam read all five with a rapidly sinking heart.

> Hey, where are you? Dad is here. We want a family photo to mark the moment.

> Hey, seriously, Sam. Where are you?

> We're heading to the club after dinner.

> Can't you just answer me! Come on, Sam.

> Thanks for sticking around to celebrate, sis. I thought you'd at least have been happy for me.

Sam put the phone down. It wasn't that she didn't wish Leo and Becky well, it was just all too much right now. The Valestré deal. She couldn't stop thinking about how it should have been hers. It really hurt, and what was worse, clearly Becky, Leo and her dad all had known about it before tonight—and not one of them had bothered to talk to her about it.

The Valestré deal had been talked about for months. Becky had been lined up for another less lucrative deal, so what had happened to make Valestré choose her over Sam? Sam groaned. Her dad had always said that Becky had the "*media polish that brands were after*", which Sam interpreted as a warning for the way she spoke up about the inequality within their sport.

Time and again she'd rowed with her dad about the unfairness of it all. Although it was true that the bigger and more well-known events were pushing for equality in prize money, there were many smaller competitions—*ones that everyone had to start from*—where the guys' prize money was substantially more than the women's. One prize she'd won in her time competing had been particularly insulting: five hundred dollars and a gift bag. A freaking gift bag!? Her male counterpart had been awarded almost ten thousand dollars. It had felt like a slap in the face and had been the moment that had made her speak up. But speaking up was costing her now.

No matter how much her dad told her to keep her mouth shut, she couldn't stay quiet about how women in sport were treated badly. She just couldn't! It was hard enough being a woman without having more odds stacked against you. But her outspokenness and her agenda seemed to be going against her. She'd lost two smaller contracts after that last interview where she'd been very clear on how she felt about it all, and now she was feeling the pinch. Competing at this level didn't come cheap. Her dad was footing the bill—and he never let her forget it.

Her big hope now was to take home a medal—gold preferably. The National Olympics Committee had paid a bonus to the summer Olympic gold medal recipients, almost forty thousand dollars for their win, and there was no reason to think they wouldn't pay similar bonuses to the Winter Olympic medalists. Then there was the fact that any endorsement that followed a win would be priceless. That kind of money wasn't just about the paycheck, though. For Sam, it was an opportunity to stand out on her own, to break free from her dad's shadow. But it hurt like hell knowing that he'd spoken up for Becky over her, especially as whatever medal Becky won, her National Olympics Committee bonus would be topped up by Valestré as per the contract. It was like he wanted to keep her under his control.

And Sam knew her brother well. Leo wasn't going to enjoy being second to Becky who was clearly being seen as first in many eyes on the circuit. He'd once been the golden child; she supposed they had that much in common. Her heart softened a little as she remembered the dark time after the car accident that had left Leo, and her mother, forever changed. While her mother had somewhat adapted to her injuries, Leo had fallen apart. His left leg had been shattered, and no amount of operating had changed the fact that his leg was now noticeably shorter than the other. His recovery was painful, but the physical pain had been nothing compared to the mental and emotional turmoil he'd gone through. He'd refused to ski since then, said that he couldn't. He'd been so angry about that, for so long. Skiing had been his whole life—he, unlike her, had made a five- *and* a ten-year plan—and it was all about his career. Now he didn't have that anymore.

Sam grasped her hot water bottle tightly. She was glad he had Becky. She'd somehow managed to get through to Leo in a way that no one else in the family had. And he did love Becky, Sam acknowledged, and she loved him. These days he was mostly fine, but sometimes his bitterness and anger raised its ugly head again. Sam sighed. These Games were proving to be a challenge to Leo as much as they were to her.

Sam's phone lit up again. An Instagram notification from the team's Insta account. Intrigued, she opened the app to see a photo of her and Finn standing staring up at the mountain with their arms around each other. Maya must've taken it before they'd realized she was behind them. It was a gorgeous photo. Maya had really captured the tension and the hope that Sam was feeling inside, and the snowy mountains looked amazing. Like a challenge to be overcome. The caption read:

> High stakes! Higher hopes! As the pressure builds and the snow heats up, Sam and Finn are chasing that gold with fire in their veins and snow in their hearts. 🏔️ 🤍 ❄️ ⛷️ 🛷 What's their #MeltingPoint #WinterOlympics2026 #FinnAndSam

Snow in their hearts? Sam's nose wrinkled. That sounded as if she and Finn were cold and calculating. Ignoring the rapid increase of likes on the post, and the comments that seemed to be coming in faster than snow in a blizzard, Sam, once again, put her phone down. She was too tired to think, and her early call to train was in the back of her mind. All she wanted was to snuggle a hot water bottle and make a hot chocolate.

Back in the room Maya, skin glowing and with two eye patches sitting on her cheeks, hummed happily while Sam made two hot chocolates.

Maya glanced at her phone. "Looks like half the gang have gone clubbing with Leo and Becky. Practice in the morning will be interesting."

Sam nodded. "Not to mention the qualies tomorrow night."

"Let's hope they don't wake us up when they get in," Maya said. "For a fancy hotel, these walls are thin! And Becky is next door."

"Are you kidding me?" Sam sipped her hot chocolate.

"Nope." Maya draped her comforter around her shoulders. "I'm cold, aren't you?"

"A little, but I think it's tiredness that's making me feel it more." Sam nodded to her phone. "Great pic, by the way."

"You saw the post?" Maya said opening the Instagram app on her phone. "It's getting a ton of likes."

"Yeah, but *snow in their hearts*?" Sam frowned. "What's that supposed to mean?"

"That you both love snow." Maya wrinkled her nose. "What else would it mean?"

"That we have cold hearts." Sam dragged a comforter across her knees.

"Only you would think that," Maya said with a huff. "Look at the comments. No one else thinks that at all. In fact, they think the entire opposite."

Sam took the phone from Maya and scrolled through the comments, her eyes flying over the words:

Go Finn and Sam! Win Big!

Watching from Montana. Go Team!

Gorgeous couple—with that chemistry they should be a real couple #MeltingPoint

Hell, yeah they'd make the perfect couple and I want to see exactly what their #MeltingPoint is! Hehehe! Bet it's hawt!

Imagine their babies! Too cute #MeltingPoint

> The way she's leaning against him makes me think that there's something in the air in Italy #MeltingPoint #FinnandSam

> I'd melt too if he looked at me the way he looks at her #MeltingPoint #FinnandSam

"Oh God." Sam handed the phone back to Maya. "That's crazy."

"No, it's not, and so what. Let them think it." Maya was busy liking each comment. "It can't do any harm. It's a good thing really—look what happened when Becky started posting photos of her and Leo."

"What happened?" Sam said sulkily, annoyed that people were calling her and Finn a gorgeous couple. They couldn't be a couple; they'd promised that they wouldn't ever be.

Maya didn't look up. "It increased her exposure, and it's only a matter of time before she gets a big deal." Sam winced but Maya didn't notice. Maya continued, "And everyone loves a love story. And being with Leo too—he's handsome and he's still supporting her even though he can't ski anymore. It's like a love conquers all story. Beautiful."

Sam stared out of the window as the snow swirled down. "True. But I have my suspicions."

"Don't we all." Maya tapped away on her phone. "But at the end of the day, Sam, it must be really hard for him not being able to be out there."

"And one of the reasons he hates me so much." Sam

sighed. "But it wasn't my fault. I wasn't driving that day, and I can't change what happened."

"I'm not saying that." Maya looked up at her. "Just try to see it from a different perspective."

"I don't have your sunny outlook," Sam said. "But I'll try."

Maya glanced at her phone as it pinged. She squealed. "Wah! Oh, you won't believe who's just liked . . . and commented on the post! Only Salvaro AND Montalier."

Sam sat up, almost spilling her hot chocolate. "What!"

Salvaro and Montalier! Never in her wildest dreams had she ever imagined two of the biggest and most prestigious names in sportswear noticing her Instagram, let alone reply to any of the posts.

"Yes . . . Salvaro said: 'Looks like Finn and Sam are already a perfect team on and off the slopes! 😊 ❄ We'd love to see what magic they create—both in sport and in life. 😊 Maybe it's time for a #MeltingPoint partnership? 🖤 ❄ #SponsorshipGoals #WinterOlympics2026'."

Sam gasped. "No way."

"Yes." Maya giggled. "And Montalier replied: 'Well, it looks like the perfect match just found its jacket! ❄ Finn and Sam, are you ready to take your partnership to the next level? We think you'd look very good in Montalier. 😊 #MeltingPoint #MontalierXFinnAndSam #WinterOlympics2026'."

"Leo is going to hate this." Sam smoothed the comforter with her free hand. "Dad is going to hate it."

Maya waved her hand as if shooing away a fly. "Snaps to Salvaro and Montalier for not telling you to shut up though! This is brilliant, Sam. You need to reply to them!"

She carried on commenting and liking replies to the post. Sam twisted her almost empty mug in her hands. Maybe it was time to stop caring about what her dad and Leo thought. After all, she was almost twenty-four. It was time to grow up, and Finn was right, it was time to think beyond the Olympics, whether she liked it or not. Sam allowed her thoughts to wander back to the night that had changed everything, the night that an elk had run into the car Leo had been driving, forcing him to drive off the road and down into the ditch. It hadn't seemed to be a bad accident, not at first sight, but the car had rolled a few times before smashing into a boulder where it stopped. Sam had been the only passenger to walk away without a scratch. Leo had been black and blue for months, and he'd broken both of his legs in more than one place.

Remarkably, her mom hadn't sustained any obvious injuries, at least that's what they thought at first. It was only when they took her mom from the wreck that they'd discovered she couldn't move her legs. She'd been too worried about her son to even register that she was in pain. Sam pushed the memory away. Leo shouldn't have been driving that night, but their dad had stayed back at the ski center to talk to some big-deal suits. Leo would hate that she'd gotten the attention from that post, but that was another thing she wasn't responsible for. Maya was only doing her job. He'd just have to get over it, and so would Dad.

"I think I'll go to sleep. Don't stay up too late." Sam got up and took Maya's empty mug as her friend worked away on the team socials. Sam rinsed their mugs in the bathroom handbasin before going to close the curtains. She paused and looked out of the window. Finn had been right about the snow. It was falling steadily and would be perfect for tomorrow's qualie. Tomorrow she'd get out there and win a gold medal—not just for herself, but for every other girl and woman who'd been told they couldn't win.

5

Finn

Finn trudged down to the gym. The lobby was deserted but outside he could see that it was dark and looked bitterly cold. The snow had stopped, leaving the most perfect powder on the mountains. He might take a chance on glade skiing later before Sam's qualie that evening. There was nothing quite like getting out on fresh pow and being the first to leave tracks. With a happy heart he pushed through the doors, and stepped into the snow and headed toward the gym.

A few hours later, wrapped up in his new Zero Below jacket and hat, Finn carried his skis toward the chairlift. The sun was beaming down, and the sky was a cracking bright blue. Glad that he had his goggles in his hand, he squinted, adjusted his hat and joined the queue.

Last night had been strange. He'd almost done it, almost told Sam that he didn't care about the medals—gold, silver or bronze. He cared about her, he wanted her, but he didn't know how to say it to her. That's what had held him back. Anyway, she wasn't ready to hear those words. She'd been surprised when he'd asked her about what might happen after the competition, and her reaction had shaken him. Clearly, she hadn't thought about him at all, in any capacity, least of all in a romantic one. If she had, she'd have said something, wouldn't she? It seemed that snowboarding took up all of her life. There was no room for him, not in the way he longed for.

Lost in thought he automatically took the chairlift, not seeing Sam waving at him from below. Gazing at the dazzling snow-covered mountains, Finn pulled a deep breath down into his stomach. His shoulders broadened as the fresh, icy air filled him. His mom was visiting in a few days, hoping to see him compete in the finals. A wave of pride washed over him. Last summer she'd moved into the house he'd bought for her just down the street from his Uncle Henry and Aunt Miranda. It still felt unreal, that he'd managed to get his mom a real house, with a garden and a garage. It was his dream, and he'd made it come true. It wasn't a house anything like Uncle Henry's—there was no way he could afford a house like that—but it was a house all the same.

He had Henry to thank for getting him into skiing after his dad's death. Henry had taken him out one day to give his mom a break, and that's when it had all started. From the moment he went down that hill, everyone had said that he was a natural. He'd discovered that out on the slopes he felt free and strong and in control, a complete change from how he'd felt when he wasn't skiing, and in all honesty, he'd found it easy. His ballet training had set him up for the sport.

All the exercises had given him a steel core and powerful legs, perfect for maintaining the balance and stability skiing demanded. While his aunt had said that watching him ski was like watching choreography, it was freestyle skiing that had really gotten him excited. He occasionally missed dance, having given it up as his mom couldn't afford to pay for classes after his dad had died. Sometimes he wished that his uncle had paid for dance lessons instead of ski lessons, but wishing never changed anything and, as his mother always said, there was no point in looking back. All they had was each other, here and now, and whatever the future brought them.

Finn sighed. There wasn't a minute that went by when he didn't miss his dad, and he was grateful for all his uncle and aunt did for him and his mom, but they couldn't replace his dad. They'd been such a great family: him, his dad and mom. The three amigos, always and forever—even now. He patted his pocket where he'd tucked away his lucky river stone, the one his dad had given him. Maybe he'd give it to Sam for her first qualie later; she seemed nervous, and it might help calm her.

Looking down at the scenery around him, Finn smiled. Once again, he had Henry to thank for introducing him to the seller of the house. True, the house was a fixer-upper, but he could get it right with a bit of hard work and some scrimping and saving. It'd be a test of his creativity, DIY skills and imagination, but he was up for it. He'd bought it for cash with all of his savings before it had even gone to market, having offered the seller the asking price on the spot. It had taken years of competitions to save the right amount, but that wasn't important. What *was* important was that his mom loved it. She'd fallen in love with it the minute she'd walked in the door. Upgrading her from her tiny apartment gave him a huge sense of achievement, and in the meantime, he'd moved back into the apartment, which was perfect for him, for now.

He twisted his lips. Maybe it'd be perfect for him for the rest of his life, seeing as his love life was non-existent. A bachelor pad, that's what his aunt had said when he'd told them his plans. Finn sniffed and rubbed his nose with his gloved hand. At the time he'd hidden his upset at those words. He'd laughed along with them—Uncle Henry, Miranda, and his mom—although he had a sneaking suspicion that his mom knew he'd been hurt. But what did he expect them to think about him? He'd a bit of a reputation, not as a bad boy, but as the one no one could pin down. It was the one thing he had in common with Taylor Swift— well, back when she was famously single. He sure as hell couldn't sing or write songs like she did. He couldn't even write a diary let alone really think about telling anyone his deepest wishes and dreams.

He had though—he'd told Sam. Not only that first time the night of her prom, but in many of the conversations they'd had over the years—just in a roundabout way. Not straight up to her face that he was in love with her, but other things, like how he was proud of his achievements, and that he was afraid to fail and lose it all. It was easier to tell her that kind of stuff; she had the same desires as he had. Easier than thinking about what might happen if he was brave enough to tell her how he really felt, that from the very first moment he'd laid eyes on her he'd been hooked. He cringed at the memory, his cheeks flushing thinking of how awkward he'd been that day.

It had been the day after his seventeenth birthday and Henry, generous as always, had given him the best birthday present ever: a whole week's ski coaching and instruction from the legendary Coach Jake Harrington. Which was why he'd arrived at the Silverpeak Ridge Ski Center in the heart of Colorado while the snow was still fresh and no one else was even awake—or at least he'd thought no one else had been awake. He remembered squinting as the sun crested the mountains and bounced off the fresh pow, and then his surprise as the metallic sound of a board on metal carried across the silent terrain park. Someone was there even earlier than he was, and that someone had been Sam.

He'd leaned against the barrier, mesmerized as she'd finished the course without a hitch. Every trick was perfect, and he'd been glued to every move this tiny, explosive and confident snowboarder made. He'd never seen anything like it. She was unreal—she hadn't missed one trick—even at speed. He'd felt like he was watching a champion, and he'd started clapping even before she'd lifted her goggles from her face. Blonde wisps of hair fell around sharp green eyes that had immediately snapped up to look at him. A button nose, pink from the cold, had wrinkled as he'd stopped clapping, his mouth an O of surprise. Blushing to the roots of his dark curls, Finn swallowed. He'd never seen any girl as cute, as pretty, or as self-composed. The girl had smiled as if she knew he was smitten, and his heart had pounded in his chest the same way it still did anytime he saw Sam.

Expertly getting off the chairlift he made his way up the mountain a little to a quiet spot before surveying the glittering white landscape around him. Below him, skiers laughed and chatted. Some lounged outside the cabin, drinking hot drinks or beer. As always, the place was busy, too busy. He needed some space to think about something other than the Games, medals, training, winning, and maybe losing Sam. A swoosh of snow flew into the air nearby as a man came to a halt beside him.

"Hey!" The man removed his goggles, a huge grin on his face. "I thought it was you! Good to see you, my friend!"

Finn shook hands with the older man, laughing and shaking his head. "Davide, man, it's good to see you! Still working away?"

"Busy as ever," Davide said. The man brushed back his graying hair from his tanned, weather-worn face. "I'm surprised to see you here. I thought you'd have been down there—with the pack—getting ready for the events."

"Skeptical as ever, Davide." Finn laughed. "But you're right. I probably should be down there but . . ."

"You needed to clear your head." Davide nodded knowingly. "This is your big chance, eh, to show them what you're made of."

"You know it." Finn shrugged. Not to mention the bonus if he won a medal, or two.

"I do." Davide looked down the mountainside toward the town where he had a ski store that sold everything a ski bum could ever want. "I don't miss it; I have to tell you that. Now life is different. I do ski touring now. You should join me

61

sometime before you go home. Stop by the store. Valentina can show you the timetable."

"Sounds great." Finn smiled. "I'd love to. I'll do that."

Davide looked around. "Heading down?"

"Thinking of going through the trees," Finn said pulling a face as Davide frowned at him.

"Alone?"

Finn shrugged.

"Bad idea," Davide said. "You know this. Was there no one else to . . . ah, I see."

Finn shifted his weight from one leg to the other, feeling Davide's scrutiny.

"You're in a dilemma." Davide nodded.

"Not quite in a dilemma," Finn said, smiling at the Italian's choice of words. "But yes, I do have a lot on my mind."

"Come on," Davide said. "I'll go with you. Let's see if we can ease your worries."

Finn's shoulders relaxed, releasing a tension he hadn't been aware he'd been carrying. Davide was right. It was dangerous to ski through the trees on your own, and he knew that. Hell, he'd even made sure others didn't do it. After fixing his goggles on more comfortably, he followed Davide to their starting point and off they went.

The cold air rushed past them as they skied through the forest, dodging branches and tree wells. Finn kept his eyes firmly on his line, anticipating anything and everything that might happen. Concentrating on the immediate future felt good, it felt manageable, like he was in control. Like he didn't have to make any decisions other than which way to turn and to just enjoy the ride. Sam would've loved this route. She'd have had a blast. He must ask her to do it with him, that's if Davide would take them. From the confidant way he moved, Davide obviously knew the area well and was ahead of him, and Finn was glad to have come across his old friend.

Breathless and exhilarated, he followed Davide more fully as they wound down the mountainside, and back out onto the piste as they came closer to the end of the run. Seamlessly they joined the other skiers and came to a stop near the cabin.

"I needed that." Finn puffed as he clicked out of his bindings and picked up his skis. "Thanks, Davide, for not letting me go alone."

"No problem. Next time you want some thinking time just call me, okay?"

"I will."

"And, Finn, if you need to talk, I'm here. I know the pressure you're under."

Finn shifted his skis to his shoulders. "I'll keep that in mind. Thanks."

"And go in to see Valentina," Davide called as he slid away. "She'll be angry if you don't!"

Finn waved and laughed before turning toward the cabin where everyone was hanging out. Sam broke from a crowd of friends and hurried toward him, her hair, usually in a braid, hung long and free down her back. Dark circles under her eyes made him stop smiling. She shouldn't look so exhausted on the day of a qualifier.

"Where've you been?" she said as they reached each other.

"Hey," he said. "You look . . ."

"I know, but don't you say it too," she said. "I didn't sleep much—Becky's room is next to mine and well . . . she and Leo . . . I'll leave the rest of that up to your imagination."

"But you and Becky have the qualie this evening." Finn took his skis from his shoulders and put them away. He caught a flush creeping over Sam's cheeks at the mention of sex. "She's going to be tired."

"Tired?" Sam rubbed her nose, which had turned pink from the cold. "They're still at it!"

Finn rolled his eyes. "Boy has stamina."

"Euw! Finn! Stop it!" Sam groaned. "Anyway, when he takes a break from . . . um . . . getting it on with Becky, he's texting with me over my disappearing from the celebrations last night and not going out with them."

"Well, that's childish."

"And he's over in my hotel now. Still with Becky." Sam blew a strand of hair from her face. "And the qualies are tonight. It's a big deal and instead of preparing for it, Becky is hung-over and in bed with Leo. They haven't stopped riding since they fell in the door last night. Dad is calling all my family to tell them the 'good news' and I . . . I . . ." She broke off as a tear rolled down her cheek. "I can't take it anymore, Finn. I heard Leo and Dad talking this morning in the hallway outside our rooms, about Becky and how things are going to change for her in the future. And I get it, I do. Things have to change but . . ."

Finn nodded. "It's hard."

"It is hard." Sam sniffled.

64

"As my mother is fond of saying: *change comes from within*." Finn offered.

Sam rubbed her nose again. "I hate change. And now I have to think about everything, and I don't want to. Why should I? Why should things change? Can't we just go along the way we were? What's wrong with that?"

"It's called growing up, I believe." Finn pulled Sam in for a hug. She leaned against him, sending his pulse racing as she wrapped her arms around him. Relishing her touch, he leaned his chin on the top of her head. "You'll get the hang of it soon enough."

Sam mumbled, her face buried in his jacket: "Do I want to?"

"You have to." Finn squeezed her. "Come on, I need a drink."

"Me too." Sam leaned back to look at him. She blinked away some tears. "Do you know what really scares me? It's the change that I can't control that upsets me the most. Being ruled by my dad forever—that seems to be out of my control and it's driving me insane. I can't seem to get away from him. He pays for everything, coaches me, does all the paperwork . . . I mean, take Becky for example. He's been Becky's coach since she could walk. Now he'll be her father-in-law, and then she'll have kids, probably. And he'll be a grandfather, and the kids will learn to ski before they can walk too! Argh! There's no getting away from him."

"He's not a bad man," Finn said. "He means well, you know."

"Well, that's debatable." Sam's jaw set.

Finn could've kicked himself. Sam had never forgiven her

father for walking out on her and her mother after the car crash. Rightly so. The man had left his wife struggling to adapt to her paralysis, with two kids—even if Sam had been eighteen and Leo was twenty-four, the same age as Finn was now—while he shacked up with the receptionist at the gym. Sam kept walking as if she was fine.

"And you, you're ready for change too," she said quietly as they went inside and joined the queue for food. "Or at least that's what it sounded like last night."

"Ah I was just having a midlife crisis." Finn nudged her, unwilling to burden her any further. "Feeling the pressure. You know how it is—are you feeling okay for the qualie later?" He picked up a tray and passed it to her. Sam threw him a side glance, and he crossed his fingers that she believed him, then grabbed a tray for himself.

"Yeah, I think so. There's nothing more I can do to prepare, so I'm trying to keep my mind off it until I'm up there ready to go."

He nodded. There was nothing like the day of a heat. It was always a strange mixture of calm and nerves, of feeling like it was your moment while also hoping you didn't wipe out. "At least the forecast is good. Great visibility."

"Did you see Maya's Instagram posts?" Sam said as if she was dying to change the subject. He silently kicked himself for momentarily forgetting that waiting around to compete was Sam's weak point. How could he have brought it up? Swiftly he ordered food and drinks for them both while Sam waited. Then she grinned at him, her phone gripped tight in her hand as the server called back the order to Finn.

"I didn't see the post." Finn turned to her. "Is it important?"

"Well, yes, if you think that Montalier and Salvaro commenting is important. Finn, it sounds like they're both interested in sponsoring us, or something!"

"Are you serious?" Finn tugged his gloves off and pulled out his phone. Sam snorted and laughed.

"You still have that old thing? It must be . . ." She counted on her fingers. "A bajillion years old."

Ignoring her, Finn opened the app and scrolled until he found the post. The photo of him and Sam was breathtaking. They looked so good, side by side, together. Raising his eyebrows at Sam who was watching him, he pushed a smile on his face. Did she like the photo? Was this the reason she was so concerned about change? His eyes scanned the comments until he found the ones from two of their favorite brands. His mouth dropped open as he read them. Looking up he locked eyes with Sam who was dancing on her toes now, all worries seemingly forgotten.

"Wow," he said. "This is . . . is this? Do you think this is a real offer?"

"Sounds like it." Sam scrunched her nose up. "Doesn't it?"

"Do you think we should reply?"

"Oh my God, that's a great idea." Sam hopped up and down as her food was placed on her tray. "But we should do it together, at the same time. That way everyone will see it."

Finn took his food and moved down the line. "What should we say?"

Paying for both trays, Sam shrugged and brushed Finn

away as he tried to pay. "You can Revolut me, or can you? That phone . . ."

"I can Revolut you," he said. "Give me a minute."

"Don't worry about it," Sam said. She slid into an empty seat and nodded for him to sit down. "We have work to do first. We need to craft the perfect reply—"

Finn added salt to his already salted fries. He dipped into the mayonnaise and popped the fry into his mouth. "God this is delicious."

"Pay attention!" Sam mock-frowned at him.

Finn absent-mindedly ate another fry. He watched Sam as she took a huge bite of her chicken, chewed it and swallowed.

"Finn—hear me out, okay, this is a little crazy, but I was thinking last night—when I couldn't sleep. And I have a plan." Sam glanced around and leaned forward. "We need to make them believe that we *are* the perfect athletes for their partnership. If we land deals with Salvaro and Montalier—without any help from my dad, or anyone else—it means that we don't need them, that we can do things on our own."

"Now who's *not* afraid of growing up." Finn picked the tomato from his burger and ate it. "Seriously, Sam, what's going on? What do you see happening?"

"This is more than just a partnership or a sponsorship deal. I feel it." Sam paused. "Finn, you know how much I want to be free from my dad, but he pays for everything, controls everything."

Finn nodded. "You know how well I understand that feeling."

"Yeah, I know. Well, think about it—we've never considered striking out on our own, before now."

"Sounds ridiculous now you say it." Finn sat forward. "I had the odd thought, but I never really gave it serious consideration. It seemed sort of rude—like I was throwing it all back in my uncle's face, you know."

"I hear what you're saying, and I want you to hear me out before you say no," Sam said. "The reality is that we're not kids anymore. I'm almost twenty-four for crying out loud. You already are, come to think of it. We should be standing on our own two feet. Well, four if we do it together."

"Four feet." Finn loved how serious she was looking.

"Finn. Be real, for one minute." Sam frowned. "Think about it. If we play this right, we can start to manage ourselves, call the shots for once."

"You really *do* think this is real—that there's a chance for a big deal for both of us?" Finn leaned in. "This could change everything, Sam, everything."

"I know!" Sam excitedly whispered. "Becky can keep Valestré. They're not a patch on these guys. The whole world would look at us differently too."

Finn nodded. It was a strange place to be, on the edge of huge success but still being treated as if his sport wasn't his main career.

Sam carried on, almost echoing his thoughts. "I could show everyone that snowboarding isn't my *hobby*—that it is a real career, and that women can have it all."

"Wow. This is huge. The potential . . ." Finn grew quiet.

"It is, isn't it?" Sam put her chicken down. "Like, Finn, if

69

we get a medal we get a bonus payment—but imagine what would happen if we had endorsements."

"I could fix up my mom's house," Finn said quietly.

"At the least," Sam said. She reached over and wiped mayonnaise from his lips. "But it's *how* we get the deal—how can we convince them that they should choose us? We've only the Olympics to convince them."

Finn nodded. "Yeah, we need to make the most of this time frame. We have . . . what's your timetable like?"

Sam looked down at her phone. "Well, tonight is the big air qualie, and the final for that is tomorrow—Monday."

"You'll walk it," Finn said with conviction. "It's your best game."

Sam smiled. "Then I have the halfpipe qualie and final on Wednesday and Thursday. That's the big one for me. What about you?"

Finn pulled out a creased and crumpled piece of paper from his pocket. He reddened as he smoothed it out. "I'm not as organized digitally as you are."

Sam shook her head. "Why am I not surprised?"

Sheepishly he pointed to some dates he'd highlighted. "My first final is this Tuesday."

"I'll be there." Sam twisted the paper from his hands. "Oh! Your last competition isn't until the 13th and 14th! That gives us . . . um, today is the 8th . . . oh crap! That gives us just under a week to make the best impression that we possibly can."

Finn frowned. "Is that even possible?"

"I don't know." Sam folded up his crumpled timetable. She smoothed it into equal folds. "We need a USP."

"A what?"

"A unique selling point—that's what Maya always says. We need an angle that gets their attention."

Finn nodded. He picked up his phone and read the comments from the brands again. The text seemed to jump out of the phone at him, but something niggled at him. The brands seemed to think that he and Sam were a *couple*. The fans too. His stomach twisted. Not in a bad way—more like the way it did right before a jump: tense, weightless, uncertain. He focused on the words again— *perfect couple . . . chemistry . . . real couple . . . something in the air*. The emojis—love hearts, heart eyes . . . it was all there in front of him what the fans wanted. What he wanted too. They needed to be a couple—even if it was just pretend. But would she go for it? Was it too much? What if it ruined everything?

He looked up at Sam, who was fiddling with a loose thread on her sleeve, her brows lowered in concentration. She seemed oblivious to the whole obvious answer.

He cleared his throat. What did he have to lose? He didn't have her now anyway. It was risky. Blurring the lines between the friendship he treasured and playing at being her boyfriend . . . so many things could go wrong. But so what? The worst thing that could come out of pretending to be a couple would be what? That they tried and failed to secure the deals—which was likely. The best thing would be if she actually wanted him—or they got the deals they so badly both wanted. He nodded to the screen.

"This is very leading . . . Maya made it seem as if we are already a . . ." He hesitated.

"A couple!" Sam said. Her eyes widened. "Yes! That's it, Finn, you got it—you found our USP! We *need* to be a couple."

"Do we?" Finn's heart pounded in his chest. *Please say yes!*

"Well yeah—or let everyone think that we are," Sam said. She sat up dead straight. "And that's how we should reply to the comments—as if we're a couple."

"A fake couple?" Finn watched as her fingers flew over the phone screen.

Sam nodded. "Sure—what else can we be? You know what we always said—our promise—don't you?"

"Of course, yes, don't mind me." Finn bit the inside of his cheek to stop himself from saying anything more. Sam was lit up with excitement at his idea, her cheeks flushed, and her eyes sparkled. She looked like she did that very first day they met. "What's going on in that brain of yours?"

With a grin she held her phone out to him. "Pick one of those for you to post; I'll send the other."

Finn felt his neck warm up as he read what she'd written.

Guess you caught us—teammates on the slopes and off! 😊 Thanks, @Montalier and @Salvaro for the kind words. Let's make some magic this season! ❄️ ✨

"It's very suggestive, this one." He kept his eyes on the phone, unwilling to look at Sam in case she could see how important this was to him. He read the second one, his mouth dry as Sam tapped the table with her fingers.

Perfect couple? You *might* be onto something. 😊
Thanks for the love, @Montalier and @Salvaro! We're
just here to break records and hearts. 🏂🎿❄️

"Break hearts?" He looked up at her.

"Well, we can change that, but I like it," Sam said taking her phone back. "Maybe we should add in the hashtag MeltingPoint. It seems to have a following."

Finn nodded. "Okay, I'm not sure which one to choose."

"You take the second one," Sam said. "It sounds more like you—the heart-breaking bit."

Closing his mouth Finn nodded. It did sound like him, he supposed. He'd had seven girlfriends in five years—well, seven that had been reported on. Seven because not one of the women, fabulous and all as they had been, had made him stop thinking about Sam. And not thinking about Sam had become his benchmark—if the woman of the moment could make him forget about her then she stood a chance. And one or two of them had—for a while, but the amnesia never lasted for long and invariably he'd found himself back on the market again, single and Sam-less.

His phone pinged as Sam sent him the reply to post.

"We're really doing this?" he asked. He gripped his phone tightly.

"Yes. We are. It's a great plan. Let's do it now," Sam said without looking up. "Ready?"

Finn nodded, then copied and pasted the text she'd sent into the reply space on Instagram. He glanced up at Sam. She winked at him, and he felt a warmth spread across his body. He'd do anything for her, even pretend they were

73

a couple, although it was going to annihilate him deep inside.

"Ready."

"One, two . . . no wait!"

"What?"

"Press reply on three or after three?"

"On."

"Okay, let's do it. One, two . . ."

"Reply!" Finn pressed the screen and instantly his reply popped up alongside Sam's. The words #MeltingPoint jumped out at him and his chest buzzed with a strange mixture of adrenaline and dread. There was no backing out now. They'd done it already. All he could do was pray it worked, because he couldn't bear to think of the disaster his life would be if it went wrong, and he lost Sam.

6

Sam

Later that day Sam lay on the thin mattress, her hands jammed over her ears and her eyes closed tightly. The big air snowboarding qualie was that evening and she was trying to take a nap and had been since she'd gotten back from lunch with Finn. Wondering where Maya was, she rolled over and pulled her pillow over her head. Leo and Becky were in the next room and from the sounds of it, their enthusiasm for bedroom cardio was nothing short of Olympic level. It sounded as if they were giving a spirited performance of *Passion* in surround sound.

A loud creak and a crash made her bolt upright and laugh. Had something broken in there? The groaning and cries of *Oh God, yes! Harder! Faster!* stopped. Silence filled the air. Then Becky's bathroom door squeaked open. Footsteps traveled across the room and into the bathroom where the sound of running water and the turn of the key in a lock made Sam roll her eyes. This was hard to take. They'd been like rabbits since the engagement. And it was driving her insane. If they weren't having sex, they were all lovey-dovey—sharing morsels of food, laughing over memes and snuggling together on the same chair beside the fire in the lobby, sickeningly feeding each other.

Maya had rolled her eyes earlier and dubbed their feeding each other "energy food", which Leo had taken offence to. Not to mention that Leo had been quite cool with Sam since last night, even though she'd apologized. She hadn't offered an excuse; there wasn't one he'd accept anyway. Instead, she'd bought them a congratulations card and a small gift of matching His and Hers towels with the Olympic rings embroidered on them that she'd picked up early that morning when she hadn't been able to find Finn. But she hadn't had the chance to give the gift to them as they were otherwise engaged. Now she wondered if she could get them matching fake medals and have them engraved with the words *Outstanding Achievement in Loud Applause Without an Audience* but wasn't sure if Leo would see the joke in it. Becky would, but it wasn't worth the risk.

Maya came into the room as the cries of *Oh God* started up again. She rolled her eyes and flopped onto her bed, exhaling hard as she hit the thin mattress.

"Ooof! I forgot this bed was like a rock," she said. "Have they been at it since I left?"

"Well, I got back an hour ago," Sam said. "And they were busy. So, who knows?"

"They sound like they're having fun," Maya said wistfully.

"Want me to knock and see if you can join them?" Sam laughed.

"No!" Maya stuck out her tongue. "It's just been a while. Like you might I add."

"Ugh."

Maya sat up. "Genius move, by the way—you and Finn—on Instagram. Everyone is screaming about it!"

"You saw our replies?" Sam twisted her hair into a braid.

"The real question is who hasn't." Maya got up and finished the braid, securing it at the bottom with an elastic. "Is there something going on that I should know about?"

"What? No! Nothing at all. We just thought that we might get some attention if we played up the whole *partnership* thing."

"Ah, I see." Maya sat down and picked up her phone. "Sounds sneaky—can I help?"

Sam twisted the end of the braid with her fingers. "Maybe—I don't want to get you in any trouble though."

"Honey, I *am* trouble, and you know it. I can more than handle whatever comes my way." Maya put her phone down. "Now spill the tea."

"Maya, have any DMs come in from anyone, offering a partnership or sponsorship?"

"No, not yet."

"And you're the only one with access to that account?"

Maya nodded. "I think so. Why?"

"If I tell you this you can't tell anyone."

"You know I won't."

Sam took a breath. "Finn and I are trying to . . . we're . . ."

"Oh my God! Are you two finally dating?" Maya clapped her hands.

Sam's mouth dropped open. "Wait—what?! No! We're

just pretending. Or at least that's what we're going to do from now on."

"Oh." Maya stopped clapping. "I'm sorry. I don't know what's happening here."

"Listen," Sam started, her heart hammering as Maya's eyes grew more and more round as she laid out her and Finn's plan. "We figured that the best way for us to get noticed by a brand is if we are a brand as well—me and Finn—pretending to be a couple. It's like you said, everyone is loving the idea, and it's getting a lot of attention. We just want to play the game and win for once, you know?" she finished up as Maya pressed her lips together. "I suppose what I'm asking is that if you do get any DMs from Montalier or Salvaro, will you tell me first? I'd like to know before my dad does—that is, if anything happens."

"Sure," Maya said. "But, Sam, are you sure about this— it's kind of a dangerous game to play. Pretending to be a fake couple . . ."

"What do you mean?" Sam said, ignoring the way her pulse jumped in her veins. "We're best friends; we want the same thing. We've agreed to do this."

"Okay," Maya said. "As long as you're sure you can handle it, I'll do my best to get you guys all the attention you need." She shrugged and giggled. "It's a great idea, by the way."

"I know, right!" Sam smiled. She jerked her head toward the door. "I can't listen to this any longer. Becky should be getting ready for the qualie this evening, not getting banged like it's going out of fashion. Leo should know that. Come on, let's go—leave them at it." She pulled on her boots.

"And are you ready for this evening?" Maya grabbed her coat and followed Sam out of the room and down the hallway.

"As ready as I can be." Sam stepped into the elevator. "Seeing as Leo is here invading my space, making it more uncomfortable than it already is, I'm going over to Finn's. Coming?"

"Oh God, yes!" Maya grinned as they stepped out into the lobby. "I've been dying for a nose around the place. I'm going to take so many pictures, and it sounds like the perfect location to catch a few shots of the world's new favorite couple!"

Sam opened her bag, looking into it briefly to make sure she had everything she needed. Then she followed Maya out into the snow, hoping that her dad wasn't at Finn's hotel right now. She really didn't need to have him in her ear before the qualie, barking advice and telling her to hydrate, to mentally plan how she was going to take the jumps, asking if she had seen the weather forecast . . . as if she didn't already think about all of those things. There was nothing else she thought about these days.

The streets were busy, the town crammed full of competitors, families and tourists. It was a nice distraction after the morning she'd had, although her dad would tell her to not get distracted, to concentrate on mantras, positive thinking and warming up. She hated that aspect of the sport. Snowboarding was fun—that's what made it mean something to her. If she couldn't have fun, then what was the point? Her best scores had always been when she'd gone out there relaxed and ready to enjoy herself. It was something her dad never seemed to understand. It wasn't the same as skiing, she supposed. Maybe that's where the difference between them lay, but she highly doubted it. The difference was that she'd never leave her family, and he had. Even though he coached her, paid for her school, never left them without, he'd left them at one of their most vulnerable moments. Black memories swarmed against her as she pushed her way through the crowd. Maya was a step too far ahead for her liking. Struggling to catch up Sam turned a corner, bumping into a tall stranger. Her bag slipped from her shoulder and fell to the ground, her things scattering across the snow.

"I'm so sorry!" Falling to her knees she began frantically grabbing her things and shoving them back into her bag, while apologizing to the stranger. "I didn't see you."

"It's fine, don't worry." A deep voice made her look up. "Ah, it's you."

"Gabriel?" Sam didn't notice the cold snow melting into the knees of her jeans.

"The one and only." Gabriel offered Sam his hand.

"Of all the gin joints in all the world," Sam said with a laugh, taking his hand up. "What has brought you here? I thought you'd retired from skiing."

"I did, after Japan, at the grand old age of twenty-seven. It feels so weird to say that. I'm here for the Games, of course," Gabriel said, brushing snow from her jacket with an easy smile. "I got a new gig—I'm doing some commentary— easier on the knees, harder on the ego."

"You're going to smash it." Sam grinned. "I've no doubt you will." Gabriel shrugged, and Sam caught sight of Maya over his shoulder. She was grinning—her eyes wide and trained on Gabriel's broad shoulders. She'd had a thing for him since Sam had introduced them in Japan last month. Maya was fanning herself dramatically in the background now. Smothering a grin, Sam pulled her gaze back to Gabriel. He stood by the lodge she'd just hurried around, casually smiling that signature, heart-stopping smile that Sam was sure looked great on TV—it was probably one of the reasons he'd gotten the commentating job. She mentally chastised herself for that thought—it was wrong and unfair, and exactly the kind of comment she was actively trying to eradicate in her sport. It wasn't Gabriel's fault that he was easy on the eye.

"I hope so. My nerves are far worse than they ever were when competing. The public can really tear into you if you mess up." Gabriel ran a hand through his dark hair. "Hey, I caught your interview with *Vertical Drop* last month—the one about prize money disparities."

Sam winced. "Yeah, that one got me a few strongly worded emails."

"I'm sure." Gabriel pressed his lips together. "But it also made headlines. Good ones. You said what needed to be said—that took guts."

"Tell that to my dad." Sam squinted up at him. She bit her lip against anything else she might say. Gabriel was easy to talk to, but he was a commentator now—who knows what he might say that could land her in trouble one day. Was he an ally? She wasn't sure.

Out of the corner of her eye she caught someone taking a photo of her and Gabriel. It wouldn't do to have a photo of her and Gabe together, not when she and Finn were trying to win some sponsorship by pretending to be a couple.

Taking a step back away from him she closed her bag. "It's good to see you, Gabe. I'd better get going though, I need to prepare—"

"I know," Gabriel said. "I'm commentating."

"Oh!"

"Don't worry—I'll be nothing but generous." He crossed his heart and smiled. "I promise—and Sam, if you need anything, someone to lead with a good question at a press conference, you can rely on me."

"Appreciate that, Gabe. Thanks." Sam nodded.

"Well, good luck to you, Sam, and to Finn, of course." Gabriel was gone before she could even say goodbye. Maya dashed over to her.

"Oh my God!" Maya gushed. "He's as hot as ever. Although I think Italy suits him better than Japan—that man sure knows how to dress! Did you see him—he looks like he came straight off a catwalk. I don't know anyone else who can pull off wearing a cashmere sweater the way he does—and charcoal is so his color."

"Cashmere? You could tell that from over there?" Sam laughed as Maya linked her arm.

"Honey, I devour runway shows the way you do a cab double cork 1080—in my sleep!"

Sam burst out laughing. "That tracks! Remember how you convinced me to wear that blue dress to my prom?"

"Do I?" Maya lifted her chin. "Can I just say—I wasn't wrong about that dress. You looked like an ice princess in it—and Finn couldn't take his eyes off you that night."

A warm glow wrapped around Sam. Prom night with Finn had been magical and completely unexpected. She allowed Maya to lead her down the snowy streets as the memory of being stood up on that night came back to her.

* * *

"I can't believe this." Sam had flopped down onto the sofa. Blue sparkly fabric had billowed around her like a cloud of blue candyfloss. "Prom is ruined! How could Will do this to me?"

"Get up!" Maya had grabbed Sam by the hand and dragged her into standing. "You'll crease it!" She'd smoothed down Sam's prom dress before carefully hugging Sam. "What do you want to do?"

Sam looked down at her dress, then at her best friend. Maya looked so beautiful. Her chestnut hair had been coaxed into curls in a half-up half-down style, her makeup was flawless, and her red dress made her brown eyes sparkle.

"You should go, go before you miss the photos," Sam had said generously as a lump had formed in her throat.

"Without you?" Maya's forehead had wrinkled, making Sam sigh.

"I don't want to go alone." Sam had twisted her hands together.

"You won't be alone! You'll be with me and Ryan, and the rest of the gang too."

"Everyone else has someone, you know. I'm always the third wheel. For once I thought that I'd have someone too—and I thought that it might be the start of something with Will."

Maya had nodded. "I'm sorry, Sam."

Sam had shaken her head. "It's okay, it's not your fault. Now go—have a great night and tell me everything tomorrow. Everything!"

"I promise." Maya hugged Sam carefully again before leaving.

From the living room window, Sam had watched through a film of tears as the limo had pulled out of the driveway. She'd been moving away from the window, intending to go upstairs to get out of her dress, when her mom and dad had come into the room.

"Bradley, get your ass to my house . . . yes now! Immediately. Hurry up." Coach Harrington was gripping his phone to his ear. "What size are you in a suit?" Her dad had hung up the phone with a firm nod. "Clara—get Leo's old suit ready." Sam's eyebrows had shot into her hairline as her mom had dashed upstairs. *What on earth was he doing? Calling Finn in to take her to prom?*

"Dad? What did you do?"

Her dad had frowned at her quizzical expression. "I said I'd let you go to prom, and I don't want you missing out on this. Bradley will take you."

Sam had gasped. Her mouth went dry. Finn? He'd roped Finn into being her prom date! *Oh God.* With a sinking heart Sam had stared at her dad. *This day truly couldn't get any worse. Not only had her prom date bailed, but now her dad was arranging an alternative for her! No way.*

But it was Finn Bradley . . . maybe this would be okay.

He'd piqued her interest from the moment she'd first seen him. It had been so hard to get him out of her mind, especially after training daily with him for the last few weeks. He was dedicated, strong and every day he looked even better than the day before. Sam remembered how her cheeks had grown red that night as her father had barked down the phone. Finn had always been fine—even back then. To this day he still looked outrageously hot in gray sweatpants, although now he knew it. Honestly, there wasn't one inch of Finn that hadn't made her blush at some stage or another during all these years they'd been friends. With a sigh she remembered how she'd wished with all her might that he felt the same about her, but he'd kept his distance from her.

Sam grimaced, remembering how she'd feared he'd think she was a loser, that her dad was in charge of her whole life. But instead, he'd been the perfect gentleman and that had been the beginning of the best friendship of her life. Maybe this fake-dating relationship idea they'd had would change that though. As Maya said, it was kinda dangerous. But what if it wasn't dangerous—what if it was the start of something? And even if it wasn't—how far was she prepared to go to convince everyone they were a couple? She tucked her arm into Maya's and set off toward Finn's place again, as the question of how far was *he* prepared to go formed in her mind. And what if it all went wrong?

*　*　*

Finn, in a bathrobe and slippers, shivered as he opened his suite door wide and let them in.

"I was in the hot tub," he said before she could even ask. Sam's eyes rested on the light stubble on his jaw and neck, before sliding down the V of the robe. He looked every bit as good as he had when she'd walked in on him naked last week in Milan. Her cheeks grew hot, and any thoughts of what she wouldn't do if she got the chance melted away like frostbitten hands held out in front of a roaring fire. She really should check her period tracker and see what the hell was going on with her hormones because the past couple of weeks she'd been practically drooling over Finn and catching him in a bathrobe just now had her ovaries dancing a foxtrot, *and* doing a handstand *and* a cartwheel. Shuffling in she averted her eyes.

His suite was huge. The hallway was a large square space; the flooring was tiled with beautiful Italian marble, and it was bright and airy. Leaving her boots and jacket in an empty space on the hanging rail, Sam sighed. It would have been nice to have this luxurious space to train from, but she had to stand her ground. If she allowed lodgings to sway her then her dad would think that he'd won her back, and that wasn't going to happen. Not ever. He owed her mom an apology, at the very least, before Sam would even consider allowing him to be a major part of her life again.

"Oh my God! Sam, get in here!" Maya's voice carried in from the living room. Sam glanced up at Finn. Standing on a step that led to the living room, he shrugged, his gown gaping slightly revealing his toned chest. Sam looked away.

"I guess Maya's found the flat-screen TV," Finn said. His ears turned red, and he tightened the belt on his robe. "It's a monster. It's like a private cinema in there."

"Monster?" Maya's head popped around the doorframe. "It's one large popcorn, heavy on the Reese's please, away from being an actual theatre."

Sam ran up the step, past Finn and into the living room. Maya was right. The television was huge. It almost took up the entire wall opposite her and was showing the events live.

"Remind me again how you managed to get this room," Sam said as Finn stood next to her. "Cos a girl could get used to this."

"I've actually never asked." Finn cleared his throat. "I was too embarrassed to."

"This is amazing." Sam stared at the screen. "You can almost see individual snowflakes!"

Maya said as she sat on the arm of a huge comfortable-looking armchair: "You can see all of your competitors here, in detail, and in the warm."

"Maybe," Finn said quietly.

"Are we disturbing you?" Sam asked, suddenly realizing that they'd landed on Finn's doorstep without warning or explanation. "We thought it'd be okay if we came over."

"What she's trying to say is that we can't listen to Leo and Becky banging each other nonstop anymore." Maya didn't even look up from her phone.

Finn flushed bright red. He pulled his robe over his chest. "Jeez. Of course you're welcome here."

"I'm sorry," Sam said. "I didn't think you'd mind."

"I don't," Finn said. "Honestly. I was feeling a bit lonely, actually. But now I'm just feeling cold."

"Back to the hot tub with you," Maya said, waving her

hand in the general direction of the stairs. "I'm making some tea if it's all the same to you."

"Work away, the kitchen has everything you'll need." Finn looked at Sam. "You coming up to the hot tub? It's gorgeous and the view is spectacular. It might help you relax before tonight."

"I've no swimsuit," Sam said. "Otherwise, it'd be a hell yes."

"You've come to the right place," he said. "Come with me."

Sam followed him up a small flight of stairs to another floor, marveling at the size of his suite and the panoramic view of the mountains. He opened a dressing room door, leaned against the doorjamb, and gestured to a suitcase. "Aunt Miranda arrived last night, a day early, and left one of her cases here as she doesn't need it—it's just the extras she brings when she travels. They're staying with friends until tomorrow. She always brings fresh new swimming suits for anyone who might forget theirs, go figure." He shrugged. Sam slipped by him. "She won't mind you grabbing one, I promise. Grab something and put it on. I'll be out there." He pointed to a sliding door and left Sam to change.

Sam looked around. The dressing room was larger than her bedroom back home. One wall was taken up with hanging rails, shelves and drawers. Towels, toiletries and slippers filled baskets arranged neatly on the bottom shelves. Robes hung from the rails. So, this was what it was like to be a star. Opening the suitcase Finn had pointed to, she found a selection of new swimsuits and rummaged through until she found one that might fit. A few minutes later she stared at herself in the full-length mirror. The pale pink one-piece swimsuit was far skimpier than she'd realized, with high-cut legs and a low-cut front complete with zipper that went down to her belly button. She tugged the zipper up and it promptly unzipped itself until it was half open revealing a sizeable amount of her cleavage. Under normal circumstances she'd have been delighted with an opportunity to look sexy in a swimsuit, but not today. Not now Maya had alerted her to the dangers of their secret plan, and especially now that her hormones seemed to be hijacking her entire body and mind.

A vision of Finn pulling the zip down the rest of the way before slipping the straps from her shoulders made her gasp and dash for the suitcase to check if there was another suit that might better fit her. But there were none. The rest were all much too big, or just bikinis. And there was no way she was putting on one of those—they seemed tinier than the swimsuit. She took a last glance at herself in the mirror, steeled her shoulders and pulled herself up tall. All she had to do was to go out there and be normal.

"Friends," she said quietly to her reflection. "You are friends, remember that. That's all. The pretending thing doesn't have to change that." Shaking her shoulders, she left the dressing room and tiptoed out into the hall. Through the glass sliding doors she could see the back of Finn's bare muscular shoulders. He was facing the mountains, chest-deep in bubbling-hot water. Sam shivered. His arms were tanned, and the tattoo on his forearm that she'd noticed when she'd walked in on him naked was clearer now, but she couldn't quite make it out.

Opening the door Sam stepped into the cold afternoon air, her eyes glued to Finn's tattoo. His forearms flexed as he bent his arms and stretched before turning around. The tattoo mesmerized her: a small compass with the outline of a mountain ridge inside the circle. North was marked with a tiny snowflake. Sam longed to touch it. Would it be so bad if she did? Finn looked up, and waved, and the tattoo disappeared from sight. A hot wave of longing beginning in the base of her stomach took Sam by surprise. Shivering, she pulled the zipper on her suit up, again, and quickly went to the tub before her nerves got the better of her—it would be impossible to explain the crazy zipper to Finn without drawing his attention to her breasts. Saying nothing Sam stepped in.

The water was hot, and Sam felt her face glow red as she caught Finn's jaw drop open a little. He shut his mouth, and she caught his Adam's apple bob before he leaned back with a grimace. Sinking into the water Sam blew out a long stream of air. Despite the embarrassment of the unzipping swimsuit and actually getting into the tub, she was glad she was there. The cool air on her face was refreshing while the hot water massaged her body in places that she hadn't realized she was tense in.

"You're right," she said after a few minutes of silence. Leaning her head back against the timber surround, she allowed her shoulders to drop from their tense position by her ears. "This is exactly what I needed. I'd say it's helping you after yesterday's qualies. You'd some tough competition."

"Yeah, it's working magic on my muscles." Finn rolled his head to look over at her. "This is goals, isn't it?"

90

"Sure is." Sam smiled. "Who can we get to give us a hot tub?"

Finn laughed. "Yeah, that's a good one."

"Finn," Sam began. She had the urge to tell him that she was crushing on him, that right now it wasn't hard to pretend to be his girlfriend because that's what she wanted more than anything else. But that wouldn't be fair. They'd made their pact not to let their feelings for one another ruin their chances of an Olympic gold, and she had to stick to it.

"Yeah?" Finn had his eyes closed, and his head leaned back on the timber, his chest, wide and dusted with hair, was practically begging for her to reach over and run her hands over his chest and shoulders. Sam gazed over him, wondering when he'd gotten so broad, so fit, so ridiculously hot. She longed to kiss and lick his exposed neck, nibble on his ear, straddle his thick thighs. Gulping, she sat on her hands to stop herself from acting out on her impulses. Random, hot, vivid impulses about her best friend, the one friend she'd never be able to live without. Maybe Maya was right—maybe this was a dangerous game to play. Finn opened his eyes and looked at her. "You okay?"

"Oh!" Sam blinked and snorted. "God. Yes. Sorry . . ."

"Worried about the qualie later?" A furrow appeared between Finn's blue eyes.

"No, well, yes, I suppose so." Sam grasped onto his explanation for her blatant ogling and for her sudden apparent lack of ability to string a sentence together. What else could she do? "I think I'll be fine."

"You'll be more than fine." Finn sat up. He slid closer to Sam, his eyes filled with concern. "Sam, don't stress this. Don't freeze. Remember to have fun—that's what you always tell me, and it works—every time."

"Have fun." Sam nodded. Her lips parted and she breathed in sharply as her eyes wandered down Finn's torso, then back to his lips before she blinked and looked into his eyes. His eyes seemed to dilate as she whispered the word again. "Fun."

Steam curled around them, rising into the crisp mountain air. The water bubbled softly as Finn leaned back, casually draping his tanned arms along the edge of the tub. His hair was a little damp, tendrils curled, and droplets of water clung to his stubble and eyelashes. His eyes flicked from Sam's eyes to her lips and back. He looked a little confused but intrigued, exactly how she was feeling.

"Yeah, have some fun—you've been way too serious lately." His voice was low, teasing. He cocked an eyebrow, as if testing her out. "You're at your best when you loosen up."

Sam's heart, and between her legs, gave a traitorous flutter. How was she supposed to loosen up when he was there, bare-chested, gorgeous and staring at her like he wanted to have fun with her in ways that made aprés-ski look tame. The heat from the water did nothing but send her feverish thoughts into overdrive. Her skin prickled, not from the cold air, but from the way his gaze seemed to linger on her for just a fraction longer than necessary.

She swallowed hard, focusing on the conversation, not the sharp line of his jaw, the way the muscles in his forearm flexed as he tapped his fingers on the edge of the tub, or where she imagined his fingers might be if she leaned in to this flirtation. And what if she did, what if she leaned right in to this flirtation—what would happen? They were adults now, on the edge of achieving—or losing—everything they'd worked for. But . . . surely if they crossed a line, it *could* be seen as something inevitable, couldn't it? It was only a stupid childish promise they'd made to each other, way back when they hadn't understood the weight of it, that was holding them back. That was all. And anyway, their fake relationship could explain a slip. A touch. A kiss. A night. And God, how she wanted a night—just one night where she didn't have to remember it wasn't real, and that stupid promise.

They had promised each other no romance, no falling in love, no distractions—but all she could think about was how much she wanted to cross that line. Would he kiss her if she made a move? Or would he be horrified?

"What is going on in that head of yours?" Finn grinned playfully. "You look like you're thinking of something you shouldn't be."

"H-hah!" Sam stuttered. She'd forgotten how easily he'd always read her. "What makes you think that I'm thinking anything other than about the qualie?"

"Because I know you." Finn leaned forward slightly, the water between them suddenly charged with even more heat. "And right now, I know you're not thinking of the qualie at all. You're thinking of something that you absolutely shouldn't be—you have your filthy mind face on."

His voice was teasing, but there was an edge to it, and almost a challenge in his eyes that made her stomach flip. Was he thinking of them too? Thinking of pinning her beneath him, her arms above her head, her wrists held in one of his huge hands while the other ran down her body? Was he imagining how it would feel to have her legs wrap around his hips? Sam gazed at his eyes, then his soft lips, and back to his gorgeous blue eyes again. Maybe he wanted her as much as she wanted him. Heat rushed up her neck. Damn it. She needed to know if there was a chance.

"What if I am thinking of something I shouldn't be?" she said, her voice stronger than she felt. She pushed her shoulders back. The zip on her bathing suit loosened of its own accord, revealing almost everything.

Finn's smile faltered for a second. His eyes dropped to the zipper and to the deep V that revealed almost all of Sam's breasts as they jiggled in the bubbling water. He looked back up at her, his blue eyes serious.

"Careful, Sam," he said quietly. "That sounds like you want to break the rules."

"Maybe I do. Maybe it's a stupid rule." Sam's heart pounded. He looked so grim, as if he was weighing up the pros and cons of their stupid pact. The air between them crackled, charged with tension. Sam felt as if she were about to jump from a plane, and Finn was there with her—would he jump too?

"Stupid?" he said. He gazed at her lips, just for a moment before staring intently into her eyes. "Sam . . . I . . ."

Sam held her breath. She'd made a mistake; her heart dropped heavily in her chest.

"Forget I said anything," she said. "I was just . . ." Closing her mouth she swallowed hard. If only she'd kept her mouth shut. Finn was looking at her as if he'd never really seen her before. His eyes, steady and piercing, roamed her face, like he was seeing something new in her, something that he hadn't let himself notice until now. Was he noticing how flushed her skin was? Did he see the way her lips parted with longing for him? His gaze softened, lingering on her mouth for a moment. She felt her pulse quicken. *He's going to kiss me!* But instead of leaning in, Finn pulled back ever so slightly. Sam could see it now, the conflict written all over his face. He was fighting with himself—she was sure of it—wrestling with the same storm of feelings that she was. *Would he give in? For God's sake, give in!*

"So," Finn said, his voice casual, forced. "Qualies, later. You going for that double cork 1260?"

Sam blinked, the abrupt shift in his tone hitting her like a bucket of icy water. She forced a laugh to mask the sting of his rejection. She felt her chest tighten, a bitter mix of embarrassment and hurt rising in her throat.

She shrugged. "I guess you'll find out later." She lightened her voice. There was no way he was going to see how he'd hurt her. "Oh, Maya and I bumped into Gabe on the way over."

Finn's head turned toward her. "Gabe? The guy who's retired now." He kept his tone neutral, but she was aware of the flicker of something in his eyes—recognition? Maybe even the slightest hint of annoyance. Gabe had beaten him in Japan last month. Obviously, it still stung.

"Yeah. He looks great, he really does. Like he's still training, you know, or as Maya would say 'a walking Dolce & Gabbana ad'." She let the words hang in the air.

Finn snorted. "That sounds like Maya—she always had a type."

"Yeah, that's true. He was sweet, and they'd make a cute couple, wouldn't they?" Sam said quietly, looking out across the mountains then back at him. When he didn't answer she said quietly, "He wished me—and you—luck."

"Mmmm." Finn's gaze drifted to the water. "Good for him." He gave a small shrug, as if he was brushing the thought of Gabe away. "Let's hope Maya doesn't accidentally propose to him. Another proposal is all we need."

Sam smiled, but her heart was still caught in her throat. She hadn't meant anything by mentioning Gabe, not really. And anyway, he knew it was Maya who had a thing for Gabe. Not her. He kept his gaze on the bubbling water. The silence stretched long and heavy. Awkward.

"Anyway, I should go, get ready. Big evening ahead." She stood up and grabbed a towel. The heat of the water clinging to her skin did little to chase away the cold knot in her chest. Why the hell did she have to mention Gabe at all when he meant nothing to her?

Finn looked up, his expression unreadable. "Yeah," he said, his voice quieter now. "Good luck."

Sam nodded and turned away, biting back the disappointment that threatened to overwhelm her. She'd put herself out there, hadn't she? She'd let him know that she was . . . willing to . . . She tightened the towel around her. She didn't know what exactly she was willing to do with Finn. All she knew was that things had changed between them and now that they had, she desperately wanted more from him. But he didn't seem willing to play ball.

7

Finn

Finn's gaze followed Sam as she tiptoed across the balcony, her towel tightly wrapped around her body, and whoa, what a body. He ran a hand through his damp hair, leaving it standing on end, feeling what he was starting to recognize as a familiar tension around his chest. *What just happened?* He'd been *so* close to kissing her, to changing everything between them—forever. The way her eyes had locked on his when they'd— He took a breath. And the way her cheeks had flushed as he'd stared at her— Oh God—she was stunning. More beautiful than he'd really ever noticed, which felt strange. This wasn't the first time they'd seen each other in a hot tub, but somehow it had felt far more intimate than anything else he'd ever experienced. More private. Loaded. Like something between them had shifted without permission.

That swimsuit—he groaned quietly. He'd another raging hard-on—thank God for the bubbles hiding how hard he was. It was starting to become a regular habit, getting turned on when she was around. He pressed his lips together, unhappy at how he was thinking about her. Sam wasn't just some girl he wanted to get with. She was more than that and had been from the moment they'd made their pact. She was more than how she'd looked; he knew that. It was everything that she was: the way she thought, the questions she asked him, the way she inspired him to get up and keep going even when he wanted to just give it all up. What he loved about her most was the way she was always just herself. His head snapped up. That was it—she was acting very unlike herself this evening . . . even down to the swimsuit she'd worn.

Had she chosen that suit on purpose—maybe she'd wanted him to unzip it, to run his hands over her smooth skin, to grasp her hair and tilt her head back so that her only option was to kiss him. He groaned. He'd wanted it, but *no*, she clearly hadn't wanted it. She couldn't have. Sam had never been backwards about being forwards—she didn't believe in that. She believed in equality, especially in love, or lust. All that talk about breaking stupid rules though . . . had that been her making a move? *Damn*. Had he misread the signs?

His mind raced. He had a sinking feeling that he'd made a mistake, like he should've shut his mouth about the qualies later. He should have ignored his mind telling him that if Sam wanted him then she'd have made the first move because that's what she'd always done—he'd seen her do it so many times with other men. Finn stared at Sam's back as she straightened her shoulders. There was something in the way Sam was holding herself that made him feel she was upset, and whatever it was, he couldn't let her leave this way. His erection subsided as he watched her shoulders slump.

"Sam?" His heart hammered as he shifted in the tub. She didn't turn back, just adjusted her towel, wrapping it like a shield around her gorgeous body. "What's going on? Why are you acting like this?"

"I'm not acting like anything," Sam said, her words guarded. "I need to go, that's all." She shook her head as if shaking away the words she truly wanted to say to him. And it hit him, like a snowplow doing ninety in a fifty zone—unexpected, forceful and impossible to ignore. He couldn't love her more. Her face was tight with emotion, her eyes bright, too bright. She'd pulled the towel up around her shoulders now as if she didn't want to expose anything of herself to him anymore. Her eyes flicked to him, and she gave a small smile. Before he could say another word, she'd opened the door and stepped inside. The door behind her closed with a soft click.

Finn was left in the steam, his mind racing a thousand miles a minute. Was it possible that Sam—

The door opened and Maya bounded out onto the balcony, waving her phone. "You won't believe the amazing shots I got of you two. The fans are going to love this—you guys are hot! I predict a sponsorship deal in no time."

"She told you?" He slipped lower into the hot water.

"Oh, she did, as you should've guessed."

"Right."

"Listen, I am here for it, Finn. I got you and our girl all the way. Cross my heart." Maya leaned a hip against the outer wall of the hot tub, holding her phone in front of Finn.

Steam billowed around the phone but through the misty air Finn could see the photo Maya had captured so perfectly.

Him and Sam, their skin tinted warm peach by the hot tub lights, were leaning toward each other, wholly engrossed in one another. Sam's zipper was low; his tattoo was bold. The mountains in the background were a blur and the steam swirled around them enticingly. The caption read:

> Steam, stars, and stolen moments. Steaming up together before heating up the competition. 💧❄️ #QualifyingForYourHeart #HotTubConfessions #MeltingPoint

Already the replies and likes were coming in hot and heavy with suggestions as to what exactly qualified as a hot tub confession. Finn half laughed, his mind still on Sam.

"Maya, this is crazy."

"It's brilliant," Maya said. "Marketing 101. Sex sells."

"There wasn't any sex!" Finn blurted.

Maya looked at him, her face scrunched up laughing. "I know! Bet you wanted it though. I can see it—the camera never lies."

Finn rubbed his hands over his face, scratching at his stubble as the bubbles rolled around him. "Ah, Maya, that's . . ."

"Sorry." Maya laughed. "But who wouldn't! It's so romantic out here, and you two are bloody gorgeous. Why you're not actually together is a mystery to me."

"We're friends," Finn mumbled, his heart low. "Best friends."

"All the best couples are," Maya chirped. "Anyway, I wanted to tell you that I'm on your side—I want you guys to get what you deserve. Valestré should've been Sam's, and now she's got to fight twice as hard as before."

Finn closed his eyes briefly. "And then some."

Maya nodded. "I know, but I promise you that I will make sure you guys get your sponsorships."

"You're a star, Maya, thank you," Finn said. "I really appreciate that. I just hope that no one sees through us. And that Coach Harrington doesn't catch wind of it either."

"Intriguing." Maya smiled. "First off, no one will know this is a fake situationship. Second—what is going on with Coach Harrington?"

Finn pursed his lips for a moment before coming clean. "Sam doesn't know this, Maya, and she can't find out."

Maya nodded. Finn continued, "Coach warned me to stay away from Sam."

Maya's eyes almost popped out of her head. "I'm sorry?! What? When?"

"Funnily enough, it was the first time Sam and I were in a hot tub together."

"Okay, what is happening here?" Maya gasped. "I can't keep up."

"It's nothing," Finn said. "It was after my first session with Coach—he caught us in the hot tub and ordered Sam out, then he pretty much told me to keep my hands off his daughter as she was, and I quote: *the best of the best*. And that he'd drop me if I even thought of crossing the line with her."

"Wow." Maya leaned against the hot tub wall. "I bet that was scary—Coach is terrifying."

"Scariest thing ever, Maya." Finn breathed out. "The man is a legend and built like a tank. I was seventeen and hadn't a clue. I almost walked away then and there."

"If you had, you could've dated her back then," Maya said.

"But then I wouldn't be here now."

Maya's brows knit together. She looked right at him and half smiled. "Does this mean you have always had a thing for our girl?"

Finn nodded miserably.

"Oh my God." Maya's eyebrows rose. "Finn, you poor baby—all these years?"

"Don't say anything," he said quietly. "I'd rather be her friend than lose her. And if Coach finds out—or even gets a whiff of what we're doing—I'm screwed six ways from The Rockies."

Maya gave a low whistle and then mimed zipping her lips before words tumbled from her mouth. "Okay, first up, that man gives everyone the fear. Second of all, we've got this—you and me."

Finn nodded.

"Hey, listen up, you're not the only one who wants to help Sam. If this plan works, and she gets the sponsorship she deserves . . . then you'll get the chance to show her how you really feel."

"Without losing everything?" Finn looked at Maya.

"Yes. We do this smart," Maya said, eyes lighting up with purpose. "We control the narrative. We make it bulletproof—well, I will—I am the best content creator for this job, and you . . . you've got the digital skills of a potato in airplane mode."

"Thanks, I think," Finn snorted.

"You are welcome!" Maya laughed. She grew serious. "Listen, I will make this so perfect, Finn. I've got all the angles, captions, filters and hashtags to make this whole fake dating thing look *chef's kiss* believable. By the time I'm done the world's gonna be shipping #FinnAndSam harder than a FedEx truck in a snowstorm." She leaned in, her voice dropping conspiratorially. "And what's more, I'll make it so airtight that even Coach Harrington couldn't call it out without totally exposing himself."

Finn frowned. "Exposing himself—how?"

Maya smirked. "Basically, I will make every post of you guys look spicy hot but also ambiguous—it'll be hard for him to say anything because we let the fans do the talking—let them make it happen. And after that, if he kicks off, he'll have to admit that he's got a personal problem with you and Sam being together." She tossed her hair. "Trust me, he'll look like the bad guy if he says anything—and he knows it. And you and Sam—you guys can go and live happily ever after."

"Wow. I love it, but hell, Maya—I wouldn't want to cross you. You are far more conniving than I ever realized." Finn shook his head.

"Honey, you know nothing," Maya said as her tummy rumbled. She rubbed her belly. "I really shouldn't have had all that Prosecco last night."

"You should eat," Finn said. "There's plenty of food in the kitchen."

"I saw that," Maya said. "Coach Harrington likes his stars well fed, so it seems."

"You could say that," Finn replied, he glanced over Maya's shoulders to the dressing room door. Was Sam still in there—possibly upset? He was so stupid, now that he thought of it. He'd basically pushed her away. No wonder she'd gotten out of the tub. What kind of an idiot was he? How could he, of all people, he who was the biggest flirt he knew, not have seen it for what it was when it happened? Sam had made a move on him. He squinted. The truth was he *had* known, and he'd been scared. A fool. His attention was drawn back to Maya as she turned to see what he was looking at.

"I'm going to make a sandwich, toasted. Yes, I think that'll help." Her stomach grumbled again as she turned back to him, shrugging at the empty hallway. She laughed. "Want one?"

"Yeah, I do, thanks." Finn climbed out of the hot tub and reached for a towel. He didn't want a sandwich, but he wanted Maya to leave. He needed to talk to Sam—alone. "I'll be down in a few minutes."

"Sure thing." Maya ran her eyes down his long frame. "Looking good."

"Maya!" Finn wrapped the towel around his waist, laughing as she blew him a kiss before heading downstairs to the kitchen.

"Toastie in twenty!"

Finn barely heard her call back up the stairs. He walked down the hall toward the dressing room door. Pausing, he laid his hand on the warm oak panel and closed his eyes. Was this a good idea—talking to Sam? Telling her that he'd messed up by not kissing her in the hot tub, by not taking her hint? Her lips had been ready to be kissed, plump and pink. He should have kissed her. At the very least they needed to talk about what had happened between them, now more than ever. Especially as Maya was in on the charade too. They clearly had some tension between them, and they needed to clear that up or else, as Maya had said, the camera never lies, and they'd fool no one. Opening his eyes he pushed the door and stepped into the dimly lit space.

*　*　*

The sound of running water drew him to the back of the room where the shape of Sam's curvy body was just about visible behind the steamed glass door of the luxurious double shower. She was facing away from him, still wearing her swimsuit, the pale pink almost the same color as her skin. She almost looked naked. His cock flickered into life thinking of Sam's soft skin, of touching her and having her come alive in his arms. Stepping closer, he cleared his throat. Sam turned her head; her blonde hair, wet and dark, clung to her shoulders. She wiped the steamy glass leaving a clear streak. Her eyes ran over his body.

"Finn!" She swiped water from her face. "What . . ."

Finn opened the shower door. Steam billowed out, engulfing him, making his body goose-bump all over. "Can I come in?" His voice rumbled in his chest, thick with the words he wanted to say—and everything he was terrified to.

Sam nodded mutely. Her eyes widened as he dropped his towel, before stepping into the shower.

"I messed up." He locked eyes with hers. He felt his cock

105

rise, the ache unmistakable, but it was his words that made his pulse quicken, hoping she'd understand. "I think the rules are stupid too."

Sam gasped. "You do?" She glanced down, then back up again. A surprised smile on her lips. Water sluiced down her shoulders and over her breasts. His throat went dry, and he cursed his cock for giving him away. He cleared his throat.

"Rules are made to be broken." He couldn't tear his eyes away from her, from how delicious she looked, all wet and wide-eyed. His fingers twitched to touch her, but he fought the urge, even as his mind screamed at him to reach for her. He breathed out unsteadily. Every nerve in his body on edge. "What do you think?"

"Finn . . ." Sam swallowed. She brushed water from her forehead before laying her hand on his chest. He gasped, loving how soft and tiny her hand felt. What would it feel like wrapped around his cock?

"Tell me if you want this, Sam," Finn said, his voice hoarse, his pulse thundering in his ears. He forced himself to stay still, to wait for her response. It was torture. Hot water splashed against his chest as Sam took a half step toward him, stopping inches from her body meeting his. It took all his resolve not to reach for her. He swallowed, feeling his Adam's apple bob, and wondered if she knew the effect she was having on him. *Please, Sam, don't make me wait.* His hand itched to grasp her and pull her against him. His skin longed for hers against his. He wanted to hold her face in his hands, to kiss her, taste her sweet mouth before nipping down the side of her neck and . . . Lord, how he *needed* her.

"I do." Sam looked up at him, blinking as the water splashed up at her face. "God, I really, *really* do. Touch me, Finn. Please."

Finn growled. His heart pounded as he lowered his lips to hers, his hands tangled in her hair as she sighed against him. Her mouth was warm, soft and tasted like cherries, ripe and sweet. She pressed up against him, her whole body hot and eager, and he almost cried out. This was the moment he'd been longing for, for as long as he'd known her. Her hands were in his hair, grasping and pulling him closer. Leaning her back against the marble wall, he pulled back for a moment, marveling at how responsive she was to his touch. As if she'd been waiting for him too.

Sam raised her eyes to his, looking at him with desire and hunger from under her lashes leaving him with no doubt that she wanted him. Her cheeks were pink, and she bit her lip before pulling him back to her. Her tongue gently pushed into his mouth. His cock strained against his shorts, as if demanding to be noticed, demanding that she use her mouth and tongue down there too, longing for her touch. As if reading his mind, Sam's hands slid down his torso, over his tight abs and down the front of his shorts.

"Jesus, Sam," he groaned as her kisses trailed down the side of his neck. "Fuck."

He felt Sam smile against his neck, her hands stroking him through the fabric, making him harder than he'd ever been in his life. He'd never wanted someone more than he did in that moment. She ran her fingertips along the waistband of his shorts, pulling them down inch by inch. Panting, he reached down and pushed them down in one quick movement. His cock sprang up and he groaned as the water and her hand found it.

"You're impatient," she whispered, glancing down at her hand. "And impressive."

"Oh God, Sam." Finn leaned his forehead against hers. "You have no idea how impatient . . ."

"I think I do," she said before letting him go.

"Don't stop!" He reached for her, tilting her face so he could kiss her again. She ran her hands along his hips, up his back and down to his ass where she grabbed him and pulled him hard against her soft belly, his cock pressed into her, pulsing with want.

"You're a witch," he moaned as his hands ran along her shoulders and down her arms. Leaning away from her, he reached for the zipper on her swimsuit, slowly tugging it down to her navel.

Sam arched her back as he slipped the straps down her shoulders, her breasts pressing against his chest as he held her waist.

"Finn." Sam looked up at him.

"Yeah?" Finn took a breath. She looked concerned, a tiny furrow between her eyes. "You okay?"

She nodded. "This is crazy."

"Crazy good or crazy bad?" He brushed a strand of hair away from her cheek, hoping to God she'd say good.

"Good," Sam whispered. "Better than I'd imagined."

Finn felt a warmth spread inside him. "You imagined this?"

Sam shrugged. "Once or twice."

"Oh." Finn leaned over her. "What exactly did you imagine. Show me."

Sam blushed even harder. "That you'd do this." She took his hand and laid it on her breast. Her hand pressed down on the back of his, urging his fingers to squeeze her nipple. Her hot lips found the base of his throat, but only for a moment before he pushed her back against the tiles.

"What about this?" he said, his voice a deep growl. Without waiting for a reply, he pressed a hand against her chest, his fingers splayed around her collarbones holding her in place. His other hand caressed her breast, rolled her nipple, squeezing and pulling as she gasped and moaned.

She nodded. With a grin he lowered his head and took her nipple into his mouth, sucking and nipping gently while she writhed against him. His cock throbbed as he smoothed his hand down her body, finding where her swimsuit gathered at her hips. She reached to push it down, but he grasped her hands and held them over her head.

"Now who's impatient?" He smiled, his voice low and tender, as he ran his hand over her quivering lower belly and down over her mound. Sam cried out as his fingers massaged her through her swimsuit, her arms above her head. Finn kissed her deeply again, catching every sound, every breath, every cry of pleasure, holding her up as she softened and moved with and against him. Her moans grew deeper as he pressed her clit, sending a shiver of pride along his shoulders. God, she was amazing, so perfect, so sweet, hot and damn beautiful. She was incredible, and it was mind-blowing that she seemed to be loving this as much as he was.

Her knees began to give way as he tapped against her mound, varying the tapping from soft to hard, then harder as she cried out: "Yes, oh God, yes! Don't stop!" He flicked the shower over to the gentler rainwater setting, before slowly guiding her to the floor. Then, kneeling beside her, he reached for her swimsuit and began peeling it from her hot, wet body. He slowed down, reveling in the moment he'd never thought he'd have.

Seeing Sam gloriously naked before him, her elegant curves, her legs slightly open revealing her swollen lips, her mouth parted and panting, trusting him—it made his chest ache—part lust, part love. God, how he wanted her completely and utterly, forever. He stroked himself a few times, his eyes locked on her half-lidded gaze. The way she looked at him almost made him come. He released his cock and ran his hand up her trembling thigh before his fingers found solace between her swollen lips. Her hot silkiness, the way she lifted her hips to allow him to reach deeper into her, drove him almost to the edge of insanity. Spreading her legs, he lowered his head to taste her. His tongue flicked against her clit before he gently sucked on it. Sam bucked beneath him, raising her hips higher as if she wanted him to eat every last inch of her. Happily, he savored her, letting his tongue explore her until it dipped right into the core of her. Her hands were in his hair, grasping his head tightly while water ran over her body.

Glancing up at her, to watch her face, needing to witness what he was doing to her, he felt a thread inside him tighten, binding him to her in a way he didn't think he could ever undo. The way she gazed back at him, so intimate, so honest and raw, it almost broke him. Slipping a finger to her entrance, he watched, his chest swelling with pleasure as she squirmed against his touch.

"Please, please," she moaned as he teased his finger in a little of the way. "Finn!"

"You like this?" He leaned over her. His finger slid slowly along her again as if he was memorizing her.

"Uh, yes!" Sam begged, her eyes shut tight. "I'd like more."

"More?" Finn's throat tightened. He grasped her thigh gently and pressed her legs open even more. "Like this?"

He slid two fingers up inside her, curling them to press against that smooth, sensitive spot deep within her. Sam's cries echoed around the room, softened by the steam. Her back arched as he stroked deep inside her, his thumb massaging her while the hot water gently fell on her breasts and belly. She tightened around his fingers, and he knew she was on the verge. Leaning over her, he continued caressing that sweet spot inside her as she bucked hard against him, her whole body writhing and twisting beneath him. She shuddered to a climax, her hands in his hair as he dipped his head to taste her again, his tongue rasping hungrily against her now soaked skin. She was so swollen and pink that he couldn't get enough of it. She tasted fresh, new, and yet familiar.

"Finn." Sam gasped. Her voice weak and breathy. "Oh God . . ."

Sam's heat tightened around his fingers even more and she came again as he sucked and stroked her. Her body bucked, her legs trembling as her cries reverberated around the shower room. Looking up along her glorious body, Finn's heart filled with joy as he watched her fall apart—she was so beautiful, so uninhibited. Sam was beyond anything he'd ever dreamed of. This first time was like nothing he'd ever imagined—it was so much better, so amazing . . . His cock bobbed as she opened her eyes and stared at him. He almost cried. This was more than sex. This was Sam—the girl who made him laugh when he didn't want to, called him out relentlessly, and who knew him better than he knew himself. And she was letting him see her—all of her—not just her body, she was baring what felt like her very soul to him. He held his breath, his mind reeling from the beauty of it all. *So this, this was love.*

"Finn . . ."

"Yeah." His voice rasped. He moved over her until he was positioned between her warm legs, his cock brushing against her hot, wet silkiness, making him suck in his breath. What would it be like when he plunged inside her—to have that tight, heat around him? He looked down into Sam's face. She was staring at him, water droplets clinging to her eyelashes, her eyes questioning.

"You all right?" he asked, concerned. What if he messed this up—or hurt her? What if she'd changed her mind?

"Never been better," she whispered. Her tongue ran along her bottom lip. "You?"

"Thank God," he whispered. "I thought for a minute you changed your mind."

"No." Sam wrapped her legs around his hips, pressing his hard length against her softness. "I most certainly haven't changed my mind."

Groaning, Finn rocked against her, loving how she gasped and tightened her whole body around his. "I don't want this to end."

Nodding, Sam bit her lip. She tilted her hips upward, crying out as his cock slid down to her entrance. Finn pressed his tip lightly against her. God, she was irresistible. She closed her eyes and whispered "please", and he almost plunged deep into her then and there. There was nothing more he wanted than to be moving hard inside her, to feel her tight around his cock, nothing. But with a moan he pulled away.

"Just give me a minute," he murmured, his voice thick with desire. "I want this to be perfect."

"It already is." Sam touched him and he almost gave in.

"Condom," he panted, wishing he could be reckless for once and not care.

"What?" Sam fully opened her eyes, blinking against the water that was beginning to run cold.

"Come on." Finn got up and reached to help her up. "My room."

Sam followed him out of the shower. He wrapped a warm towel around her and pulled her into his arms, kissing her passionately. The click of the dressing room door broke their kiss. Stepping back from Sam, Finn felt his heart race as footsteps grew louder the closer they got to the shower room. Sam stared at him, frowning. She reached for him, but he raised his finger to his lips. Shaking her head she called out, "Hello?"

"Toasties! Sam—I made you one—sustenance before the qualies," Maya's voice called out. "You still in that shower? There'll be no hot water left."

"Just out," Sam said. Finn reached into the shower and turned off the running water. "I'll be down in a minute."

She winked suggestively at Finn. He grinned and shook his head to hold back a laugh.

"Tell Finn," Maya called from the dressing room. "I can't find him—but he's probably in his room—and I know how much you'd like to relive that naked moment you guys had a few weeks ago." She giggled. "And if I were you, I'd take this chance!"

Finn's eyebrows shot up. He grinned at Sam and dropped his towel. Sam's eyes immediately lowered to his cock, then, as her face reddened, rose back to his face, then just as quickly she looked away.

"Eh, yeah," she half stammered. "Thanks for that!"

"See you in the kitchen." Maya left the dressing room.

Sam turned to Finn, who was standing, in all his naked glory, with his hands on his hips. She stared at his shoulder as if there was nowhere else she could look. "I can explain . . ."

Finn twirled slowly. "No explanations necessary."

Sam started laughing. "Finn! Come here!"

"Happy to!" He picked up his towel and wrapped it around his waist.

Sam leaned against him, laying her head on his damp chest. "I, eh, I wasn't expecting this to happen."

"Me either." Finn leaned his chin on her head. "It was . . ."

"Yeah." He could feel her smile against him, hear the happiness in her voice. "Well . . ."

"Well," he echoed. He ran his hands down her back, settling on her waist. "We'd better get moving, before she comes back to find us."

"Yeah. Can you imagine the Insta post?"

"There's that," he said happily.

"See you downstairs," Sam said, planting a kiss on his chest.

Finn squeezed her tight. "Downstairs in five." He let her go and walked to the door. Resting his hand on the handle, he turned back to look at her. She was so beautiful. It was like he'd never seen anything as perfect or wonderful before in his whole life. Not Bernini's statues, not the Northern Lights rippling across the sky, not the mountains covered in the freshest snow. His heart swelled as she smiled shyly at him, her hair tucked behind her ear and her towel clinging to her curves. He'd never forget this moment, *never*.

8

Sam

It was dark, the sky filled with stars and the wind nonexistent. Down near the base of the competition slope, sponsor banners barely moved, and the crowds gathered. Livigno's snowy peaks were shadowy silhouettes against the brightly lit terrain, the snow sparkling under the floodlights. Sam stood at the top of the slope, holding her board tightly. With a sigh she smoothed down the *Ohana* sticker her mom had given her years ago after a family holiday. She didn't care that it was meant for a surfboard—it was the meaning that she loved. Now it was fading, scratched and the edges were curled. Sam pressed down again on the sticker, willing it to stay on. She'd peeled it off every old board and set it on every new one. It had survived snowstorms, competitions, and tears. But there was no way she could compete without it. She kissed two fingers and touched the sticker, praying it wouldn't come off. She needed it.

"Sam!" Her dad stalked over to her. His voice was low but sharp as his eyes flickered over the sticker. "Get it together. You look like you've never seen a slope before."

"Okay," Sam snapped. "I'm with it. Ugh." She struggled with her goggles and her helmet.

"You're not." Jake fixed her with a hard stare. "You haven't been with it since we got here. This isn't some backcountry practice run, Sam. It's the damn Olympics."

"I know what it is." Sam's tone cracked sharper than she intended.

"Then act like it," Jake said. "You can't let your mind wander—not now. This isn't a season—it's your career."

The words hit like icy water, but Sam didn't flinch. Jake continued. He stepped toward her. "You were made for this, Sam. Don't throw it away because you're too stubborn to talk to me."

Sam kept her eyes on the slope. "You know what day today is?"

His silence stretched.

"Five years ago," she added quietly. "The drive home from the Breckenridge qualies. Leo driving, Mom singing those country love songs . . ."

Jake looked away, jaw working.

"She always said qualies were her favorite." Sam's voice caught just slightly. "I'm not distracted, Dad. I'm focused—on more than you think."

Jake's shoulders shifted, like he might feel something, but he leaned backwards, as if he was suddenly burdened by emotions. His eyes flickered with a mix of sadness, grief, and hope. Sam searched his strong, angled face. Maybe he'd reach out, just once, like he used to, before everything changed. But instead, he raised his chin, his eyes on the course she was about to run.

"Land the 1080 clean, no flair, no distractions. Keep it technical." Jake turned away.

Sam nodded as he glanced back at her, fighting the tightness in her chest. How was he able to do this—focus so clearly on the competition without thinking about Mom and how happy she'd been to see where they were today?

She watched as he stood to one side, scrutinizing the competition, his face still, his eyes slits. Then she turned her attention to the slopes as Lila Chambers got in position for her final run. The British woman kept her eyes on the slope and ignored Jake Harrington and Sam saluted her for that. It wasn't an easy task ignoring Coach Harrington's presence. Lila took off and Sam held her breath as the young woman zoomed down the approach, then up over the jump. Everything looked great, but Sam knew Lila had ruined her chances as soon as she'd gone into the air. She cringed as Lila seemed to lose her balance midair—she gripped her snowboard for a moment too long and paid the price. Her mouth grimaced and her arms waved wildly as she fell, missing her landing badly.

There was an audible collective intake of breath from the crowd as Lila crashed down, sliding and tumbling to a stop. She lay in a crumpled heap for a minute before moving slightly. Sam hugged her board and watched in horror as a number of officials hurried toward Lila, while a medical crew with a stretcher came into sight. Lila slowly got up, shook herself off and dejectedly slid down the slope to the relieved cheers of the crowd. The medical crew checked her over and she left with them, not even waiting for her score.

Sam swallowed. She loved snowboarding, but the sport

was unforgiving when you made a mistake, and you could get broken up really bad if you made one slight error. Her mouth went dry as she went through the trick she was thinking of pulling off. If she managed to do it then she'd certainly get a place in the final, but if she messed up then she'd be out. This was her final run of the qualifiers for the big air section, and while her score so far was good, she needed this run to be brilliant—if even just to boost her confidence. Pulling her gaze away from the slope, Sam listened to the commentator. Gabriel's deep voice rang out clearly, his concise commentary fair and accurate, and Sam was sure that Maya would be hovering around the media room trying to catch his eye.

But all of that didn't matter now. Now there was Finn. At last.

A pleasurable shiver made Sam bite her bottom lip. Finn! FINN! The way he'd said that he thought the rule was stupid too . . . Oh God, the way he'd stared into her eyes as he'd said it. It had been perfect! So perfect! She broke into a huge smile as Becky made her way past. Becky smiled back and Sam nodded, the smile leaving her face.

Becky had completed two of her three runs and was already ahead of her on the scoreboard and definitely destined for the final. If she kept up this spate of good luck, she'd take the gold in the final, that was for sure. This was her third run, and she set off with the confidence of someone who knew she was winning. Sam watched Becky slide down the approach, holding her breath as Becky picked up speed. She flew up over the ramp, and Sam breathed out. Becky executed a perfect frontside double cork 1080 finishing her run off in style and with a punch in the air. Becky was ecstatic, as were the other competitors. That run had just given Becky a shot at the podium—she'd already claimed her first finals place.

Sam clapped as they cheered Becky on. She was thrilled for Becky but her mind was racing. That was exactly what she'd planned on doing. It was what her dad had told her to do—had he told Becky the same thing? Should she do it now or would it look like she was copying Becky? Her dad caught her eye, and she waved at him, seeking his coaching advice. Originality was a key element, and she didn't want to get penalized for being a copycat. She waved again, but her dad turned away and started walking toward the way down as if he was done with the competition. Sam's heart pounded hard in her chest, her breath billowing into clouds before her. What was going on—wasn't her dad, her coach, going to guide her? What was she to do now? Sam glanced around. There was no one near her, not one of her teammates. What would Finn say?

Her eyes skimmed the crowd, searching for Finn. Finally, she spotted him, near the break in the barriers where the competitors left the run-off. His tatty orange beanie almost glowed in the crowd. Her knees went weak thinking of what had happened between them earlier. Her breath caught in her chest. It had all happened so fast, it hardly felt real—but the ache between her legs that was begging for it to all happen again made her realize that it most certainly had happened, and it had been so damn good. God, he'd made her come twice, twice! And this was just their first time together. Her heart pounded as another competitor set off.

Sam barely noticed how that competitor scored. She couldn't stop thinking about how when she'd left the hot tub, she'd been sure he wasn't interested. But then he'd followed her into the shower . . . and oh my God . . . the way he'd kissed her, the way his hands had possessed her, the way he'd hoarsely whispered her name over and over—it made her think that he'd always known exactly what he wanted to do with her if he'd had the chance. And he'd made that chance happen—and boy, he'd taken it with both hands. The way he'd buried his face in her, tasting her as if he were starving, God, just remembering it was almost enough to make her come. Again.

Gabriel's voice rang out, announcing the score of the previous competitor. Sam blinked and shook her head. She had to stop thinking of Finn, and how he'd touched her . . . She shook herself again and stamped her feet, getting her blood flowing and warming up her muscles. She knew what Finn would say, he'd say *so what if Becky did a loop-di-loop-fandango and the can-can, get out there and have fun and do whatever feels like the right thing to do when you hit that ramp.* But he wasn't standing here with her. He hadn't seen how her dad had practically turned his back on her as if she had no chance now that Becky was definitely on the rise. No, she had to try it. If Becky could do it then she could too. She just had to do it better. She had to get that medal. She clenched her jaw.

Finn's voice rang in her mind, *have fun* he'd said, and she knew he was right, but competing wasn't just about the fun. She had to make this count—she just had to. Her dad was right: she'd worked her whole life for this moment, and she just couldn't let it be a moment of fun. She had this one chance because as much as she didn't agree with her dad, she was afraid that one bad fall, or simply one missed opportunity, would be the thing that would take her out of snowboarding for the rest of her life—like it had for Leo. Maybe she should change it up—add on to the run that her dad had first told her to do—the run that had given Becky a place in the final. But was that trying too hard?

Taking a breath, Sam closed her eyes and imagined completing the run perfectly. She imagined going for the triple—then went back to the double—the triple was too hard. It was too risky. Or was it? Sam tried to think what her dad would say. Then she opened her eyes, took her position, and went for it.

9

Finn

The crowd had thinned out and Finn was relieved. The qualies were nerve-racking enough without them resembling the finals, and the competition was tough this year. Becky had surprised everyone with her flawless execution. Maya had caught the whole thing on her camera and was sharing it on all the team's social media platforms. Becky was glowing and had almost flattened Leo when she'd run into his arms afterwards. Someone near him said that she must've been extra stoked because of her engagement, which didn't make any sense to Finn.

He'd shifted away from them just as Coach Harrington joined them, patting Becky on the back and smiling. Finn frowned. Why wasn't Coach up with Sam? He turned to watch Sam who was looking a little peaky. Finn crossed his fingers as Sam settled herself. He found he was smiling as he squinted up at the big screen to get a closer look at her. She had her eyes closed, doing her usual gearing-up ritual. When she opened her eyes, he was struck by how beautiful they were, but also by the slight flash of fear in them. He'd seen Sam do this before, but never had he seen fear in her eyes like tonight. This was her first qualie for her dream—was she really that afraid of failing? Around him people chatted, laughed and complained about the cold, but he couldn't move. Sam looked off, somehow. He held his breath, anger stirring in the pit of his stomach as the loudspeakers above his head broadcasted Gabriel's commentary, and unnervingly, Gabriel was saying aloud everything he was thinking.

"Sam Harrington, tipped for a medal in this year's big air and in the halfpipe, is looking good, if a little awkward today. Let's hope she can keep her cool on this, her final run for this big air qualification."

Finn's heart leaped into his mouth as Sam took off. His eyes never left her as she flew into the air over the jump. Finn's hands balled into fists by his sides. Gabriel continued.

"She's got the height—definitely has hit the highest in this qualifier—this could be the triple we've all been waiting . . . No! What was that? Sam Harrington has followed her teammate, Becky Stanford. A double cork 1080—what a statement."

Finn grimaced as Gabriel went quiet. He didn't need to say that "*what a statement*". Sam would be kicking herself, and she'd probably want to thump Gabriel for saying it. In a sport where creativity was applauded, bringing attention to Sam copying Becky was a real sucker punch. Something was wrong with Sam. Finn's mouth went dry. Was it what had happened between them earlier? Had that thrown her off form? He stood still and watched the big screen as the camera followed Sam.

He stared up at the screen, hardly able to breathe, as Sam snapped out of her bindings. She knew she'd messed up. She was stomping away, head down, her goggles still on. She paused, waiting for her results. Her mouth was pressed together so hard that her lips seemed to have disappeared. Gabriel was back commentating, and Finn mentally tuned him out. He didn't need Gabe's voice and opinions in his head telling him—and the world—that Sam Harrington had just made the qualie, by the skin of her teeth, that her trick was lacking in her usual confidence and pizzaz, and that maybe there was some old injury possibly playing havoc now. Pulling his old orange beanie off his head, Finn hurried to the break in the barrier where Sam was moving away, her eyes downcast and her dad hot on her heels. Stopping, Finn stood in the snow as people drifted away. The event was over, and the sky had clouded over. It was dark and the lights were blinding.

Maya, in her satsuma coat, came over to him, her mouth pursed and her steps quick.

"What happened to our girl?" She slipped a phone into her pocket. "I've never seen her so rattled."

"I don't know," Finn said. "She was really solid this evening, and then, right before she took her turn, I saw something in her change."

Maya nodded. "She's going to be so pissed about this."

"Yeah."

"Vodka pissed, I'd say." Maya shrugged.

"I guess I would be too," Finn said. "Come on, Mai, let's go find her, see what's going on?"

Walking beside Maya, Finn's guts churned. This was

because of him, because of what had happened in the shower. He should have left her alone, shouldn't even have flirted with her in the hot tub—it was selfishness, pure selfishness and pity for himself that had made him go after her. It was the evening of one of the biggest competitions in her life, and he'd let his stupid ego and his desire for her take over.

"She's lucky she made it into the finals," Maya said. "What do you think put her off? I saw her dad down here—when he should have been up there, with her. I think that didn't help. Not on top of Becky getting Valestré."

Finn nodded. "That did cross my mind."

"I don't like this, Finn." Maya's face clouded over. "Coach wasn't at Sam's training this morning either."

"What?" Finn's mouth dropped open. "That's unheard of."

"I know. Yikes—that doesn't look good."

Ahead of them, at the entrance to the ski center, Jake Harrington stood, glowering like a bull ready to charge. His eyes flashed when he saw Finn. Finn groaned inwardly.

"What now?" he muttered to himself as Maya scarpered by Jake, into the warm and cozy ski center. Louder he said, "What's up, Coach?" as Jake stood in his path.

"You and I need to have a talk. Now." Jake's shoulders went back. Finn backed away.

"Sure, is everything okay?"

"No, everything is not okay." Jake stormed around the side of the cabin. "Explain this to me." He shoved his phone under Finn's nose, the Instagram post of Finn and Sam in the hot tub dazzled Finn's eyes.

126

Crap, crap, crap. Finn swallowed. How the hell was he going to explain this? Maya had posted the pic before their conversation and it was as hot as hell, and definitely something Finn had never wanted Coach to see.

"I told you, on day one, to stay away from Sam." Jake's voice was low and charged with anger. He towered over Finn. "I told you she was on track for a medal. That nothing was to get in her way. You told me you wouldn't mess with her. Am I right?"

Finn nodded. Damn. He'd never even thought of what might happen if Jake saw the post. He hadn't realized he had Instagram. Jake had never liked a post, posted a comment, or mentioned it in real life. Now that he saw it through his coach's eyes—through Sam's dad's eyes—he could see how it looked.

It looked like they really were together. Just as they'd planned. He kept his eyes on the screen as the post gathered more and more likes, as comments rolled in. Jake swiped his hand away and started reading out the comments while Finn cringed.

"Have you something to tell me?" Jake snarled.

"No." Finn pressed his lips together. What the hell was he going to say? That they were pretending to be a couple on social media so that they'd get a deal that would give them both some control over their own lives? That they'd had a steamy shower room session earlier? That he'd fallen in love with Sam the moment he'd first spoken to her, and deeper every day since? There was nothing he could say that would make it right in Coach's eyes.

"I sincerely hope so," Jake said. He took a menacing step

toward Finn. "Because what happened earlier shouldn't have happened."

Finn paled. Shit. Did Jake know about them in the shower? Surely not. If he did, then he wouldn't be so calm, if you could call his *I'm going into battle, and I will annihilate you if you get in my way* stance calm.

"Coach—"

Jake continued. "Something put her off tonight. If it was you, I swear to God, Finn, you won't compete in this sport again, because . . . shit." Jake rubbed a hand over his face, dragging his features down, making him look a decade older than he really was. "Keep away from her. I mean it. I'm not losing anyone else."

Finn blinked. That hit somewhere between *what the* and *totally unexpected*.

Jake quickly looked away, like he regretted the slip. He squared his shoulders before trudging away through the snow, his shoulders down and his face grim.

What the actual . . . ? Finn breathed out and leaned against the cabin, the cold seeping in through his jacket. No one seemed to have noticed the altercation between them, thankfully. It had clouded over, and tiny flakes of snow had started to fall. On the slopes the groomers were out preparing for the competitions tomorrow. The ski center lights switched off as the last of the staff left for the night. Pushing away from the cold wall, Finn trudged through the snow in the direction of the town. Lingering near the ski lifts, he looked down at the yellow glow of the lights that made the town look alive. Music and singing from the nearest bar carried up the snow-covered mountainside. People seemed to be in couples, everywhere he looked.

Coach's words kept coming back at him. *Stay away from Sam. Keep away from her. I mean it. You won't compete in this sport again . . .* Shit. What was he supposed to do now? He'd promised to keep his distance—promised not to mess it up for her. And now here he was, falling apart after just one make-out session, one super-hot, intimate and unreal make-out session, with Sam—the one girl he wasn't supposed to touch. His head spun. Had that moment meant the same thing to Sam—because if it hadn't, then what? Had she gone along with it as a part of their fake-dating plan? Nothing about it had felt fake to him. Not even for one second.

Kicking up some snow, Finn trudged onwards, a thought forming in his mind. He groaned, annoyed with himself imagining it was real. Sam had never said anything about wanting it to be more than fake dating—and stupidly, neither had he. No. He'd just hopped into the shower with her and said that rules were stupid. *Damn—that could mean anything.* He shoved his hands into his pockets. He'd been talking about that rule they'd made—that stupid pact to stay away from each other—and in the heat of the moment, he'd assumed she knew that. But he hadn't actually said it. And neither had she. *Crap.* He felt stupid. He'd been floating around all evening imagining that she'd wanted him as much as he wanted her. He'd even pictured a life with Sam by his side, not as a training partner, but as his best friend and lover. *Wow!*

Lover.

A warmth flushed through him from his toes to his face,

129

making his hands tingle. He buried his nose down into his neck gaiter as a smile suffused his face. Sam. God . . . she was the most wonderful, warm, loving and adorable girl—no, woman, he'd ever known. His chest swelled with love as he pictured her smiling shyly at him earlier. Somehow Maya hadn't picked up on the vibes between them even though Sam's eyes had shone, and she'd been soft and silly in the kitchen while sharing his toastie, before she'd grown serious and calm as the time for the qualies had approached.

He loved silly Sam as much as serious Sam; in fact, there wasn't a thing about her he'd change, not even when she was sassy Sam. He quickened his pace as he got closer to the town. Well, there was one thing he'd change—her father—he wished Sam had a more understanding and supportive father, one who hadn't just flat-out warned him off his daughter.

The smile fell from Finn's face. Coach Jake Harrington knew every single person in the industry. Young, old, whatever sport it was, he'd contacts everywhere. Something told Finn that his coach didn't make threats lightly. Not once in all the years he'd been under Jake Harrington's guidance, had he ever seen his coach go back on his word. At the start of their coaching relationship, Uncle Henry had warned him not to step out of line with Coach Harrington, and he hadn't. He'd been afraid to. All these years he'd jumped when Coach said jump, had followed every rule, gone to every training session, and more especially, he'd kept away from Sam even when his heart had told him otherwise.

But today everything had changed. He and Sam, they were both at the pinnacle of their careers, with new great and previously unconsidered opportunities opening up for them at every stage. Sam was fitter than she'd ever been—he was too. There was no doubt that they'd both go home with medals . . . if they didn't mess things up by concentrating on the wrong thing. Each other. And that's exactly what had happened earlier—he was sure of it. She'd been fine until he'd selfishly followed his heart, and his cock. She'd planned to outdo herself in that qualie, he knew it. Big air was one of her favorites and she'd be feeling crap now. If only he'd had some sense and hadn't asked her to join him in the hot tub.

A shadow walked toward him as he reached the town, waved and then ran. Finn's heart leaped in his chest. *Sam*.

"Hey!" He waved back as she got closer. Puffing, she pushed back the faux-fur-lined hood of her jacket as she ran toward him. Her face was pale, her mouth unsmiling. He knew that she was probably kicking herself over that last run. She always did when she knew she could have done better. How the hell was he going to tell her that it was his fault? That he shouldn't have distracted her that way—that had been very unfair, and exactly what Coach had been warning him against. He couldn't say that last part, not about her father, but maybe he'd have the guts to say the rest, and maybe his heart would withstand the inevitable pain.

He stopped walking, pushed his hands deep into his pockets, and waited for her to reach him. She gave him a half-smile as she stood before him, slightly lower on the slope beneath him.

"Hey, where did you go?" She laid her hand on his arm. "I saw your beanie then nothing. It was like you'd disappeared! I searched everywhere for you—don't leave me like that again, d'ya hear? I needed you."

Finn's heart sank. "Sorry, sorry—I had to run to the bathroom. I thought I'd be back on time." Some excuse, pathetic, useless. He shrugged, disgusted at his half-ass attempt to smooth things over. "I didn't mean it."

"Well, of course you didn't." Sam squeezed his arm. "You gotta go when you gotta go."

Finn half smiled. "You okay?"

Sam's lips, those plump, glossy, pink lips he'd kissed only hours ago, twisted into a grimace. "Not really. How much did you actually see?"

"All of it, well, most of it . . ." He almost forgot about his running to the bathroom lie. "Hey, I know what you're thinking, but Sam, it's just the first competition *and* you got through to the finals. That was the goal, wasn't it?"

Sam rolled her eyes. "Yeah, but I very nearly didn't. I scraped through, Finn. I knew I'd messed up the minute I hit the air. Knew it."

Finn took her hand and tucked it into his pocket. They started walking down the street.

"What do you think went wrong?" he asked tentatively. He crossed the fingers of his other hand, praying that she'd say anything other than what had happened between them.

"I, uh," Sam started. He felt her hand tighten in his. "My head wasn't in the game and my mind was racing—I couldn't concentrate."

Finn steeled himself. He took a deep breath, hauling the icy air down into his lungs before speaking.

"Was it . . . was it because of what we did earlier?

Because if it was, then we should probably not . . ." A heaviness wrapped around Finn's shoulders, settling in his chest, deep in his heart as he said it, completely at odds with the hum of excitement that spilled from almost every bar in the small town. The bars overflowed with people, the air thick with lively music and chatter. Finn couldn't shake the feeling that he didn't want to be there anymore. He just wanted to be alone, with Sam. Alone somewhere where they could talk it all through.

Sam shook her head slowly. She seemed to take a minute before she answered him.

"No. It was all me. I was indecisive up there. Honestly, Finn—it wasn't about . . . us."

"Indecisive?" he croaked, then cleared his throat. The heaviness in his chest lightening a little but returning again as he looked down the street that was heaving with winter sports fanatics. In the distance he saw Coach Harrington stomping through the crowds. It looked as if he was heading to their hotel, but in the dark Finn couldn't be sure. It also looked as if he was walking toward them. Finn pulled his hand from his pocket, Sam's too, and let her hand go. Immediately he regretted it as Coach Harrington's back came into view beneath a streetlamp. He was walking away from them and probably hadn't seen them. From the corner of his eye, he caught Sam's hurt expression. Her little frown disappeared as quickly as a shooting star skims the sky. She pulled her mittens on and readjusted her hat.

"Oh, nothing," Sam continued as if nothing had happened. "Just what to do, I suppose, what trick to do . . ." Finn flinched. He knew that tone in her voice so well. She was covering something up, not telling him the truth. And the truth was, in his opinion, that he'd been the cause of her indecisiveness. He'd caused her to double-take up there, and that had nearly cost her a place in the final.

Sam carried on talking. "And then there's my dad. He really laid into me when I got to the center. He said I've been slacking off—and that I need to smarten up because the way I'm going it looks like I won't get a medal—and apparently this is my one chance. And telling me that I'll be too old for the 2030 Games or something ridiculous like that—2030! I'll be only twenty-seven by then. That's not too old!"

Finn looked down, hating that he agreed with Jake, hating that Sam seemed to be considering what Jake was saying—that she wouldn't win a medal this time. "Maybe you should listen to him. You have to make the most of this opportunity." Finn cringed as Sam stared up at him. "You can't be indecisive, you just can't. One bad fall, Sam, that's all it takes. One. What if you got injured? Then you're out—possibly forever. This might be your only chance."

"Not you too," Sam blurted. "Between you and my dad—you'll both have me in a geriatric ward before I'm twenty-four." Her voice rose. "Why do you guys think, that I won't want to try, at least, for the next Games? What do you think will happen to me after these ones? I won't be giving up anytime soon, you know. And, by the way, in case you didn't know, plenty of athletes compete in the Games more than once, and plenty are over twenty-three—I'm not getting too old! It's like you men all think that a woman can only be interested in one thing at a time! Well, I'm *not* interested in babies and weddings and being a bridesmaid or whatever other crap you all think a woman should be interested in once she hits a certain age. I'm not! I will never want to stop doing this—whatever it is!"

"Shit, Sam, I didn't mean that." Finn stopped walking. Reaching for Sam, he pulled her to him, closer than he normally would. Wishing he had the balls to kiss her right here, among the crowds and the buzzing streets. She leaned up against him, her mouth inches from his. It was like she was begging for his touch, wanting him to kiss her too. *Damn*. If only he could tell her how much she meant to him, and that he didn't want anything to get in the way of her dreams—not even him. His breath caught under his ribs as his heart hammered so loudly, he was sure she'd feel his pulse. Her breath warmed his lips. God, he wanted to kiss those lips . . . "You know I didn't mean that. I said it all wrong."

Her green eyes glared up at him, then softened. "I know. I'm sorry."

Her arms tightened around him, and he closed his eyes as he pulled her close, snuggling her in under his chin, her hat slipping backwards on her head. Her hair smelled like the shampoo she'd used earlier, sweet vanilla and warm jasmine. This was heaven. It was better than winning any gold in any games. A giggle from someone nearby broke the moment. He glanced up. A huddle of friends stood across the street, phones out, were grinning like they'd just stumbled across a celebrity. It would be everywhere in minutes, this private moment between him and Sam. Instagram reels. TikTok edits with sparkles and romantic music. Maya would be thrilled. Coach less so. He stiffened as another small group of people stopped to see what was going on. He heard his name, then Sam's. Someone laughed, excitedly. More phones raised in the air. Finn's stomach dipped. This was weird. It wasn't like the press shots or sponsorship reels he was used to—the kind where you knew the angle, held the smile, controlled the story. This was raw, messy, and real. He loosened his arms around her as she peeped over her shoulder at their accidental paparazzi.

Sam pulled away from him slightly, her head lowered as she turned back to him, ignoring the delighted fans who were still snapping away. Quietly she said, "I know you didn't mean it, and you're right—I did make the final." She stepped back and pulled her hat back down over her hair, then tugged her hood up as if to hide her face. All traces of her smell disappeared as she zipped up the funnel of her jacket. "That should be my next focus. Tomorrow will be a good day, don't you think?"

"I do," Finn said while fighting the urge to pull her back into his arms. She was right. Going for gold was all they should be thinking about. "And you're right. Focus on tomorrow's final. That's exactly what we—you—need to do." He looked up at the crowd around them. "Come on, let's go."

10

Sam

Walking beside Finn, Sam swung her arms a little more energetically than usual, trying to shake off the strange surge of anxiety that flooded her body. Between Finn holding her like that, and the crowd of fans snapping them, she wasn't sure what to do. She lowered her head. Should she reach for him? Hold his hand? Link arms? Or would that attract attention to them again? Attention that she felt ill prepared for. Finn was walking fast through the snow and grit, as if he couldn't wait to get away from the crowds. She shoved her hands into her pockets. They walked quickly through the town, passing loud bars filled with music and people. Everyone was cheering or dancing or having some sort of fun, but all she felt inside was fear and confusion as question after question formed in her mind. What were they now? Friends? Fake-dating teammates? Shower . . . associates? What!? Her brain spiraled, and Finn wasn't helping. He was a maddening step ahead of her, like he was avoiding matching her stride on purpose.

Sam frowned and tried to narrow the gap between them.

"Will you stop walking like we're late for a race?" she muttered under her breath as his pace increased. Finn stopped walking and Sam caught up to him, kicking herself as a crease of worry formed between his eyebrows.

"Sorry," she said. "I didn't mean to snap."

"I know." He rubbed his chin, his mouth stern. "Sam, we should talk—"

Sam didn't get to hear what Finn was saying as a satsuma flash of chaotic energy barreled into her.

"There you are! Finally!" Maya threw an arm around each of them, drawing them closer and grinning like she'd just won the lottery. "Why do you two look like you're heading for a breakup instead of the hottest bar in town? Come on! You guys are trending! You've got a job to do!"

Sam blinked. "We're what?"

"Oh my God, haven't you seen?" Maya steered them into a packed bar glowing with fairy lights, blasting tunes from the Nineties, and smelling like Christmas. She flung her coat over a stool and whipped out her phone while still talking a mile a minute. "The team *loves* you right now. The comments—the reposts—you two are melting the snow off the Alps."

Sam glanced at Finn, catching his cheeks redden. Maybe he was cold, or embarrassed, she couldn't tell. His face was otherwise pretty normal. Then he seemed to visibly relax in front of her very eyes. His shoulders broadened, a hitch down from the stressed position they'd been in only moments ago. His stance loosened, and his forehead smoothed out. She felt her own body relax in response, and a smile formed on her lips. Finn winked at her before turning to Maya.

138

"You're kidding," he said as Maya waved at the barman.

"Nope." Maya handed him a shot that appeared as if by magic and then handed one to Sam. "Only one for you—you've got to be ready for the final tomorrow. Now come on—act natural—be charming. Make the people swoon!" Maya raised her phone like a director.

"Are you recording this?" Finn tried to see around the phone, but Maya leaned away from him.

"Of course," she said. "It's for the story—it'll only be up for twenty-four hours. Don't worry. Come on, Finn—I need to get this shot, and then get our girl to bed early. Just pretend you two are on *Love Is Blind* and have seen each other for the first time ever."

"That's playing dirty." Finn laughed. He looked at Sam and waggled his eyebrows at her. "But I like it."

Sam let out a strangled laugh, and then Finn, damn him, wrapped an arm around her waist. Sam gasped as he leaned in close and whispered in her ear, "Smile for the camera."

Sam quivered as his arm tightened around her. It wasn't fair how her body wanted to melt into his, or how his seemed to fit right into hers. Her breath hitched as he looked down at her, making her hope that this wasn't fake at all—and for the moment she forgot that it was.

"Cheers!" Finn clinked his shot glass to hers, and she knocked it back in a blur of confusion, longing, and want.

"This is gold!" Maya cheered. "You two are pro at this—look—the chemistry—are you seeing this? Give me a minute. Just tagging the team here. There. Done."

"You're tagging them?" Finn paled. He let Sam go. His arm, warm and steady, slipped away from her, leaving a chill behind as if a gust of wind had come through the bar. She watched, heart sinking as he took her empty glass and set it on the table right next to them.

"Don't worry—I'm not tagging Coach," Maya said quietly to him. She waved her hand and nudged Sam. "You should see the comments, the reposts—and you should have seen the team earlier today—they were practically high-fiving over the analytics. You guys are gold-medal marketing right now."

Finn's mouth opened, then closed again.

Sam tried to process it. *Wait—Coach isn't being tagged?* Her stomach twisted. *Since when did Maya start filtering posts for his sake? And why did Finn look like it meant something more? What did this mean for their fake-dating-get-a-sponsorship plan?* "Are you saying . . . the team are okay with this?" She gestured at Finn and herself.

Maya shrugged. "Not officially but also not unofficially. I've been told to milk it for all it's worth. Don't take offence to that though—it's great for all of us. It's getting people talking, and getting you noticed by all the right people. Now come on—give me one more shot—and make it look as if you want to jump each other's bones."

Finn choked. "Maya—"

Sam let out a breath—half laugh and *half what even is my life now*. But Maya was right. It was brilliant that the team was on their side. It made it *feel* like it was real—and not fake. Finn was smiling at her now, and for a minute he looked just as dazed as she felt, like the world had shifted into a new timeline, one where they were together and where everyone was happy about it. Then Finn slipped his arm around her waist again and leaned in like it was the most natural thing in the world, and her breath quickened. Her hand reached for him before she could stop herself and rested on his chest.

Maya gave a victorious squeal and snapped the photo. "God. You two are addictive."

Finn didn't move away from her; his thumb caressed her lower back as she trembled in his arms.

Sam raised her face to Finn. "You're enjoying this way too much."

He grinned. "Doing my best for the camera—right?"

For the camera. His words thudded in her chest as he moved away from her. The bar suddenly got louder as someone climbed up on the bar and began dancing as if they were auditioning for a part in *Coyote Ugly*. It wasn't long before someone else joined them and then another shot was in Sam's hand. With a laugh of disbelief, Sam looked around, slightly stunned to see how crazy the crowd was. It was almost a physical enactment of what she imagined was going on in her brain right now. Her thoughts were all over the place, on her sport, her father, and most of all, on Finn and how he'd just said: ". . . for the camera—right?" so calmly, because she wasn't calm at all.

Someone bumped into her, and she staggered against the barstool, grasping the bar to steady herself. Her eyes flickered around the room. Everything was loud, too bright, and beating way too fast, but her heart, it felt as if it was slowing down.

"Sam?" Finn called her. He dipped his head to speak in her ear again. "You okay?"

She nodded. "Yeah." She took a breath, her heart hammering. "I just didn't think pretending would feel so real."

Finn's smile faltered, just for a second. His eyes dropped from hers, like the weight of something unsaid pulled at him. When he looked back up, the light in them had dimmed slightly, and his jaw tensed—like he wanted to speak but couldn't.

"Same," he said. Then after a beat: "But we're still pretending, right?"

Sam downed her second shot. She didn't answer him, not because she didn't want to, but because Maya was taking the shot glass from her and reprimanding her for drinking before a final.

"Girl—what are you doing? I said just one!" Maya gave her a pointed look. "Final tomorrow. Remember that little thing—the actual reason why we're here."

"Urgh, you're so right." Sam relinquished her shot glass although all she wanted to do was to have it refilled immediately. How could Finn be so cool? She really wanted to talk to him, to clear up what they were playing so dangerously at. She zipped up her jacket and touched his arm softly. "You coming?"

Finn hesitated, then shook his head. "I think I'll stick around for a bit. If you're okay with that?"

"Sure, of course." Sam nodded; a flicker of sadness flared inside her. She really wanted to talk to him, to try figure out what they were now. Something between them had shifted, and she needed to talk to him, her best friend, about it.

Just as she turned away, Finn reached for her hand. She

looked back, startled—and then he stepped in, close, one arm pulling her to him, his other hand gently under her chin, tilting her face to his as if he'd done it a hundred times before.

"Don't worry about tomorrow," he murmured, his voice barely above the music. "Go to bed, rest, and have sweet dreams."

Before she could reply, he leaned down and kissed her, a soft gentle brush against her lips. It was simple, natural, and it lingered long enough for her to touch his face, her thoughts scrambling as he smiled against her mouth. Her heart twisted as she pulled away slowly, her eyes searching his face for some clue as to what he was thinking—no—*feeling*. But Finn just smiled, soft and unreadable.

"Night, Sam."

"Night," she said quietly, then turned and stepped out into the cold night air, questions trailing after her like falling snow.

Behind her the fun was only getting started in the bar. The heavy beat of a club classic started up and the crowd roared in appreciation. Sam walked away, loneliness curling in her stomach. She didn't want to leave Finn. Touching her lips softly, she wished he'd come with her. She wanted his arms around her—for real—not for their plan. She power-walked past other revelers and bars that were filled to capacity. It was as if everyone was in party mode. The town was electric. Sam sighed as she caught a couple kissing passionately outside a closed store, unafraid of who saw them. She wanted that—wanted to kiss Finn in front of everyone out in the open. Her shoulders drooped. Clearly, he didn't, or he'd be right beside her, walking her back to her hotel, but here she was, striding through the bitterly cold night alone, her heart longing for him and feeling more heartsore with each passing moment.

Maybe this fake-dating idea wasn't the best plan, and there was no one she could talk to about it, because Finn was the person she always went to when she needed someone— and now she couldn't. A flash of anger flared up inside her—this was the first time she'd ever felt like she couldn't talk freely with him, and it was horrible. She cringed at her own pathetic behavior, at how she'd simpered and fallen completely for his act.

Her hands curled into fists as confusion and frustration built up inside her. Hell, back in the shower he'd behaved as if they were together. But that was when they were in the shower and not seen by anyone, and then there was earlier— he'd walked as fast as he could, as if he couldn't wait to get away from her. He even let her go when his fans had been taking photos of them and then had put on an act in the bar on Maya's command. It was as if it was all for show, that there was nothing else to it.

It hadn't always been like that though. Once upon a time he'd been crazy for her, but that was years ago. Prom night. That one moment she should've seized, but instead she'd made him a promise to put their careers first. Huffing, Sam felt tears prickle at the backs of her eyes. Maybe he didn't remember that night the way she did. Maybe he didn't remember saying that they could revise the plan later. She'd tucked that little nugget of hope away in her heart, waiting for the moment he would say it was time to think about it all over again. Had she imagined him saying it—had she projected her own desires on her memories for all these years?

"Sam! Hold up!"

Sam turned around and inwardly groaned as her brother gamboled toward her, his limp more pronounced than it had been in a while. The last thing she wanted right now was company, but he seemed a little down, as if he really didn't want to be alone.

"Hey," she said as he fell in step beside her. "Your leg—is it sore?"

He grimaced. "It's the cold—it makes everything ache like it happened yesterday."

"Oh." Sam glanced at Leo. "I'm sorry."

"It's okay, thanks." Leo didn't look at her. "I'll be fine. Well done today, by the way."

"I sucked." Sam shrugged. "And got an earful from Dad."

Leo nodded. "Don't let him get to you, Sam. You have what it takes."

"Thanks," Sam said. "But shouldn't you be rooting for Becky?"

"I am rooting for Becks." Leo smiled. "Doesn't mean I can't root for you too—you're my only sister, and I know what it's like to have Dad come down on you so hard."

"It's like he's angry with me, or something." Sam sighed. "I mean, Valestré?"

"Becky was shocked to get it. And she's a little afraid to talk to you now."

"What?" Sam shook her head. "She shouldn't be. It's not her fault."

145

"No, it's not." Leo nodded. "But you've not been as friendly with her lately, and she—we—figured that was why."

Sam gaped. "No! Well, yeah, I was put out by it, but Leo, I blame Dad. Not Becky."

Leo shrugged, his gaze distant as he adjusted his weight, the old hurt in his eyes flashing briefly. "Kinda hard to know that, Sam, when you weren't talking to us."

Sam's chest tightened. She hadn't realized how distant she'd been.

"I felt like everything was slipping out of my control, Leo. Between Dad pushing me, and then Becky getting the deal—" She cut herself off, hurt bubbling up inside her like a hot spring. "It was like he was trying to replace me, you know."

Leo stopped walking, his jaw clenching. "You think that's bad? Imagine how it felt when *you* started taking my place. When everything I'd worked for was . . . just gone." His voice was low, almost a whisper. It hit Sam like a sudden wipeout on the slopes. Hard, sudden and painful. Guilt flooded her chest.

"What do you mean?"

Leo swallowed hard. "I told myself never to tell you this . . . but God, Sam . . . the car accident, and my leg—it ruined my life. I had my shot—my dream. And then just like that it was over—and he turned to you almost immediately. I'd barely had time to recover before he was talking about you and your chances, your training sessions, your talent." He gestured vaguely, his voice cracking. "And it killed me a little, you know. I was supposed to be the one. I wasn't supposed to be sitting on the sidelines. And he never ever, not once, said sorry for that day—the accident shouldn't have happened." He swiped at his nose, his eyes glistening with tears. "He was supposed to be driving, and I should've said no when he told me to, but I didn't. I couldn't. And then Mom . . ."

"Leo. It wasn't your fault. I know that," Sam choked out, tears welling in her eyes. Watching her brother fall apart like this made her feel sick. She wanted to apologize, to say something to make it better. "And I didn't want to take your place—you must know that. But I felt like Dad . . . he made it clear that I had to carry the torch." She paused, meeting his gaze. "I never wanted to replace you, Leo. I just didn't know what to do when everything changed."

Leo's face softened, but there was still an edge to his voice. "I know, Sam. But sometimes it feels like that's exactly what happened. I don't blame you—no more than you blame Becky. Dad has always had his own agenda, and I guess that now we've both been on the end of his ambitions."

Sam looked down at her boots. They started walking again, slower this time, as if they didn't want to reach the hotel too quickly. "Do you ever wish it had been different? That Dad hadn't pushed us so hard? That we could've just . . . skied and boarded because we loved it?"

Leo gave a quiet laugh. "All the time. I used to sneak away to glade ski with Ryan, and it was heaven—no Dad yelling at me like it was life or death."

"You never said that before."

"Didn't feel like I could." He hesitated. "And after the accident . . . I didn't know who I was anymore. It was too

147

painful to get back out there, and after a while I didn't want to. You were on the rise, and I'd faded away like a ghost."

Horrified, Sam wiped tears away from her cheeks. "You're not a ghost. You're my big brother. And I miss you—I miss *us*."

"I miss us too." Leo's voice was gentler. "Look, I'm sorry. I didn't want to dump this on you—that wasn't my intention. I just wanted to say good luck tomorrow."

Sam nodded, a small breath of relief catching in her throat. "Thanks, brother."

"Anytime, sister." Leo smiled.

"You coming in?" Sam nodded as the hotel came into view.

Leo shook his head. "Trying to soak in as much of the atmosphere as I can, seeing as I can stay out as late as I like."

Sam laughed. "Now that's what I call looking on the bright side."

"That's me! Mr. Brightside." Leo looked sheepish. "Thanks, Sam. For talking. See you tomorrow."

Sam climbed the hotel steps, pausing to look back at Leo as he walked away. Her eyes stung in the cold, her cheeks too, where her tears were still damp. That was a conversation she'd never imagined happening. She rubbed at her cheeks, hoping she didn't look as emotionally shattered as she felt. The hotel doors slid open, and a blast of heat greeted her. Pausing to check her face in a lobby mirror, Sam spied Gabriel behind her in the reflection. He was sitting alone at the hotel bar. She turned around. His lanyard swung lightly around his neck: *Gabriel Hawke, Global Sports Network*. He raised his glass at her, and she nodded back at him, then

148

glanced behind her as his eyes flicked past her. *What on earth . . . ah*, she smiled. He was looking for Maya—he had to be. Why else would he look behind her like that? The only answer was for Maya, especially as she was usually at Sam's side. Her phone buzzed with a text from Maya.

Are you still awake? I'm coming back to the room.

Sam smiled and fired off her reply.

I'm awake all right—I'm walking into the hotel bar and about to say hello to Gabriel Hawke.

Maya's reply was almost instantaneous.

Do not move! I am on my way. Hubba hubba SMASH!

Sam giggled, glad to have something lighter to focus on. Maya had had her eyes on Gabriel since Finn had first competed against him a few years ago, long before she'd had the nerve to get Sam to introduce her to him last month. And since then, the pair seemed to create sparks whenever they were in the same room, but so far neither Maya nor Gabriel had made any move toward the other. Maybe this time *something* would happen.

Sam stifled a grin as she waved over at Gabriel where he stood casually leaning against the bar, one foot raised on the foot rail, and a crystal glass of whiskey in his hand. In the twinkling fairy lights Gabriel looked as if he was posing for a *GQ* article. His well-fitted deep blue cashmere sweater contrasted beautifully with the twinkle-lit background; his jacket hung open effortlessly. He took a sip from his whiskey as she made her way over to him, then slipped his hand into his dark jeans pocket. As usual, he exuded a quiet, comfortable yet commanding presence, and an elegance that only someone with his Italian heritage could get away with. The whole scene looked like it belonged on a postcard. The warm spicy scent of his whiskey mingled with something richer—dark chocolate and spice, maybe even a hint of clove. His aftershave was bound to make Maya's mouth water. Sam smiled as his dark eyes still searched behind her. Yes, he was definitely keeping an eye out for Maya.

"Gabe," she said. "Hi, fancy seeing you here. I thought you'd be with the rest of the press crew."

Gabriel shook his head. "That scene isn't for me. They're . . . how can I say this without getting myself into trouble . . ." He paused, glancing around to make sure they weren't going to be overheard.

"I won't tell anyone." Sam smiled, leaning in slightly. "Promise."

He smiled and she could see why Maya was so into him. His smile was energizing, his laugh deep and real. "Let's just say that the press room has more egos than the changing room ever had."

Sam giggled. "That's saying a lot."

He nodded. "Isn't it? Honestly, I don't fit in there—they think I'm not one of them."

"I get it," Sam said. "Strange way to be when they'd be out of a job without us. Do you ever regret retiring?"

"Good point, and no, strangely enough. I thought I would

150

but I'm enjoying this side of things, being able to analyze jumps without being in competition with anyone." He nodded to the barman. "Can I get you a drink—to celebrate you getting into tomorrow's final?"

"No, thanks though." Sam shrugged. "It wasn't my best run. Not much to celebrate really."

"What?" Gabriel squinted at her. "Don't be silly. You're at the Olympics, dealing with the most amount of pressure you'll ever be under in your career—and your very first run got you a place in the final. That's huge."

Sam looked down. How could she explain it to Gabriel Hawke? The man had won his first Olympic medal in the very first event he'd competed in, and he'd been only twenty-two. He'd always seemed so self-assured, calm and collected, whereas she felt like a hot mess ninety-nine percent of the time.

"We're not all as put together as you are," she said, gently smiling at him. "I remember when you took that gold—you were as cool as a cucumber."

"I wasn't," Gabriel said before taking a sip of his whiskey. "I was lucky, but you—you have what it takes. No one in this competition has what you have—they're all watching you and measuring up to you. You remember that tomorrow."

A warm sensation washed over Sam. No one had spoken so positively to her about her performance today. Not even Finn. She opened her mouth to reply, but Gabriel's attention wasn't on her anymore, which could only mean one thing: Maya had entered the building.

Gabriel cleared his throat, and Sam bit her lip, loving how his eyes lit up on seeing her friend.

"There you are!" Maya blazed into the hotel bar, causing heads to turn and conversations to falter as her undeniable energy and sassiness filled the room. "Look at you." She paused, mid blaze, to look Gabriel up and down. "A real-life, walking, talking *GQ* spread. What do you think about my girl here?"

Gabriel gave Maya the once-over in return. "I was trying to buy her a drink to celebrate—"

"Uh-oh—no," Maya said, waggling her finger at him. "She's already had her quota for the night, and she needs to go to bed."

"And what about you—do you need to go to bed too?" Gabriel raised an eyebrow suggestively at Maya. Sam watched in awe as her friend fluttered her eyelashes at the man of her dreams and as Gabriel all but melted in front of her. *How did she do that?*

"Need?" Maya pouted. "Maybe. Not right now though. Right now, I'm heading upstairs with my girl to plan her big day tomorrow. Goodnight now, sweet dreams." Sam struggled to hold back a giggle as Maya blew Gabriel a kiss while simultaneously pushing Sam toward the exit.

"You are one class act, Maya Adams." Sam broke into peals of laughter as they stood by the elevator. "How do you do it?"

"Watch and learn, honey, watch and learn." Maya sashayed into the lift, leaving Gabriel Hawke watching her every move. "Now, bedtime for my girl—let's get that medal tomorrow!"

11

Finn

Finn lay in his extra-large king-size bed. He kicked the duvet off, swung his legs over the side and sat up. Shivering in the dark, he wished he'd put on a T-shirt before going to sleep, then he reached for his phone in the darkness—3:55 a.m. He didn't have to get up for another hour, but he couldn't sleep, especially knowing that Sam was competing in her first final that day. At least he had another day before his next qualie. He stretched his arms high above his head. Maybe she was awake too? Probably not. Hopefully not. She needed all the rest she could get.

Thumping his pillow into shape, he pictured Sam in bed. She was a messy sleeper—he knew that from Maya's jokes. Arms and legs all over the place, farting and talking in her sleep too. He laughed out loud. He couldn't help it. There was something adorable in that and he wished he could witness it. Lying back down he stared up at the ceiling.

Waking up beside Sam would be magical. He sighed. He was a morning person; she wasn't as much. If he ever got lucky enough to wake up with her, he'd bring her breakfast in bed. Coffee, black with two sugars. That was her wake-up drink. It was the only time she drank black coffee. She didn't like to eat much but loved a croissant with chocolate spread and strawberries. Easy.

From the few times that he'd stayed in the same accommodation as Sam he also knew that she was mostly incoherent until she'd had a long hot shower too. Picturing her in the shower made him reach for himself. Stroking himself, he closed his eyes. He'd never had as many hard-ons in one day before. Idly he wondered if it was dangerous, then took his hand away, preferring to imagine what a perfect day with Sam would be like.

They'd get out on the slopes after her shower, and they'd do a glade run, and she'd be brilliant. He saw her sweep into the air, land perfectly, smiling at him as he led the way. Then they'd have some lunch, probably pasta in a cheesy sauce— steaming hot and peppered with paprika—it would warm them up and fill their hungry bellies. Then maybe they'd get another run in before picking up the kids . . .

Finn's eyes burst open. *Kids. What the? They had kids. How did that happen? What the . . . but . . . they'd be gorgeous kids—a girl and a boy of course.* Throwing his hands behind his head he settled back, smiling as he imagined what their kids might be like. They'd be fair-haired, like Sam; hopefully they'd have her green eyes too. He hoped she wanted kids, despite what she had said earlier about not wanting babies. It would make his world complete if she did.

Grinning in the dark, he pictured teaching his son how to ski. One thing was for sure, he wouldn't be the kind of father Jake Harrington was, nope. He'd be there for his kids, not telling them what to do, who to do it with, and how to do it.

The conversation with Jake at the ski center came back to him, word for word. An icy shiver made him move, tuck his arms down and pull the duvet up over his bare shoulders. Jake Harrington—there'd be no kids with Sam if Jake Harrington had his way, but he could hardly stop them from having as much fun as possible in the meantime when the team was behind them. A sense of resolve settled into his chest and made him sit up and get out of bed.

There was no point in lying there dreaming about things that he wanted. He may as well get some training in, maybe catch some Z's later if he needed to. Forgoing a shower, Finn pulled on his sweats and trainers, grabbed his backpack and tiptoed down to the lobby. The breakfast room was empty, but he grabbed a pot of yogurt, and a bottle of orange juice for after his workout before heading off.

Jogging along the snowy road, Finn pulled his neck gaiter over his face. It was freezing and, in the distance, he could see the groomers out already making sure the snow was perfect for later. The usual excitement he felt when he saw fresh powder sparked up inside him. He pushed all thoughts of Sam, Maya, Jake Harrington and the team out of his thoughts, and paused. He completed a few stretches then turned his attention toward the road. Running along the sparkling snow he concentrated on his breathing, letting the rhythm of his steps clear his mind. Sam's face kept coming back to him no matter how fast he ran. Her worried expression as she ran to him after her qualie, then the anger in her voice as she'd called him out for not supporting her—and finally, the way she'd looked at him when she'd said goodnight. She'd looked as if she had a million things to say to him and like she didn't know where to begin.

Rubbing his face, he slowed to a walk. What the hell would he say if she asked him how he was feeling? There was no way he could tell her about her dad warning him off. Things were bad enough between Jake and Sam already. He groaned. And then there was Maya and her social media posts—and the team's official yet unofficial support of them. It couldn't have come at a better time. Since he'd gotten up, he'd received what felt like hundreds of Instagram notifications from fans who shipped him and Sam so hard it felt like they'd hit an iceberg. It was exactly the attention they both needed—Sam with her sponsorship hopes, and his dreams of proving he could stand on his own two feet—it was a win for them both.

Finn smiled. Maya was unrivaled when it came to content creation. Her last posts of him and Sam had been so carefully orchestrated that he'd found himself wanting to congratulate her. He laughed, just as his phone buzzed again. This time it was Maya.

> Where are you, lover boy? The team have asked for more content, and I've got a plan for some hot photos—get your tight buns to the gym pronto. I need you and my girl looking like you want to pump more than iron.

Finn couldn't help but grin as he rounded the bend in the road, the gym just in sight.

The gym was just opening; yellow lights were flickering on all over the building. Pushing down his neck gaiter he squinted in the darkness. A shadowy figure stood outside the gym as if they weren't sure about going in. He picked up his pace a little, sure that he knew who it was.

Maya must've really worked some magic to get Sam out of bed at this hour. They'd joked often enough about how she hated dragging herself out of bed early—even for fresh powder. Sam, looking like she was barely awake, hid a yawn as he hurried toward her.

The soft crunch of snow beneath his boots made her look around. Her eyes flickered over him before looking down and focusing on the travel mug she held in her hand. The heady coffee aroma cut through the icy air, inviting and warm. Sam's expression changed from grumpy bear to sleepy bunny as Finn approached her.

"Hey," she said, her voice still gritty from sleep. "You made it."

"Maya sent me a text," Finn said, his voice gruff from the cold air. "Shouldn't you be in bed, resting for tonight?"

Sam sheepishly smiled, raising her eyes from her coffee. "I'll rest later, I promise. Maya was awake at a crazy hour, plotting, scheming and developing ideas for us. She was fizzing with so much energy that I couldn't stay in bed—this was really my idea, although the team jumped on it when Maya messaged them—I was hoping she'd save it for later though." She stifled another yawn.

"Your idea?" Finn burst out laughing. "Who are you—and what have you done with my Sam?"

Sam's eyes flicked to his, and his mouth went dry. *My*

Sam . . . had he really said that out loud? Her cheeks turned pink as he studied her, wondering what she was thinking.

A soft laugh escaped from her, breaking the tension. "I'm still me, just me. I swear." She nudged him, the sleepiness in her eyes dissipating a little. "Just trying to keep the momentum going—that's all."

Finn smiled, feeling a rush of warmth at the sight of her flushed cheeks. "Well, if this is your idea, explain to me what exactly pumping more than iron means . . ."

"Oh God!" Sam squeaked. "Did she really say that? I was joking!"

"Oh, she did." Finn grinned. "And I cannot wait to see how this plays out."

"What can I say?" Sam pulled a face. "Maya thinks that more photos of us as a couple will sway it for us. Especially if we add some heat to the photos."

The way she said, *us as a couple* made Finn's chest tighten. He could feel it, something igniting between them, something sparking and flaming up, ready to set them both alight. *Did she feel it too?*

He scratched the back of his neck. "I'm not complaining, if we're gonna play this fake-dating thing, we might as well do it right—right?"

"Right," Sam agreed, her voice suddenly more serious. She sipped her coffee, then said: "So . . ."

"So, what about serenading you in front of the gym?" He raised an eyebrow and placed his hand on his chest in true Nineties boy band style. "Maybe we should slow dance—right here—your call . . ."

Sam rolled her eyes, but the hint of a smile tugged the

158

corner of her lips. "Get your ass inside, Bradley. Slow dancing . . . singing . . . stick to the slopes—that's where your true talent lies."

Finn burst out laughing. This was the Sam he knew so well, quick with her comebacks and always keeping him in check. He saluted her then motioned to the door. "Come on, let's show the team what #MeltingPoint really looks like."

Sam met his gaze as he held the door open for her, and for a moment the teasing was gone. There was something real in her eyes, something unspoken. It was the kind of look that made his heart skip a beat.

"Right," she said softly as she ducked under his arm, "#MeltingPoint—let's do this." She spun away from him and into the atrium before disappearing into the dark gym. Lights flickered on as he followed her.

Dumping his bag beside Sam's, he dragged off his hat and ran a hand through his hair, leaving it standing on end.

"Good Lord." Sam half smiled at him, making his heart soar. "Finn. Your hair!"

Finn felt his cheeks heat. "I could do with a cut." He flattened the spikes of hair that had been standing up all over his head. Sam tugged her sweater over her head, emerging perfect, as if she'd just had a blowout. She was wearing a sleek one-shoulder crop top that highlighted her toned arms and shoulders. He sucked a breath in as she swooped her hair into a jaunty high ponytail. How was he going to make it through a training session—fake or otherwise—with her looking like that.

"You promise to take it easy on me?" He blustered as she bent down to slip out of her sweatpants, revealing the high-waisted leggings she had on beneath. His heart pounded as she smoothed her hands over her hips, the leggings accentuating her strong curves.

"I will," she said, leaning into a stretch. "Nothing strenuous, I just need to loosen up. Maya is on her way. She said she'd be down soon to take a few photos. I think we should try to concentrate on catching a good few shots of us. That way she can post over the next few days. She said Salvaro are more active at liking and commenting on them, so they might be our best bet."

"Maya's not here yet?" Finn snorted, trying to get to grips with the idea of posing for photos with Sam looking like that. How could he hide how he felt from the camera? Because it was sure to pick up every little detail. "I thought you said she was up."

"I said she's up, not awake," Sam joked.

Finn breathed out. She was making jokes; that was a good thing.

"Listen, about yesterday," Sam started. Her eyes dropped to the floor. "At your suite. I think it's best if we put what happened aside. We need to stay focused—on what's real and what's not."

Finn nodded. His words caught in his dry mouth so that nothing came out. Sam's big green eyes were staring up at him, her face pale and drawn. He could see the signs of exhaustion beneath the focus she was wearing. It would be wrong to add to her worries and tell her that he wanted her more than anything in the world.

"Of course." He forced a light-heartedness into his voice that he didn't feel. "You're one hundred percent right. Focus.

Train. Win." He mentally rolled his eyes. He sounded like a bad cheerleader.

But Sam didn't seem to notice. Her face relaxed and her shoulders lowered.

"Thanks, Finn. You've no idea what this means to me."

Finn swallowed, his smile sliding from his face as she dropped to the floor and started rummaging around in her gym bag. She sat back on her heels. "I've forgotten my towel. Back in a minute."

She smiled at him, then turned and walked toward the ladies' changing room.

"I do know," Finn said to the empty gym, before picking up the battle ropes from their rack. "I know all too well."

Five minutes later Maya lumbered into the gym. Flinging her satsuma coat over the first treadmill she met, she yawned and rubbed her eyes.

"This time of day should be banned." Her gravelly voice made Finn laugh. "It should be illegal."

"Poor Maya," he grunted as he dropped the battle ropes he'd been shaking. Wiping sweat from his brow with a towel, he moved toward the bench, placing his leg on it and squatting.

"Oh my gosh! Finn! What fresh hell is that?" Maya groaned as she watched him. "Stop it right now. It looks painful, and you're making me feel like a loser."

"Can't stop," Finn breathed out heavily. "Almost done."

"Where's Sam?" Maya strolled around the gym, stopping to nudge a hand weight with the toe of her boot. "I thought you'd be together."

"Nah, we're not together, Maya, you know that. It's

all for show." Finn gritted his teeth through the last of his squats.

"Well, you *should* be together." Maya tried to pick up the weight but couldn't. "That—" she pointed at the dumbbell "—should also be illegal."

Finn collapsed onto the bench with a grunt, wiping his hands on his shorts. "Tell me about it. My legs are gonna fall off."

Maya eyed him skeptically. "You're the one who uses his own free will to come here even when I don't demand it. Me? I'm just here to make you look great on the 'gram."

Finn raised an eyebrow.

"Don't give me that eyebrow," Maya said. "You know it's on fire—the whole place is watching you two, and you have them all in the palm of your hand. The two of you are pure chaos and I'm here for it!"

"Chaos?"

"Sam is busy looking all gorgeous and like a snow angel, and you—" she gestured dramatically at his form on the bench "—are the definition of 'I forgot how to sit down after leg day'. Everyone loves it, and everyone loves you two—together."

Finn chuckled, but Sam's voice played back in his head. He said: "We're just focusing on training now, Maya. We have to."

"I know you have to." Maya sighed. "But it doesn't change the fact that you guys have so much *unresolved tension* that if I threw a match, I could start a fire. Ohhhh, could that make a good hashtag? Firestarter. I could add the music too . . . The Prodigy."

Finn scoffed. "Please, we're just—" He picked fluff from his shorts.

"Just what? Playing hard to get? Like I haven't seen this rom-com before." Maya flopped down onto a balance ball, almost falling over as it bounced her back up. "Another illegal monstrosity!" Glancing at Finn, she righted herself. "And just for the record, I'm team 'just get it together already'. You guys are meant for each other." She pressed her fingers together in a hashtag sign and gave him a dazzling smile. "#FinnAndSamForever."

"I swear you think in hashtags." Finn snorted. "Maya, it's just not that simple."

Maya looked at him for a long moment. "Hmmmm what is going on here?"

"Nothing, Mai, nothing." Finn sighed.

"And that sounds like a problem," she said softly.

"No, it's not a problem." Finn pursed his lips. He had the urge to tell her how he really felt about Sam, and the hot tub, and the shower—but what good would that do? She couldn't do anything about it, and it wouldn't be fair to land her in an awkward position either, especially as she was Sam's best friend. No, better to keep his mouth shut. That way no one got hurt.

"So, where is our girl?" Maya scrolled through her phone.

"Here," Sam called. Finn looked up—his breath blew out in one huge stream. Sam was in the doorway, looking stunning, her skin glowing. She looked a little more refreshed than before. His heart pounded.

"I was about to go through my ideas for content with Finn here." Maya tried to get off the balance ball. She slid onto the floor, her arms flailing as she went. "Oooof! Don't mind me—just testing gravity."

Sam giggled and ran over to help Maya up. "You okay?"

Maya nodded and dramatically rubbed her backside. "Peachy!"

Sam laughed. "So, what's the plan?"

Maya waved her phone. "Oh yeah, we're aiming for Olympic-level greatness with our posts. He's not much help though." She nodded at Finn. "Me, however, I am an absolute genius."

"Spill it, genius," Finn deadpanned. He swallowed, nervous about what Maya was going to say. She stuck her tongue out at him and put her hands on her hips.

"You guys are brilliant for photos, honestly. It's not even like work, taking pics of you together, so I've been mostly concentrating on hashtags and captions. #FrostyButFabulous for example although #MeltingPoint has really taken off—like through the roof taken off. Also, what do you think of this for a caption: *When your training is on fire but you're still cute enough to post about it.* I'm not sure. Sounds a little preachy maybe? Like you're not supposed to look sweaty or whatever it is that happens to you people when you exercise."

Sam chuckled. "I like it, but I get what you mean. Maybe we should actually just work out. Just a bit. Finn already looks the part. That way it gives strength and honesty to the caption?"

Maya tapped her phone thoughtfully. "That's brilliant! All right, here's the shot. Sam, stand here. Do that thing you do—what do you call it—your routine or whatever. With

164

the weights." She danced around taking shots as Sam began her arm workout. "Unreal! Now—be fierce! Be flawless and sweaty! Grrrr! That's it!"

Sam stood with her feet hip-width apart, a dumbbell held steady at shoulder height. Stray strands of hair stuck to her face, and she looked powerful and in control. Her leggings hugged every flexed muscle as she braced for the next rep. Her expression was fierce—focused. Just like that, she was totally in the zone. Finn watched, completely forgetting to breathe. She was so good at this. A flush crept up her neck as her eyes locked on his, but she didn't look away. Just squared her shoulders and adjusted her grip like the damn pro that she was. Maya's voice cut through the moment like a whip. She waved a manicured hand at him.

"Earth to Finn! Hello!" She pointed to behind Sam. "Get in the frame! Act amazed at how amazing she is!" She flashed a mischievous grin. He shuffled into his place behind Sam, his face a mix of mild horror and amusement. "And you know, just put your hand on her waist, no—the other side. I want people to think you're a team—in the gym and outside it—smolder! Yes! Come on, Finn—work it! Flex that bicep—just enough to make it look natural. Perfect! Oh, I can see it now: #TeamWorkMakesTheDreamWork."

Finn gently placed his other hand on Sam's hip. She flinched slightly and he swallowed.

Then Sam ever so slightly tilted her hips backwards toward him as Maya took photo after photo. He groaned and glanced down. Her ass looked so good in those leggings, and she felt ripe under his touch.

"That's it! Ooooh, it's giving 'supportive but slightly

possessive boyfriend' vibes." Maya ran around them taking shot after shot. "I can see it now #SheLiftsHeLusts." Quickly he removed his hand and stood back. Surely Maya had enough photos by now.

Maya looked up from her phone. She caught Finn's eye and for a moment he thought that she could read his mind. The twinkle in her eye, the smirk she couldn't suppress, it was all too much. He crossed his arms and waited for Maya's appraisal. She was scrolling through the photos.

"See?" Maya looked up with a grin. "I knew it'd work—there's not one bad photo. Not one. This needs to be a carousel. You look strong and fit, the two of you, which obviously you are being fitness freaks, but also . . ." she paused and clapped ". . . you both look hot in these—like sizzling, like an erupting volcano, no—more! Like hotter than whatever hot sauce Jennifer Lawrence ate when she kept saying *what do you mean?* This is going to blow up big time!"

Sam danced on the spot. "Let's hope it spurs Salvaro into action!"

"Just you wait," Maya teased. "You guys will be even more famous before the day is out. Another pose before you go—I want to give your fans choices! Finn—pick up that skipping rope thingy and do what you were doing when I came in earlier. Not gonna lie—you looked hot as hell and if I thought it, well, you can be sure everyone else will too."

"Yes, sir!" Finn picked up the ropes, his head shaking. *Skipping rope? How long has it been since Maya was in a gym?* He gripped the battle ropes, muscles tight in his

166

forearms, veins prominent as he began to slam the ropes in rhythmic waves against the padded floor. His T-shirt clung to him, darkening in patches between his shoulder blades as he worked the ropes. He grunted and felt a flash of heat cross his cheeks at the sound. His arms burned but it felt good to be doing something physical. He kept the rhythm steady, his eyes locked on Sam who seemed to be doing her best not to notice his occasional grunt or groan. It all sounded a little too . . . primal . . . raw. Sexual.

He felt the muscles burn in his chest, almost as hot as Sam who was nearby on the balance ball, pretending to stretch. Her eyes kept flickering to his, then to his arms, his thighs. It was hard to concentrate on the ropes with her eyes on him like that. Her lips parted and he caught the quick dart of her tongue on her lower lip. *Damn. Was she checking him out?* Spurred on, he threw the last of his energy into the moment as Maya danced around them.

"That's it! YES! Sam! That face—hold it! Oh, hell yes—you're looking at your man like he's the last protein shake in the universe—now *this* is what I got up early for!"

Sam blinked as Finn gritted his teeth behind a smile. Laughter building up inside him as Sam tried to straighten her face.

"I was not!" Sam cried out, picking up her towel from the floor.

"Yes. You. Were." Maya was relentless. "The camera saw everything. You looked like you wanted to climb him like a rock wall."

"Maya!" Sam buried her face into the towel.

"No point in hiding now," Maya said. She whipped the

167

towel from Sam. "It's okay to think your boyfriend's arms should have their own Insta account."

"I do not!" Sam burst out laughing, as Finn guffawed and dropped the ropes. He lost it. Laughter burst from him so hard he couldn't breathe.

"These arms?" he said between chuckles. He flexed dramatically and walked slowly toward Sam. She was grinning so wide now his heart was about to burst with joy. There was nothing better than having her look at him the way she was looking at him—as if she was his—as if this was real. "Their own Insta account?"

Sam's eyes widened, dancing, as he moved quicker. "Finn! Don't you da—"

He chuckled again, loving the way her eyes sparkled at him, as if she was full of fire—and daring him to do it. With a playful growl, he swooped in, employing his old ballet school technique to lift her from the floor as if she weighed nothing. God, she felt good in his arms. Soft, warm, and precious. This was everything he'd ever wanted. He spun her around once, his eyes on her as she threw her head back and laughed, her hands on his shoulders, her body pressed against his chest. Sam squealed as he set her down, half laughing, half scolding him as he gently set her on her feet. His hands lingered on her waist as she caught her breath.

"This is *gold*!" Maya shrieked, practically vibrating with joy. "I think we can call it a done deal—if *someone* doesn't sign you guys up after these, I will quit my job because . . ." she paused and looked at them, her brown eyes glinting; she held up her phone ". . . these are unreal. You two are officially illegal levels of adorable."

"Do you hear that?" Finn said softly to Sam. "We're adorable."

"Yes, yes," Maya interrupted. "I said it first though, and I also said illegal. Now listen—I have to go do a few press interviews, maybe line up a few for you two."

12

Sam

Spirits lifted, Sam listened happily to Maya's chatter as they made their way out of the gym. Likes and comments on the Instagram carousel were coming in hard and fast since Maya had posted it only minutes ago. It was as if people were waiting for any news of her and Finn.

Sam sucked on her bottom lip as a teeny bit of guilt made her stomach flutter. She'd purposefully tilted her hips backwards fully knowing that Finn would be uncomfortable, or maybe even turned on, and Maya had fully got his reaction, and now the whole world knew his reaction too. But it was for their cause—they had to get a sponsorship deal, and soon. Finn would understand, wouldn't he?

"I'm heading this way," Maya said, pausing as they walked down the main street. "What are you going to do?"

Sam paused outside a store. Throwing a glance in the window she nodded toward the door. "I think I'll mooch around a few stores, might pick up something to remind me of all of this."

"Great idea." Maya had her head back in her phone again. "I'll see you at lunch."

Sam watched Maya stroll away. Twisting her lips she turned back to the window and almost laughed when she realized it was the Montalier outlet store. Moving away she strolled down the street, half paying attention to the crowds and stores. A young girl pointed her out to the woman she was with. Sam waved and the young girl jumped up and down while the woman smiled and gratefully mouthed *thank you*. Sam nodded her head and walked on. It was the first time she'd ever been recognized in the street. It felt good, and weird. For a moment she had an inkling of what Finn felt when people pointed him out on the street. Her heart beat a little faster when she thought of him, and the sense of guilt she'd had earlier grew larger inside her. She shouldn't have done that, not when she'd told him they needed to concentrate on the Games. Although why exactly it wasn't fair, she couldn't quite figure out. Was it unfair to her—or to him? He hadn't said anything about what he wanted from her. The little voice in her head piped up again with a *neither have you*. Shoving her hands into her jacket pockets she tried to silence the voice, but it kept making comments on how she'd behaved: *you're sending him mixed signals; you should say how you feel, tell him what's in your heart. What have you to lose?*

She walked faster, as if she could outwalk the voice, but the question kept popping back up. What did she have to lose? *Him!* She'd lose him if she told him everything that was in her heart. And she'd never do that. It was dangerous. Memories of her mom in the months following the car accident flooded her mind. The painful therapies, the tests, the final diagnosis that she was paralyzed and needed a chair and assistance. Her mom's sunniness in spite of her obvious pain. And then Leo's darkness and how he'd turned in on himself, refusing counselling and blaming himself for everything.

She remembered the day she'd found her mom's ice skates in the trash—the fact that her mom had preferred throwing out her practically new skates instead of putting them in the charity box hadn't been lost on Sam. But it had been the distance her dad had put between them all as he struggled to deal with his wife's and son's injuries that had hurt them all the most. Then it was the day he'd moved out, without any warning or explanation. He'd just packed his things and rented an apartment near the gym and that was that. He was gone.

All the years of their marriage seemed to have been thrown in the trash, just like her mom's skates had been. That had been what had broken her mom the most. The way he'd bailed on her when she'd needed him, the way he wouldn't answer her calls and only came by the house when she was gone to her doctor. It had sent her mom into a deep depression, but it had pulled Leo out of his. His rage had been unbelievable, and he'd had to be held back more than once when he'd met his dad on the street, or at the snow park. He'd finally broken down and seen a therapist. Maybe it was something she needed to do too.

Sam looked down at the dirty snow at the edge of the street as she marched along. She'd never understood how her mom had let her dad back into her life. It was almost as if she'd forgiven him—something Sam would never do. Leo seemed to have calmed down over the last few years and seemed to have a decent relationship with their dad. Sam huffed as she came to the end of the pedestrian zone. He'd more than a decent relationship with their dad when she really thought about it. Lately they seemed thick as thieves.

Shaking her head she pushed that thought aside. It was none of her business what kind of a relationship Leo and their dad had. With some effort she looked around. She'd been to Livigno before, and had always loved it, but this time she'd hardly spent any time absorbing the picturesque and lively town. The store she was outside was new, and interesting. Peering in the window she saw that it was filled with all sorts of ski wear. Most of it wasn't like anything she'd seen outside of her parents' photo albums. Squinting she tried to make out what was in the far corner of the store but couldn't. The only thing for it was to go in.

The warm air inside made her nose and cheeks tingle. The place smelled amazing, like her home used to before her dad moved out. Spicy cinnamon and calming lavender. With her nose in the air, Sam wandered further into the room. Geometrically patterned rugs scattered across the wooden floor reminded her of the rug in her bedroom back at home. Nineties music played quietly in the background and the lighting was golden and gentle. Looking around, she didn't see anyone, so she started rummaging through the jackets and coats that had caught her eye from outside. *Everything was vintage!*

A huge smile spread across her face as she pulled out a jacket that was almost identical to the one her mom had worn when she'd come to watch her first snowboarding competitions. It was neon bright, blousy. The color clashed, and the fabric crinkled and rustled as she ran her hand down over it. Laughing, she plucked the tag from the sleeve and then gasped. It was a fraction of the cost she'd been expecting it to be. Tucking the jacket under her arm, Sam flicked through the other pieces. Each one made her smile. They were all so individual and had personality and even felt a little sassy. Finding a mirror, she held a jacket up to her chest and turned back and forth.

"You can try it on, if you like," a woman's voice called over. Sam jumped. The woman raised her hands, almost dropping the load of coats and jackets she was carrying. "Oh, I'm so sorry. I didn't mean to startle you."

"No, it's okay," Sam said. "I was lost in my own world here. These are amazing."

"Thank you." The small, neat woman put the stack of clothing on the counter and blew some dark hair from her brow. The rest of her hair was swept back into a French braid, making her look elegant and serene. Her face was open and friendly. Her own clothing appeared to be vintage too. Sam hoped that there was another sweater like the navy one the woman was wearing. It was giving Swiss vibes with white snowflake motifs and a cozy crew neck. "I hope you find something you like."

"I have already," Sam said holding up the jacket.

"Oh, that's one of my favorites." The woman came out from behind the counter. "There are matching pants too. Let me find them for you. Here . . . yes, here they are. They look like they'd fit you. Why don't you try them on?"

Sam took the pants and held them up to herself. They were unreal! The hot pink and bright holly green colors were so different to what she normally wore. The pants even had suspenders on them and a zip around the back that attached to a zip on the jacket that made them a one-piece.

"Ah, I'm a snowboarder," Sam said handing back the pants. "These look quite fitted. I'm used to a looser-fitting style."

The woman smiled. "You'd be surprised how roomy these are. Trust me."

Sam took the pants back, feeling a little pressured. Biting her lip, she picked up the jacket. "Sure, why not?"

"The changing room is over there." The woman pointed to the back of the store. "Take your time."

Hanging her jacket up, Sam sighed. She'd never mastered the art of avoiding a salesperson, ever, although she'd stood no chance in a store that had no other customers in it anyway. Stepping out of her pants and boots, she shivered slightly before tugging on the vintage pants. They slid up over her hips comfortably, the suspenders on her shoulders making it easy to twist and move. Pulling on the jacket she caught sight of herself in the mirror. Her eyes widened and she stifled a giggle. Her hair had loosened from the braid she'd put in that morning and was wild around her face, which was pink and blotchy from coming in from the cold. She truly looked like an Eighties ski diva. Just as her mom had when she'd come to watch her compete. Zipping up the jacket she was surprised at how easy it was to move. Twisting and bending was easy, she could still lay her palms flat on the floor too. Crouching down she found the pants didn't restrict her like she'd thought they would.

"Well, how do they fit?" the woman called.

Sam came out of the changing room and did a twirl. It was strange, she'd never imagined that the outfit would make her feel so good. It was as if she'd forgotten who she was, and they'd reminded her. "They fit like they were made for me." She walked toward the full-length mirror near the front of the store. "I love them!"

A man outside the window turned and she caught his eye. His rugged, tanned face lit up and he bounded into the store.

"Samantha!" He grabbed her in a bear hug. "I was wondering when you'd call in. Let me look at you—hahaha—this look suits you very well."

"Thank you, Davide!" Sam laughed as he twirled her around. "I like it too."

"You've met my Valentina?" Davide smiled at the petite woman who'd come over and wrapped her arms around his waist. He planted a kiss on her head and held her close.

"No, I didn't know!" Sam beamed at Davide. It had been a long time since she'd seen him so happy. "Hi, Valentina, I'm Sam."

Valentina took Sam's proffered hand. "Ah, now it makes sense. I've heard so much about you so it's lovely to finally meet you."

Davide looked past Sam. "Where's Finn?"

"Finn?" Sam's brow furrowed.

"Yes, I told him to call in. My store is next door—did he not tell you?"

Sam shook her head. "No, but . . ."

"You are busy. Please, don't mind me. I am forgetting how busy this time must be for you, for both of you. What a fantastic experience this is, no? The Olympics, here, and I get to see you again." Davide laughed as Valentina playfully slapped his chest.

"Davide!" she admonished. "It is not always about you!" She turned to Sam, a twinkle in her eye. "He's always making it about him—thank God he has me to keep him humble."

"Good to see he hasn't changed," Sam said with a wink. "But yes, it is an incredible experience, Davide. I'm loving it." Her stomach dropped as he smiled widely at her. The truth was, she wasn't loving it as much as she'd thought she would.

"I don't want to keep you from shopping," Davide said. He spun her around. "And this . . . this you must buy. *È perfetto su di te.*" His warm eyes crinkled as he smiled again, making Sam's heart happy. It really was good to see him. He waited for her to nod before pulling Valentina back into his arms. "*Amore mio*, come see me for lunch. I cannot bear to be apart from you."

"Of course, but you must leave in order for me to do that!" Valentina kissed him on the cheek and ushered him out the door. Davide waved in the window as he passed by, blowing kisses too. Sam laughed.

"You guys are so sweet," she said to Valentina as the woman blew kisses back to Davide. Valentina shrugged. "He's cute. How could I resist him?"

Sam looked at the enraptured expression on Valentina's face. She was lit up and humming as she tidied the rails. Sam went into the changing room and picked up her clothes. She couldn't stop thinking about Davide and Valentina. Cute wasn't how she'd describe Davide. Rugged, charming, no nonsense, straight talker, kind, outdoorsy, and yes maybe dashing—those were the kind of words she'd have chosen. Cute didn't quite match up with his broad shoulders, height and general papa bear image but if Valentina thought he was cute then maybe he was—maybe there was a soft and snuggly side to Davide that she'd never seen. The thought of him being in love cheered her up. It was as if he'd won the lottery. His obvious joy was infectious. Sam grinned as she closed a button on the jacket. There was nothing quite like an Italian man in love. They were so in the moment. She should take a leaf out of his book. With a grin, she decided to buy both the pants and the jacket. They made her feel good and might make Finn smile when he saw them. And they were a bargain price too, so it really wouldn't hurt her bank account too much.

"Ah, you made a wise choice." Valentina rang up her purchases. "Can I wrap them up for you?"

Sam smiled. "No, I'm going to wear them now. Live in the moment."

Valentina clapped her hands. "Yes! You will look amazing out there in these."

"Thank you!" Sam tapped her phone to pay as Valentina carefully snipped the tags from the clothes. She crossed her fingers and hoped that Finn would think the same thing. The outfit was loud and very different to the loose, dark and somewhat somber snowboarding clothing that most of her peers wore. Wearing neon pink and green would attract a lot of attention. Attention that Maya was sure to make the most of. Swinging the bag that Valentina had packed her own clothes in, Sam hurried toward her hotel, a huge smile on her face.

In the hallway outside her room, she noticed Becky's door was ajar. Sam rolled her eyes. Leo had moved over to Becky's room as soon as their engagement had been made official, and Becky's roommate had happily moved in with another athlete. Sam sighed. It had happened so fast it was almost indecent, but who was she to judge. They were happy and not hurting anyone. It was about time her brother had some fun and happiness in his life. If only she didn't have to listen to them banging each other hour after hour as if it was training for an Olympic sport.

With a huge grin, Sam opened her room door and flung her bag on her bed. She pulled the engagement gift she'd bought them from her suitcase. If they were both in the room, and not riding Olympic rings around each other, then this was the perfect time to give it to them, especially as she and Leo seemed to be on better terms than ever. With a happy dance, Sam hurried out to the hallway.

Through the half-open doorway, the TV blared. Sam paused. Gabriel's voice came across the airwaves, smooth and calm. He really did know what he was talking about—he had that going for him. Sam rolled her neck to try relieving the tension that was building up in her shoulders.

She thought about the trick she'd in mind to do later. It would be a tough one to pull off, but she'd done it once before. Surely, she'd be able to do it again. She went through the motions she'd have to take to hit the sweet spot on the ramp as she walked toward Becky's room. She'd have to make sure that . . . the TV went quiet and Leo's voice broke her concentration, and she stopped inches away from the door.

"Look, there, that's the moment she messed up."

"Oh, yes, I see. You're right." Becky's softer tone was a little harder to hear, but in the silence, Sam heard every word. Her mouth dropped open. *What was going on?*

"Look, one more time."

The TV came back on, and Sam heard Gabriel's commentary again. His voice loud and clear.

"*. . . this could be the triple we've all been waiting . . . No! What was that? Sam Harrington has followed her teammate, Becky Stanford. A double cork 1080—what a statement.*"

Sam's hand flew to her mouth. They were rewatching yesterday's qualies. More specifically, they were rewatching *her* performance at yesterday's qualies. Bile rose in her throat.

"She's off her game," Leo said.

"Uh, no . . ." Becky sounded confused.

Leo continued. "Look at her face even before she set off. She's not feeling it—"

"Listen to your fiancé." Jake Harrington's booming deep voice cut Leo off and made Sam jump. "This is your chance to step up."

Her dad was there too? Shredding her reputation to pieces with her brother and her teammate? A throbbing in her temple made her reach for the doorjamb to stop herself from staggering back. After all he'd said to her, not just at the Games but over the years . . . about how this was her chance, and how she was born to do this, that she had to

180

work harder to be better because he knew she could do better. She'd better not let him down, his reputation was on the line . . . He'd said these things to her at every single competition she'd gone to. And she'd listened to him, she'd done her best—well it looked like her best wasn't enough. And it never would be.

Choking back her tears, Sam quietly went back to her room. She threw the matching His and Hers towels onto the suitcase, and changed into her team gear, flinging her new vintage ski wear to one side. The final was just hours away, but she couldn't stay in her room—not next door to where her dad and brother were talking badly about her. She needed to walk, to clear her mind. Her stomach lurched as she zipped up her jacket. What was the point of even trying when she clearly wasn't meant to win?

13

Finn

The stars were hidden, and the sky the darkest blue as Finn stared up the ramp, hoping to spot Sam among the other finalists. She was at the back, facing away from the event. Not a good sign. He twisted his old orange beanie in his hands, the spotlights dazzling him a little.

The announcer's voice echoed over the slopes as the big air final kicked off. Each rider launched down the massive ramp, the crowd roaring with every gravity-defying trick. Finn barely registered the scores—until Becky appeared at the top of the run.

Becky. Sam's future sister-in-law, her teammate and also her competition. Becky oozed confidence as she dropped, her body fluid and in control. She soared off the ramp with a smooth backside double cork 1080, grabbing her board with precision. The crowd erupted as she struck the landing perfectly, raising her arms in triumph.

"Strong run from Becky Stanford!" The loudspeakers blared as Gabriel's voice rang out across the snowy terrain.

Becky's score flashed on the screen—solid, but not unbeatable. Finn swallowed hard as Becky grinned and waved to the crowd. She was top of the leader board, for now, and it looked like she was going to enjoy every single second of it.

Finn glanced toward the ramp, easily spotting Sam. Her jaw was tight, her expression unreadable. Finn's heart dropped. To anyone else it looked as if she was preparing hard, but he knew her too well. She was good at hiding her feelings, but that tension in her posture was giving her away and would mess her up if she didn't loosen up. Sam stood back as Harper came forward. Gritting his teeth, Finn turned his attention to the ramp as Harper set off. Her fearless style had made her a crowd favorite, and she didn't disappoint. She launched into a massive frontside triple cork 1440, holding the grab longer than anyone else had dared. Finn couldn't help but be impressed as she landed with the faintest wobble, straightened out and skidded to a celebratory stop.

But Gabriel's commentary made Finn press his lips together. He hoped Sam wasn't paying any attention to it. "Harper Reynolds, Canada's golden girl, may have struck gold with that fearless display of dexterity and skill. She's going to be a tough one to beat." Finn watched as Harper's score pushed Becky down into second place. He crossed his fingers. *Come on, Sam, you can do this! Show them what you've got.*

Maya sidled up to him, her phone in her hand recording his expression as Sam stepped forward to the top of the ramp, her fingers on the chin strap of her helmet. She looked composed, but he'd seen the way her eyes had darted around the crowd just now. She'd never done that before. Gently

183

pushing Maya aside, Finn moved to the barrier, his eyes never leaving Sam. He pulled his orange beanie on. If she saw it, she might feel better.

"Let's go, Sam," he murmured, willing her to get it together.

Then she dropped in. Her approach looked smooth, but as she reached the ramp's edge, Finn saw it—that split-second hesitation. She still went for the trick, a backside double cork 1260, her grab clean, tight, but her rotation was just a fraction too slow. She landed with too much weight on her back foot, the board slipping slightly. Her hand shot out, dragged in the snow to keep her balance. The crowd gasped. Finn gripped the barrier, his bare hands white and cold. Sam recovered quickly and rode the rest of the way, but the stumble was impossible to miss. It would cost her.

Gabriel, at least, sounded disappointed. "Ohhhh, a valiant effort from Samantha Harrington, but that landing, it's going to hurt her score. If she'd landed cleanly, we might have been looking at a new leader on the scoreboard." Finn closed his eyes. Gabriel's analysis was right.

He opened his eyes, his heart racing. Sam skidded to a stop and yanked off her helmet, her chest heaving as she watched the scoreboard. Finn didn't need to see the numbers to know the truth, but they flashed in front of him regardless. Fourth. Gabriel's now flat commentary confirmed it: "With a clean 1260, she'd likely have topped Harper Reynolds' 1440 and taken gold. An incredible run, but such bad luck. That tiny mistake has cost Samantha Harrington the podium."

Finn rubbed his face, wishing he could turn back time. She'd been so close—so damn close. If she'd only landed that trick—she'd not only be on the podium, she'd be on the top of it—and all her dreams would have come true. He couldn't take his eyes off her. She stood frozen, staring at the board as if willing it to change until the podium was set up right in front of her. The winners were clapping each other's backs, hugging and cheering. Sam stared. Her shoulders slumped, and she hurried away, swinging her helmet as if nothing mattered, as if her heart hadn't been shattered.

"Sam!" he called out as she stormed toward the break in the barrier, not even looking left or right as the medalists took their places on the podium. She was being rude—no one left until the medals had been awarded. "Sam!" he called again, but she barely glanced at him. Her face was hard and blank, but he could see beneath the surface. She was destroyed. She didn't stop or look at him again. He dragged his beanie from his head and pushed it into his pocket.

The crowd cheered as Becky received the silver medal and Harper the gold. Finn didn't care. He turned away as Becky shook her champagne bottle and sprayed it everywhere. All he wanted was to find Sam and tell her it didn't matter, that everything would be okay. If she'd listen to him. If only he could think of something to say that would make things right. His legs moved before his mind could catch up, following Sam out of the athletes' area. She was hurting; he knew she was, and she shouldn't be alone right now.

He spotted her just beyond the crowd, walking fast, her head down. Her shoulders had risen up to her ears again and each step was sharp and deliberate. No one was getting in her way as she left the scene.

"Sam!" he called, picking up his pace.

She didn't stop, didn't even look back.

"Damn it, Sam!" he muttered under his breath as he broke into a jog. She glanced back and saw him but turned away and kept on walking. Jogging, he finally caught up with her as she rounded the corner to the street.

"Hey!" He touched her arm gently, slightly out of breath. His chest ached as he saw the dark and teary expression on her face. "You always storm off in the middle of a medal ceremony?"

She rolled her eyes and didn't answer. Just kept walking, her hands jammed deep into her pockets, her head down as if watching her boots crunching over the snow was the most interesting hobby in the world. The silence between them was strange. She'd never been so closed off, so unreachable— not with him.

"You don't have to say anything," he said, quieter. "I just didn't want you to be alone."

She paused. Her mouth pressed together even more tightly. His heart ached for her disappointment. His head whirred with what to say to her, but all he could think of was that she should have had it today—she should've taken that gold. She'd gone for it, but she'd pulled back as if someone had said something to her midair. Christ, she'd been so goddamn close. Why had she done that—pulled back like that? He knew she had it in her—he'd seen her pull off that trick before. He was gutted for her.

They turned a corner, and she glanced up. "Look, a bar. You buying?"

"Always," he said. It came out too fast. He held open the door for her, eager to do something to help. She went

186

in, no thank you, no come on, hurry up. Nothing. She was like a zombie.

The bar was warm, and wood-paneled. Firelight flickered and low conversation filled the air. Finn glanced around, relieved that it seemed that there was no press in the place.

"Booth or barstool?" Sam shrugged her jacket off with the kind of fluid precision she should've used on the run.

"Booth." Finn nodded toward a quiet space near the fire. He watched her go, taking in the terse, tight line of her back as she walked away. She didn't seem to want him around. Had he made a mistake by following her? She seemed to want to be alone.

At the bar he ordered two beers, but he couldn't take his eyes off her. She sat in the booth, her arms leaning on the table, her hands gripped together like she was trying to stay calm. Her face was tightly composed, but he knew she wasn't happy. She was far from it.

The bartender placed two beers in front of him, just as he caught Sam ordering from a server. The server was back with two tequila shots just as he reached their table. Sam threw one back as if it was medicine. No salt. No lime. No pause. Finn placed their beers on the table as she reached for the second shot.

"Don't look at me like that," she said, keeping her eyes on the tequila. "A girl has to drown her sorrows every once in a while."

"Fair enough." Finn took a sip of his own drink. He sat next to her, watching her grimace as the second tequila went down. "Does that make you feel any better?"

"Oh, come on, Finn." Sam scowled. "Can't you cut me some slack?"

"Sure," he said. "But I don't think that's a wise thing to do, Sam."

"Don't tell me what I can and can't do."

"Okay, so that's how it is." Finn sat back. "For crying out loud, Sam. I'm just looking out for you."

"Sorry," she mumbled as she wiped her mouth with the back of her hand. "I didn't mean to snap at you."

Finn looked down for a moment before answering. "It's okay, Sam. I get it."

"I know you do." Sam touched his arm. "Look at us: two fools in a bar . . ." She gestured around the almost empty bar. "It's actually very nice in here. Posh. Table service, mood lighting, olives . . . very demure, mindful blah blah." She spluttered a laugh.

"Come on, Sam," Finn said softly, wishing she'd just talk to him. "You don't need to put on a brave face for me."

Sam rolled her eyes at him. "Me—brave face—hahahah!"

Finn watched in horror as her face crumpled. She looked down and wiped her face with her hand. "This is too much; this whole damn day is too much."

Tears fell in great big drops, onto the oak table.

Grabbing the tiny black napkin that had come with her tequila, she tried to mop up the tears that wouldn't stop falling. "You're right. Tequila is not a good idea."

Finn moved closer, gently pulling the napkin from her hand and offering his sleeve.

"Here," he said, voice low. "Use this—I don't mind."

Sam huffed a laugh through her tears. "What, and ruin your designer hoodie?"

"It's not designer." He shrugged. "And you can ruin anything of mine, Sam. I mean it."

He didn't know what else to say, didn't know how to make any of this better—what could he do to bring her back to herself—the brave, talented and unstoppable Sam he thought he knew.

"Want me to see if they can whip you up a *Samwich* or a *Finnomenal*?" He nudged her.

The tiniest smile on her lips made his heart soar. "God, not the *Finnomenal*. Cream cheese, jalapeños and *pineapple* in a wrap . . . I haven't had one in ages."

"No time like the present," Finn said, happy to see her smile.

"Um, Finn," Sam said. "Maybe not here—it's Italy—they don't put pineapple on anything."

"You're so right." Finn chuckled. "How do you think they'll feel when they hear you put banana into a sandwich?"

"It's a dessert sandwich," Sam said, her lips quirking into a smile. "Like banoffee—which sounds Italian, doesn't it. I think I'll be fine—you on the other hand, as the inventor of the criminally and insanely delicious Finnomenal—you might actually get arrested."

Finn laughed. This was the Sam he recognized: witty, funny, and so easy to talk to. For a second the tension in his chest loosened. She shifted and suddenly her hip was close to his, her warm, soft body leaning into him.

"What would I do without you, Finn?"

She leaned against his shoulder, her hair tickling his chin. A surge of protectiveness filled him as he slid his arm around her and pulled her in closer, holding her like he was shielding her from everything, even herself. He smoothed her hair back from her face, inhaling her scent as if he'd never get to see her again.

"Thank you," Sam said, looking up at him. "I just hate this feeling. I thought I could do it. I really did."

Her breath warmed his neck, making his blood heat up. She was so close.

Her lashes were wet, her face blotchy. It made something inside him twist sharply. What had happened to make her doubt herself?

"You can do it," he said quickly. "You're the best out there—you are what the Finnomenal is named for."

She giggled and shook her head. "Finn!"

"No—you are, Sam."

"Finn—I messed up today," Sam said quietly, as if she was hearing someone else say it. She wasn't smiling anymore. Her whole body seemed to deflate right next to him. "I messed up. I always mess up."

Her words sliced through him. His heart sank. Where were these words coming from? This wasn't Sam. Sam was unrelenting, and she'd always picked herself up whenever she'd made mistakes before. What the hell was hitting her so hard? Didn't she know how good she was? He turned to her, taking her hands in his.

"You messed up," he said. Her body stiffened; a frown formed on her brow. He sat back. He wasn't even sure what he was trying to do—comfort her or snap her out of it. But whatever it was, it hadn't worked. She scooched away from him, taking her warmth and scent with her.

190

"Thanks." Her eyes didn't meet his, her hands scrabbled around for her jacket. "I'm tired, I'm going to go to bed."

He didn't move right away, and she huffed.

"Finn." She kept her eyes down. "I need to get out."

He slid from the booth, slowly and confused. She slipped past him, pulling her jacket up on her shoulders.

"Sam—" He reached for her, but she shrugged his arm off.

"Goodnight, Finn." She finally looked at him. Her green eyes were puffy and red.

"Sam, please," he tried again. "What did I say? Talk to me. Please."

She shook her head slowly. "I really need to go, Finn."

Finn's stomach knotted hard. He opened his mouth to say something—anything—but nothing came out. *What did I say?* She didn't wait for him to try to fix it between them; she was gone, moving toward the door, leaving him behind.

"Sam, wait—" A rising panic swirled in his gut. She was gone, and it was because of something he'd done, something he'd said. He sat down hard, staring at the table. Two untouched beers. Two empty shot glasses. A napkin damp with her tears. Shit. He grasped the napkin and folded it up. He'd been the one to mess up. He was an absolute idiot, even if he didn't know what he'd done.

For the very first time, Finn wondered if maybe Sam didn't want him to be the person she ran to, and it felt like the searing, breath-stealing pain of falling through the ice of a dark, frigid lake.

191

14

Sam

Sam drew her knees up to her chest as Maya handed her a coffee.

"Urgh, Maya. It's too early."

"It's six thirty. I've been up for hours. Here you go, two sugars, black. That should wake you up." Maya, fully dressed and perfectly glammed up, sat on the edge of the bed. "Do you want to talk about it—yesterday?"

"About what?" Sam groggily blew on the surface of her coffee.

"That sounds like a no," Maya said. She leaned forward and gently touched Sam's hand. "I'm here, when you need to talk."

Sam shrugged but smiled. Maya was being so kind to her, so warm and supportive. She'd left a hot water bottle in her bed last night and had been fast asleep by the time Sam had come to the room. This was the first time she'd spoken to her since messing up yesterday.

"Thanks for the hot water bottle," she said. "And thanks—I know you're here for me. I'm just not ready to talk about it." She shouldn't have listened to her father in the qualies. She should've gone with her gut and let herself have fun. Just as she should have yesterday. But every time she thought of going out there as herself, she froze as the words *messed up* and her father's voice telling Becky to listen to Leo drowned out everything else in her head. She knew she'd messed up the qualie, but she'd been sure she'd have been placed. Fourth—no one remembered fourth. She'd have settled for third, even though it wouldn't have been enough for Jake Harrington. Anything less than gold didn't rank with him when it came to Sam.

"Do you remember Breckenridge?" Sam said quietly. "The year Leo took first place."

"Yeah, he was unstoppable." Maya blinked.

Sam looked down into her coffee. "That night . . . we didn't go to the lodge right away. Dad stayed behind, talking to some suit about Leo. Celebrating and pushing for a deal." Her voice tightened. "I hadn't placed at all, but Dad didn't care. He was locked in on Leo and this deal. Mom had had a few glasses of wine so . . ." Sam paused. "So, Leo drove."

Maya's head shot up. "Wait, what. You never told me Leo was driving."

"I wasn't able to." Sam's tone was flat. "It was . . . oh God, Mai. It was such a great night, you know. We were all on a high and so hopeful for Leo."

Maya shook her head. "And then the accident—and he never skied again."

Sam nodded. "It was snowing hard, and then out of

nowhere this huge elk was in front of us. Everything spun. It was like we were moving in slow motion and all I can remember is the sound of metal screeching, crumpling against the trees, country songs on the radio, and then silence."

Maya's eyes welled up. "Sam."

Sam wiped away a tear. "I walked away without a scratch, Maya. But Mom . . . Leo . . ." Sam put a hand over her mouth, choking back her tears. Maya took the coffee cup away from her and hugged her tightly. Sam leaned on her friend. Her shoulders shaking as tears streamed down her face. The sensation of being in that car surrounded her again. The realization that her mom wasn't moving, just crying quietly. That Leo was screaming. He'd been destroyed that night, physically, emotionally and mentally.

Maya held her, quietly and gently. Her hand rubbed Sam's back in circles until she calmed down. Then, slowly, Sam pulled back and wiped her face on her pjs' sleeve, as Maya dabbed under her eyes, trying not to dislodge her makeup.

"I'm sorry," Sam said.

"Girl, I don't need your apology for being real." Maya pulled a tissue from her pocket. "This I can fix." She pointed to her face. "But as for the rest, today we just get up, get some air."

Sam gave a watery laugh. "Sounds solid."

Maya stood up, sniffling. "Step two though." She smiled. "Is a little more fun. Explain to me—what is this?" She reached down behind the bed. A flash of hot pink and deep green caught Sam's eye. The ski jacket she'd bought in Valentina's store. "This is outrageously beautiful. And you—you are putting this on."

Sam half laughed. "I am not."

"You are. It's too cool to sit here in this room. And don't tell anyone I said this, but I'm not a big fan of the team's kit." Maya pressed a finger to her lips while shaking the jacket. Her eyes widened in delight. "Hello? Did you see this?" She tugged the label from the inside of the jacket. "This is a sign, girl—it's a Montalier! A vintage Montalier!" She flung the jacket at Sam.

Sam caught it with one hand. Gripping it tightly, her stomach fluttered as if filled with a blizzard. Should she wear it? It was a million miles away from what she'd normally wear. She squeezed it, loving the softness of the fabric, the fluffiness of the down.

"What's that?" Maya was beside her, pulling at the ski pants from behind the bed as Sam laughed. "Wow! This is . . ."

"It's crazy." Sam breathed out. "I don't know what I was thinking. I saw them in Valentina's store and had a mad moment."

". . . bloody fabulous!" Maya gasped. She held up the ski pants. "And it matches! Ooooooh please wear it."

"No," Sam spluttered. "It's too much. It's all wrong and too bright."

Maya scrunched up her face. "I get ya, but . . . it's so great—will you at least try it on for me?"

Sam hid her face in her hands, then peeped out from behind her fingers. Maya grinned at her and held out the ski suit.

"Pretty please—remember when I picked out your prom

195

dress? Uh-huh, yeah you do. I never get it wrong, and I know this is going to be amazing on you. Please try it on, please!"

"Fine!" Sam slipped out of her pjs. "Give it here."

Shimmying into the ski suit, she caught a glimpse of herself in the mirror. Her face was glowing, her eyes sparkling. She didn't look like she'd been sobbing her heart out moments ago. Anyone looking at her would think she was full of confidence, brimming with brilliance. Zipping up the jacket she spun around to face Maya.

"Tah-dah!" She flung her arms out wide, then did a twirl as Maya clapped.

Maya walked around her, her five-foot-two body bouncing as she failed to suppress a grin. "Oh, Sam—it's like it was made for you."

"Do you think?" Sam grabbed her hairbrush and dragged it through her hair. "I really do like it but it's not really me, is it?"

"I don't know." Maya stood back, her hand on her hip as she looked Sam over. "You *look* like you, and you're smiling, and you seem . . . well, do you want me to be honest?"

Sam nodded. Maya wouldn't say anything to hurt her. "Please."

"You look like fun and the Sam I know *is* fun." Maya's eyes beseeched Sam's. "And ever since we got here you've been not as much fun and I'm worried. That's all."

Sam pulled the zipper down. Finn had said something similar to her. She needed to relax, to find the joy in the moment or else she was going to lose it all.

"Fun?"

196

"Sam," Maya said, stepping toward her. "I'm sorry, I didn't mean to hurt you."

"You didn't." Sam pulled the zipper back up. "You're so right, Maya. I need to have fun. And if this damn gorgeous outfit isn't fun, then I don't know what is!"

"Damn right!" Maya hollered, jumping up and down. "You're wearing it?"

"Can I?" Sam plaited her hair, then grabbed her gloves. "Won't the team have something to say about it?"

Maya shook her head. "Uh-no. I know the rules inside out, back to front. You are obliged to wear the kit for all competitions, events and anywhere else you're representing the team, but your own free time is catwalk time, baby! You can wear what you want then." She hopped up and down. "I have had the best idea ever. You are going to love this."

Sam laughed; Maya's energy was contagious. "What now?"

"Let's make this a moment. A photo shoot—me, you, and that Slay Queen of a ski suit." She snapped her fingers in the air. "This outfit is too good to not be seen."

Sam's heart raced a little. "But why? You can't post it to the team socials."

Maya's eyes twinkled mischievously. "No, but you can post it on your own page—take some control of things for yourself."

Sam bit her lip. "Oh, okay."

"And no one can say a thing, and what's even better is that your page has almost as many followers as the team page," Maya burbled. "And it's brilliant. I'll accept your thanks now—you're welcome!" She dipped into a quick bob of a curtsey.

Sam scrunched her nose up.

"Well, I do look pretty damn good in this . . ."

"That's my girl!" Maya ran to the window. "Now come on. This light is great."

Standing in front of the mirror Sam couldn't help but grin. Her father was going to hate this, but that didn't matter. All that mattered was that for the first time in months she was feeling like herself again. Maya was right. She needed to take back her own power, and everyone needed to see her do it.

* * *

"Are you done yet?" Sam tried to not laugh at Maya. She was lying face down in the snow, awkwardly angling the camera up at Sam.

"Shhhhh! Hold that pose. Don't move! Do it for the grid." Maya's voice was muffled. "Got it! Look at this— man, I am good, and I don't get paid nearly half as much as I should."

Sam breathed out as Maya staggered to her feet, snow stuck to her coat and hair. Brushing her friend down she spontaneously hugged her.

"Thanks for this, Maya," she said. "I didn't realize how much I needed it."

"No biggie," Maya said, her eyes warm. "What are friends for? And speaking of friends—I promised Finn I'd call in this morning and make him my famous smoothie. You coming with?"

198

Sam shook her head. She wasn't ready to face Finn yet even though the right thing to do would be to go and apologize for being such a diva.

"Sam." Maya sounded slightly sad. "It's his final today. You should come with me—wish him luck."

"I'll catch him later," Sam said quickly. "I just don't want to show him this." She glanced down at her ski suit.

Maya squinted at her. "Did something happen between you two?"

"No," Sam was quick to answer.

"Because I think he'd love to see you in that particular ski suit." Maya grinned. "Your ass . . ."

"No." Sam poked Maya before pulling on her gloves. "But I'll walk you to his hotel. I need to stretch my legs."

"Damn, I've lost one." Maya pulled on one of her mittens and double-checked her pockets as they walked. "Well, that's annoying—they match my coat perfectly."

Just as they reached the hotel, Sam saw Gabriel, standing to the side, holding something and looking a little on edge. Sam tilted her head. It looked like a satsuma-colored mitten that could only belong to one person: Maya.

"You forgot this?" Gabriel's deep voice was low but clear. There was a softness to his tone that made Sam's throat constrict. Her chest tightened. She recognized that kind of tone. Love. Gabriel was giving off a quiet affection that was hard to ignore, while Maya was sparking like a firework on the Fourth of July.

"Aren't they adorable?" Sam said, flashing a grin. "Perfect together—the mittens—I'm talking about the mittens." She raised an eyebrow, watching them both as they smiled at one another.

Maya flushed, a subtle shade of pink spreading across her cheeks as she shot a look at Gabriel. "Look at you," she blustered. "Keeping my mitten hostage."

Gabriel's cheeks reddened, but his eyes twinkled at Maya. "Your . . . mitten . . ." He held it out to her, and Sam held her breath. It was like some kind of alternative Cinderella scene, and she was here for it. The way their eyes lingered on each other for a moment made her heart flutter.

Maya broke the silence with a laugh. "It seems you've got my mitten—and my attention," she teased, her voice light but warm. She slid her hand into the mitten he held open, her fingers brushing against his. She smiled up at him. "You're too good to me."

Sam blinked rapidly and covered a smile with her hands. Honestly, Maya was the best flirt she'd ever seen. And Gabriel was falling for it. Sam watched in amazement as his smile softened into a bashful grin. This was the most romantic moment she'd ever seen.

"Just doing my part," Gabriel said. "Wouldn't want you to lose anything—especially not this mitten."

Sam had to turn away to hide her smile. What was happening? Gabriel Hawke, known for his calm, cool, and collected personality, his ability to remain unruffled no matter what the occasion, was melting under her friend's attention.

Maya raised an eyebrow, a playful smile tugging at the corners of her mouth. "You're starting to sound like a knight in shining armor."

Gabriel laughed, his cheeks still tinged with a soft pink. "If the glove fits . . ."

Maya snorted, and Sam couldn't hold back a laugh either. The tension between them melted away in the shared humor, and for a second, it felt like the three of them were part of a world entirely their own.

"Okay, okay, I'll let you two have your moment," Sam said with a teasing wink, stepping back. "But seriously, if I get dragged into one more *Cinderella* scenario, I might start looking for my own glass slipper."

Maya rolled her eyes, but her grin never faltered. Glancing at Gabriel, she gave him a mock-serious look. "If I catch you keeping any more of my stuff hostage, there'll be consequences."

Gabriel held his hands up in faux surrender. "I'll keep that in mind."

"Well, I hate to break up beautiful things, but duty calls." Maya smiled at Gabriel. "I've got a Finn to annoy."

She winked at Sam. "I'll catch you later—and don't worry. I'll log in for you and post the best pics. Ciao!" She waved her hand and disappeared into the hotel, leaving Sam and Gabriel standing in the snow.

He turned to her, his smile faltering. "Sam, about yesterday, I'm sorry you missed out."

"Thanks," Sam said. "I messed up."

"No. It was bad luck, that's all." Gabriel shoved his hands into his coat pockets. "You had it right up until that last second. I never saw anything like it. You made everyone sit up."

Sam hunched down into the neck of her jacket. "No, it wasn't bad luck. I hesitated."

Gabriel looked at her steadily. "Ah, I've been there too. You didn't trust yourself?"

"Something like that. How'd you know?" Sam looked at him. They were friendly with each other, and had met on the circuit many times, but he'd never been as open about his career before.

"Been there." He nodded. "Messed up too. Qualifiers in 2018. Didn't you know?"

Sam shook her head. She'd been so wrapped up in herself, acting as if no one before her had ever failed in anything, that she felt a hot wash of shame creep up her neck. "What did you do?"

A smile tugged on the corner of his mouth. "The same thing you're known for—I got up. And the next day I showed up, and the day after."

Sam kicked the snow at her feet. "I feel like a fool."

"You're not a fool." Gabriel's tone was firm but kind. "But you are if you let this get to you. Sam, you're not even close to being done. Get back out there and show them that."

Sam swallowed hard, his words settling somewhere deep beneath her ribcage. The sting of shame was still there, but it was softened now by something steadier, respect maybe. Or even hope.

"Thanks," she said quietly. "You've no idea how much that helps."

Gabriel smiled. "You don't owe anyone anything, remember that."

Sam nodded, not trusting herself to speak.

Gabriel looked at his watch and Sam smiled, knowing

it was an accessory that Maya would love to see. "Look, I have to go—media team meeting. Apparently, I'm supposed to know what I'm doing up there." He grimaced.

"I've no doubt you'll hit those marks," Sam said, hiding her hands in her pockets so he wouldn't see her trembling. His words were hitting home hard. She didn't owe anyone anything. It was about her—her love of the sport and her joy, and it always had been.

She watched Gabriel run lightly up the hotel steps and into the lobby. The street was quiet around her now, the cold less biting than before. Her heart still ached for yesterday's loss, but she had tomorrow waiting for her, and moping about it wasn't going to get her anywhere. Nope. Sam Harrington wasn't done yet. But first she needed to change into her kit and get out there to cheer Finn on.

15

Finn

Finn sat at the breakfast table in his suite watching Maya, in the kitchen, as she poured a thick, pink, almost purple, liquid into a tall glass.

"Here you go, my famous Freestyle Fuel Smoothie," she said as she placed it in front of him.

Finn stared at the smoothie. "Mai, this is huge—it could feed a giant."

Maya shook her head and laughed. "I know what you're thinking, but you will be glad of it later. Today is too important—and I know you won't eat your snacks before the final."

"You know me too well," Finn said, picking up the glass. He took a deep sip and licked his lips. Having Maya here was making a huge difference, especially as his family now couldn't come. His mom couldn't make it due to catching a really bad flu, but she'd promised she'd call him before the competition later. Uncle Henry and Aunt Miranda had come down with the same thing and had sent him messages rather than come to see him, afraid of him catching the same horrible bug. Today was his first chance to go for gold. The final for freestyle slopestyle ski competition would take place just after midday and he was nervous.

"Have you seen Sam?" Maya called over her shoulder as she dropped a coffee pod into the Nespresso machine. "I waited up for her but eventually I had to go to bed. What time did you get in?"

"I was in bed by ten." Finn took another mouthful of the smoothie, unwilling to share what had happened last night with Sam. "I didn't see her."

"Oh," Maya said. She sat down at the table with her coffee. She picked up the room service menu.

Finn looked down into the smoothie. He tried to push down the image of Sam leaving him in the bar last night. And, if he was honest with himself, it was killing him not knowing what had gone wrong between them. He sighed deeply trying to think about how Sam was feeling. "You know Sam—she won't want to talk about it."

"For sure." Maya twisted her mug on the table. "I think Sam is reliving a lot of things."

Finn's head shot up. "Yeah, I think you're right."

Maya nodded, still playing with her mug. "It really kills me to see our girl hurting so much. I know she never says anything—to anyone. Not even me. It's like she's afraid to ask for help—Little Miss Independence all the way. It's like she's afraid she'll lose a part of herself if she admits she can't do this alone."

Finn's thoughts drifted to Jake, to the words Jake had said: *I'm not losing anyone else.* A chill went down

Finn's spine. Sam wasn't the only one struggling here. The conversation was starting to feel too heavy. He shifted uncomfortably in his seat, his gaze flitting around the room.

Maya let out a soft sigh. "All right, enough of that. Today is your day. So, eggs? How about an omelet?" Maya held up the room service menu. Finn pulled a face. "Never mind. What about you—are you doing okay? Worried about your qualie today?"

"A little," Finn said. "But I'm okay. Are you sure there isn't alcohol in this?" He raised his smoothie and took another drink, eager to change the topic.

Maya giggled. "You know, the very odd time I wonder what might happen if I added just another dash of vodka—would anyone even notice? No, Finn! Of course there's no alcohol in that! Sheesh!"

"Any news from Montalier or Salvaro?" Finn leaned both elbows on his knees. "Things seem to have been a little quiet."

"Yeah," Maya breathed out. "There's been some news, not great. Salvaro have signed a deal with Harper. I'm worried how Sam is going to take this."

"Crap. Wow. How did Harper bag that one?" Finn flopped back on the couch. This was going to hurt Sam so much. Of course Harper had got the deal—she'd taken the gold medal. Finn groaned inwardly. This was another nail in the coffin of Sam's seemingly depleting confidence. "Don't say anything to Sam. She'll only beat herself up for it. Blame herself."

"Don't I know it." Maya swiped the glass from under his

nose and took a sip. "Damn, this is good. I am a domestic goddess."

Finn laughed and reached for his glass. "You? In all the years I've known you, I have never seen you do anything in the kitchen that didn't start with a coff and end with an ee."

"Cheeky. Listen, back to business—the real reason why I'm here," Maya said with a dramatic hand gesture as she whipped out her phone. "I want to share this with you." She swiped through Instagram showing Finn post after post of him and Sam, including the video of him watching her lose her podium place yesterday. "Despite crickets from Montalier, people are eating this up, Finn. It's unreal. You two are picture-perfect."

Picture-perfect. Finn frowned. "Should you have put that one up?" He pointed at the post of Sam looking devastated at her loss, the pit of his stomach heavy as he wondered if she was still angry with him.

"Yes," Maya said brightly. "It's showing the world how real this is, and people really respond well to vulnerability."

"Maya." There was a warning sound in Finn's voice. "I think that might be overstepping the mark. Sam wouldn't like this."

Maya's face fell. "Oh. Do you really think so? I thought she'd be okay with it."

Finn gnawed on his bottom lip as Maya stared at the phone in her hand, her finger hovering over the delete button. Shaking his head, Finn put his hand on hers.

"Don't mind me. Why don't you just ask her?"

Maya gave a pained smile. "I will. Thanks, Finn."

Maya took a sip of her coffee. Throwing a side glance at Finn she grimaced.

"So, what's actually eating you? It can't be just the final. You're like a skater on thin ice, all antsy and on edge."

"Nothing." Finn slurped the last of his smoothie.

"Liar," Maya said with a laugh. "I've known you a long time. Spill the tea."

"There's nothing to spill." Finn lowered his gaze and picked at a crumb on the table.

Maya sat beside him in silence. Her phone pinged, once, twice, then a dozen times. Opening Instagram, she sighed heavily. "Everyone is liking the posts. Everyone but you." She peered at Finn. "Why?"

Finn fidgeted with his empty glass; his lips twisted as he tried to think of something to say. Finally, his voice low and his eyes trained on the table, he said, "It's Sam."

"Oh."

"She should've been up there on that podium. She deserved to be. It's my fault she wasn't."

"She made a mistake," Maya said, frowning. "That's not on you."

He shook his head, his words catching in his throat. "No, it is on me. I—we—Sam and me . . . Look. These posts—they're all anyone is talking about."

Maya blinked, taken aback. "What? But that's the point, Finn. You know that."

"I know." He ran a hand through his hair. "Look, Mai—the thing is that pretending to be with her—to be her boyfriend—it's killing me." He took a breath not daring to look at Maya's face. "Because I actually do love her. I'm *in* love with her. And

208

we had a moment the other day and I think it's messed with her head and now she's . . . now she's losing her dream."

"Oh, well that changes things." Maya sat back, her face soft on hearing his words.

"Look, don't say anything to anyone, will you?" Finn said miserably. "I'll be fine, in time. And Sam deserves to win a medal."

"What are you going to do?" Maya took his hand and squeezed it.

"I'll get through this week as best I can, then I'll stay away from her," Finn said flatly. "What else can I do?"

"I don't know, I think that's a bad idea." Maya leaned back; her brow furrowed. "You can't stay away from her, Finn. If you stay away from her, it'll just make things worse. She'll think you don't care—and the reality is that the Montalier reps are keeping tabs on you both. This 'couple' thing is working. If your heart isn't in it then I can't help you. I can post a million photos of you guys looking all cute and spicy, but people will know. They always do. Now that I know this, I think that's what your magic ingredient has been all this time—it's what everyone else has seen. If you pull back, even a little bit, it's going to fall apart for you both."

Finn rubbed his temples. "Great. So, what you're telling me is that I have to keep this up even though it's killing me."

"Hey," Maya said sharply. "Don't get me wrong, I have a lot of sympathy for you, but Finn—Sam has worked her ass off to get noticed. And whether you like it or not, the fake-relationship thing is what's making it happen. You're the one who has always said she deserves her dream. Don't blow it now because you're scared of your own feelings."

Finn squirmed in his seat. "I've been scared of these feelings since the day I first saw her."

"Wow!" Maya took his hand. "That's a long time to be scared of love."

"The thing is, I'm not scared of love," Finn said. "I'm scared of losing her if she doesn't love me back."

"Sounds like the same kinda thing to me," Maya said.

"No, it's not." Finn was adamant. "Anyway, I think I've lost her completely. We had a bit of an argument after her final yesterday. And she stormed off, and she hasn't contacted me since."

Maya's mouth dropped open. "Wait—what? That's not like our girl. She hasn't even texted you good luck this morning?"

Finn shook his head. "Nothing. And the worst thing is that I have no idea what happened."

"This is not good," Maya said shaking her head.

"No, it's not," Finn started. He shook his head and grimaced. "What if I've ruined everything—how can I fix this?"

Maya played with her phone. Throwing a side look at him she said, "Leave it with me."

Finn groaned.

"I'll get to the bottom of it," Maya continued. "But, seriously, Finn. You've, um, you've loved her—forever and you never said anything?"

Finn shook his head. "No, we knew we liked each other, but we made a pact not to mess up our careers by dating each other. We both thought it was the best thing at the time, and it worked, for a while."

"Oh." Maya's brow furrowed. "What changed things?"

Finn shrugged. How could he explain that while he'd loved Sam since that first day, seeing her here, so close to achieving her dreams, had brought it all back. He hadn't been able to stop thinking about Sam in a way that he hadn't done since they'd first met—in a way that took over his every last waking moment and all of his dreams too. And, in his opinion, that had been the beginning of this heartbreak. Because he'd started paying more attention to her then, more than he'd ever given her. He'd given in to his desire to be around her, and it had backfired. It had backfired because it had worked—it had seemed that she'd started liking having him around too, and then they'd ended up in the shower, and she'd lost the gold. He put his head in his hands and rubbed his eyes.

"I don't know. I just know that it has."

Maya pulled his hands down from his face and patted his arm as her phone pinged, but she didn't pick it up. "What are you going to do?"

"Nothing." Finn sounded even more miserable. "Absolutely nothing."

Finn jumped up from the couch. "Anyway, that's where my head's at." He grabbed the smoothie glass and rinsed it out before putting it in the dishwasher. Leaning on the counter with his two hands he dropped his head low. "Maya, you can't tell anyone, okay? Not even Sam."

Looking up he pressed his lips together and waited for Maya's nod.

"Not a soul." Maya stared at his hunched form. "Cross my heart."

"Thanks," Finn said. "And thanks for listening."

"Anytime." Maya gave a small smile. "But Finn?"

He looked up. "Yeah?"

"The Instagram posts?" She paused. "How do you want to do this now?"

Finn stood up, his hands on his hips. He stared at a spot behind Maya for a moment before replying: "We carry on with the plan. It's important to Sam, so let's get her this part of her dream."

"Okay," Maya said with a downturned mouth. "If you're sure."

"I am, Maya, it's the least I could do for her." Finn pushed his hands into his jeans pockets. "Look, I'd better go. I should get ready—it's almost time."

"Best of luck, Finn." Maya picked up her phone. "I really mean that. This is your gold—don't forget it."

* * *

From the top of the slope Finn could see Maya in the crowd. Her satsuma coat was a great way to spot her. He smiled, wondering if she was aware of how visible she was. Scanning the crowd around her, he searched for Sam's face, but she didn't seem to be there. His heart sank in his chest. She wouldn't stay away from his first Olympic final—his first chance at going for gold? He pulled his focus back as the crowds cheered and then hushed as the first competitor took off.

Finn watched, his breath tight in his chest as the young Norwegian landed his trick. A new kid on the scene, he was definitely one to watch, confident and strong and setting the bar high. His landing had been clean and his fist punch in the air made everyone cheer. The crowd buzzed, their energy rippling through the air as the score flashed up. Good, but not good enough. Finn breathed out.

Next up was Henri Duval. Known for his bold tricks, Henri took off and he didn't hold back. The crowd seemed to hold their breath as one entity as Henri flew into the air. Finn gasped as the Frenchman flipped and rotated in the air. His cork 720 was perfect, but his landing wasn't quite as sharp as it should have been. His knees buckled slightly, and the crowd were silent, watching as he regained his balance. He skied to a stop to polite applause. This wasn't the moment the crowd had been waiting for—the gold was still up for grabs.

Finn's mouth went dry as the next skier made his way forward. This was the one he really had to beat. Viktor Laurent already held two gold medals and had a reputation for perfection. He tore down the course, a blur of motion and power before he propelled into the air. Finn couldn't tear his eyes away as Gabriel's amazed voice rang out over the loudspeakers.

"A flawless cork 1080! And one, two, no three rotations! Laurent isn't here to play—he's here to win!"

The crowd erupted! Cheers and whistles vibrated through Finn's chest as Viktor's score flashed on the screen. He'd set the bar now, and it was high. Finn swallowed as his name echoed over the loudspeaker. Searching the crowd one more time for Sam, he made his way to the starting point. He couldn't see her, but he had no choice. It was now or never. Pulling on his goggles, Finn narrowed his eyes and focused.

His skis cut through the snow as he raced down the hill, the cold whipping against his face. This was the moment he'd been waiting for—a chance to take home an Olympic gold medal. His heartbeat hammered in his neck as he reached the ramp and then the world fell away as he spun into the trick. The crowd fell silent, watching him defy gravity as he performed a double backflip, gripping his skis midair with a mute grab. His body twisted, his core tight as he navigated the flips with precision. The ground rushed up to meet him faster than expected, his breath bursting from his lungs as his skis touched down with a slight wobble. Recovering instantly, he kept his head high as he surged forward and finished with his arms above his head. He'd done it! He was sure of it.

Ripping his goggles off, then his helmet, Finn punched his fist in the air as the crowd cheered loud enough to set off an avalanche. His face lit up and the crowd roared again. The commentator could barely contain their excitement. "Finn Bradley, ladies and gentlemen! He has nailed it! That's surely taken the gold! A risky trick but a brilliant one!"

He pulled off his skis and stared at the board. His score flashed. His heart leaped into his mouth. He'd done it! He'd taken the gold! Punching the air he looked around, hoping that Sam was there. And she was—she ran across the snow toward him, her arms wide and her smile huge. He flung his helmet away and ran into her arms and lifted her into a swing that made the crowd roar even louder.

"You did it!" Sam screamed as he put her down. "Finn!"

"I did it," he said quietly, then again more loudly. "Hell yeah! I did it!"

He grabbed her and pulled her into his arms, kissing the tip of her nose before running his hands through his hair, leaving it standing on end. He'd done it. He'd done it. Yeah! All the hours of training, the long days and the arguments he'd had with himself about whether it was going to be worth it or not . . . the sacrifices . . . He looked at Sam as she ran to high-five Maya who was filming it all. She was his biggest sacrifice. A hollow feeling began to form in his stomach. He'd won gold, but Sam still needed hers. He'd always imagined that she'd have hers first. She looked back at him, her face lit up with a genuine smile, her eyes sparkling with pride. She pointed and he turned around. They'd brought the podium out. Turning back to her, he pulled a silly smile and shaped his hands into a heart. She blushed, and then he was on the podium, the crowd was cheering, cameras flashing.

Someone placed the medal over his head and the weight of it surprised him. The ribbon on his neck was sharp. Lifting the medal, he looked at it, tears in his eyes. His mom would be so proud. Blinking away the tears, he tried to keep his composure. The air sizzled with energy as someone pushed a huge bottle of champagne into his hands and he followed the other medalists in shaking the bottle and spraying it everywhere, much to the crowd's delight.

His eyes darted to Sam. Surrounded by their teammates she was cheering and clapping him on. He grinned back, his head light as he picked up the gold medal and looked at it before looking at Sam again. She gave him a thumbs up, her face bright and smiling. His heart almost burst. Seeing Sam smile at him like that, like he was hers and she was his, was the real gold, and felt special, almost secret.

Out of the corner of his eye he caught Maya filming them and he forgot all his misgivings. She could record them all day long if Sam just kept smiling at him that way. Stepping down from the podium he waved to the crowd, the medal comfortably heavy against his chest, but his heart as light as a snowflake. Maya was beaming, nodding at him as he moved toward Sam. She had that sparkle back in her eyes, one that he hadn't seen in days now. Finn started walking faster, closing the distance between them in no time. There was no one else he wanted to be with.

"Hey," Finn said, his focus on Sam.

Sam slipped her arm through his, her bright smile warming his heart. "Come on, let's go celebrate! Do we have to call you Goldie from now on?"

Finn burst out laughing. "Sure, if that helps you remember who I am now."

Sam shoved him. "Oh, I know who you are, now—Mister Goldie McGold Medal Winner!"

Finn playfully pushed her back, laughing as she scooped up a snowball. Dodging her throw, he fell over. Jumping up, he grabbed a handful of snow before running toward Sam. Her giggles and shrieks as she ran, ducking from a possible impending snowball, made him smile. Catching her, he held the snow above her head, his eyes crinkling as she cringed.

"No! Don't! Finn!" She gasped, laughing as she tried to catch her breath. He stood there, watching her, her cheeks flushed with cold and joy. He could still feel the sting from last night—her walking away without any explanation at all. He still couldn't work out what he'd said or done, but what he did know was that everything was better now she was here. Everything. He grinned and lowered the snowball, loving how she wriggled in his arms, how she laughed and threatened to cover him with snow if he dared drop it on her.

Laughing, he held her tightly, until a familiar shape grabbed his attention.

From the barriers, Coach Harrington was watching them intently. A sharp pain twisted in Finn's chest. He looked at Sam, at her beautiful smile, the way her hair escaped her braid no matter how tightly she plaited it. He longed to brush her hair back from her eyes and feel her shiver under his touch. He wanted to count the tiny freckles on her nose just so he knew how many there were. His heart contracted. Everything about her was perfect. Dropping the snow, he laughed and hugged her instead. Deep down he knew he'd never do anything that might hurt her. In fact, he'd do anything to protect her.

16

Sam

Sam brushed snow from her collar, relieved that Finn hadn't rubbed it in her face, and that some of Finn's die-hard fans had found them and interrupted their snowball fight. The way he'd looked at her . . . the way his lips had parted. God, if he hadn't let her go, she'd have kissed him. And that would have been a huge mistake—fake-dating plan or not. One kiss could turn this whole moment on its head, and this was Finn's moment. He deserved to celebrate his win without her stealing it away from him. And she deserved it too. Kissing him now wasn't going to make anything any clearer. Not when she was still thinking about how natural it had felt to be with him in the shower, as if they were meant to be together. What did that moment mean to him? Did he feel the same way?

She tugged at the cuff of her jacket, her fingers restless as she watched Finn talking with some fans. He posed for a photo with a couple of young teenagers who'd been waiting for him after his win, and her chest ached. He was focused, yet something was off. There seemed to be a slight change in his manner. His jaw was tight despite his smiles and laughter. Every time their eyes met, she felt like she was burning up inside with desire. But she didn't see that reflected back from him, not even in a fake way. Maybe she was overthinking things, but she shook her head. Was she? It wasn't like he was angry with her, but there was definitely something there, something unspoken now between them. She exhaled slowly as he smiled at her, trying to push the feeling aside. She *must* be reading too much into it.

One of the kids tapped her arm and asked her to take a photo of them. Nodding she took his phone and cajoled the group into laughing and smiling. Finn caught her eye; his expression was unreadable. It was driving her crazy.

"How's my girl?" Maya's voice cut through her thoughts, soft and careful.

Sam turned, smiling, glad to see Maya. "I'm fine," Sam lied. "I'm so happy for Finn."

"Me too." Maya seemed a little tense. "I was worried . . ."

"Worried?" Sam handed the boy back his phone and turned her full attention on Maya. "What about? Finn?"

Maya pulled a face. "You know me, I'm always worried."

Sam tilted her head and raised her eyebrow. "You literally never worry. You're the most chilled person I've ever met."

"Fine," Maya admitted. "I had a moment when Viktor pulled off that trick that made me panic, but our boy, well, he did it—he really did it!"

"He did, didn't he?" Sam said. "I never doubted him."

She could hear giggles behind her as more fans arrived to ask Finn for a photo. A frisson of jealousy flashed through her as a glamorous woman handed her a camera to take another photo. She huffed as she looked at the small screen, wishing she could take the photo without the woman in it.

"If she was any closer to him, she'd be in his boxers." Sam sniffed as the woman wrapped her arms around Finn, squealing about how fit he was.

Maya nudged Sam. "Should we tell her that it's not a *Build-a-Boyfriend* workshop that's going on here, or do we let this play out?"

Sam grumbled as Maya laughed. Finn seemed to be enjoying the moment. His wide smile wasn't lost on Sam. She squinted at the screen and took just one photo as the breeze blew a strand of the woman's hair across her face.

Maya raised an eyebrow at Sam and giggled. "So this is how we're playing it, is it?"

Sam wrinkled her nose and huffed again. "One more," she called. "That one wasn't good."

"Do you want some of my chill?" Maya whispered as the woman practically wrapped herself around Finn's toned torso again.

"Nope," Sam said. "No chill needed. I am chill personified."

"Yeah, in your dreams." Maya took the phone and handed it to the woman who was trying to get Finn's number.

Sam crossed her arms as Finn wrangled his way out of more photos, promising he'd be around to watch the men's freestyle moguls and that he'd have more time then. He ambled toward them, his eyes darkening as he got closer.

Sam shivered and wished she knew what was going on in his head.

"Oh! I almost forgot." Maya pulled out her phone. "You two have a dinner date—the team has arranged it all. I'm using all my amazing caption skills for this one, so prepare yourselves to thank me profusely: *a candlelit dinner so magical you'd think Cupid himself cooked it*—in the fabulous and exclusive Monteluce. This Friday, I assume you both are free."

"Ooooh Friday!" Sam said, as they began walking back to town. "You know this Friday is Friday the thirteenth."

Finn shrugged. "I don't believe in superstitions."

Maya snorted. "Excuse me? Says the guy who wouldn't ski without his magic pebble—remember that? Yeah, I thought so."

Finn gawped. "It was a lucky stone—not a magic pebble. Big difference."

Leaning on Maya, Sam stage-whispered, "He made me carry it in my bra once, in case he lost it."

"That was *one* time!" Finn shook his head, grinning. "One time!"

"What I want to know, is where is it now?" Sam giggled. "In your . . . ?" She glanced down at his pants.

"Hell no!" Finn feigned horror. He pulled his glove off and held up the small flat stone, the one he carried everywhere. Its deep gray color was flecked with white spots and there was a smooth indentation on one side that seemed to hug Finn's thumb. He'd always had it on him when he competed. He said it was lucky because it was the last thing his father had given him before he'd passed away. Sam smiled, glad to see he still had it.

"Well, the moral of the story is: don't claim not to be superstitious when you are," Maya said. "And speaking of magical things, do you know what it took me to get a reservation at Monteluce—three charms, spells and a minor miracle. You all should be worshipping me like the Slay Queen that I am."

"All hail Queen Maya!" Finn chanted as they walked. Sam smiled. It was beginning to feel normal again, as if nothing had happened. She was right—she'd been reading too much into things.

The snow crunched beneath their feet as the three friends walked and chatted.

"Well," Maya said brightly as they reached the bar where everyone seemed to be waiting. She yanked open the door, a mischievous grin brightening her face. "Time to celebrate!"

The bar was alive with energy. The upbeat music had everyone in a good mood. The delicious smell of spiced wine and coffee wrapped around them as they squeezed in the doorway. People were tightly packed around rustic tables, laughter and chatter mingled with the music, and fairy lights were strung along beams adding a cozy charm to the otherwise upmarket ski lodge vibe. Sam spotted Davide and Valentina waving from a corner table.

"Looks like they're already celebrating you." She nudged Finn. "Think you can handle the attention for another while, Mister Goldie McGold Medal Winner?"

Finn grinned. "I think I could get used to this, yeah."

"Let's grab drinks," Maya declared, grabbing both Sam and Finn by the wrists and pulling them in from the entrance. "My shout. What are you having?"

"Anything with bubbles," Sam said, as if injected with celebratory energy.

"A beer, please," Finn called as Maya wriggled her way to the bar. He turned to Sam, a soft quietness in his eyes that hadn't been there earlier. The noise of the bar faded just enough for Sam to catch his words.

"I feel kind of weird," he said. "Getting a gold. Standing up there. You should have your medal too."

Sam shook her head quickly. "No, Finn, stop. This is your moment—you earned it." She touched his arm and squeezed it gently, her heart filled with love as he gazed down at her. "You were incredible out there, honestly, Finn. You were the best, clearly—you won!"

Her mouth dried up. He'd managed to make half of their dream come true.

Finn's eyes found hers again. "It will be your turn next," he said. "I believe that, more than anything—and Sam, I'm sorry—for whatever I said last night to upset you."

Sam's throat tightened. "You didn't say or do anything."

"Liar," Finn said. His blue eyes filled with concern, the edges crinkling as he offered a soft smile. "I know you, Sam Harrington. You can't hide from me."

Sam's mouth fell open slightly. She stared at him, then forced a smile. If he really knew her so well . . . then he would know how she felt. Wouldn't he see that he was— and always had been—the one person she loved more than anything? If he did know—why wasn't he saying anything? Her heart hammered in her chest. Her palms grew sweaty. Maybe his silence said it all. She smiled wider and shrugged as if she wasn't breaking apart inside.

"Fine. Apology accepted."

"Good." Finn's eyebrows lowered as Maya reappeared, carrying three drinks awkwardly in her small hands.

"Tough crowd over there," she announced as Finn helped her. "But here we are, one bubbly, one beer, and one mystery cocktail that will apparently change my life." She grinned and raised her glass. "Cheers to gold medals, sponsorship deals, and cute barmen!"

Sam clinked glasses with Maya and Finn, who seemed to have managed a genuine smile for the first time since he'd gotten his gold medal earlier. His smile, however, faded away as his ex, Harper, glided over to them.

Sam stiffened but managed a small smile. "Hey, Harper."

"Hey." Harper tilted her head, her blonde hair cascading over one shoulder. She laid a hand on Finn's arm, her perfectly manicured nails glinting under the twinkling fairy lights. "Congratulations, Finn. I always knew you had it in you. Gold suits you."

Finn pulled his arm back. "Thanks, Harper. I guess it does."

Harper smiled widely, her gray eyes flashing over Finn. "Aren't you going to congratulate me too?"

Finn frowned. Sam glanced at Maya and caught a flicker of worry in her eyes. *What was going on?* She turned to Harper with a light laugh. "You have *more* to be congratulated on?"

Harper lowered her tone. "You haven't heard? Oh, I feel strange telling you my news, and it's not a brag. I never expected it, and I'm just so thrilled and honored . . ."

"Heard what?" Sam said, while glancing from Finn to

Maya who were looking stunned. *Would she ever just get on with it?*

Harper brushed an imaginary piece of fluff from her arm, her eyes sparkling. Glancing up at Sam she beamed. "It's not public knowledge yet, only those in the know, know, but I thought you knew?" She turned to Maya.

Before Maya could retort, Finn interjected, "No, Harper, we haven't a clue what you're on about."

Harper raised an eyebrow, her smile wide with happiness. "Well then, I'll tell you!" She winked at Sam. "I know how you feel about women in sport, and how we always get second dibs when it comes to anything, so I think you'll be happy for me—it's a step in the right direction for us women." She wrinkled her nose and did a tiny dance on the spot. "Salvaro want me to head their next campaign—can you believe it!?"

Sam's throat constricted. *Salvaro had gone and chosen Harper?* A ringing sound in her ears made her stagger a little. She felt Maya's hand on her back, steadying her. Through the ringing sound she just about made out Finn and Maya murmuring congratulations to Harper.

"I know, right," Harper said as Sam tuned back in. "I can hardly believe it. I never thought it was possible—for me, you know? We're signing tomorrow, before our qualie."

Sam choked out the words. "Oh my God, Harper—wow!"

Maya caught hold of Sam by the elbow and pinched her. Sam pulled her arm away but smiled wider at Harper. "Huge congratulations!"

"Thank you." Harper looked as if she was about to cry.

225

"I knew you'd be happy for me—for women. This really is amazing."

"It sure is," Sam said. She felt like crying too. "I'm happy for you, Harper. But we have friends waiting . . ."

"Oh! Of course," Harper said with a wave of her hand. "Have a great night."

Sam watched as Harper slipped away into the crowd. The room suddenly felt too warm, too loud. She turned to Finn and caught his arm. "She got Salvaro."

Finn nodded. "I got that."

"Urgh," Maya said. She frowned.

Finn took a mouthful of his beer, and a long look at Sam before speaking. "Don't let it rattle you. Not now. Don't let it get in the way of your qualie tomorrow."

"Easier said than done," Sam said. "When she's a gold medalist who has the deal I wanted."

"She's a gold medalist by chance," Finn said quietly, his eyes on Sam's. "And you know it." Sam was about to interrupt when she caught the deep warmth in his eyes. "And tomorrow, imagine that gold medal in *your* hands, because it's yours, Sam. It's your gold medal. You're unstoppable, and you need to remember that. Look at us—look at how far we've come."

A warmth bloomed in Sam's chest, spreading like adrenaline before a first jump. He was right. His words made her feel like she really could do it.

"Thanks for that, Finn. I needed that."

"You're welcome." Finn spread his arms wide and took a bow. "I'm here all week. Now come on, let's go over to Davide and Valentina."

226

Weaving their way between people and tables, Sam felt butterflies in her stomach. *Finn believed in her*. She couldn't stop smiling as they sat at Davide's table. She almost believed in herself too, and it felt so good. A fizzy joy wrapped around her. Valentina was pouring wine, Maya was sampling the fresh bruschetta, and even Finn seemed to have cheered up as Davide hugged him and demanded to try on the medal. Laughing, Sam brushed her hair back from her face, soaking up every moment. Harper forgotten, she smiled at Finn, loving how he blushed under Valentina's compliments. She couldn't stop watching him. He was laughing at something Davide was saying about Valentina flirting with Finn. He brushed a hand through his dark hair, and she remembered how his hands had felt on her naked waist, on her breasts.

He glanced at her, caught her looking at him, and smiled at her—and it felt like Christmas morning when you'd gotten everything you'd asked for. Maya nudged her, her phone in her hand. Sam dragged her gaze away from Finn and looked down at the Instagram posts Maya was showing her. They were all of her and Finn, and they were beautiful. Sam's breath caught in her chest as she flicked through the images of her and Finn hugging, their smiles only for one another, their arms filled with each other. Their love was obvious. She started and looked up. *Love. Was that possible?* Looking back down at the images she bit her lip. *Love, of course.*

Slipping from her seat, she wriggled past some people until she was next to Finn.

"Do I get to try it on, too?" she asked him, her fingers touching the gold medal that lay on his chest. "It might be my only chance."

227

Finn looked down into her face, his expression serious, but soft. Wordlessly, he lifted the medal from his neck and gently placed it over her head. "It won't be your only chance," he said so quietly that Sam thought she'd imagined hearing it. Touching the medal, she felt a fire stir inside her. This was why they were here, and so far, they'd managed to get one medal. In two days she'd have hers. Then, and only then, would she feel able to talk to him about them, about the possibility of a *them*—and in that moment it all felt so very achievable. She felt light and free—until she heard it. A sudden burst of laughter from a nearby table, a man's voice cut through the air.

"Well, looks like I'm out—I had Harrington pegged for gold, but I guess I was wrong."

Another voice joined in, chuckling, "Come on, you didn't really think she'd win, did you?"

"Well, no, but I drew her name in the lottery, so I was hoping," the first man said. "At least I only put five on the bet."

"Five!" someone squealed. "Five? Why bother?"

The first man spoke again, and Sam could picture him shrugging, "I don't know—I mean, we all know who the real contender is."

"Yeah, someone who doesn't flunk out and come in fourth place—I drew Sasha Mitford—an unknown but I bet you an extra twenty she scores higher than Harrington in the qualifier tomorrow."

"I bet Harrington doesn't even make it through the qualifier." The sound of hands slapping down on the table behind her made Sam jump.

She bit her lip, tears smarting in her eyes. Her breath raggedly escaped her as she held back the lump in her throat that threatened to escape. She didn't dare turn her head, terrified to face the people who were talking so callously about her. Her pulse drummed loudly in her ears, and she closed her eyes, praying that no one else heard. Opening her eyes she felt the blood drain from her face. She stood still, as if frozen.

"Sam?" Finn's deep voice cut through her thoughts. Without looking at him or even saying a word she pushed away from the table and through the crowd toward the door.

Outside, Sam stood still, the cold seeping into her bones as snow fell softly all around her. Finn's gold medal sat heavy on her chest. She yanked it off and stuffed it into her pocket. Everything was going wrong. A shiver ran over her body, and it wasn't just from the cold. Staring in through the glass, she saw Finn pull on his jacket as if he was coming to find her. The cold air bit her cheeks as she shook. She flinched as someone came out of the bar, loud music reverberating against the snowy street. Her jaw clenched as Finn came out onto the street. To hell with those idiots. She didn't need their approval. She needed to take control. Control of everything in her life—for once.

Finn wrapped her jacket around her shoulders, his warm fingers brushing against the back of her neck sending shivers down her spine. Her mouth parted; heat stirred deep inside her. She stared at him. His dark hair was tousled, his blue eyes warm and focused solely on her, the way they had been in the hot tub. Could she have him? Maybe not forever—but just for this moment? No competitions, no expectations, no jackasses in a bar slating her as if they owned her. No. Just her, taking what she wanted—Finn—for once. Her fingers curled around the collar of her jacket, as she stepped close to him. His eyes darkened as her breath curled against his chest.

"I'm okay," she said, her eyes locked on his lips.

"You sure?" His voice was quiet, his breath mingling with hers.

"Yeah." She lowered her gaze and squeezed her hands into fists to stop them from reaching for him. "I really am. You should go back in. Celebrate."

"Not without you," Finn said quietly. "I'm not going anywhere without you. You're not alone, Sam. I'm here."

She looked down at the snow.

"Sam, look at me," Finn said. She shook her head. With a sigh, he slipped his arm around her waist, tugging her closer to his solid, warm body. He hooked a finger under her chin and made her look at him. "Maybe you just need a change of scenery."

Sam nodded breathlessly as his eyes scanned her face. He really was beautiful. "Yes."

"Somewhere . . ." He hesitated.

"Somewhere where I can be me." Sam stared into his eyes, mesmerized by the sensation of his hands on her face and body. *How had that happened?* She leaned closer, upwards, hoping he was thinking the same thing as she was.

He brushed a strand of hair from her face. "Yes."

Sam's breath hitched. Without thinking, she leaned up, closing the small gap between them.

His lips were as warm and soft as she'd remembered, and for a moment he didn't move, as if he was caught off guard. Then his hands were in her hair, cradling her head as his lips moved over hers and his tongue tasted her mouth. Moaning, Sam slid her arms around his neck, pulling him closer, her body melting against him. She deepened the kiss, her fingers curling into his hair at the back of his neck as his hands, inside her jacket, grasped her waist, his fingers finding a sliver of skin as her top rode up.

Finn broke the kiss first, but only to whisper against her lips. "Sam . . . is this what you want?"

She nodded fervently, her lips longing for his again. "Yes." She pulled him close again and this time her kiss was hungrier. Finn groaned softly and she could feel the hard length of him pressing against the soft warmth of her lower stomach. Thoughts of what he'd do to her made her shift closer to him so that he shuddered under her touch.

"Sam." His voice was hoarse, gritty. "What are you doing to me?"

She ran her hands down his back and kissed the side of his neck. "What do you want me to do to you?"

"Come with me," he murmured, kissing her again before taking her hand. "Let's go somewhere quieter."

Sam nodded, breathless as he led her around the corner to a dark doorway in a side street. He held her hand, caressing the back of it with his thumb as they waited for some people to pass them. She could sense his frustration as another couple, laughing and joking, walked by. She dragged him further down the side street until they were completely out of sight of anyone on the main thoroughfare. She giggled as his eyes widened as she pushed him against the wall, her breath heavy with want. Then she was in his arms again, kissing him deeply while her fingers fumbled with the closings on his ski pants.

He growled, his hands reaching for hers. "Sam, stop."

She pulled back, dizzy and captivated by the moment.

"Sam," Finn groaned, pulling her into his chest, his arms holding her tight. He whispered into her hair, "Not here."

She pushed against him. "Not here?"

"No." He grasped her hips, then spun them around so that she was against the wall. Leaning down, he kissed her deeply again. Sam wrapped her arms around him, her body weak as his scent enveloped her. His hands ran down her sides, making her shiver and press against him. His skin was warm where his hoodie opened at the neck, soft and tantalizing against hers. With his hands on her waist, he carefully steadied her as she swayed against him.

"God, Sam." His breath was ragged as he touched his forehead to hers.

Sam nodded gently, afraid to break contact with him. She smoothed her hands down along his chest and stomach, reveling in the hardness of his body. Wanting to rip his clothes off. He groaned as her fingers began loosening his pants again. His hand, warm and big, took hers again.

"Come on, Sam. Not here. Not in public." He swallowed and Sam blushed. He was right. This was not a good idea.

"Where then?" She bit her lip, watching him carefully for his reaction.

He looked down and shook his head before shoving away from the wall, his hands in his hair, a look of torment on his face. Her stomach plummeted as he looked at her and shook his head.

"Oh, Finn," she breathed out, her voice unsteady.

"Sam?" His voice was quiet but firm, a raw edge to it. He stood back, putting space between them as she stepped forward. "You've—we've really crossed a line here. Tonight—the other night . . . what are we doing here?"

"I-I didn't mean—" Sam started but her voice cracked. She reached for him, but he was already a step away from her. "Finn . . . I just wanted to take some control. No, that sounds wrong. I didn't mean it that way."

"You don't have to explain." His voice was tight, but gentle. He rubbed the back of his neck, turning away from her. "Sam, I'm sorry—and it's not that I don't want to. I can't."

"What?" Sam was at his side in a flash. "If this is because of that stupid promise we made, I don't want to hear it! I think it's nonsense and I *want* to break it. I do."

Finn grasped her hands and kissed them. "Me too, Sam. I swear to you that I do. But not tonight. I just want it to . . . to mean something."

Sam's heart twisted painfully, and for a moment, she thought she might collapse. But Finn pulled her in again, tucking her head beneath his chin like she belonged there. And God, she really wanted to belong there. Her thudding heart slowed down as his arms held her, his warmth seeping into her. For a while they just stood there, in the quiet hush of the night, the hum of the town muffled by falling snow. Sam breathed him in, her mind going over the whole thing. She felt his lips press a kiss to the top of her head, and she pressed her face closer to his neck. He was right. They'd already had the passion—the shower—and she still ached

233

for more, but this . . . this was different. This was choosing not to lose herself in the moment. All she had to do was to kiss him again and he'd give in to her. It was a powerful feeling, but it wasn't control. It was the opposite. *This* was restraint, *not* rejection.

"Walk me back?" She eased herself out of his embrace, smiling as the crease between his brows smoothed away. She slipped her hand into his, letting their fingers twine together as they started walking. His hand felt right in hers, and as they stepped out into the street, Sam felt a rebellious streak rise up within her. This was taking control, this moment. Holding hands with the man she loved on the street—in front of the world—and tomorrow . . . tomorrow she was going to take back the dream she'd allowed to slip away from her these past few days. One thing was for sure, no one was going to save her from anything—if she wanted to win, she was going to have to do it herself.

17

Finn

From his hunched-up position against the barriers, Finn watched the women's qualifiers for the halfpipe snowboard. It was bitterly cold. The sky was gray and threatening snow, and yet, judging from the crowds in the stands, everyone in Livigno seemed to be there. He wrapped his hands, cold even though he was wearing gloves, around a hot coffee and took a look around. His stomach was in knots, but he still took a huge bite of his brioche. Something had come over Sam last night, and it was both electrifying, thrilling and making him worry. She'd been fearless on the walk back to her hotel, with her chin raised and a steely determination in her eyes that he'd never seen before.

Gabriel's commentary infused the snow-filled event space as huge screens flickered on high stands. Finn scanned the closest screen for Sam's form. As usual, she was at the back of the group, but unusually, Jake Harrington wasn't hovering

235

around his daughter. Instead, he was talking animatedly to Becky while Leo stood nearby nodding and smiling. The camera just caught Sam's calm and set face before Gabriel's chiseled face filled the screen. Finn shoved the rest of his brioche into his mouth as the camera zoomed out.

Gabriel's co-commentator, five times Olympic Gold medal winner Seb Whittaker appeared, wrapped in a tight, shiny yellow puffer jacket and an overly long vivid fuchsia scarf that clashed horribly with the yellow jacket. The jacket caught the lights most unflatteringly, highlighting the tightness of the jacket around the man's slightly paunchy middle. The material bunched awkwardly around his shoulders as the end of his fuchsia scarf flapped dramatically in the wind. He fussed with it, tossing the end over his shoulder as if he thought he was Lenny Kravitz. His face, haggard and red, was set in a smug expression, as he posed for the camera. A strand of graying hair flopped across his forehead, and he flicked his head back before beaming a gallant smile directly at the camera.

"Sam Harrington really hasn't shown up for the Games at all," he said confidently with a cheeky grin. "It's like she's skipped the Games, again, this year. Maybe we're just not fashionable enough for Sam Harrington, the current darling of Instagram."

Gabriel, commanding and elegant in his tailored black wool coat, his collar turned up against the cold, his trademark charcoal turtleneck hugging the strong line of his neck, shifted away ever so slightly from Seb, his face closed but dark. "Fashionable?" He flicked his eyes up and down Seb's body, a small smirk barely evident on his lips. "Well,

Seb, not everyone needs to make an entrance as dramatically as you do. Sam Harrington prefers to let her performances speak for themselves."

Seb's eyes narrowed momentarily and Finn, from his position at the barrier, watched, mouth open in surprise as the exchange on the screen continued. Seb laughed tightly. "Ah gallant Gabriel, always the stoic protector—does the lovely Sam know that you've become her unofficial spokesperson?" His grin widened, self-assured and cocky.

Before Gabriel could respond there was a sudden commotion to their left. The camera caught Maya, juggling two steaming cups, hurrying behind them. A sudden gust of wind caught the end of Seb's ridiculous scarf, whipping it into the air and into Maya's face. Finn gasped, gripping his own steaming cup, as the spectacle unfolded in a split second.

Maya, unable to see, stumbled, and like a cartoon character, kept on stumbling. She tried to catch her step, but couldn't, and she staggered, blindly and directly into Seb. A fountain of hot chocolate burst into the air, landing all over his pristine pink scarf and shiny puffer jacket. Finn burst out laughing as she floundered against the rotund man.

The picture shook as if the cameraman was laughing, then zoomed in on Seb's shocked face. His mouth was frozen in an O as he rapidly blinked while the steaming hot chocolate dripped onto the snow at his feet. The camera zoomed out to show Maya, in her satsuma coat, frantically dabbing at Seb's chest with a rapidly disintegrating tissue, only to leave little chocolate-colored flecks of tissue stuck to the man's jacket so that he looked like an overripe banana.

"I'm so sorry," she kept saying. "It just . . . the scarf . . . the wind . . . *why is that scarf so long?*"

Seb snatched the tissue from her, his grin painfully fixed in place. "No panic. It's all fine. Don't worry."

Gabriel's lips twitched. "What was that you were saying, Seb? Something about fashion?"

Finn choked on his laughter, doubling over on the barrier. Sam would love this. It was TV gold!

Maya, now in the background, was offering to get the jacket dry-cleaned, but Seb dismissed her with a broad wave. "No need, sweetheart. I'm a professional—these things happen."

Finn grinned. Seb deserved every drop of hot chocolate he got. Seb, visibly tense as he flicked a tissue ball from his scarf, laughed harshly. "And now, back to the slopes, before I drown in hot chocolate."

Gabriel, ever composed, shifted his attention to the monitors. "Looks like we have to move away from our fashion advice expert and back to the slopes as our next rider is at the top of the run. Let's see if Harper Reynolds can keep her lucky streak and take home another medal by landing something as bold as Seb's wardrobe choice."

Seb's laughter was forced, but the sound of the crowd swelling drew their attention. The camera feed cut to the glistening halfpipe as snow softly began to fall. Harper adjusted her goggles and smiled in preparation for her turn.

Seb's voice cut over the crowd. "Canada's golden girl, Harper Reynolds, looks set to add to her gold medal collection. She has come to this competition ready to show us what she's made of."

Finn grimaced and pushed up from the barrier as even Gabriel sounded impressed.

"You've got to give it to Harper Reynolds, that was a sick and flawless frontside 720, and there she goes—did you see that! Straight into a corked 1080—a daring move. And there it is—the highest score yet in this round of qualifiers. Harper is one hundred percent in the final."

The crowd cheered. It sounded like Harper had aced it. Finn wrapped his fingers around his mug and leaned back against the barrier. His foot tapped and he bit his lip. Sam would be looking for him, possibly. He tweaked his orange beanie hoping she'd spot him. A slight tone in Gabriel's voice made him stop tapping his foot.

"Becky Stanford. A fashionista if I ever saw one. I'm sure you know all about Becky's newest aprés-ski clothing collab with Valestré, Seb."

Finn raised his eyebrows as he listened to the commentary. If he didn't know better, it seemed as if Gabriel had a bone to pick with Becky. His voice had been borderline acidic. Finn leaned forward on his elbows and watched as Becky took her turn. She didn't make one mistake, but her performance was lackluster. Nevertheless, she had done enough to grab a coveted place in tomorrow's final.

Sam's face appeared on the screen. Her chin high, her eyes focused. Finn breathed out hard. Good, she looked ready, she looked . . . angry. Finn's toes scrunched tightly in his snow boots.

"Here we go." Seb's voice filled the air. "Harrington, looking for redemption and a place on the podium after failing to make the cut in the big air round. Can she pull it off under such pressure—both Reynolds and Stanford are already set to compete in tomorrow's final. It's a tall ask."

Finn's jaw clenched. Gabriel's voice, smooth and measured, took over. "Don't write her off just yet, Seb. Everyone's allowed an off day, and history shows us that Sam Harrington is capable of pulling out the magic when it matters."

"Let's see if she can channel her past energy today." Seb's tone was slightly skeptical.

Finn frowned, his eyes glued to the screen as Sam dropped into the pipe. He leaned forward, his coffee almost spilling from his cup. The cup was hot, but his hands felt cold. Quickly he put the cup on the snow at his feet, afraid he'd crush it.

"Come on, Sam!" His foot tapped up and down. His stomach flipped as Sam's first hit was okay, not enough for her to catch her usual trick, but enough to catch attention from the crowd. Finn's stomach sank as Sam's second hit was cleaner, but safe. He knew that behind her goggles she was frowning, squinting, and calculating her next move— very unlike her normal exuberant and feisty runs. Her body language was off, she seemed stiff, controlled and not fluid. Wringing his hands together, Finn bit his lip. This wasn't Sam's game—she thrived on spontaneous moves, on how she felt on the board.

"Playing it safe," Seb said theatrically. "I was expecting more from Harrington. This is one of her best disciplines."

Gabriel cut in sharply. "Safe is smart. She knows exactly what she needs to qualify."

Finn bit back a smile. Gabriel wasn't wrong.

In a swirl of snowflakes, Sam's last hit sent her high off the lip into a clean frontside 720. A pit formed in Finn's stomach as he registered the crisp, cleanness of her run. It was uninspired and she landed smoothly and solidly. But there was no doubt she'd make it to the final now. Finn dropped his head forward, running his hands through his hair as Sam unclipped herself from her board. A heaviness settled over him. He should be glad Sam would make it to the final, but her run had been . . . He rubbed his hands over his face and groaned as the word *heartless* came to mind. Heartless was something Sam most certainly was not.

The scoreboard lit up. She'd come in third highest score, but if she was happy, Finn couldn't tell. Sam's jaw was set, her eyes down as she lifted her board and headed out. The screen filled up with Gabriel and Seb once again and Finn moved away from the barrier and toward Sam.

18

Sam

Sam barged her way through the crowds, ignoring the well-wishers and fans calling out to her. Her eyes darted about searching for Finn. She drew a breath deep down into her lungs and held it for a second before pushing it out hard and fast. She'd made the final! Her heart was thumping, but her brain was calculating what was next—how was she going to make the cut tomorrow.

Finn fell in beside her, taking her board without a word. She glanced at him, loving how he smoothed down her battered *Ohana* sticker every now and then, and suddenly so glad that they'd been so civil to each other last night. He'd been right—she knew that now. He'd had her best interests at heart and now here they were, walking side by side in the snow, and all she could think about was that after this—the Games—she was going to ruin him. In the best possible way. The snow crunched beneath their feet as they made their way to the ski center. For a few minutes they didn't talk, Sam's breath coming in short bursts as she rolled her neck from side to side as if she was stiff.

"Another final," Finn said. "I knew you'd do it."

Sam shrugged. "I knew it too, but . . ."

"Yeah." Finn nodded as he held the door open for her. "It was clean. Possibly too clean."

"It was supposed to be," Sam muttered as she went inside. "That was the point."

"It's just . . ." Finn started, then stopped. "It didn't look like you out there."

"Oh, come on," Sam blurted. She waved her arm. "Finn! I made it, didn't I?"

"Yeah," Finn said again. "But you don't look happy about it."

"Well, I am happy!" Sam snorted.

"Show it then!" Finn laughed and poked her arm.

Sam grinned and stuck out her tongue at him. "How's that?"

"It'll do." He passed the board to one of the team support crew, smiling his thanks. His expression softened as he turned to Sam. "You know, it's not always about landing the tricks. Don't forget to have fun."

Sam sighed. "You're right." She pursed her lips as Finn's shoulders relaxed. This was a conversation she wasn't willing to have with him right now—now she just wanted to imagine those douchebags from the bar choking on their words. She bet they were speechless after the run she'd just pulled off—even if it was that little bit too clean, too controlled. She glanced over Finn's shoulder and nodded.

Over by the receptionist's desk Maya was dabbing Gabriel's chest with a tissue, trying to get hot chocolate

243

splatters off his wool coat. Sam watched them as she moved through the room. Maya laughed, and Gabriel's lips twitched into a small smile. He didn't seem to notice anything or anyone other than Maya as she folded the tissue. Gabriel took the tissue from Maya's hand and put it in the trash can beside the desk, then slowly he removed his coat before folding it carefully. Sam watched as Maya's eyes ran over Gabriel's broad and toned torso. In his cashmere turtleneck, every inch of his physique was clearly defined, and, judging from her wide eyes and the way she subtly licked her lips, Maya didn't miss one tiny detail of it.

Sam shook her head. "I have been waiting for this to happen," she whispered under her breath to Finn who was just as mesmerized at the situation as Maya seemed to be. Maya laughed, her nervous laugh, the one she always did when she found someone to be extremely attractive, which made Sam grin. It took a lot to make Maya laugh like that— she generally needed someone with brains as well as brawn, and well, now that she thought of it, Gabe had both. A glimmer of warmth, of curiosity even, passed over Gabriel's face and Sam grinned wider. *Wow! Something really was going on!* She bit back a sigh. Maya and Gabe . . . that was one to watch.

Bending down to unclip her boots, her attention zoomed in on Becky who was being interviewed by Seb, minus his chocolate-stained fuchsia scarf, just outside the gym doors. Becky was beaming and loving the attention. Her hands gestured excitedly as she spoke, her new diamond engagement ring flashing under the bright lights. Leo stood slightly away from her, watching the interview with a huge smile on his face. Jake Harrington too. Sam snarled quietly in the back of her throat. Those two . . . her heart pounded hard in her chest as anger rose in her stomach. Leo caught her eye and nodded at her, but Sam turned away, biting back the words she wished she could say to him. How could he—her own brother—think so little of her? And her dad too.

Turning to Finn she managed a smile. "You don't have to wait for me. I'm going to take some time and freshen up." She nodded toward the changing room. "I'll catch up with you for lunch—grab us a table somewhere."

"Rustico?" he asked. She nodded.

"Should I ask Maya and Gabe to join us?" There was a mischievous twinkle in Finn's eyes. Sam laughed.

"Sure! See ya there." She smiled until Finn left, then took one last look at Leo and her dad. They were deep in conversation, looking as if they were strategizing, and like none of their plans included her.

Trembling, she pushed through the changing room doors, a lump in her throat making her cough. Had they always felt that way about her? She'd always felt that her dad, at least, had believed in her, but now, now maybe that wasn't true. Maybe she'd thought it because she wanted to think it was true. Because before Leo's accident, it had all been about him.

Shoving her helmet into the locker, she recalled the strict training schedules and diets she'd adhered to after Leo had decided never to ski again. How she'd anticipate Jake's reactions to her every trick, and how she'd push herself harder just to hear him tell her she was the best. The pressure had been—and still was—immense. Leo was right—he'd been dropped, and Sam had had to pick up the reins so that Jake wouldn't look like a failure.

Now he was telling Becky that *she* was the best, and he'd dropped Sam, just like he'd dropped her mother as soon as she became too much to take care of. A tear slid down Sam's face as she grabbed her towel and headed for the shower. At least no one could see you cry in there.

Soaping her body down, Sam let the tears flow. All the good times she'd trained and skied with Leo came rushing back to her. He'd been such fun, before the accident, sweet and witty, and spontaneous. Afterwards he'd been bitter, angry, and resentful, and why wouldn't he be? His whole life had been ripped away from him. Everything he'd ever wanted to do, to be—it had all been destroyed. All of his hopes and dreams—gone—in a heartbeat. There'd been a time when she'd had to sneak out to train so that he wouldn't get upset. He'd been devastated; she knew that. Until that moment he'd been aiming for the Olympics too.

Her chest tightened as steam filled up the tiny shower cubicle. It hadn't been his fault, but he'd blamed himself, and probably still did, she realized as she wiped her face. But it wasn't hers either, and she deserved better than how they were treating her. Snapping the water off, Sam grabbed her towel. The changing room was silent. If she was quick, she'd get out before anyone else came in. Talking and smiling and pretending everything was okay was too much right now. She just wanted to get home. She snorted. *Home*. Home was currently the small messy hotel room she shared with Maya. Throwing her towel into the hamper, Sam sighed. She had nowhere else to go but to the hotel.

At least there she could hide away in her room, away from the noise and the crowds.

Pulling up her hood over her woolly hat, Sam slunk through the ski center lobby toward the doors.

"Sam!" Sam stopped and bit her lips. Every instinct screamed at her to keep walking, to pretend that she hadn't heard Jake calling her. But his voice carried that sharp, commanding edge that she'd spent a lifetime obeying. Slowly, she turned to face him.

"Sam," Jake said with a frown. "Where were you? I searched everywhere. I wanted to talk to you."

"I was here," Sam said dully. "All the time. You were too busy with Becky to see me."

Jake's gray eyes scanned his daughter's face. "I see."

"It's okay, Dad," Sam said. "It doesn't matter."

"You got a minute?" he asked, shoving his hands into his pockets in a way that she barely recognized.

Sam folded her arms across her chest. Really, he wanted to give her a minute—now—when he'd spent every other waking moment hyping up Becky. "Not really."

"You need to be smart tomorrow," he said. Sam rolled her eyes. He hadn't even heard what she'd said. Just kept on talking at her—not to her. "Don't let emotion drag you off course."

She stared at him. "You mean, like Leo?"

Jake stiffened. "Leo made his choices," he said after a beat. "I didn't stop him, Sam. I told him he could still compete. Paralympics, coaching, anything. It wasn't me who quit."

Sam sucked in a breath. "He didn't quit. He broke."

247

Jake flinched, the guilt flashing so fast she almost missed it.

"But you quit—you quit Mom, right when she needed you most." Sam swallowed hard, her voice thick. Her hands balled into fists, and she shoved them behind her back, shaking and sweating. She'd never even dreamed of speaking to her dad like that before.

Jake shifted awkwardly. "I know." His voice was low, frayed. He rubbed a hand over his jaw. "But I can't change the past, Sam. I did what I thought was best, at the time."

Sam said nothing. Gripping her hands together behind her back, she clamped her lips together. Her chest tightened painfully. Part of her wanted to forgive him, but the other part remembered missed birthdays, constant training, early mornings and putting herself second. Her eyes stung as he stood before her, suddenly looking smaller and older than she'd ever realized he was. He'd given his life to this sport. He'd won awards and accolades, but he'd also lost so much.

Jake shifted and shrugged. "Tomorrow—"

"Tomorrow, I'll do it my way." Sam cut him off, her voice stronger than before. "I think I've earned that right."

Jake's eyes met hers. For once, there was no judgment, no anger, no power. Only something raw and lost. He nodded.

Before she could say anything else, Sam spun away and walked as quickly as she could to the exit. Her heart didn't race; she didn't long to turn around and apologize for speaking out. A quiet resolve warmed her, from her feet up. She was done being told what to do. It was going to be her way from now on—and that meant she was going to focus on herself. A sliver of sadness made her stop for a moment. She glanced back at Jake. Something softer gripped her heart. For a second she wanted to run back to him, to tell him it was okay, and that they could fix it—that she could fix it. But she couldn't. She turned away. Her face crumpled. Wiping her nose with her cuff she blinked back her tears. It wasn't up to her to fix it anymore—in truth, it never had been. She'd taken on that role blindly, trying to make everyone happy, not seeing that it was like putting a Band-Aid on a brain hemorrhage. It was never going to work, never going to mend them all. No, she had to fix herself, and hopefully her dad would learn that he had to do that too.

Crowds milled around outside, and she skirted the larger groups, pausing every now and then to pose for a photo, her hands trembling as the conversation with her dad rattled around inside her. She felt awkward, like an imposter, but no one seemed to notice or care. The crowds dispersed and she spotted Maya and Gabe by a hot food stand.

"Sam!" Maya waved both arms like she was directing traffic. "Over here! Emergency carbs!"

Sam made her way over, smiling and nodding to people as they called out to her.

"Look!" Maya shoved her hand under Sam's nose. She rolled her eyes playfully. "It's called a Würstel, sounds exotic, I know, but it's basically a hot dog—though it tastes far superior to a hot dog."

Gabriel snorted. "I tried to have a panini, but now . . ." He held up his hands, a Würstel in each. "She couldn't decide on toppings."

Maya beamed at him. "Well, I needed expert advice. And

who's more qualified than a man who treats mustard like a life decision?"

For a second, Gabriel stared at her, like he couldn't quite believe she existed—and then, to Sam's astonishment, he laughed. "Some of us like a more understated approach to . . . chaos." His eyes glimmered as he handed Maya a Würstel.

"Ooooh what are these?" Maya picked up what looked like a pepper.

"Peperoncini—a little pickled spicy pepper," Gabriel said, leaning heavily into his Italian accent. "A little like you—you should enjoy them."

Maya lowered her chin. "Is that a promise?"

"So, this is how it begins." Sam laughed, her mood picking up. Gabriel's face froze and Sam burst out laughing. "Don't say I didn't warn you!" She slipped her hands into her pockets. Her fingers brushed against something cold, hard. She frowned, curling her hand around it she pulled it from her pocket.

Finn's medal.

The gold glinted under the bright lights, the ribbon hung loosely from her hand. She bit her lip. She'd shoved it into her pocket last night and had forgotten about it—it looked like Finn had too. But how could anyone forget they had an Olympic gold medal? Sam turned it over in her palm, her finger tracing the surface lightly. The weight of it pressed against her skin—a reminder of how his body had pressed against hers last night—real, hard—and within her reach. She pushed his medal back into her pocket. Finn—she really needed to see him—to talk to him about *them*. And now was as good a time as ever—maybe even the best time.

"Enjoy your . . . Würstels." Sam grinned. "I have to go. I'll see you later." Sam pulled her gloves from her pockets and tugged them on as a swirl of butterflies danced in the pit of her stomach.

Inhaling the cold, sharp air, she slipped away, avoiding the crowds and cameras by dodging down a quiet street. The snow hadn't stopped since this morning and had only gotten heavier as the day progressed. Now it was beginning to really come down and she tilted her face up for a moment, letting the large, soft flakes land on her nose and eyelashes. This was what she loved, the stillness after the adrenaline, and the sense of achievement. But right now, she couldn't wait to see Finn, to see his warm, open face—and how he seemed to smile in a certain way only for her. She wanted to share his space, her tummy rumbled, and his food—and if it went well, then she'd maybe tackle that she wanted more than friendship. She'd have to wait and see how he took some normal conversation first before launching into how much she wanted him. Crossing her fingers, she quickly turned the corner and dashed across the road to Rustico.

19

Finn

"Davide texted me," Finn said as he added sugar to his latte. "He said you'd called by and met Valentina."

Sam nodded. "You never told me you'd bumped into him."

Finn grimaced. "Sorry—I meant to. But Valentina, eh, what about that?"

"She's lovely," Sam said. "Perfect for that big old grumpy bear."

Finn laughed, making Sam smile again. "You're so right. She's a honey."

"I see what you did there, Finn Bradley—bear, honey." Sam grinned.

"I can't eat any more." Finn dropped his pizza crust on the plate. He leaned back and patted his lean belly. "That was the best pizza I've ever eaten."

"You've said that about every pizza you've had since you got here." Sam laughed. She picked up his crust and took a bite. Finn shook his head in wonder. Who was this Sam sitting beside him—relaxed and calm, with a hint of something about her that he couldn't figure out. It was as if she'd won the lottery and hadn't a care in the world, and it was a far cry from the Sam he'd left at the ski center not long ago. He gazed at her, as she watched the world pass by around them.

The snow was still coming down, and the server passed them some warm outdoor rugs so they wouldn't get too cold. They were sitting at an outside table, cozy, under an awning and outdoor heaters. She looked adorable with her blonde braid sat on one shoulder and her nose matching the cute pink hat she was wearing. She seemed to be lost in a daydream, staring into space, sipping her hot chocolate and wrapped up as if she was about to set off on an expedition to the North Pole. She smoothed out the outdoor rug that she'd pulled over her knees. A smile lit up her face as she watched a couple walk down the street, arms wrapped around each other and oblivious to anyone else. He knew it, always had since the very start—she was a romantic at heart. The way she looked right now, it was the way she'd looked that very first day that they'd met.

She'd been wearing a pink hat that day too, and her smile, her voice, her laugh, the way she'd stomped that course without breaking a sweat. He stretched out his legs and reached for his latte, sighing happily. Sam turned to him, her smile making her eyes sparkle.

"What?" She nudged him with her knee. He nudged her back.

"Nothing," he said. She slow-blinked at him, and he laughed and ran his hands through his hair as he sat up. "Okay! Okay! I was just remembering the very first time we met."

Sam's smile widened. She looked down and traced the rim of her mug, as if she was trying to distract herself.

"At the park." She bit her lip. Finn's heart beat a little faster.

"You stomped it," he said, his voice low. "Every feature—you owned it. I'd never seen anyone make it look so easy."

Sam glanced up at him, a gleam of recognition in her eyes.

"You," she said, nudging his knee again. "You were standing at the barrier—trying not to look impressed."

"Oh, and I failed that. Mightily." He laughed. He licked his lips and took a breath. "How could I not be impressed by you?"

Sam looked up, her green eyes wide and searching his face. "Finn—"

He raised his hands. "I know, we're not supposed to talk about it—or think about it, or break the pact we made, but hell, Sam—I can't do anything but think about it. The other night, and last night . . ."

She sat back, her eyes still locked on his. Damn, his mouth went dry. *God, how had it all gotten so complicated?* And why the hell had he opened his mouth—talking about those two moments—as if that was all he wanted from her. He picked up his latte, and put it back down again, trying to find the right words, trying to find the perfect way to tell her that yes, he'd fallen for her the moment he saw her, but that it was the years since that had made him fall in love with her. He ran his hand through his hair again and sighed deeply.

A tight knot formed in his chest as Sam, facing him, scooched closer and reached up to smooth down his hair.

The scent of jasmine and vanilla, of her, took him by surprise—he closed his eyes and inhaled. Her hand brushed his cheek. Without thinking, he grasped it as if to steady himself and pulled it to his lips in a fleeting kiss. Opening his eyes he caught a change in her expression, like someone had lobbed a bomb between them. *Wait, don't say it, don't tell me to back off.* His stomach lurched at the thought that he'd messed up. She took his other hand gently in hers.

"Wait," she said before he could say a word. "Let me talk."

Finn nodded, his hands tingling as she squeezed them gently. She looked nervous, biting her lip and blushing. She took a deep breath and looked down at their hands. He stiffened. *Please don't, please don't say there's no hope.*

A gentle smile played on her lips as she raised her eyes to his. "You have no idea how weak at the knees you made me that day. You were a smash!"

"What?" He gaped.

Sam gave a small shrug, her cheeks reddening adorably. "I could hardly string a sentence together. Remember how I stammered?"

"I didn't notice," Finn said, his stomach lightening. "I was too afraid that I was making a fool of myself."

"You weren't," Sam said. She scrunched her nose and leaned forward. "I was too busy wondering who this hot guy was and trying to figure out why my body was on fire—in places I'd never realized could go on fire. And if I would ever see him again, and if I did, what would happen. Because all I could think of was that I really wanted to kiss you—I still do."

255

Finn's mouth dropped open. His hands felt as if they were clammy, but he didn't want to let go of hers. He couldn't let go of her now, not if his life depended on it. She tilted her head and smiled at him. "Say something, please. Don't leave me hanging."

He was hoarse when he spoke. "You know I fell for you that day, but Sam . . ." He paused and let out a small laugh. Shaking his head he continued, "Gah! I can't seem to get the words out right."

"Take your time," Sam said softly. "I'm not going anywhere."

Her quiet voice stilled him. "Do you promise? Not to go anywhere? Because, Sam, I can't imagine a world without you in it—next to me. And it's got nothing to do with what's happened between us here, and everything to do with the fact that from the moment I met you, you felt like home to me. And every day since, every time we talk, train, or just hang out, I fall deeper in love with you—it's you, everything about you. How you see things, how you challenge me, how you live—even when you're struggling—every minute of you makes me want to be a better man, one that you might one day take more seriously." He stopped talking and flopped back in his seat as if worn out from saying what was in his heart.

"Damn," he said suddenly as her face changed from soft, to smiling, to puzzled. "I didn't mean to tell you all of that. Forget about it."

"Are you kidding me?" Sam asked, her voice gritty. "Hell, Finn, that's a speech for the ages. Wow."

He looked down, rubbing his chin. "I don't want to put pressure on you."

"You're not putting any pressure on me." Sam leaned forward, her hands on his chest, until she was inches from his face. "Look at me, Finn Bradley. Please."

Raising his eyes to her, Finn swallowed. It was beginning to snow even heavier, almost a blizzard, and everyone was getting up to leave, but Sam just leaned against him, her face tilted to his, as the rug slipped from her knees.

"I have one regret," she said. "We should never have made that pact."

"No?" He quivered as her arms slid around him.

"No," she said with a giggle. "Finn Bradley, how can you declare yourself so damn passionately to me one minute, and the next act as if nothing was said. Put your arms around me, for God's sake." She laid her head on his chest. "It's not as if we don't know one another."

Finn didn't need another invitation. He pulled her closer to him, snuggling her down into his arms as if she was the missing part of him. Her soft sighs against his chest filled him with pride, and joy, and the urge to tell Coach Harrington exactly what he could do with his threats. Finn pressed his cheek against the top of Sam's head, and the outside world faded away.

"Sam," he whispered.

"Yeah?" she murmured back.

He paused, letting the moment settle in his heart. Held back the words he was longing to say to her. Was this the place to do it—a rustic little bistro in a side street of a small Italian town on a snowy day? He couldn't hold in the smile that took over his face. If this wasn't the most perfect place in the world then nowhere was.

"Sam, I love you."

Sam sat up. She gazed at him, her eyes lit up with that emerald glitter that he loved. She grinned at him. "About time."

A bubble of laughter burst from him, and he held her tighter as his shoulders shook.

"Agreed."

"Finn?" She touched her nose against his. He held his breath as her lips brushed against his. "I love you too."

The surge of joy that filled him at the sound of her saying that to him was immeasurable. He wanted to punch the air, to kick up the snow, to yell until the whole of the Alps was an avalanche.

"In the great words of Taylor Swift," she said as he grinned like a Cheshire cat. "*It's been a long time coming*."

"And I promise you this—you always will be." He laughed gently, ducking as she slapped him playfully.

"You said it wasn't about . . . what we got up to!" Sam joked. "But I sure as hell hope that some of it is . . ."

Finn shifted in his seat. Something low down in his stomach began to wind tightly. "Like I said—I promise," he murmured into her ear, hoping he wasn't scaring her. Was this too much too soon?

Sam's hands slid up his chest, her fingers soft against the stubble on his jaw. "Show me."

"Sam." His voice was hoarse. "What are you doing to me?"

She ran her hands down his back and kissed the side of his neck. "What do you want me to do to you?"

"Come with me," he murmured, kissing her again before taking her hand. "Let's go somewhere quieter."

20

Sam

The walk back to Finn's hotel was a blur. Faces, stores, snow, that's all she could remember. Someone called out *good luck* and she laughed wondering how on earth they knew what she was about to do. Then she laughed again because of course they didn't know that she was about to rip the clothes off Finn Bradley's fine body, run her hands over every inch of him while she lost her mind. All she could think of was how he'd held her in the shower, how he'd devoured her as if he'd been starved of her all his life, and how she wanted to do the same for him.

Her heart pounded as they stood in the elevator. He held her hand, caressing the back of it with his thumb as they waited for their floor, and she could sense his frustration that they had to share the lift with another couple.

Within minutes they were in his suite. The door had barely clicked shut behind them before Sam was in his arms again, kissing him deeply while her fingers fumbled with his shirt buttons. He pulled her jacket roughly down her shoulders, breaking their kiss only long enough to fling it away. His hands were everywhere—in her hair, on her throat—rough and desperate. They ran down her sides, making her shiver and press against him. With his hands tight on her waist, he backed her carefully against the wall, steadying her against it as she gasped for air.

"God, Sam." His breath was ragged as he tore his shirt off. Tossing it aside he groaned. His eyes were the darkest she'd ever seen—there was a hunger there that took her breath away. She gasped. This Finn—shirtless, hair tousled, his usually sunny face replaced by something fierce and serious—had no idea how undone he was making her. Sam stepped back. The crease between his eyes deepened, telling her that he wasn't playing games. He was going to ruin her. She raised her chin and hoped that he would.

"What do you want?" his voice was low, lethal. He stepped away from her, leaving her aching for his touch.

Blinking, Sam dragged her eyes away from his low-slung gray sweatpants and the deep V of muscle at his hips, acutely aware of how her pulse thudded in places that she yearned for his touch. She blinked again and cleared her throat. Helplessly, she said, "I don't know . . ."

He reached for her, sliding his hand around her shoulders to cradle the back of her neck, dragging her toward him. "You don't have to," he rasped, his breath hot against her ear. "I'm fine figuring out every goddamn thing that you need."

Sam's heart hammered in her ribs. Her eyes devoured him, the stubble on his jaw, the tension in his shoulders. He looked so strong, virile and completely unlike his normal soft, funny self. "Finn?"

"Yeah." He pulled back just enough to see her, his hands cradling her like she was something precious.

She slid her hands up his bare chest, feeling the frantic thrum of his heartbeat in his throat. She smiled, a small but sure thing, filled with honesty.

"I don't want you to figure it out alone," she whispered.

He stilled, his arms tightening, flexing in the dim light.

"I want us to do it together," she breathed. "Every last messy, scary, stupid thing. With you."

A harsh, broken sound ripped from Finn's throat—half laugh, half groan. Then he was kissing her again, but slower. Tender. Deep. Like he was memorizing the taste of her, binding her onto his very soul. He broke away, leaning his head on her shoulder, his bare chest rising and falling in uneven breaths. "I love you, Sam," he whispered hoarsely against her skin.

His words made Sam shiver. Her pulse pounded in her throat.

Finn didn't speak. He raised his head; his gaze locked on hers.

Sam's breath hitched. "I love you too, so damn much."

Finn closed his eyes.

Sam had barely time to process the emotion that swept across his face. One second, she was standing before him, every cell in her body screaming at her to move—to touch him. Every heartbeat ringing in her ears, every muscle in her body weakening under the moment. The next his bare chest was warm against her palms as he pressed her back against the wall. His hands, familiar and strong, ran up her arms, rested on her collarbones for a moment before tilting her face up to his.

"Say it again," he murmured, his voice low and rough.

Sam swallowed hard. She whispered, "I love you."

A muscle ticked in Finn's jaw; his eyes darkened. His hands cradled her face; his thumb swept across her cheek. He laid his forehead against hers, his breath warm and minty as he whispered, "Sam, is this real?"

Before she could answer, his mouth was on hers, hot and hungry, taking her without hesitation. Sam groaned against his insistent lips. Finn deepened the kiss, as if he was reclaiming something he'd lost, something he refused to lose again. His body was solid against hers, heat radiating from his skin through her shirt, sending shivers down her spine.

She melted against him, her hands skimming over the hard planes of his chest, nails digging in just enough to make him growl with pleasure. *He liked that.* Good, she needed him to feel what she was feeling, how much she wanted him—how much she'd always wanted him.

He broke away from their kiss as her hands grasped the waistband of his sweatpants. His hands pulling hers away as his cock pressed hard against her belly. "Say it again." He grasped her wrists tightly while leaning deeper, harder against her. "I like how you say it."

"I love you, Finn. I want you." Sam pushed back against him, willing him to understand how much she wanted this. Her eyes strong on his. "Finn."

He let go of her wrists, his mouth tantalizingly close to hers. "You're mine, Sam," he breathed raggedly. "It's always been you. Even when I tried to let you go, I couldn't."

Sam pulled him to her. She clung to him, her fingers threading through his hair, her entire body melting into his.

Finn swept an arm around her waist, lifting her just enough that she had no choice but to wrap her legs around him, gasping as his cock, hard and rigid, pressed against her most intimate parts. She looked down into his face as he carried her upstairs to his room.

"Sam," he said, staring up at her with a heat that made her skin tingle as if she was already naked. "I see you. I want to see all of you. Tonight, and every night. Forever."

The door slammed shut behind them.

Finn carried her across the lamplit room in a heartbeat, his hands holding her ass, his mouth on hers. They tumbled onto the bed, his hands reaching under her shirt as if he was desperate to touch her skin. Sam arched her back as his fingers found her nipples, coaxing them into stiff peaks beneath the silkiness of her bra. His touch was everything she'd ever wanted, and now it was almost too much. Grasping a handful of his hair, she moaned into his neck as he kissed and caressed her. Her body pulsed as they ground against each other. Eager to have his skin on hers, she pushed him away, fumbling with her shirt buttons as he kissed her neck, sucking and nipping at the tender spot beneath her ear until she groaned and hastily pulled the shirt open, not caring that two buttons flew across the room. His hands scorched against her waist as she pushed him to lie back on the bed, his eyes drinking her in as she stood up to tear her pants off. For a moment she stood still, unable to believe they were doing this. Leaning up on his elbows, he raised an eyebrow at her and her stomach flipped.

"You okay?" he asked, his eyes roaming down her body. Sam caught a movement in his sweatpants. She nodded, breathless, her eyes taking him all in as she reached for his waistband.

His quick intake of breath as she tugged down his sweatpants made her heart race. He kept watching her as she climbed on top of him, her long lean thighs straddling his waist while his hard cock pulsed against her softness.

"I'm okay," she said, loving how his hands felt on her waist, her ass, slipping into her panties and pulling at them gently. His hands moved back to her waist, grasping her tightly.

"You feel incredible," he groaned as she ground down on his thick length. "Christ, Sam." He grabbed her more tightly then in a flash she was beneath him, his full body— hard and urgent—pressed her into the mattress in the most intoxicating way.

His lips ghosted kisses along her jaw, down her throat, his strong legs nudging hers apart. "Tell me," he murmured. "Is this what you want?"

"I don't want anything else." Sam scraped her nails across his shoulders, arching her back as his mouth, fevered and wet, traced kisses down her neck and to her breast. She slipped her bra straps down, as he reached behind her to unhook it. His tongue rasped against her nipple, sucking and biting gently while his fingers tugged her panties off. He touched her lower belly, his eyes darkening as she sucked her breath in.

"Tell me again that this is what you want?" he growled, looking up at her. She nodded, mute at the desire evident in his eyes. He smiled wickedly at her, and she gasped as his fingers slipped lower, gently seeking that sensitive bundle of nerves that was aching for his attention. His fingertips massaged her swollen mound, dipping to tease her clit as she fought to keep from begging him to fuck her. This was too good, and if it lasted forever, it wouldn't be long enough. A flush burned across her cheeks as he lowered his head to take her nipple into his mouth, his tongue licking her before he sucked hard. Crying out she threw her head back, unable to keep watching him. His fingers kept moving against her, stroking and teasing her, creating a deep ache low inside her. Arching her hips, a guttural groan escaped her throat, and she blushed even harder, suddenly nervous about the intimacy between them. No one had ever made her groan like that before. She laughed a little before whimpering as his fingers found her hot, wet center.

"Stop!" she gasped, rising to her elbows to look at him. Finn stopped exploring her body, raising his head to look at her from under sexy, heavy eyelids. Sam's heart fluttered; her stomach clenched with desire. "You'll make me come."

"I want to make you come," Finn said huskily. He smiled mischievously. "Isn't that the point?"

Sam giggled. "Well, yes . . . but not so soon."

He raised an eyebrow at her. "Oh?"

"No, not so soon," she whispered as she slipped from under him so that they were lying down, facing one another. "Let me take a turn."

Finn's eyes widened as she pushed him to lie on his back. He stretched out before her, not once breaking their gaze. His lips curved up slightly, as if he was curious about what she was going to do while his smile made her think that he knew full well what she had in mind. His body was perfection, strong yet supple, lean and honed by years of discipline, every inch a masterpiece. He quivered slightly as she smiled back at him. The smile drifted from his face as she ran her fingers along his thigh, a groan escaping his lips as he tilted his head back, his forearm covering his beautiful eyes. His stubble was dark against the golden tone of his skin, his lips parted as she lifted her hand from his body. He shivered as she shifted closer to him, his stomach rising and falling gently with every inhale and exhale.

Sam's eyes trailed down his sculpted body, taking in the taut muscles of his chest, the soft dusting of hair that made her bite her lower lip, the deeply etched muscles that formed the V-lines that disappeared into the waistband of his shorts, like a damn arrow directing her to exactly what she was looking for. She ran one hand down his chest, pausing to caress his lower stomach, relishing how he caught his breath as she scratched her nails gently lower and lower in a circular motion. She hesitated, for a brief moment, until he uttered her name.

"Sam." His growling whisper sent a delicious shiver along her spine. Sam traced the V shape slowly, then ran her fingertips along his waistband, lifting the material ever so slightly. His cock bulged and flickered beneath the soft cotton. She ran the tips of her fingers down along the hard length of it, reveling in how he writhed and groaned.

"Yes?" she whispered back to him.

"What are you doing to me?" he groaned as she stroked his pulsating cock.

"This," she said as she pulled down his shorts. "Lift your hips. Now."

Finn groaned and complied, sighing as Sam tossed his shorts to one side. Kneeling beside his stretched-out body, Sam touched him, sliding her fingers around his swollen member, learning the feel and the size of him as she leaned forward to press soft, fiery kisses along his hip bones.

Her hand stroked his cock up and down. His skin was soft, silky, and enticing as she varied the tightness of her movements. Her lips carried on kissing his body closer and closer to his cock. Finn lifted his hips, and Sam pushed them back down.

"Wait," she said. "Wait."

"I can't," Finn moaned. "Touch me, Sam."

"Well, if you insist," she said playfully, stroking the entire length of his cock before licking it. "More?"

"Please . . ." Finn's words were barely audible as she licked and stroked him, her tongue tasting and teasing every inch of his impressive length. Vaguely she felt him touch her ass, then gently, but firmly, ease her kneeling legs apart so that he could touch her wet, warm core. His fingers dipped into her, and she gasped, pushing against them until his fingers were deeper inside her, slipping in and out of her while his thumb pressed tantalizingly against the tender skin of her inner thigh, forcing her to open her legs wider. With a deep moan she licked her lips and fully took him into her mouth, going deep and tight, loving how he shuddered and groaned, crying out her name as if he was about to come.

"Oh, Sam." His groan sent a molten spiral of desire through her. One of his hands was on her head, holding her braid gently as she took him even more deeply into her mouth. His grip on her hair tightened. His hips moved gently as she gripped the base of his cock with one hand, the other cupped his balls. He slipped his fingers out of her and pressed against her clit, making her cry out. Grinding against his hand, her mouth hot and wet and full of his huge cock, the tension tightening in the base of her stomach, with his hand gently guiding her up and down, Sam shuddered. She was so close, and so was he. His thrusts were more determined, his hand on her head was firm. Suddenly he pulled her away from him.

"I need us to stop," he panted, his face contorted with pleasure. "I'm too close . . ."

Shakily, Sam sat back and brushed a strand of hair from her face. Finn moved, fast. Standing above her where she knelt on the bed, he smiled and softly touched her lips with his fingers.

"Lie back. Your turn."

21

Sam

Dazed, Sam shivered as he took her face in his hands. "What?"

"Lie back." Finn murmured against her pouty lips, tasting her mouth deeply as she leaned in for more. She reached for his cock again, but he stopped her with a groan.

"Sam," he growled and took hold of her shoulders. "Lie back. I want you to enjoy this."

She stopped kissing him and leaned back onto her elbows, her eyes on his. He smiled knowingly at her, and she bit her lower lip as he nodded at her as if asking her to trust him. Lowering her body back onto the warm brushed cotton sheets, Sam gasped as his hands grabbed her hips and pulled her toward him. His hands were warm, rough in places. They felt good, right, against her softness. He settled between her thighs, his powerful legs holding hers apart, heat radiating from his skin. The rough scrape of his hair against her soft inner thighs sent a delicious shiver through her, making her breath come in gasps. Panting, she glanced up at him through her eyelashes, almost not daring to look at him at all. His gaze was unrelenting, almost pinning her in place. The urge to look away battled with the desire to wrap her legs around him and stare into his eyes as they met. But she didn't move. Without touching her, or saying anything, he'd made her feel more desirable than she'd ever felt before.

He leaned over her, his cock heavy against her belly as his eyes sought hers. His arms framed her, his hands planted either side of her head, keeping her beneath him but never trapping her. He lowered his head to her ear. "Sam?" he whispered, his voice low, rough but warm. "You want this, don't you?" His murmur melted her inhibitions completely. She nodded, her hands moving, seemingly of their own accord, to skim the sides of his body to cradle his face.

"Yes. Finn." She pulled him to her, kissing him deeply as his body pressed down gently on hers. Wrapping her legs around his waist she cried out as his hand ran down her body to grab her ass, his mouth still on hers. Moaning, she moved gently against the hard length of him, loving how wet and slick they both felt. Tangling her fingers in his hair, she arched beneath him, her hips silently urging him closer. As the heat spiked between them, he pulled away, breathless. He chuckled, his eyes gleaming with mischief. Before she could protest at his pulling away from her, he caught her wrist, and guided it above her head, his grip a teasing contrast of restraint and invitation. Sam fluttered her lashes, a smile on her lips. She willingly offered her other wrist, her heart pounding as he wrapped one large hand around both, effortlessly holding her beneath him. His other hand stroked her face, then grasped her chin as he kissed her deeply. His hand grazed her throat, her collarbones and traced a gentle, teasing trail down her body, skimming over her nipples as his mouth pressed down on hers. His hand settled on her hip, holding her in place as she writhed beneath him. Lifting his head, he opened his eyes.

"I need you." His hand left her wrists, slowly and deliberately exploring her body, leaving her breathless and dizzy. He lowered his head to between her thighs, his hands lifted her hips, his mouth tasting her with searing, wet desire. Sam cried out as his tongue found her clit and he gently licked and sucked it. Raising her hips higher, his hands moved down, his finger finding her opening, slipping inside, stroking her as he moaned against her. He slipped another finger in, and she contracted around it, loving his invasion of her most private place. Heat gathered in her belly, swelling and surging with every stroke. She tensed around his fingers, her hips gently moving in rhythm with his mouth, her movements begging for more of the wicked and unrelenting pleasure he was giving her. She raised her hips higher, her hands fists, gripping the sheets, pulsating and moaning with desire. Finn shifted away from her, his touch dragging across the tender skin of her thighs as if he didn't want to move.

"Finn?" she called shakily.

"I need to grab something." Finn stroked her thigh, slowly and promising. His voice was ragged, his gaze dark and devouring. "Don't move."

He was back before she could even consider moving, his weight pressing her into the mattress once more.

"Miss me?" There was no time to answer, his mouth was

on hers once again, his kiss stealing any answer she might give.

The sharp crinkle of a foil packet opening barely registered with Sam, but somehow the sharp tearing and rustle made her pant, anticipation curling low in her stomach.

"Super-efficient," she murmured against his lips as he carefully and quickly smoothed the condom over his cock. "Damn."

"Last chance to change your mind." His voice was pure gravel. His fingers tightened on her hips as he leaned over her. "Because once I start, I'm not stopping until you come."

Sam nodded, dragging him to her, her body answering for her as his hard, taut body burned against hers. Wrapping her legs around his hips, she rubbed against his massive cock, whimpering as he placed his tip at her entrance. He pulled away, his forehead on hers, his breath unsteady. "Say my name."

Opening her eyes, Sam stared into his. Licking her lips she gasped as he slowly entered her, stopping before going all the way. She grasped his shoulders, crying out as he pulled away.

"Say my name," he growled as he pressed back into her, slowly and surely.

"Finn," Sam cried out as he filled her completely, his swollen staff sliding in and out of her slowly, teasingly. He slid all the way in, and held himself there, as if claiming her. She pushed against him, relishing how they seemed joined as one, loving how even the slightest movement sent her spiraling into oblivion. His lips were on her throat, his hands on her wrists. His thrusts steady and deep.

"Fuck, Sam, you're . . ." Finn gasped, ". . . you are amazing."

Unable to speak, she tightened her legs around him, bucking and thrusting against his steel sheath as the heat inside her began to boil. Pleasure crackled through Sam, starting at her core and racing outwards. Every cell in her body burned as he pounded into her, his balls pressing against her as he buried himself in her. Her cries echoed around the room as she passed the point of no return, her hands pulling free of his wrists to wrap tightly around his shoulders. Clinging to him, she screamed his name as her orgasm peaked, her fingers digging into the hard muscles of his shoulders. His thrusts went deeper, harder, faster against her wetness. He grabbed a handful of her hair, her braid long since undone, and held her tightly as his movements became more deliberate. Sam gasped as the heat she'd thought had gone began to gather deep inside her again. Panting she writhed, begging him to fill her again, but he continued his slower, deeper sliding in and out of her wet center.

"Fuck me, Finn." The words slipped out of her without warning. He paused, as if stunned.

"You mean that?"

"Fuck me. Finn," Sam said, firmly. "I want you to fuck me."

"Say please," Finn teased her, sliding out slowly.

"Please!" Sam shifted her hips, her legs pulling him back inside her.

A guttural groan escaped from Finn. He surged against her, plunging into her as she cried his name over and over, her climax building for a second time with each eager thrust until she was bucking uncontrollably beneath him, her breath coming in gasps, her cries rasping in her throat. Everything faded except for the feel of him, the heat, the intensity. She broke, pleasure surging more intensely through her than she'd ever felt before—hot, crazy, like wildfire. With a cry of his name, she tumbled over the edge. He held her gently as she came, his body shuddering as she shook beneath him. Her hands found his hips, then his ass, and she pulled him deeper into her, rocking against him, begging him to come with her.

Suddenly he grabbed her, grasping her tightly as he stilled slightly, then his body convulsed, shaking as he reached a crescendo. He held his breath as he came, his body stiffening as he cried out her name. Gasping, he laid his forehead against hers and pulled in a ragged breath. Lying down beside her, he threw his arm over his eyes, as if embarrassed. Sam snuggled closer to him, almost unsure what to do next. She'd never experienced this kind of feeling before, this sensation of closeness, and of being completely safe. At home even. She slowly released a breath. Was he feeling the same way? Was he nervous too? She felt the muscles on her forehead relax—she wasn't nervous, she was with Finn, the place she always should have been. The place she'd been longing for. She'd the strangest feeling that he felt that too. Gently she slid her arm over his chest and held him close, shocked to find him trembling.

"Finn?" she whispered as his breathing returned to normal. "You okay?"

"More than okay." He rolled over to face her, his arms holding her tightly. "I feel like I'm soaring—flying. I feel . . . like I never want to move. You?"

Lying in his arms should've felt strange. Weird. This was her best friend after all, but it didn't. It felt as if they should have been together already, like this was meant to be.

"Me too." She nodded. "You . . ."

"No, you—" He kissed her softly. "You are perfect."

Sam dipped her head, away from his loving gaze. In his arms she felt perfect. It wasn't a sensation she was used to feeling.

"Come up here," Finn said, moving them both until they were settled against the pillows. Curling in beside him, Sam sighed deeply, as if the weight of the world had been lifted from her shoulders. Finn drew the duvet up over them, carefully tucking it in around Sam's shoulders. Sam sucked on her bottom lip as he pulled her closer to him, his arm felt protective and loving. His chest rose and fell gently beneath her head. His fingers toyed gently with her undone hair.

Their eyes met in the dim light, and for a long moment neither of them spoke. Then, Finn brushed a strand of hair from her face, his touch soft, delicate. Sam exhaled softly, her fingers tracing absent patterns on his chest.

He stroked her cheek. "Sam. I am here for you. I will never let you down. I couldn't even if I wanted to because . . ." He took a deep breath. His eyes glanced down and then back up to hers. "Because I love you. I've always loved you."

Sam stared at him, tears stinging the backs of her eyes. All these years she'd pretended that he was just Finn, her friend, the person she could tell anything to, the person who knew what she was going through, the first person she wanted to share things with . . . all these years she'd pushed away the love she'd felt for him because of that stupid promise.

"Finn." She squeezed his hand. "We made that promise . . ." She could still see them, that night walking home from prom, swearing to win before anything else. It felt silly now, but very real.

Finn's expression flickered, just for a second, as if he couldn't believe she was talking about a stupid pact they'd made when they were teenagers. That promise—career first, friendship second, then nothing. Well, nothing wasn't good enough, and time was going by too fast.

"Yeah," he said, his voice quieter now. "We did, but that was a long time ago."

"We meant it then, didn't we?" Sam almost choked on her words.

"Sure, but Sam, why did we ever make that promise in the first place?" He sat up, pulling the duvet closer to them both. "I know now—I was scared. Weren't you?"

Sam swallowed, suddenly feeling light-headed.

"We were kids," he said, watching her gently. "We thought love would ruin everything. What if we were wrong? Maybe we were."

Her heart twisted. He was right. All those years, wasted. But what if he was wrong? What if the promise was keeping them safe, and focused and winning? She took a deep, shaky breath. If she told him how she really felt there'd be no going back to before. She could lose him if it all fell apart. She plucked at the cotton sheet, her mind racing.

"Sam," Finn whispered. "It's okay if you don't feel the same." His voice cracked and he cleared his throat. "I'll be okay, I'll survive. But if you do—if you're just scared—Sam, don't let a promise we made as dumb teenagers stop you from saying what you really feel."

Sam gasped. Her pulse pounded in her throat. She'd lose him if she didn't say something—lose him forever. She couldn't—not when it seemed like she'd just *found* him. She stopped picking a thread from the sheet and sucked a breath in.

"Back then." Sam let out her breath. "I seem to remember you said that we would revise it—the promise. I think that maybe, maybe we *should* revise it."

His whole body stilled. His hands stayed by his side. Nervously she raised her eyes to his. "I love you, Finn. Always have, same as you." She smiled weakly. "And yeah, it's scary."

"It is, it's terrifying." Finn stared at her. He breathed out then opened his arms. "Come here."

Sam settled into his arms, loving how he seemed custom made for her. He settled his chin on her head, sighing deeply before snuggling down deeper into the pillows. Closing her eyes, Sam sighed. She'd had never felt more seen in her life.

22

Sam

Thursday, 12th February

"I can't believe you're still not going to tell me what Finn did to make you smile like that. You've managed to say nothing all day—it's driving me insane!" Maya said, her head buried in her phone. "And I can't believe I didn't open the door a minute earlier this morning and snap a photo of you two. Your fans would go wild!"

The two women stepped out of their hotel, zipping up jackets and pulling on hats, ready to stroll along the snowy street toward the ski lifts.

Rolling her eyes and choking back a giggle, Sam pulled her neck gaiter on. "I am so glad you didn't! It definitely wasn't a photo you could put on Insta without the account getting banned."

"Hey, don't tell me that!" Maya raised her head, her eyes wide and twinkling.

"Anyway, what's going on between you and Gabe?" Sam slipped her gloves on.

"Nothing." Maya half smiled. "Having some fun, that's all. I mean, he's so damn hot."

"He's unreal," Sam said. "And my take is that he's very into you."

"Yeah, he is, but before this I was into my beachy blond, all-American boy next door kinda guy, you know, a little preppy and a little built at the same time—looks good in Ralph Lauren and his daddy's Porsche. But oh, my, gosh . . ." Maya let out a low whistle, fanning herself with one hand ". . . Gabe is all man—he's got leaning against a wall off to a fine art, and man, does he smell of expensive cologne and bad decisions—hell yeah. He makes me want to make nothing but bad decisions." She winked at Sam. "I bet he even has his own car."

"Vroom!" Sam doubled over laughing. "I bet he does, and I bet it goes fast."

"I don't know though," Maya said, wrinkling her nose. "I get the feeling that he's far more serious than everyone thinks. He's giving serious Finn vibes."

Turning away so Maya couldn't see her face glow with embarrassment, Sam nodded. "Yeah, maybe. I mean, he's intense enough at the best of times."

"I'm not into serious right now," Maya said. "I just want some fun—and some of whatever you two were up to all night."

"I'm not going to tell you!"

"Argh, you are so irritating right now." Maya playfully

279

pushed Sam. "And by the way, your personal Instagram page—the posts of you in that vintage suit—wow!"

"What?" Sam turned to her, her brows raised. "For real?"

"Girl, it has blown up! Haven't you checked?"

Sam shook her head. "No, I didn't have time—"

"You seriously cannot give me that comment and not tell me what is making you smile like the cat that got the cream today—what *did* that boy do to you?" Maya shook her head in wonder.

Sam laughed. "I will leave that up to your imagination, but let's just say—this girl is living her best life right now—and then some!"

* * *

There were no other competitors at the top of the course. Sam was early; this was the earliest she'd ever been to a finals, but this was her last chance to try for an Olympic gold, and she wanted to savor the moment. Breathing in deeply through her nose, she leaned her board against the railing, her eyes suddenly drawn to her *Ohana* sticker. Running her hand over it, she frowned. The sticker was smooth, flat to the board as if freshly glued in place. Sam chewed on her bottom lip, her frown deepening. The sticker had been barely stuck in place the last time she'd looked at it, and now . . . she laid her palm flat on the sticker and took a deep breath. Finn must've done it for her, although when he'd found time, she couldn't quite figure out. She looked up and surveyed the sky. It didn't look good. All day it had grown darker and more like snow. Now, in the darkness of the winter evening, the heavy, gray blanket of clouds made the edge of the halfpipe hard to see even with the defining blue paint lines and the bright lights. If they made it even halfway through the competition before the snow started, they'd be doing well. Her nose smarted from the cold, but deep inside her a fire was burning. She didn't even notice Maya taking some shots before slipping away as the competitors started arriving.

Harper was the first of the other competitors to spot Sam. She strolled over, her eyes on the clouds. "Not great visibility."

"No." Sam didn't move from her position. "These later event times, they're tough." She held her board in one hand, the other was warm in her pocket. She gripped Finn's lucky stone, although she knew she didn't need it. It was simply good to have something of his with her. Turning the soft, warm stone in her hand she looked away from Harper, vaguely aware of the young woman's eyes on her, waiting for her to say something.

Sam felt a smile tug at the corners of her mouth as Harper smoothed a hand over her hip, her face tight, her brows low. She seemed nervous. Sam had seen Harper's latest Instagram posts. In every photo Harper had been decked head to toe in fresh Salvaro gear, the spoils of her latest sponsorship deal. Sam allowed the smile to surface. Harper had looked great, no, she'd looked amazing. The pressure was on, Sam realized. Salvaro had chosen Harper, and now she couldn't fail. Harper was clearly on edge. Sam didn't want to add to Harper's discomfort, after all, there was no point in being bitter about it, not now when they'd bigger things to think about.

"I love your Instagram—I think you're perfect for

Salvaro," Sam said, her voice as smooth as fresh powder as Harper chewed on a fingernail. "Best of luck. See ya later." She shifted her board in her grasp and moved away from Harper, eager to get away from the nervous energy Harper was radiating. It was very off-putting, and she didn't need to try competing against that as well as the course.

Lowering her head, Sam sniffed and took a half glance at the course again. She could easily do this—in her sleep. She knew it. But what was even easier was to guess what Harper . . . and Becky would do. They were predictable, and with the weather the way it was, she was sure she was right. All she had to do was relax, remember that she loved what she did, and have fun.

Marching toward the back wall as the area became more and more busy with athletes and their teams, Sam brushed shoulders with another competitor. Staggering slightly, she automatically called out, "Sorry!"

"No worries." Becky's warm voice made Sam look up. She adjusted her glove as Sam blinked.

"Oh, I didn't mean that."

"I know, it's just so crowded up here." Becky smiled. "Good luck, by the way."

"Thanks, you too." Sam moved on, aware that Leo was watching their interaction from the gate. Glancing back at Becky, she rubbed the stone in her pocket. *It wasn't Becky's fault that Leo and Dad had made her their golden girl now.*

Leaning against the barrier, Sam rolled her eyes as Leo sidled up to her, stopping within earshot. Sam pressed her tongue against the inside of her cheek to stop herself from telling him to get lost. Now wasn't the time. But she'd damn well make sure that there would be a time—and she wouldn't mince her words when that time came around.

The speakers above their head crackled and Gabriel's voice carried out onto the still, cold air.

"Tonight's women's halfpipe final includes some of the best snowboarders I've ever seen, Seb," Gabriel's calm and strong voice proclaimed over the speakers. "Take Becky Stanford—she's really showing the world how good she is, here in Livigno. Her progression has been amazing, and such a turnaround from her slightly off and, dare I say, messy performance in Japan in January. She's got a real shot at the podium here, if she can keep it clean."

Leo's eyes narrowed. He glanced down at the bottom of the slope, then back at Sam as Gabe continued.

"Now Sam Harrington, she's something different. She's one to watch—mark my words. Where Stanford is all about powering high into her tricks, Harrington is more fluid—she's got an effortless style that makes me think she was born for this. You wouldn't know it—as both women are so different in their styles—but they are both trained by the legendary Jake Harrington, and we all know the kind of champions that man creates."

Sam's head snapped around before she could stop it. Her gaze landed on her father's back, where he stood with the other coaches drinking coffee. She shivered. *Damn him.* He wasn't getting into her head, not tonight, not ever. He turned around as her eyes narrowed. His face was set, grim and solid. Sam closed her eyes for a moment. She didn't have to listen to his shit, not anymore. He'd built her up only to drop her the moment she was in need. That wasn't what a good coach should do. Bracing her shoulders, she stood tall, a knowing smile on her lips. He nodded at her to come to him, but she didn't move.

"Aren't you going to talk to him?" Leo watched the exchange, his eyes flickering from his sister to his father.

"No." Sam raised her chin. "Why should I?"

"He's your coach," Leo said, a hint of confusion in his voice.

"A real coach sticks with their athlete through thick and thin. Don't think I don't know what you and Dad have been saying about me." Sam exhaled, unable to keep her promise to herself. "I heard you two, in Becky's room. How do you think that made me feel, Leo, you two saying that I'd messed up—that I had no confidence in myself?"

Leo looked down at the snow, nudging it with his boot. "I'm sorry you heard that, but Sam, that's not what I had been trying to say to Dad—what I did say—listen, I was trying to get Dad to see how hard you were working, and to tell him a few things I thought might help. But Sam, Becky was there too, and I'm supposed to be her number-one fan. It's complicated, and you know Dad—his listening skills need updating."

Sam squinted at him. "But you let him say that . . ."

Leo glanced up. "I should've said more. I'm sorry, Sam. I didn't want to make it worse—I feel like I'm walking a tightrope sometimes, between you and Becky, and then Dad. He doesn't take me seriously at all."

Sam sighed, the frustration starting to ease. "This all sucks."

"I know, right," Leo said quietly. "Are you nervous?"

"Not really." She breathed out strong, realizing that it was the truth. "You?"

Leo's smile faltered. "Not my sport anymore, as Dad reminded me that night." His voice was softer, quieter.

"Oh God," she said. "Leo, he shouldn't have . . ."

A grim shiver washed over Sam; one she didn't like. Skiing had been his life, before the accident. She let out a slow breath. "It must be weird, watching everyone else go for it."

Leo's jaw flexed. "Yeah well, this is my life now."

"Leo." Sam stepped forward, Jake's face and words in her mind. "It doesn't have to be. You could get back out there, couldn't you? The pain—is that what's stopping you from skiing?" She paused, her mouth dry. "I wish you'd try, because you loved this, and I really wish you could get something of it back."

Leo exhaled sharply. He pulled his hat down over his ears, and for a split second something like regret flickered across his face, but it was gone in a heartbeat. He smiled and for a moment he looked like the Leo who'd always cheered her on.

He shook his head. His eyes glistened as he looked up at Sam. "What I came up here to say was that you're gonna crush it."

Sam's stomach churned. "You sure about that? My last few performances . . ."

"They don't mean anything," Leo said, his tone serious. "Trust me, Sam, you have what it takes, but pressure gets to you, it always has and then . . . listen, when that happens I've noticed you lean back too much. You need to drive through your front leg for more pop, something I figured out after my accident. I can't rely on this leg." He tapped his left leg. "I had to learn to make every other movement count. Use your core, and your arms to control the air time."

Sam stared at Leo. He never spoke about his injury, ever. "Front leg, huh?"

He nodded. "Push up, not back. You've got the strength, Sam—use it."

She felt a little twinge of nostalgia. Leo was offering real advice, like he used to when they were kids. It wasn't something to ignore or laugh about. She nodded. "Okay, I'll give it a shot."

Sam watched him for a second, then glanced up as the next rider was announced. *Becky.*

"She's going to go big," she said to Leo, her stomach twisted as he nodded. "And it's her downfall."

Leo looked at her, then over at Becky where she stood at the drop-in.

"Dad's trained her well, but she isn't clean enough." Sam nodded toward Becky, who was checking her helmet strap.

Leo rubbed the back of his neck. "Yeah, damn, you're right. She'll have the height, but . . . it won't be enough."

Sam nodded unhappily toward Becky. "First hit: huge method air—massive but simple, and the crowd will love it. But it'll lack complexity."

Leo's brow furrowed. "I never really thought of it that way."

"Next, double cork 1080," Sam continued, almost reluctantly, her voice calm. "Clean in the air, but the landing—not so clean. She'll push for a backside 1260— again it won't be clean. Finally, the moment that might work: she's gonna go for a frontside 1440." She glanced at

Leo, catching the flash of realization in his eyes as he turned to face her.

"She'll land it, but not well." Sam stared at her brother. "And the judges will dock her for it. And that's why she won't take the gold." She let that sink in for a beat. "That's what he's told her to do, that's what he thinks it takes to win this competition. But he's wrong, Leo. And Becky will pay the price and there's not a thing we can do about it."

Sam turned away as Becky dropped in, her heart pounding. Becky deserved better. She was a brilliant and instinctive snowboarder, but she had to learn to trust her own gut and not listen to so many opinions sometimes. A shiver ran down Sam's spine as Gabe's commentary called out Becky's tricks. She'd predicted the entire run, to a T.

Pulling herself up tall, she applauded for Becky, knowing that every eye in the place was on her. Becky's score was good, but not good enough for gold. Sam's heart sank for Becky—she'd been led to believe she'd take the gold, but she hadn't. And she wasn't in any other events. That had been her last chance, as it was for Sam. As it was for her biggest rival, Harper, who was next up, and more than ready to take her chance for the gold. Sam lowered her chin and watched as Harper got ready to go.

Harper dropped in, in her trademark calm and methodical way. Sam barely noticed herself speaking, predicting Harper's every move. "Backside 900, clean." Her fingers twitched. "Switch frontside 720, solid." She hitched her board higher in her arms. "McTwist . . . Frontside 1080 to finish." She blinked as Gabe's commentary followed hers, almost word for word.

Leo looked at her in amazement. "You do realize that's kind of freaky, right?"

Sam barely heard him. *Harper's run was good, really good. Safe, yes, controlled and precise, pure Harper.* A stampede of nerves trampled across her stomach. "Freaky? No, Leo, it's not freaky—it's keeping it real. Wish me luck, bro."

"You don't need my luck." Leo grinned. He shook his head. "You need to listen to your gut, Sam. That was amazing."

She nodded at him, then strode away, her pulse thrumming. It was her turn now. *Time to show them all.*

The top of the run was quiet. Sam adjusted her goggles and glanced down to the crowd below. Finn's luminous orange hat glowed under the bright lights, and she smiled. She glanced back at Leo. His face was a mess of contradictions. His brows were pulled tight, his lips pressed into a line, but his eyes were steady and locked on her. He nodded slightly, but she saw it. Then he nodded again, this time more surely. And her heart swelled. Nodding gently at him, she turned confidently back to the moment. Drawing the sharp, cold air deep into her lungs, she felt the world fall away from her. The cameras, the crowd, her father—all disappeared. Her nerves settled as a huge smile broke across her face. *Fun.* That was what this was all about. She was here to have fun, and if that meant winning too, well so be it. She exhaled. Snow started to fall, huge featherlike flakes drifting in slow motion around her, catching the floodlights and dancing on the slightest breeze. Sam's breath swirled away from her, like smoke. It was just her and the halfpipe now.

She dropped in.

The familiar rush hit instantly—the sharpness of the air on her face, her board slicing through the snow. This was where she was meant to be. She launched into her first trick, a backside 900, clean as hell. The moment she landed she felt it in her bones—*this was it*.

She barely registered a moment after that, the pipe stretched in front of her, a playground waiting for her next joyful move. She spun into a switch frontside 1080, tweaking it just enough to make it hers. The crowd roared. Gabe's commentary was electric. She was doing it her way, hitting the tricks with Becky's recklessness *and* Harper's precision— but adding her own personality to it. She let herself play with it, throwing in a McTwist so smooth she felt like she was carving the sky. The snow fell heavier now, dusting her goggles. She embraced it—it was pure magic!

The last trick loomed. She bent her knees, loving the strength she could feel in every cell of her body. She surged upwards, engaging her core and front leg as Leo's advice spun in her head. Time slowed. The crowd held its breath. A frontside 1440. But not just any 1440. She tweaked it midair, added a *little* extra style, a *little* extra joy, a *little* extra Sam—and she brought it home clean. She landed so effortlessly it was like she'd never even left the ground.

And she knew. Knew before the scores came in, before the crowd could react, and before Gabe's excited commentary blasted from the speakers.

She'd done it. She'd taken the gold.

Suddenly the noise was deafening. The crowd screaming as the scores flashed on the screen. But none of it mattered.

Sam flung her goggles and helmet aside while frantically unclipping her feet from her board. She bolted across the snow as if electrified—straight for Finn.

He ran toward her, stopping as she flung herself hard into his arms. Finn's hat flew into the air as they tumbled to the ground, a soft mound of snow breaking their fall. Laughing, Sam sat up first, then straddled Finn. She grabbed the front of his jacket and yanked him closer, crashing her lips against his. His hair was soft and his arms tight around her as the crowd cheered. She deepened their kiss, loving how warm his lips were, how he tasted of mint and chocolate, and how *damn good* it felt to let everyone see that she loved him. Finn squeezed her waist as he pulled back. His face lit up.

"About time." He winked.

"Don't I know it," Sam said, breathless.

"You looked like you were having fun out there."

"I was—"

Before she could say another word, the world around them came rushing back—the roaring crowd, the flash of cameras, the dazzling floodlights, and the fact that they were half-buried in the snow. And then, through the speakers, Gabe's voice cut in, barely controlling his laugher.

"Now *that's* what I call a celebration! Finn Bradley might need a head injury assessment after that tackle."

Seb's chuckle came across in reply, "I don't think he's complaining."

23

Finn

Running his hands through his hair, Finn spun around twice, then stood stock-still as Sam stood on the highest podium, her face alight with joy as her gold medal was placed over her head. The snow had stopped just in time for her moment. She looked amazing, perfect, where she belonged. He couldn't take his eyes off her. She was lit up, and everything he knew her to be. Valentina and Davide waved at him, and he ran over to them, his eyes sparkling.

"Look at her!" he called as he approached them. "Isn't she phenomenal!" He air-punched as he gave a little jump. Cameras flashed around him, but he didn't notice. Valentina took his face in her hands and kissed his cheeks. She was beaming.

"Ah, Finn, I think you are more dazzled by her than by the gold medal! Who can blame you? Look at her—this is how a champion looks! She is not just victorious, but alive!"

Finn turned to look, again, at Sam where she stood on the podium. He never wanted to forget this moment, how she smiled, the way the crowd cheered for her, the way she searched for him and blew him a kiss making the crowd go crazy. Laughing, he caught her kiss and blew her one back. Hell, she was beautiful when she smiled like that—like a sunrise over the Alps, golden and unstoppable. Unforgettable. He grasped Valentina's hand tightly as he watched Sam, a lump in his throat. The moment stretched, timeless. His heart pounded just as it did the day he'd first met her. Finn stood, rooted to the spot, mesmerized by her, just as he had been that day—the day that seventeen-year-old Finn had fallen for her without any explanation.

She looked for him again, her green eyes flashing, her blonde hair escaping her braid and blowing into her face. There was something in her that he hadn't seen in a while— she was glowing, radiant. Strong. She looked like she knew who she was. He took a deep breath. This was the Sam he'd fallen in love with all those years ago. She hadn't just won—she'd loved every second of it. While others chased medals, glory and attention, Sam chased the feeling—the sheer, breathless joy of it. The wind in her hair, the speed, the thrill of pulling off something new and reckless—because it made her feel alive. And fuck—she looked good. She looked like a goddess.

"She's unreal," he said quietly as Sam encouraged the crowd to cheer loudly for Becky as she received her silver medal. "She's extraordinary." He exhaled sharply, his chest tightening. What had he done to deserve such an amazing woman? Just as he thought he couldn't love her more, Sam reached for Becky. Without hesitation, she pulled her onto the podium beside her, wrapping an arm around her like they were sisters, not competitors. The crowd roared in approval, the cameras flashing to capture the moment. Becky looked stunned for a moment, then emotional, before laughing and hugging Sam back.

Finn shook his head in awe. That was Sam. She wanted a gold medal, but that never meant that she wanted to crush anyone. She'd always lifted people up. Always. She was fierce on the slopes, but off them—she was *this*. A woman who never let the scoreboard define her, who never let winning mean that someone else had to lose. And that was why she was more than just an athlete—she was the kind of person who made him want to be better.

The gold medal gleamed as Sam held it high, next to Becky's silver. But it wasn't the medal that Finn cared for. It was just her. He slowly became aware of Davide's huge, reassuring hand on his shoulder.

"True love, eh?" Davide's deep voice chuckled in his ear; his hand squeezed Finn's shoulder. "You are a lucky man, as I am. Not because she loves you—but because you now truly see her for who she is—magnificent and majestic. Like my Valentina."

"Of course!" Valentina tilted her head and pouted. "And yet, do you tell me this every day, Davide? I think not."

Davide placed a dramatic hand over his heart. "*Tesoro mio*, I tell you with my eyes, with my soul, with my . . . must I say it aloud?"

Valentina rolled her eyes and swiped at him. Laughing, she shook her head. "Men . . . always thinking silence is romantic and that the thing between their legs makes us forget how silly they are."

Finn huffed a laugh. "You two are ridiculous." But his voice was thick with emotion as he looked at Sam.

Davide squeezed his shoulder again, this time firmer. "Jokes aside, Finn, never, ever, underestimate the power of words. Tell her every day. Every single day, as I will—from now on."

Finn swallowed hard. He nodded. That's exactly what he intended to do. Starting with the minute she stepped off the podium.

"I'll be back in a few minutes," he said to Davide and Valentina as Sam stepped down. He turned back briefly.

Valentina gave him a thumbs-up sign then shooed him away.

Crunching over the snow, Finn kept his eyes on Sam. She was surrounded by fans, with Maya hovering nearby. His skin prickled as he walked toward her, longing to touch her. A red jacket caught his eye. Jake Harrington. He stood back, arms folded across his chest, his face blank as he watched his daughter sign autographs and pose for photos. The least he could do was smile; after all, his protégées had taken silver and gold, but he looked like he'd known exactly what they'd do all along, which was a total lie. A slight sneer curled Jake's lips, an expression that Finn recognized. Jake was acting as if he'd set this all up, like he was the one in control. *Like hell he was.*

Anger flared up in Finn, and he quelled it as best he could, but it got the better of him.

Changing course, he marched close by Jake, his hands shaking as his coach turned to watch him. Jake stepped in his path; his chest puffed out.

"She had to fight for that gold," Jake said. "She'd have gotten one sooner if you hadn't distracted her. I warned you to back off."

Finn couldn't help himself. He snorted. Stepping back slightly he took in the older man and shook his head before stepping forward again. "You've got it backwards, Jake." He purposefully dropped the word *Coach*, smiling as Jake's eyes fired up.

"You think you know my daughter better than I do?" Jake growled.

"No, Jake." Finn met the older man's gaze. "I think you know her well, but you've been afraid to trust her."

"Who do you think you are?" Jake blustered. "What the hell do you know about . . ." His voice trailed off as he desperately gestured at the arena.

"I'm the man who truly believed she could do this, from the day I met her," Finn said clearly. "But she didn't win because of me—or you. She won because of who she is—because of what she loves. And she loves this, Jake. How did you not notice?"

Jake's mouth dropped open. Finn continued, "I don't pretend to know her—I let her show herself to me. I see her—and I'll never not see her. You think she's great because she's won an Olympic medal, well, let me try to make this clear for you: she's not great because she has an Olympic medal, she's great because she loves this sport, and she loves people and that's what makes her a champion. You'd do well to remember that."

Jake adjusted his jacket, pulling his collar up as if to ward off Finn's words. His lips twisted as if he wanted to say something but couldn't get the words out. Then he exhaled through his nose like Finn had said something stupid.

"You're passionate," he mused. "I've always known that. Fiery. But fire burns out. And Sam—she was raised in *my* world. She *knows* what it takes to stay on top." He paused. "Do you?"

Finn shook his head. "I knew you'd throw that card down. And I'm not afraid of you. And Sam—you're still missing the point. You may have trained her to win, in a world that you think is yours, but she was always going to win—with or without you."

Jake's jaw tightened, just a fraction. Finn pushed his hands down into his jacket pockets. His stomach churned. Standing up to Jake like this hadn't been on his to-do list. A flicker of movement nearby made him look around. Jake turned to see what he was looking at Sam. Just a few feet away.

Finn pressed his lips together. *This was awkward*. Sam's eyes were trained on him, her forehead creased. *Shit, Jake is her father*. And she hadn't moved a muscle since he'd spotted her. He willed her to understand that he needed to do this, to stand up to Jake for once and for all, otherwise he'd never be his own man. But he wished she'd give him some indication that she was on his side. The knot in his stomach tightened as his hands clenched into fists deep in his pockets. Then he drew a breath and, keeping his head high, nodded at Jake once. Jake nodded back, with a hint of respect to it. Then Finn walked away without waiting for Jake's dismissal. The snow started again. It swirled around them, descending like huge duck down feathers. He blinked as they landed on his face, cold and wet. Shaking, Finn moved toward Sam. She didn't move toward him but kept her eyes on her father as he turned on his heel and walked away into the watching crowd.

Then, as if she'd snapped out of a spell, she was before him, making his heart pound and his breath shallow. What had he just done? That was her father! The man who'd raised her, and he'd basically told him to get lost. Shit. She was going to hate him for this.

She touched his arm, grasping a handful of his jacket. "You okay?"

Finn gazed into her face, surprised to see concern and worry written all over it. He shrugged, trying to play it off that it was her father he'd just gone toe-to-toe with, and that he was terrified. "Guess we'll find out when he tries to have me assassinated."

She gave a small smile, her brows relaxed. "He wouldn't."

"Oh, I'd say he has the contacts."

"Without a doubt," Sam said softly. "Finn?"

"Sam?"

She searched his face for a moment, and his mind went blank. *Please let her be okay with what I said.* He held himself steady, his chest contracting hard, as she brushed a strand of hair back from her face. His hand twitched to move, to touch her, to hold her and tell her that he'd meant it—every word—even if it ruined everything between them, because it was the truth. And he had to stand by his word.

Without a whisper, she reached for his hand, lacing her fingers through his.

The tension in his chest loosened.

"I heard everything," she said. "And you were right."

"About what?" His throat was tight.

"About me. About why I love the sport. About who I am."

She tightened her grip on his hand, then lifted it to her lips to press a gentle, deliberate kiss to his fingers. "Thank you."

His breath caught; his voice was rough when he spoke. "You never have to thank me for seeing you."

"I know." Sam shrugged, a smile spreading across her face. "It drives me crazy that I didn't know it sooner." Then she stepped into his arms. The tension and tightness flowed out of Finn's body as she held him. There was a quiet certainty in her movements, her arms wrapped around his body even more closely. Her body steady, warm and comforting, like the first rays of sun after a snowstorm. Her heart was against his, and he couldn't tell whose pulse was hammering like crazy. Pressing his cheek against her hair, he gave a shuddering sigh. For the first time, in a very long time, he didn't feel like he had to fight for his place, because Sam was here, holding space for him.

Sam raised her face, a glimmer of wickedness in her smile. "Fancy celebrating my win with me?"

Laughing, he kissed her nose. "As long as you wear something special."

Snorting, Sam gently thumped his chest. "You dirty-minded . . . well, what exactly do you have in mind?"

"You . . . and your medal." Finn leaned forward to whisper in her ear. "And nothing else."

Sam gasped but leaned against him, letting him know

298

with her whole body that he'd said all the right words. "Now that I can do."

"If you two don't get a room you'll melt the snow, and then what!" Maya's voice came from directly behind Sam. She smirked and flicked the snow from her face. "I heard that, by the way. And I'm all for it, just so you know. But can you do it later—after we open this email from Montalier?" She held her phone out to Sam as the snow came down harder.

24

Sam

Sam choked. She looked wildly from Maya to Finn and the phone Maya was offering to her. *Holy crap. No way! NO WAY! An email from Montalier. Not a DM, not a reply to a post. An actual email. What the . . . ? Had they done it? Was this what they'd been hoping for? A sponsorship deal? What if it wasn't? But they'd hardly email if it wasn't, would they?* Her head spun with all the possibilities.

Her hands trembling, Sam took the phone from Maya. Turning to Finn, she pushed the phone into his hands. He fumbled. The phone slipped and fell into the snow.

"Shit," he cursed, bending to pick it up. He held the phone out to her, as if it was a bomb. "Sam?"

Sam shook her head vigorously. "No. Noppppe. You do it."

"Nah-uh," Finn said. "This is your baby."

"It is not!" Sam pushed him gently. "It's yours too!"

Maya snorted. "Much and all as I like hearing you two talk about babies, this isn't doing us any good. One of you, read the email before I combust!"

Sam shook her head again. "No, Finn—please do it. I can't . . ." She doubled over, her head spinning. "What if they . . . what if they hate us?"

"They don't hate us—you!" Maya said, patting her back gently. "How could they?"

"I don't know," Sam cried, looking up at her from her crouched position. "Maybe we're too . . . I don't know! But they could!"

"Listen here, missy," Maya said with steel in her voice. "No one on this wide world could hate you—except maybe Harper, now she might really hate you—but no one else. Cross my heart and hope to die, I wouldn't tell you a lie."

"That's not helping." Sam whimpered. "Call yourself a friend, huh?" She rubbed her stomach to try to ease the smarting pain that jabbed her insides.

"Maybe you should stand up," Maya said, stepping closer to her. "Everyone is looking at us." She smiled broadly at a fan who stopped in her tracks and about-turned when she saw Maya's crazy grin.

Sam stood up—too fast. Black spots danced in front of her eyes. She grabbed Finn's arm to steady herself, catching his pale face as she did. "What? Did you open it?"

Finn nodded mutely. His hands were white from holding the phone so tight. Sam's mouth went dry. *They'd flunked it.* Why else would he look so devastated? Pushing her shaking hands deep into her pockets she braced herself as his eyes reached hers.

He cleared his throat and looked down at the screen.

"Tell me what it says," Sam said, hoarsely. "Please."

"Give me your hand," Finn said. Slowly, Sam withdrew

301

one hand from her warm pocket and grasped his, gasping as he grabbed her tightly. He cleared his throat again, then began to read:

"Dear Maya, I hope you're doing well! On behalf of everyone at Montalier, we'd like to extend our warmest congratulations to Sam on her incredible Olympic win! Her performance was nothing short of spectacular. Coming on the back of seeing her Instagram posts wearing vintage Montalier was an unexpected but thrilling moment for us. She and Finn, as a couple, truly embody the timeless spirit and passionate evolution of our brand, and we couldn't be more delighted."

Finn paused. Sam raised her eyes to his, butterflies swirling around her entire stomach just as the wind whipped up the falling snow around them. "Don't stop!"

He smiled, and she gave a little jump.

He continued, the smile broadening on his face as her eyes widened. "We'd love to discuss a sponsorship opportunity for both Sam and Finn, as we believe they represent the perfect blend of passion, talent, and innovation that Montalier stands for. In addition, we're keen to explore a collaboration with them on a special collection—one that not only celebrates Montalier's heritage through vintage-inspired designs but also pushes forward our commitment to sustainability with a more eco-conscious approach to performance wear. Let us know a convenient time to discuss further—we're incredibly excited about the possibilities ahead!"

Sam squealed! Her hand squeezed Finn's tighter until she had to let go. Massaging her cramping hand she jumped into the air, howling with joy. "We did it! FINN! Argh!"

"A collab!" Maya took the phone back. "This is beyond brilliant. A collab with Montalier—Sam, Finn—you guys—promise me you'll remember me when you're famous."

Sam threw her arms around Finn, kissing him soundly on the cheek and screeching in his ear. He patted her and pushed her away, gently. His face ashen and still.

"Finn?" Sam peered into his face. "Did you hear what you read?"

Finn nodded. Gradually the color came back to his cheeks as Sam rubbed his arms. Scared, but buzzing still, she led him to a bench near the edge of the pathway and made him sit down. Maya sat beside him as if propping him up.

"Finn?" Sam sat down and nudged his shoulder. "Talk to me, or I'll have to go get a medic."

He let out a short laugh. "Still breathing, don't worry. Just . . . winded."

"I hear you," Sam said. "It's a lot to take in."

"Speaking of a lot," Maya chimed in. She nodded behind Sam. "It's Leo."

"It's okay, Maya," Sam said quietly. "He's all right."

Sam stood up as Leo and Becky came into sight. He offered her his hand. She took it and he pulled her into his arms.

"Congratulations, sis." His hug was warm, tight. He squeezed her once more before letting her go. "You deserve it, Sam. You really do. That was out of this world—that last trick . . ."

"They're calling it the switch mirage." Becky laughed happily. "Sam—you're a legend. No one has ever pulled off what you did! Gabe and Seb broke it down on TV, in slow motion. Everyone is talking about you. How did you even come up with the idea?"

Sam sank down onto the bench, next to Finn. "I just did it," she said. "I don't know how. I think it had something to do with having more time in the air, pushing through on my front leg."

Leo's face reddened, his usually serious face beaming. "You think?"

"Yeah," Sam said. "I sure do." She leaned into Finn, loving how naturally he slipped his arm around her shoulders, at how his solid body offered her warmth, strength and love. Shifting through the memory of the moment in her mind, Sam remembered how strong she'd felt when she'd followed her gut and twisted into that cork, and how she'd felt when she'd landed it cleanly. Would she ever be able to do it again? Maybe if she took Leo's advice . . . maybe if he coached her . . .

"A legend. Hell yeah—I can work with that. I can see it now . . . Sam—the myth . . . the legend . . . the mirage!" Maya's chirpy voice made Sam smile before looking back to Becky.

"Maybe you and I can train together?" Becky asked, her voice more resolute, more mature than Sam had ever heard it. "Women together, in sport—lifting each other up. I'll never forget today, Sam. It means the world to me."

Sam smiled up at Becky, relishing how Leo did a double take. "I'd like that. Yeah, Becky, that would be great. But only if Leo is involved."

Leo gasped but Sam saw the way he gripped Becky's hand.

"Okay, that's a date then," Becky said. She turned to Leo, all business. "Speaking of dates, we've postponed the wedding for a few years. I think I want to try for the next winter Olympics. I won't have time for wedding dresses or babies or whatever else the world has planned for me."

Leo gaped. "Becks! We weren't going to tell anyone."

"Well, we can't keep it a secret," Becky said. "Honestly, babes, I'm not spending the next few months dodging questions and reading articles about why we haven't set a date. There's nothing wrong with a long engagement—you said so yourself."

Leo looked chastened. His face reddened but he smiled and pulled her close to him. "I did, didn't I? And you're right, I know."

"Even if it's difficult to admit?" Becky chuckled, her eyes warm on Leo.

Leo rolled his eyes in a way that Sam knew so well.

"Oh, I think he knows," she said. "Good call." She laid her hand on Finn's thigh, worried that he hadn't said anything at all. "Are you heading down to Rustico? Yeah? Great, we'll catch you up."

She waited until Becky and Leo were out of earshot before turning to face Finn.

"Hey?" she said softly. "What's going on? You haven't said a thing since you read the email."

"I don't know what to say." Finn took her face in his hands. He planted a soft kiss on her lips and drew back to look at her. Her heart contracted at the warmth and love in his eyes, at how gently, yet firmly, he held her.

"Look at you," he said. "A legend already—not even in

the making. Living in the moment, breaking the rules—and winning because of it. You're an inspiration, Sam. I wouldn't be anything without you."

"Finn!" Sam started to speak, but he kissed her quickly.

"And I definitely won't look as good in vintage—or Montalier—as you do." He grinned. "But I'll give it my best shot. I do, however, think that we have to bow down to this freaking legend beside us—" He looked up at Maya who had gotten up to capture a few shots of their sheer joy.

"Me?" Maya squeaked, peering out from behind the camera. Her satsuma coat glowed as the snowfall began to thicken.

Sam threw her head back, a throaty chuckle reaching for the sky. Finn was right—Maya was going to be an instrumental part of their future. She'd chosen her prom dress, and made her wear the ski suit, and made her do that photo shoot.

"I'm right, aren't I?" Finn said.

Maya propped her chin up with her hand, looked upwards and pretended to think about it before she struck a pose. "Damn right, you're right. But whatever—because I am not liking this baby blizzard that's happening—my hair will frizz up. Come on. Move it, you two lovebirds. There's a bistro with a bottle of champagne with my name on it and I intend to get very drunk indeed."

Finn made to move, but Sam pulled him back down. The pathway was empty now. It was the first time they'd had alone since the morning. The bistro was going to be packed. It would be fun and loud, but right now she longed to be alone with him, even if only for a few moments.

"We'll follow you soon," she called to Maya who was already trudging through the snow in the direction of the main street. Maya waved a hand in reply. Turning to Finn she said, quieter, "Can we just stay here—for a bit—before the craziness starts?"

Nodding, Finn sat back, his face serene, looking entirely like he'd carved first tracks in the most perfect pow. Sam's insides fluttered. There was a softness to his features now, the sharp angles of his face softened by the shy smile he gave her. His hair fell over his forehead, tousled—just like it had been last night when he'd moved on top of her.

"You look happy," she said.

"I am happy."

Looking at him from under her eyelashes, Sam was struck by how relaxed he was, how contentment seemed to wrap around him. He'd looked like that the first day she'd met him, the day she'd lost her heart to him. She pulled him closer to her, until their breath mingled into one steamy cloud in the freezing night air. "I love you, Finn Bradley."

"I love you, you legend, Sam Harrington." His eyes twinkled. "Always have."

"Right back at ya." Sam scrunched her nose up. "But can we save the romance for later? I'm freezing my ass off here and I'm dying for a cocktail. Let's go before they drink the place dry!"

"You said ass and cock in the same sentence." Finn groaned. "And you expect me to go to the bistro?"

Sam leaned into him, her hands skimming his shoulders, her fingers soft at the nape of his neck, tangling in his hair.

307

Her lips touched his, softly then she grinned as she felt his hands on her hips, pulling her against him.

"Nope!" She jumped up from the bench as he ran his hand down her hip and grabbed her ass. She swatted his hand away with a giggle. "Keep those thoughts for later. Come on! Race ya!"

Running through the snow, Sam looked back at Finn as he ran to catch up with her. His smile was infectious, and she laughed out loud as he outpaced her. Then he slowed down, coming back to take her cold hand in his warm one. They kept pace with each other, jogging side by side down to the street. *This was the way it always should have been.* Just the two of them. Together they could take on the world.

25

Sam

Monteluce shimmered with candlelight. The top-class restaurant was busy, the soft clinking of crystal and china, and piano music threaded through the air. The tables were draped in crisp linen, and the quiet hum of conversation enhanced the serene and calming décor. Sam stood in the foyer, gripping the side of her ankle-length, deep coral, velvet slip dress. She stared around and chewed on her bottom lip, then stopped remembering how painstaking it had been to get her lipstick on earlier. The maître d' smiled at them, his face calm and professional even though his eyebrow had flickered slightly at Sam's footwear. She smothered a smile. Maya had given her two options: ballet flats, or knee-high biker boots, which were a lot more elegant on than they'd looked in her suitcase, and the ones that Sam had chosen. There was no way she was ruining Maya's hard-earned Chanel flats in the snow.

"Now, listen to me," Maya said as she gently slapped Sam's hand away from the lace-edged strap on her dress. "Girl! No fidgeting! Just relax and have a good time. Do you hear me?"

"Yes, boss." Sam blew a blonde tendril back from her face. Maya had pulled out all the stops for this evening— her first *real* date with Finn since they'd more or less told the world that they were a couple. "Shoulders down, smile on . . . What if this all goes wrong, Maya? This place is . . . it's overwhelming."

"Tshh!" Maya rolled her eyes. "It's filled with people— people who eat, drink, and fart—just like you do. Everyone here is thinking the same thing. Don't you for one minute think that you're here to impress anyone, okay?"

"Because you are already impressing them." Finn's deep voice made Sam spin around, the skirt of her slip dress billowing slightly, the high slit revealing a little of her thigh. "Wow!" His eyes widened as he gaped at her before closing his mouth. "You look incredible."

Sam felt her cheeks heat up under his gaze. "I wasn't sure . . ."

"I am," Finn said leaning in to kiss her. "You are astonishing—and the only person I know who can pull off those boots with that dress."

"It's snowing out!" Sam playfully slapped his chest. "You don't look bad yourself."

Finn grinned and grasped his lapels. His navy-blue blazer caught the light, the rich fabric dark against the crisp white dress shirt beneath it. Sam ran her eyes down his frame as he winked at her. "I do, don't I?"

"Humble as always," Maya chimed in. "But you do scrub up well, Bradley."

"I'm glad to hear it," Finn said, a slight chuckle giving away his nerves. "I knew you were styling Sam—so I had to step up my game. Didn't want to be upstaged. Thank you, by the way—the suit fits like it was made for me."

Maya beamed. "My pleasure, now go on, you two, get in there and enjoy your evening and try to forget I'm here. I'll take just a few shots and be gone."

"That's a lie." Sam rolled her eyes affectionately. "You'll be at the bar, phone at the ready like a proud stage mom!"

"I have no shame." Maya was already stepping back, angling her phone. "Now, walk slow—give me that 'yes, you guessed it—we're a couple' vibe."

Finn offered Sam his arm. "Shall we?"

Sam took his arm, smiling shyly as people looked up and recognized her and Finn as they walked to their window table. Outside the lights of Livigno twinkled as the snow continued to fall gently. Inside, candlelight flickered, and the scent of warm bread and roses filled the air. Sam settled onto the comfortable leather seat. She tucked one boot-clad leg behind the other, her eyes on Finn as he pulled at his cuffs before sitting down.

"I guess we're not used to this," she said softly as someone poured wine for them. "Maya said that she'd sorted our menu, so we don't even have to think about it. I've a feeling she's ordered anything that might be an aphrodisiac."

"Not that I need it," Finn said, his voice husky. "God, Sam, you look good enough to eat."

"Finn!" Sam gasped. Her cheeks roared with heat, but

she smiled. She'd never stop wanting Finn Bradley saying things like that to her.

An antipasto board appeared, followed by a course of ravioli, then steak. Sam sipped her wine. She barely noticed Maya taking photos, nor the waiter as he'd smoothly placed course after course in front of her. They hadn't stopped smiling and talking since they'd sat down. This was what she'd been missing in every other relationship she'd had. She leaned forward and laced her fingers through Finn's, loving how he gently squeezed her hand as she did. He'd opened his top buttons, and his strong, tanned neck was making her wish they were back in his hotel suite. The arrival of dessert—three golden bomboloni, piled high and dusted with sugar, with a little pot of warm Nutella on the side—made Sam moan out loud.

"It's like an Italian *Samwich*," Finn said, licking chocolate from his fingers in a way that made Sam smile. "You know who'd destroy this plate in five seconds flat?"

"Leo." Sam nodded. "And he'd convince us that hazelnuts are a protein post-training fuel."

Finn burst out laughing. "He's not wrong, though, is he?"

Sam laughed. "No, he's not." She leaned forward. "He texted me on my way over—he's thinking of going back out there—skiing again."

Finn stopped laughing, he sat back in his seat, a genuine smile lighting up his face. "Seriously?"

"Yeah," Sam said, her eyes stinging with tears.

"Then that's worth celebrating." Finn raised his glass. "To second chances. To comebacks. And to Leo finding his way back to what he loves."

Maya's deep sigh from nearby reminded Sam that she was here, taking shot after shot of her and Finn. She pulled a chair up to their table and tapped her phone.

"Okay, you two lovebirds, I'm out of here. You two are *sickeningly* photogenic and I can't stomach it anymore." She grinned and pinched the last piece of bomboloni from Finn's plate. "God, this is delicious." She murmured through sugar-dusted lips. "Anyway, like I said, I'm gone. If you need me Sam, I'll be in my hotel room—seeing as you've practically moved out—editing and posting these damn beautiful and somehow *hot* photos of you guys.

"Thanks, Maya," Sam said. "But what about dinner? You've had nothing."

"No worries, girl." Maya stood up. She fluttered her eyelashes as a tall, dark, and impossibly handsome man arrived with a small bag. She laid a hand on the waiter's arm, "Gio has been taking the best care of me all night, he's spoiling me—but I'll make sure to leave him a great review." She winked, picked up her bag, and sashayed from the restaurant leaving heads turning as she went.

A rumble of male laughter caught Sam's attention.

Across the room, at a table opposite theirs, Sam glanced her father. He was seated with a number of other coaches and looked like he was out of place, for once. His usual commanding presence seemed awkward, and he wasn't laughing along with the others at his table as loudly as he used to. Gritting her jaw, she turned back to Finn, her fingers tightening around her wine glass.

Finn noticed her mood shift. He took a swift look over his shoulder and turned back to Sam, his brow furrowed.

"You okay?"

Sam took a long breath. "Yeah, don't worry. It's fine." She smiled suddenly, remembering the *Ohana* sticker on her board. "Hey, I meant to thank you."

"You're welcome." Finn smiled. "For what?"

"My *Ohana* sticker." Sam sipped her wine, her eyes warming as she remembered the small, yet meaningful detail.

Finn's brow furrowed deeper. "Sam?"

"You fixed it—it was about to come off," Sam said, a playful smile on her lips. "And I was so worried I'd lose it, because then I would actually lose it. How did you find the time to glue it on? And so smoothly."

"It wasn't me." Finn reached for her hand, his expression softening.

Sam stared at him. "What?"

"I didn't do it." Finn nodded toward Jake. "Your dad did."

Sam blinked. Her heart did a strange flip. Her gaze flew between Finn and her dad across the room. Her dad had glued her sticker? He'd known how much it meant to her? He'd never said anything nice about that sticker—he'd only ever sneered at it, saying it didn't belong on a snowboard— and now . . .

"My dad?" she murmured. The sudden warmth she felt made her pulse race. "I don't know what to say."

She pushed her chair back. Finn jumping to his feet as she did.

"You want to go?"

She nodded. Her words caught in her throat. All these years she'd thought he didn't see her.

"Okay, come on." Finn's touch on the small of her back propelled her to move. She hurried toward the exit, her ears ringing. Then she stopped. Turning around before she could change her mind, she drew herself up tall and moved elegantly between the tables to where her dad was still sitting.

"Dad," Sam said quietly. "I'm heading out, but I wanted to stop over and say goodnight."

Jake swiveled in his chair, surprise sweeping across his face. "Sam!"

Before he could stand up, Sam leaned forward and kissed him on the cheek. "See ya tomorrow."

Jake caught her hand as she straightened. "Tomorrow . . . yes. See you then." His voice was gritty. Sam turned away and swept through the restaurant, tears smarting at the backs of her eyes. Finn took her hand. His steady, firm grip grounded her, and she breathed out. It had been a small thing, but significant. And she knew she'd done the right thing. Maybe they could try to go forward now, make some sense of their relationship. Finn held her coat open for her, and Sam felt a quiet sense of closure settle in the air between her and her father. The evening had been amazing, in so many ways.

"Ready?" Finn said, pulling on his coat.

Sam nodded. "As I'll ever be."

"Famous last words," Finn said holding open the door for her. "Just wait until I get you out of that dress . . ."

Sam snorted. "What!"

"You're lucky I'm a gentleman . . ." Finn said smoothly, trying to keep a straight face as Sam giggled, ". . . most of the time."

"Don't make promises you can't keep," Sam said as she stepped out into the cold night, the snow falling softly around them.

"I see what you did there, Harrington." Finn shook his head. "Some promises are made to be broken—or revised."

Sam shivered with anticipation as he pulled her close. Their noses touched; his breath warmed her skin as he raised her face to his. His lips were soft, and he tasted like sugar. She melted against him as he gently ran his hand up her back and into her hair, holding her firmly against him with his other arm.

Drawing away she looked up at him, breathless. "What are you promising now?"

He chuckled as she swayed against him. "Oh, this is not a promise, it's a fair warning."

26

Finn

Finn woke up, the scent of a woman tickling his nose. *Jasmine, possibly. Whose perfume was it this time?* Groggily he stretched one arm over his head. The other was trapped under the woman in his bed. She was somewhat cocooned in the duvet, and barely discernible. Foggily, he ran his hand down his face, dragging his fingertips against his stubble. *Shit. Sam! The woman was Sam! Hell yeah!*

Fully awake now, in all ways, Finn gently pressed the duvet away from her face, his heart contracting tightly when his eyes confirmed that his biggest and most longed for wish had come true. Sam Harrington was in his bed. They'd spent a second night together. And he'd told her he loved her. And she loved him right back. Breathing gently, worried that he might wake her up just by being awake himself, he lay back, beaming up at the ceiling. *Damn. This was unreal, it was brilliant.* Joy and amazement washed over him. *She*

317

was his. He was most definitely hers. They were together, as they always should have been. He looked over at her again as she curled into him, somehow managing to still hog the duvet. She looked like she belonged there, tangled up in his sheets, snoring lightly. *That's because she does*. His heart gave a jolt as the thought struck him. *She is right where she always should have been.*

Pinching the bridge of his nose, Finn felt his initial euphoria flatten a little. He'd spent years waking up next to women whose names blurred together, never staying, never committing to any of them, except for Harper. She was the closest he'd ever gotten to commitment and that was only because he'd been convinced that Sam was going to make something of it with Ethan. *Christ, so much time had been wasted*. It hit him like a ton of bricks. They could have had this—this precise moment, and the last two nights—and they'd let a stupid promise get between them. Well, that and Jake Harrington. He groaned inwardly. How many times had Jake warned him off Sam? *Too many*. He should've told Jake to mind his own business long ago, but he'd been afraid. Afraid of causing a row, afraid of being blacklisted, afraid of losing an Olympic medal. Well, now he had one and its shine faded in comparison to this moment.

He swallowed and turned gently on his side so that he could look at her sleep. His gaze traced the curve of her cheek, the way her lashes rested against her skin. The way her hair draped over her shoulders, finally free from its usual braid. She snored softly and he laughed quietly, his chest shaking as she draped her arm over his waist. She moved against him, her warm, soft body sending waves of desire through him. His cock, fully awake now that he'd realized it was Sam in his bed, quivered. Finn didn't move. It was early, too early. He always woke before his alarm on competition days, thriving on the buzz and the mental preparation he loved doing before a run. Today was his last event, the men's freestyle halfpipe. Normally he'd be up, but this wasn't a normal morning, and there was no way he was going to wake Sam. They'd worn themselves out in bed last night, and she needed her sleep.

Softly kissing the top of her head, a dull ache settled in his chest. They could've had *this* years ago. He could've held her after tough days, kissed her before competitions, made her laugh, and scream, in hotel rooms across the world. Instead, he'd let other people—*her father*—convince him she was off-limits. That he wasn't good enough. Because that's what it was all about, really. He wasn't good enough. *Did Sam ever think that? Had Jake told her to stay away from him?* Finn clenched his jaw, his erection subsiding as his anger built up. Jake Harrington was wrong. He *was* good enough—he *was* damn well brilliant and perfect for Sam.

Sam shifted, letting out a small sigh as she curled closer to him, her fingers brushing against his chest.

"Morning," she whispered sleepily, her eyes still closed.

"Hey," he whispered back, his arms encircling her tightly, as if he couldn't bear to let her go. "How'd you sleep?"

"Like a log," Sam murmured. "Best sleep I've had in ages."

Finn smiled. "That's good."

Her eyes fluttered open and he stared down into them, a panic creeping over him. *This was Sam—his best friend.*

319

The person who knew him better than anyone else in the world. The one girl he thought he'd never have. Everything was different now. The weight of change settled heavily in the pit of his stomach. His pulse quickened. *What if this wasn't real—what if it was just another passing romance?* Swallowing he tried to smile as she stretched in his arms. *Please let this be real. Please let this last.*

Sam nuzzled the tip of her nose against his chest. "What's up? You look like you want to run away—please don't."

Please don't. Her words made him smile. *Run away, like hell he would.* "I most definitely don't want to run away."

"Good." She wrapped her arms around him as he lay back. "Because I'd be lost without you."

Finn closed his eyes for a second. "Pinch me, will you?"

Sam giggled. "What?"

"Pinch me—I need to know this is not a dream."

"I won't pinch you," Sam whispered, kissing his chest. "That would be mean."

She slipped on top of him, her warm body straddling him, the duvet over her shoulders casting her body in a shadow, all curves and heat. The gold shine of her Olympic medal where it lay between her breasts caught his eye. She'd worn it, and nothing else, in bed last night, as he'd asked her to. "But I will do this." She leaned forward and kissed him deeply, her mouth warm, her lips soft. Her softest, sweetest, most intimate parts pressed down on his cock as it pulsed with desire. *Shit, Sam, this moment.* She felt so good, better than he'd ever imagined. Any thoughts of competition prep dissolved from his mind as he lost himself in Sam. Her hips moved slowly, up and down, pressing his cock deeper against her slick folds. She sighed against his lips. "Does this feel real enough?" Instinctively his hands tightened on her ass, holding her as he moved gently against her. *Are you kidding me?* He gritted his teeth as she rolled her hips, dragging a helpless moan from him.

"Hell yeah," he growled. "So unbelievably real."

"I need you." She held his jaw with one hand, pushing his head back while dropping tiny hot kisses over his neck, biting him gently on that tender spot where his neck curved to his collarbone. "I need you inside me."

His cock hardened. "Damn." His hands moved to her hips, gripping her tightly. *She was destroying his resolve. She was wrecking him.*

Sam rocked against him, slow and teasing, wet and hot, her tongue dipping into his mouth before she tenderly bit his bottom lip.

"Didn't you hear me?" She grasped his hair. She pulled his head back gently and stared into his eyes. "I need you. Inside me."

His body responded before his mind could. His pulse hammered through his body as she nibbled his ear.

"Give me two seconds." His hand shot out, blindly searching his bedside locker until he found the small foil packet. Her teeth grazed his bottom lip. His pulse pounded. The crinkle of foil sent a rush of heat through him. He groaned as she shifted, then she pressed down, just right, sliding down his length as a guttural moan escaped her pink lips. The sound of her moan almost made him come. Swallowing, he ran his hands down her body as she shifted and leaned back, the duvet falling from her shoulders as she braced her hands behind her, hard against his thighs. The smooth arch of her body as she moved was bathed in the dim light. Finn couldn't keep his eyes off her. Her head was thrown back, her long blonde hair fell in waves, glimmering in the shadows. *She was stunning*. Flushed. *Wicked*. And completely in control. She raised her hips, then sank down deeper, plunging down on him, as if she couldn't get enough of him. Finn threw his head back against the pillow as her softness tightened around him, clenching and stroking him with her hot wetness. His hands clamped on her hips, desperate to keep himself grounded.

She moved, faster, harder, her hand sliding down her body to touch herself. Her fingers slipping into her folds as she tightened around his cock. *Goddamn it, she was amazing*. Finn's body was strung so tight he thought he might snap. Every muscle burned with restraint as she writhed above him, crying out as she brought herself to the edge. Her wetness surrounded him, every slick, hot slide of her body on his tormenting him. Heat coiled deep in his core, tightening as she pulsed and cried out his name again. *Christ, he'd never get enough of her screaming his name.* His breathing ragged, his eyes on hers as pleasure gathered, sharp and unbearable, rushing him to join her.

"Sam—" he growled, half a plea, half warning.

"Let go," she breathed out in a rush. "Come with me."

Her whisper sent him over the edge. Pleasure ripped through him, shattering his attempts to hold back. *Her words, her body, the way she moved. Fuck.* A ragged groan tore from his throat as his whole body tensed, then melted as he came deep inside her. Every pulse, every aftershock left him utterly wrecked. She slowed down as he all but collapsed under her, his hands sliding to her thighs as he gasped. Sam leaned forward, then slid to lie next to him, her leg thrown over his, her arm on his chest.

"Fuck." Her voice was small, surprised even.

"You can say that again." He chuckled, pulling her close against him. "You are . . ."

"A little embarrassed." She buried her head in his chest.

"Fucking awesome is what I was going to say." He lifted her chin. "Don't be embarrassed, Sam. That was amazing."

A flush deepened on her cheeks, making her look even more beautiful. Finn's heart swelled. Wrapping his arms around her he held her as she giggled softly.

"It just felt good, you know," she whispered. "Like I couldn't stop myself."

He nodded, kissing the top of her head softly. This side of Sam, this tender and gentle, almost nervous Sam, was new to him. He couldn't love her more. "Thank you," he said quietly.

"For what?" She stopped drawing circles on his chest.

"For showing me another side of you."

She blinked and wiped her face. "Oh."

Tilting her head so she had to look at him, he traced his thumb over her lip.

"Hey," he murmured, frowning as she stayed quiet. "Talk to me."

A tear slid down her cheek as she exhaled slowly, a tremble in her breath.

"It's just different—me and you." She hesitated. "Everything is different now."

"Is it?" He wiped the tear away, a knot forming in his stomach.

She shook her head. "You know it is."

"Sam?" Finn cupped her face. His heart clenched. "Please don't say that."

She looked away. "It's like . . . it's like I can just . . . just be. Does that make sense?"

Finn let out a small, relieved laugh. "Yeah, perfect sense." He brushed a strand of hair back from her face. "You can always just be with me."

"I know." Her fingers spread across his chest, pressing against his heartbeat. "That's what makes things different."

"Nah." He nudged her softly. "It doesn't, Sam. We always were with each other, only we were, well I was, afraid of being with you like this."

"This?"

"Yeah, this—in love."

Sam squealed quietly then laughed. "In love! Oh!"

"I do love you," Finn said gently. "I meant it when I said it that night. It wasn't just an in the heat of the moment thing."

"I love you, too."

Finn's chest swelled. She could say those words a million times and he'd never be tired of hearing them. He gathered her up into his arms and sighed deeply. This was perfection. Nothing would ever top this moment. Sam stirred, tension in her body.

"Stay." He held her more tightly as she moved to get up.

"I don't want to go," she said. "But I have to – and so do you. It's the halfpipe final – for you. Remember?"

Finn's eyes widened. "Crap! The final. Yes. I was ready to stay here all day. Right, let's go! Shower!" He sat up and gently pushed her to stand up, unable to not run his eyes over her body at the same time. *Damn, she was fine.*

Sam laughed, but something in her eyes shifted. *Had he done something wrong? How could he fix it?* His eyes traveled over her face. He couldn't bear to think that he might have hurt her. Grasping her hand, he pulled her back down to sit beside him.

"Sam? What's going on in your head right now?"

"Nothing." She wrapped her arms around her body but smiled at him. He smiled gently back.

"Sam, tell me what it is. I know you. I can see you're not okay right now. Don't leave me worrying about you."

Sam's breath stilled. Her eyes hardened as she chewed on her bottom lip. Finn sat up straighter. "Sam—what is it?"

Sam's body stiffened. She started to say something but stopped. Then she raised her chin and spoke.

"Look, don't get angry about this, okay."

He nodded. *Of course he was going to get angry. If something had upset her, he'd get damn well fucking angry.*

"Before the big air qualie I . . . I overheard a conversation that I shouldn't have heard, and it upset me."

Finn's fists clenched on the duvet. He worked to unfurl them before she noticed.

"What did you hear?" His voice was low, concerned.

Sam swallowed. Her posture shifted, she whispered, "It was Leo. And my dad." She looked down and shivered. "It doesn't really matter now. I've spoken to Leo. We've cleared a few things up. And it didn't matter in the end—but you know what? I think it was good for me, for a while. It gave me a lot to think about."

"Good for you?" Finn couldn't keep the incredulous tone from his voice. "How, Sam? What did they say?" Immediately he regretted sounding so sharp. "Sorry."

"It really doesn't matter now," Sam said firmly. "The thing that's come out of this is that I won't be listening just to my dad anymore. I took some of Leo's advice and it worked out for me—and if I hadn't been so stubborn and had spoken to him properly before all of this, then maybe I wouldn't have had to learn this lesson now. I might have learned it a long time ago."

Without a word, Finn pulled her into the duvet again, holding her tightly as a heaviness passed through his chest. The way her voice had cracked a little, like she was holding herself together, told him everything.

"Leo might get back out there, on the slopes," Sam said quietly against his chest. "It's something he should have done years ago too. But he thought that Dad believed he was a failure. And, Finn, that's not true either. I know that—for a fact."

Finn's jaw loosened. He had to let go of the heat that surged through him, dark and fast. His pulse roared in his ears. His hands balled into fists again. If Leo and Jake were standing in front of him now, he wasn't sure he'd be able to control himself. The desire to lash out against them both was hot and curled through his body, tensing every fiber and muscle.

But then Sam sighed, her breath warm on his chest. She was tucked against him as if he was her safe place. And he was. She'd said as much, and he wouldn't change that. But one thing was for sure, she'd never doubt herself again, not if he had anything to do with it.

"If Leo gets back out on the slopes," she said quietly, "it would be wonderful."

"You know they're idiots." His voice was gruffer than intended so he softened it. "Two, big lumbering idiots."

Sam tensed. "Yes but . . ."

"But nothing, Sam." His chest rose and fell. She didn't need his anger. She needed him to believe in her in the way they should believe in her—the way she believed in him. She needed him to support her. Love her. He rubbed her arm soothingly. "They don't get to decide who you are, Sam. You do. And the last time I checked only the best made it to the Olympics. And you, Sam Harrington, you are a gold medalist. An Olympian. You're the goddamn best with the medal to prove it. You know it!"

"Thanks," Sam said, her face pink with emotion.

"Hold up a second," Finn said, his voice softer now. "Say it."

Sam laughed. "Finn!"

"Say it," he urged, unwilling to let her go until she said it. He rolled them suddenly, pinning her beneath him, his arms braced on either side of her head. She laughed, pushing against him hopelessly. He smiled down at her. "Say it, Sam—I want to hear you say it."

Her lips parted, a flush crept up her neck. "I'm . . ."

"You're?" He kissed the tip of her nose.

Sam laughed again, this time louder. "Jesus, Finn, I'm the best!"

"What? I can't hear you!" Finn grinned.

Sam's wide smile made his heart soar. All his anger swept away, morphing into a desire to lift her up. He laughed as she scrunched her nose up and yelled, "I'm the goddamn best!"

"Damn right!" He kissed her, slow and deep. When he finally pulled back, she was breathless, and he could see the desire in her eyes.

Sam pushed him off and jumped up. "Finn Bradley if I'd known all these years that you kissed like that . . . I think I need a cold shower!"

"Make it quick." He smirked. "You've got five minutes before I come in and—"

The bedroom door swung open. Sam froze. Finn blinked.

Maya stood dead in the doorway, a huge grin on her face. "Don't mind me—I'm just here to witness history. Again. And to remind you, lover boy, that you have a final today. My famous Freestyle Fuel smoothie is in your kitchen waiting for you – but now I think it should be renamed The Railed and Refreshed! What I want to know is . . . what you two were doing that made you both not hear the blender?"

Finn laughed. He stretched lazily in the bed, not an ounce of shame in his actions. "Morning, Maya."

Sam grabbed a T-shirt and, blushing, tugged it on. "Eh . . . how the hell did you get in here?"

Maya laughed. "If I told you, I'd have to kill you."

"Does this have anything to do with that guy on the front desk?" Sam grumbled as she tried to cover her ass with the T-shirt.

"No! What do you think I am—some kind of sexy

assassin coercing hotel employees to do my crazy bidding with this delightful body of mine?" Maya threw her head back and laughed. "Girl, I simply took Finn's spare room card the last time I was in here—now, come on—you promised to meet me for breakfast—and I want all the tea. And you, Romeo, get up! You have another final to compete in today—although, from that glow on your face you look as if you've already won."

"You have no idea." Finn joked from his comfy position under the duvet. "Sam, don't tell her everything. She won't be able to handle it."

"In your dreams, buster," Maya said with sass as Sam stood in the middle of the room, her eyes and her mouth open.

Maya tossed Sam a hoodie. "Hurry up, Olympic champion! My stomach is rumbling."

Sam pulled on the hoodie and her pants and hurried to the door. Finn watched her go, warmth blooming in his chest despite the embers of anger that still glowed there. Sam was magic, always had been—determined, fierce, extraordinary, not someone to mess with. She was brilliant. She needed to understand that she was all of that, and nothing less. He sat up, wanting to pull her back to bed.

Quietly, he called her name. She turned to him, and he smiled as he caught a flicker of the old fiery, passionate Sam he knew so well.

"You're unstoppable." His voice was almost a whisper. Then her eyes met his, and he saw it. That determination, that strength he'd always admired. Belief in herself growing. He smiled.

"Yes, I sure as hell am." She nodded at him. "And so are you—go get that gold, lover!"

Finn threw his arms over his face as the door closed softly behind Sam. *Lover*. Hell. He smiled into the crook of his elbow. He could come last for all he cared; Sam Harrington had called him *lover*!

27

Sam

The snow had stopped sometime in the night, leaving Livigno looking crisp and postcard fresh. Sam strolled down the main pedestrian street with Maya, her heart sinking in her mouth. Red hearts adorned everything—lights, windows—they even dangled from balconies. Romantic music came from every café, bistro and restaurant. Men carried flowers, beaming with pride as they stopped to buy chocolates. *Valentine's Day.* She'd forgotten. She pulled out her phone and there it was—Maya's annual Happy Galentine's Day text. Sam groaned inwardly. If only she'd remembered.

Scurrying along, she dashed into the restaurant where they were going for breakfast. Red roses sat in vases on every table, and the place was jammed with people gazing adoringly at one another. Gabe was seated at a table in front of the largest window. Maya waved and hurried over to him. Sam stood in the doorway for a moment and watched them exchange good mornings. Gabe leaped up to pull out Maya's chair for her, and she blushed tenderly as she sat down. They clearly were into each other, but they seemed not to want to do anything about it. Which was a surprise to Sam—neither one of them were known for being shy. Quite the opposite really. And they'd been all over each other only days ago, but now it looked like they were just . . . friends? It seemed as if nothing had happened between them at all. Puzzled, Sam bit her lip and slipped onto the chair opposite Maya, hunching forward to read the menu on the table.

"Good morning!" Gabe placed a large matcha in front of Maya. He glanced up at Sam. "Oh, you don't look like you're having a good morning at all."

Sam felt Gabe's eyes on her, as Maya reached for her matcha.

"Are you okay?" Gabe's deep voice was low. "Has something happened?"

Sam shook her head. She scrunched her nose and looked at her two friends. "No. Nothing has happened."

A crease formed on Maya's forehead. "Well then, what's with the sudden drama?"

Sam hid her face in her hands, then popped her head back up. "Valentine's Day."

Maya nodded. "Well, yeah, that's today."

"I forgot." Sam hid her face in her hands again. She mumbled through them. "I feel like such a bad girlfriend."

Gabe laughed. "Cut yourself some slack—you're barely a girlfriend. It's only been a few days."

Sam dropped her hands and glared at him at the same time that Maya swiveled around to poke his well-developed bicep. "You clearly have no idea." She turned back to Sam. "I can't believe you forgot!"

Sam grimaced. "I know. It's just that it's been crazy, with interviews and meetings and everything. I haven't had a chance to think straight."

"That's fair enough," Maya said. "It has been a bit of a whirlwind."

"And then some." Sam plucked at the menu. "And today is busy too. Ideally, I'd have time to plan, to get him something special."

"Yeah, I suppose. What kind of something special? Finn never seems to want anything."

"I know, right," Sam said. "But isn't that all men?"

Maya nodded. "Sadly, I think it is. Socks and boxers for the win, every time."

Gabe looked in amazement from one woman to the other. "First of all—all men? Really? But I'll come back to that later—secondly. Plan? What's there to plan? You get flowers, chocolates, maybe perfume or if she's really something, jewelry. You should just wear something sexy and um just . . . you know . . ." he waggled his eyebrows at her ". . . well, that's all a guy really wants."

"You can say it out loud." Maya rolled her eyes.

"No, I can't." Gabe nodded his head to the table to his left where a family were having breakfast. The two younger kids were making a mess with maple syrup and pancakes, a teenager slumped over a mug of black coffee, and two tired-looking parents who seemed more in need of the coffee than the teen, sat staring into space. "They don't look like they have the energy to explain what I *can't* say."

"Oooooh, naughty." Maya giggled. Nudging Gabe's arm she winked. "I bet I can guess what it is you can't say."

Laughing, Gabe stood up. He slipped into his wool coat, his smile warm. "I bet you can. I've got to go. Catch up later?"

Maya nodded.

Sam watched the interaction with interest. She waited until Gabe had left the restaurant to turn to Maya, a quizzical smile on her face. "Okay, you have got to fill me in on what is going on between you two."

"Nothing." Maya took a sip of her matcha. "Nothing at all."

"Oh, come off it," Sam said. "It doesn't look like nothing."

Maya leaned forward, her elbows on the table. "So, he's gorgeous, he's kind, he's sexy and has a wicked sense of humor," she said. "But he's far too serious for me, honestly. I'm here for fun, I'm messy, I'm loud and he's . . ." she paused and gave a slight shrug ". . . he's looking for love, Sam. And it's complicated, I think."

"Oh." Sam sat back. "Poor Gabe."

"He'll be fine," Maya said. "And so will I, honestly. I'm too busy right now. I need to make a name for myself, you know."

"I do know," Sam said.

"Yeah, you get it." Maya laughed. "It's not like this job is gonna last forever. The Winter Olympics is almost over . . . I need to line up some more work for after."

"Oh," Sam said with a tiny laugh. "It really is nearly all over. It feels so strange. Like, this has been my ultimate goal, and now, now it's all over. Just a few more days and the closing ceremony and then . . . then what?"

"I know, right?" Maya pouted. "It feels like a dream, doesn't it?"

Sam nodded. There was something pulling her back to Gabe though. Thoughts of the years she and Finn had wasted lay heavily on her heart, but at least she'd been able to see Finn almost every day. It wouldn't be the same for Maya and Gabe. She was a freelancer; he wasn't the easiest person to pin down either. "Maya." She hesitated, then carried on. She owed it to her friend to say something. "Are you sure you don't want anything to happen with Gabe? Lord knows where your jobs will take both of you next—you might not see each other again."

Maya wrinkled her nose and nodded. She leaned in, a softness in her eyes that made Sam sit up. Maya was about to drop some tea. "Look, we all have them, the guys we can't stop thinking about. And girl, it's come as a huge surprise to me that he's the one I can't get out of my mind. I mean look at him, he's a hottie—and heaven forgive me, he looks like he was carved out of marble by the gods and made to go all night long—imagine the stamina." She chuckled before getting serious again. "But he's not for me, not really. The real plot twist is that I know I won't walk away with my heart intact—cos, Sam, underneath all that perfection, Gabe is the kind of man I could love so hard, I'd never recover. And let's face it, I don't really know him, but I do know that he's too serious for me—and I'm not ready for that."

Sam's breath caught in her throat. It was the way Maya said it—not teasing, not gossipy, just . . . knowing.

"Maya, I never expected all that," Sam said softly.

Maya's smile was warm, but a hint of sadness reached her eyes. "Yeah, I know. But rest assured, I'm fine." She swirled her matcha and grinned with her trademark Maya sparkle.

"Anyway, you know me. I'd break up with him in a week. I couldn't do that to him—he's a good man, a really good man. And those are like unicorns—almost impossible to find."

"Almost." Sam's chest pinched as Maya gazed down into the remnants of her matcha. "You look like you need a fresh cup."

Maya brightened. "I do, please. It's been exhausting being Gabe's emotional support hot mess but what can I say? He needed me."

A bubble of laughter burst from Sam. "You! An emotional support—what!"

"Oh yeah," Maya said, her head bobbling with mischief. "I'm basically Florence Nightingale . . . with better tits."

"That you are." Sam laughed. She smiled at the waitress who was making her way over to them before ordering her breakfast and a fresh matcha.

Maya smirked at her. "So, you're gonna fill me in on what the hot hell is going on between you and Leo—and then, the real stuff—you and Finn?"

"Looks like I don't have a choice!"

"Good." Maya flicked her eyebrows up a little.

"What—what are you looking at me like that for?" Sam pushed the menu to one side. A tiny shimmer of regret in her chest. Like maybe she'd underestimated everything just a little. "I get it. I should have seen it before—I should have listened to you way back at prom when you told me to go for it."

Maya shook her head, her smile wise. "You weren't meant to do that back then, don't you see? You were meant to find him now. And he was meant to wait for you. It was fate."

Sam's laugh caught in her throat. Maya was right.

Drumming the table with her fingertips, Sam sighed. "That still doesn't help me with today—I want to do something special for Finn. It's our first Valentine's together, and I'm in meetings back-to-back all day."

"Can't you celebrate it another day?" Maya asked.

"No." Sam was sulky.

"And do you have any ideas?" Maya took her fresh matcha from the waitress.

"Not an iota." Sam poured syrup over her waffles. "Do you know what bothers me the most?"

"What?"

Sam unfolded her napkin. "We damn well knew we were meant for each other, from the very beginning. And now here we are—finally together and I forget our very first Valentine's Day."

"I'm sorry." Maya's smile was soft, and Sam didn't catch the glimmer in her eyes that meant she was hatching a plan. "Don't let it get to you, okay?"

"I'll try," Sam said, spearing a piece of pancake and strawberry.

* * *

The day passed in a blur of interviews and meetings, fan greetings and half-eaten sandwiches. Drained, Sam trudged toward the hotel, longing for a hot shower and some time with Finn. She couldn't wait to see him—to congratulate him on his second gold. She just wished she had something to mark the occasion—his second win and their first Valentine's Day. Her heart lurched. The stores had been closed by the time she'd finished up. Empty-handed and filled with apologies, she turned the corner to his hotel only to stop in her tracks. A horse-drawn sleigh was outside. Its golden lanterns cast shadows onto the snow; a majestic gray horse stood patiently, while the driver, bundled up well against the cold, nodded to her. She hurried forward, a burble of laughter escaping her as she saw Finn in the back, tucked up under a pile of faux-fur blankets.

His face lit up when he saw her. He waved to her to hurry up, pulling back the blanket invitingly. Sam reddened as people stopped walking to take photos of them. This side of her win was proving difficult to get her head around. Since the world had heard of their Montalier deal, she'd been inundated with DMs, questions, and most of them had been about what designers she might go to see at New York Fashion Week in the fall. Finn hadn't been asked about what shows he'd attend. It rankled her, but her resolve to be more than a clothes horse had been forged at the last round of media interviews, and she was determined to be herself and to show that self to the world. If she could inspire even just one kid to stand firm in their beliefs, then she'd have done what she'd set out to do.

She climbed up into the carriage, laughing as he grabbed her hand.

"Finally!" He laughed as she slipped in beside him. "I thought you'd never get back."

Sam sat back, letting him tuck her in warmly as the sleigh driver clicked his tongue and flicked the reins. The horses' breath curled in the freezing air, hooves crunching on the snow as they glided forward, pulling them away from the crowd and onlookers.

338

Exhaling slowly, Sam felt her body relax as she leaned against Finn. He handed her a napkin, smiling as she noticed the picnic basket at his feet. He'd thought of everything. A sliver of guilt stabbed at her. She'd completely forgotten. How could she explain that to him?

"Hot chocolate, with marshmallows and a hearty dash of whiskey, or champagne?" he interrupted her thoughts. "And there's some mac'n'cheese, and a fondue set too, although I'm not sure how we'll manage that without burning something."

"What? No Finnomenals? What about a *Samwich*?" Sam giggled.

"Well, actually, yes," Finn said, shaking his head as if he was surprised. "But all in good time."

"I'll have a hot chocolate, please." Sam gazed around. She couldn't have planned this better if she'd done it herself. Love was definitely in the air. The town twinkled around them, fairy lights, love hearts, couples . . . every cliché of Valentine's Day all in one perfectly beautiful location. It was perfect. Too perfect. She sighed; a flash of satsuma caught her eye before it disappeared around a corner. And then a deep chuckle that sounded like . . . No. She was imagining things. Sitting up slowly, she bit her lip.

"How did you pull this off?" she asked Finn quietly.

"Me?" Finn's brow furrowed. "I thought you did."

Sam snorted. "Me? No—I, eh, I forgot."

Finn blinked, then burst out laughing. "Me, too." His shoulders shook against hers, warm and strong. Sam groaned, pulling him closer to her.

"What are we like!" he gasped. "We're hopeless."

"We are." She laughed, holding the hot chocolate away from her as he kissed the tip of her cold nose. "But maybe that's why we work."

"Maybe." Finn wrapped his arm around her waist, shifting her closer to him, making her heart beat even faster.

"Who do you think did this?"

"I have an idea," Finn said. "But let's not spoil it for them."

Sam grinned and kissed him quickly. "You're a unicorn, Finn Bradley, do you know that?"

"I don't know what that means, but I think it's a good thing." He smiled.

"It's a very good thing—the best," Sam said, laughing as he handed her a rolled-up wrap oozing with cream cheese and pineapple, a piece of jalapeño peeping from the top.

"As is this," Finn said, his arm tightening around her as the sleigh glided through the streets and into the countryside. Neither of them noticed Maya and Gabe lingering in a doorway, half hidden by a vending machine.

* * *

Maya hugged herself, drawing her satsuma coat tighter around her.

"They really have no idea, do they?" Gabe murmured.

Maya grinned. "That's the whole point." She nudged him. "Now let's get out of here. There's a bartender back there, shaking a cocktail with my name on it. And if you're a good boy, I'll buy you a whiskey."

Acknowledgements

Darling reader! Hello!

I love winter, I adore snow—I love *love* **LOVE** cosy places—and Italy is one of the most perfect places in all the world! So writing this book, set against the thrill of the Winter Olympics, filled with so many of my favorite things, was such a joy! It was fun, especially writing about snow, chilly days, and hot chocolate on sizzling sunny days! While writing stamina isn't quite like training for the Olympics (I wish it were!), it takes grit and endurance all the same. And not just from me—there's a list of people who made this book happen—the people who believe in possibilities, dreams and determination – and me. Without them I'd be floundering on learner slopes chanting "Pizza, pizza, pizza, French fries!" instead of feeling like I took all the golds in having this book published.

Firstly, my endless thanks and love to Nicky Lovick, my agent, for championing *Melting Point* (and all my ideas really) from the very beginning, and for believing in the fire and heart of my work. Your belief in me has me at a loss for words.

And without a doubt I am indebted to my amazing and dazzlingly brilliant editor, Amy Mae Baxter. What an inspiration. Your sharp eyes and supreme guidance helped shape Sam and Finn's journey on the slopes on in the heart, making every twist, tumble, and triumph feel real. As for cutting some of those spicy scenes (poor Gabe! hehehe!)—you were dead right! You, Maddie, Emily, Jessica, Helena, Laetitia, Helen and Sarah—what a team!

Diving deep into the world of skiing, snowboarding and the Winter Olympics was a total blast, and an eye opener. Huge thanks to the athletes and communities who inspired me with their grit, passion, and the ability to look unbelievably cool while hurtling down a slope or a mountain at terrifying speeds. I am now a huge fan of Anna Gasser, Chloe Kim and Mia Brookes—fearless, awesome and real women doing and living their best lives.

Thank you to my most outstanding friends who cheered me on—Bláithín—what would I do without you and our daily podcasts?!, Caroline, Gillian, Anne-Marie, Gracie, Bernie, Carol, Haze, Ais, Ger, Hannah, Hazel G, Amanda G, Catherine RH, Carmel H and many more writers who constantly uplift me . . . some read drafts and for that I am most grateful and entirely embarrassed! Also thanks to Mallory – my eldest daughter – who read certain passages aloud to me and gave me her stamp of approval as a dedicated reader of all of my work among other books (I'm looking at my copy of *Iron Storm* and *ACOTAR* . . .).

Huge thanks to Ellen and Jade, and David, for listening to me go on and on about my works—and never ever telling me to quit or be quiet. You're all absolute legends—your encouragement fuelled many late nights, spicy moments (in the book!), and caffeine overdoses (until my doctor told me to cut back on the coffee . . .).

Of course that goes for my husband too—Dave, you're the man, my rock, always and forever. I'd give you the last coffee pod and not only because I'm cutting back!

And finally to the readers who crave passion, ambition, and a little heat in their romance. May you always have dreams to chase—and may you always chase them! Throw caution to the wind every once in a while, and never, ever, settle for anything less than a love that fuels your fire—and your sass—and your desire!

And speaking about desire . . . wait until you read Book Two—the heat turns up, with some familiar faces and new sparks flying!

Mmmmmwah!
Ciao for now!

Already missing Sam and Finn?

Watch out for Maya's story, a spicy, fake-dating, ice-skating rom-com coming Winter 2026!